SPLAT!

Edited by
John Ledger
&
Ts. Woolard

Edited by: John Ledger and Ts. Woolard
Cover Art by: David McGlumphy

J. Ellington Ashton Press

http://jellingtonashton.com/

Table of Contents

I GOT 'DEM OLE
MONKEY MORNING BLUES
Sebastian Crow

In the alley behind The Bucket of Blood, Rooney tugged at his crotch with one filth encrusted hand, and scratched his shaggy, flea ridden mane with the other as he scurried about like a headless cockroach searching for cigarette butts.

The alley reeked of piss, shit, rotten garbage, vomit and the Aqua Velva Rooney had been drinking just minutes before. A rusty green dumpster overflowed with all manner of delectable trash that a bum could really enjoy; greasy left over fries, bags of half-eaten chips and barely gnawed hamburgers that didn't taste too bad once the stale buns were discarded and the maggots scraped off. It was one of Rooney's favorite stops but today he had to contend with an angry street monkey with an ugly penchant for lobbing balls of wadded shit at Rooney whenever he got too close to the dumpster. The monkey was under the illusion the dumpster and all its delectable goodies belonged to him alone.

"*Ain't you never heard of hobo solidarity*?" Rooney yelled as a clump of shit splattered against his cheek.

A pair of hostile eyes watched the whole horrible scene from the back window of a ratty apartment above the Mondo Bizarro Adult Book Store. The watcher was a madman, though he didn't know he was a madman. He was also homicidal, which was just something you really don't want your madmen to be. If he could just remember where he had left his .9mm, he would have blown holes in the monkey *and* the bum. That monkey had practically been begging to be killed for days. Hanging around slinging poop at anybody who got too close to his treasured hoard of garbage was a killing offense if there ever was one. As for Rooney, he was just a bum. Nobody liked bums, not even street monkeys.

The maniac, whose real name was Max, though he preferred to be called Mr. X for dramatic effect, watched in revulsion as Rooney wiped the steaming pile of monkey shit from his face, and proceeded to shovel the foul stuff in his mouth like he was feasting on Beluga fucking caviar instead of monkey poo. Even the monkey retched in disgust.

The cyborgs in Max's head were causing fluctuations in his brain waves, he was no longer functioning at a 100% and the world had taken on a strange, disjointed feel. He also believed the Borgs might have been effecting how time worked in this dimension. It had been last night just hours ago, now it was clearly next week by the color of the sky, which had been a deep purple and was now a holocaust red. *Time for dinner*, Max thought.

A light switched on in his head and he remembered where he put his gun. It was in the closet, stuffed under his old Grateful Dead albums and the Devo porn tape. Max ran to the closet and rummaged through the clutter until he found the weapon, buried at the bottom of a ratty old shoebox. He checked the clip to make sure it was loaded, chambered a round, and went to the window to mete out a little rough justice. He took aim at the monkey first, figuring it would be the most difficult target. Sure enough, his first shot went wild, hitting the brick wall, sending shards of split brick and mortar careening towards the little primate, who yowled and covered his head. The second round was the money-shot and caught the shocked simian square in the head. His brains, splattered against the dirty brick building, looked like gray cabbage soaked in red-eye gravy.

Rooney, still engrossed in his coprophagous treat, barely glanced up as Max dispatched the monkey to primate heaven. The madman smiled as he carefully lined the old shit-eater up in his sights and fired. The bullet tore into the bum's chest spinning him in a circle. Blood spurted from the wound in a thick, crimson stream. The bum collapsed to his knees, clutching his chest and babbling dying-man-crazy. A comical look of confusion crossed the bum's face, which Max erased with a second bullet.

The bum flopped backwards, landing in pool of half dried vomit. Max set his gun aside, grabbed an old canvas bag—one of those oversized military duffels—and climbed out the window, shimmying down the fire escape with the grace of an acrobat. He slunk across the filthy alley, checking his surroundings to be sure his progress went unobserved. He stooped down beside Rooney's body and began feeding him into the duffel. The bum was pretty emaciated, so picking him up was like loading a sack of sticks. The result of a monkey shit diet, Max guessed. He thought he could carry the bag as long as the straps held. He would come back for the monkey later.

Time lurched and it was six months ago yesterday. Max was eating out the maggot infested cunt of some dead whore he thinks he found behind The Bucket of Blood. Then again, he might have killed her, sometimes he lost track of these things. She didn't remind him of Daisy at all, so he didn't see any reason to kill her, unless she had been a spy. Maybe she had figured out his secret identity and he'd had no other option. Then why was he violating her in such an intimate manner?

The whore moaned and shoved his head deeper into her rotting, putrid bush.

Ah! Not dead after all, just a two dollar whore he'd pick up in the bar earlier. No maggots at all, either, just your garden variety pubic lice and an unwashed cootchie. Behind him, a monkey slings a turd at the back of Max's head. Time hiccupped again and he was back in the present.

Grunting, Max managed to wrangle the strap over his shoulder. Struggling under the weight of his bundle, he began climbing back up the fire escape, looking like a homicidal Santa Claus with his bag full of cadaver, a drunkard's scabbed, scrawny legs poking out of the top like an absurd Christmas goose. He reached his floor, shoved the bag through the window, and went back to fetch the monkey.

Back in his apartment, Max dragged both corpses to the bathroom, stripped the bum of his smelly, tattered rags and the monkey of his organ grinder's hat and paisley vest. He tossed the bum's already stiffening cadaver into the rust stained bathtub, opened the tap on full blast, making sure the water was hot enough to scald. Taking a bar of lye soap, he scrubbed the dirt off the bum, scouring until the dead man's skin was red and raw. The water quickly turned muddy brown as filth, shit and blood filled the tub. Max emptied and filled the tub several times before he deemed Rooney clean enough.

Max stood back and admired his work; the bum's corpse was squeaky clean. His tangled, ratty hair was shiny and fresh from the cucumber shampoo he had used. The beard was a problem though. It would have to go. The bum's flaccid member dangling between his legs like an ugly, one-eyed worm also repelled him. Max solved the problem with a straight razor.

Slicing neatly around the pubic region, making sure he got the testicles along with the penis, the homicidal maniac was quite proud of his crude penectomy. Where the sex organs had been was now only a gaping red hole, a makeshift vagina. Staring at the neat, bloody hole caused a vague stirring in Max's own genitals. He shook off this inchoate urge for the time being, there was still the beard with which to contend. Until it was gone, it'd be too...too...well, too gay. He might have some exotic tastes, but he was certainly no fairy. He didn't cotton to none of that fag stuff, which was strictly for those effete uptown aesthetes.

Grabbing a pair of forceps to avoid touching the ugly things, Max placed the severed genitals in a plastic bag, thinking he would freeze them for now. Later he would deliver them to someone who would appreciate the gift.

Now there was that beard to take care of, and then he needed to clean the monkey; So much to do, so little time.

* * *

The room was dimly lit; a few small lamps and aromatic candles scattered throughout the tiny apartment imbued the usual shabbiness with a cozy, romantic feel. Max, dressed in white tie and tails, sat at the dining table entertaining a special guest. He popped open a fresh bottle of champagne and poured a glass for both of them.

"Thank you," Daisy replied, taking the glass in one, black, silk gloved hand.

Her voice was as melodic and light as he remembered and she was as beautiful as ever, dressed in that black, sequined evening gown he had always loved. Her long hair, tied back in a French twist, smelled delightfully of cucumbers.

"A toast," he cried, raising his glass.

"A toast," she echoed and laughed.

"To us! May we never be apart again." They emptied their glasses and laughing, tossed them over their shoulders for luck.

Daisy fingered a cigarette from a pack of Fat Bastards. Max, ever the gentleman, leaned across the table and lighted her cigarette. Daisy exhaled a plume of sweet smoke, placed one dainty elbow on the table, favoring Max with such smile he momentarily forgot all the shit that been fucking up his life in the last few years.

"So what have you been up to, Max?" Daisy said.

"Oh, you know, the same old, same old." Max shrugged and took one of her cigarettes for himself.

"Still on the job then?"

"What else would I be doing? I don't exactly have the temperament for normal life."

"No, you never did." Daisy sounded sad.

None of that shit, Max thought. He wasn't going to let anything ruin this night.

"Hey now, I've prepared a very special dinner," Holding up his finger, he rushed to the kitchen, returning moments later with a large covered serving plate that he sat on the table.

"*Voila, singe roti,*" he announced, removing the lid with an exaggerated flourish to reveal a beautiful roasted monkey.

"Bravo!" Daisy clapped her hands in delight.

"*Mademoiselle,*" he bowed and picked up the carving knife and fork. Always a gentleman, he served her first before slicing himself a nice slice from the breast.

Tucking in, he sighed in pleasure and anticipation. There would be dinner and pleasant conversation; he would not allow it to degenerate into one of their old arguments. Later there would be love, tenderness, and a temporary respite from his loneliness.

As Max brought the fork to his lips, his mind defogged enough that he saw his surroundings as they really were. His brow furrowed in disgust and momentary sanity. He could see the bum, dressed in Daisy's favorite gown, his face clean-shaven and made up. Daisy was long dead and he was trying to seduce a murdered hobo with a stringy boiled monkey and tap water in an old champagne bottle. He loathed himself, but like any addict he knew he was powerless to stop, he would keep playing this same scenario over and over until he was caught or he finally got up the nerve to put a bullet in his own head.

Max shook his head at his poor recreation. He needed to do better with the make-up, he always overdid the rouge and lipstick so his Daisys always wound up looking a bit like demented clowns. Next time he would do better, next time he would be more selective in picking his Daisy, instead of some old stew bum, he'd try a woman. He just needed to get over his reluctance to killing women. After all, there were plenty of nasty women who deserved killing just as much as men.

The cyborgs resumed their scurrying around his brain and Daisy was back. The dingy apartment was their old place in France and they were young and so much in love it hurt. She was no longer dead; he had brought her back just as he always brought her back, just as he would always bring her back.

"Penny for your thoughts?" she asked and she was just Daisy again, the bum's features erased by the lunatic's memories.

He smiled, content once more.

CHUCKLES
Tina Piney

Step, slap, squeak. Step, slap squeak.

"Why the fuck did I ever become a clown?" he mumbled to no one in particular. "Clowns, clowns have clown cars, joyous cars filled with clowns. But not Chuckles. No, Chuckles has to freaking walk!"

He knew why he became a clown. When he was a boy he stared, eyes fixed, absorbing every gesture, at a TV clown named Bozo. When he was a kid, clowns were worshipped. If you had a clown at your birthday party you were neighborhood royalty. Bozo had millions of fans, a TV show, records, books. And what did Chuckles have? A one room apartment above a Chinese food restaurant with access to a tiny metal grate-like balcony, so he could revel in the view of the alleys and garbage dumpsters. Bozo probably even had groupies. The closest Chuckles had was the slightly semen-like smell mixed with rot, vomit, and bean sprouts that wafted up from the dumpsters. Despite the 10% discount he was entitled to, he would never consider eating at the restaurant below. He didn't miss the irony of his pickiness as he sat eating cold frank and beans out of the can, trying not to notice the overwhelming stench of the flatulence his stress had brought him.

He was returning home after a failed birthday party halfway across the city. It was his only gig this month. He wasn't even sure that he would be able to keep his shit-assed apartment at this rate. The less he worked, the more rundown his suit and props became. This was a vicious circle because the worse he looked, the less he worked.

After taking a really good look at himself in the mirror last month, he decided he needed a new horn, a way to distract from his face. He was getting old and it showed. The greasepaint accentuated every wrinkle. It made him look a little scary. A flashy new horn to honk in everyone's faces was a great way to distract from his eyes and get the party started. He actually spent two weeks going every other day without food just to afford

11

it. He was so happy to have it. The unfortunate result was that this diet caused him to look emaciated, more baggy and wrinkled... more scary. Nevertheless, that morning he rose, washed thoroughly, got his costume on and headed out the door. He had a long walk, but was excited to have a chance to showcase his new horn. He walked quickly with a smile on his face, his shoes squeaking out his favorite tune.

It was nearly two hours before he finally reached the street that the party was on. He consulted his paper for the address and realized it was the next house on the right. He brought out his shiny new horn and readied himself for the show. He rounded the corner to the backyard as the mother had instructed. He was looking for Tristan, the seven year old birthday boy. He would be dressed in all blue, his favorite color, and wearing a special birthday hat with a flashing light on it.

Chuckles, in his excitement, had not thought to check his appearance. His exaggerated smile looked sinister on his skeletal frame. A Ball Park frank with extra onion-like stink which would assault anyone downwind rose from his sweat-stained pits. His makeup was smeared and running down his face. He spotted Tristan and charged forward, horn at the ready. Parents and kids alike turned towards the commotion. He got within a foot of the boy, honked the horn, laughed and yelled "Happy Birthday!"

The boy shit his pants.

Coulrophobia was a word that haunted Chuckles' dreams. The fear of clowns. In this day and age, how could anyone be afraid of clowns? Yet kids were more likely to request zombies at a birthday party than clowns. How could a clown, full of colour, making balloon animals, be more terrifying than a creature full of rot, salivating for your flesh? Okay, maybe if the clown was John Wayne Gacy looking to snuff you out and bury you in his basement. But Chuckles? Chuckles was paid $20 to leave Tristan's party. Half the kids were screaming and the parents hurled rather unpleasant remarks about his appearance and body odor. How could he get anyone to understand how hard he tried, the effort he put into to just getting to that damned party? How could he express his creative genius without performing or making a single balloon animal?

As he was pondering all of these things, Chuckles noticed a flattened squirrel by the side of the road. He crouched down to look at it, knees cracking as he lowered himself. He stared at the squirrel, one eye popped out and stuck to the side of its face. No one knew what that squirrel had to do to survive day to day, the extraordinary lengths it went to get its food, or how it braced itself against the cold. Nor did anyone care. That squirrel fought for everything it had, every day, yet someone ran it down without a second thought and left it there to rot away.

Not me, he thought, and with an overwhelming sense of pride picked up that squirrel and put it in his bag. Renewed, he finished his long walk home with a smile, snapping his fingers in time with the squeak from his shoes.

Chuckles made it home and excitedly removed the squirrel from his bag. When he first picked it up, he wasn't sure what he would do with it; he simply knew that he had to liberate it from the gutter. Now he had time to examine it more closely. With his gloves off, he realized that the poor little fellow was still warm. He felt the fur—way softer than he would have expected for a creature that had such a rough life. His own skin was tough and leathery from all the soap he used to remove his makeup. Maybe he should stop scrubbing so hard, let the oils from the makeup sit on his skin longer and rehydrate it a bit.

It occurred to him suddenly that the best way to honor the squirrel would be to eat it...*to survive...to carry on*. Chuckles brought the cutting board and knife over to the upside down basket he used as a coffee table. He positioned the squirrel on the board, considered it for a moment, then began to cut. First he removed the fur, careful to keep as much intact as possible. He cut off a few toes in the process, but when he peeled it from the carcass he felt a sense of pride. He'd done a good job. He grabbed an old newspaper and laid it out flat on the floor where he mindfully set the fur to dry. This was definitely something he wanted to hang on to.

He started cutting off tiny scraps of meat and laying them on a plate. Upon slicing open the stomach, a mass of stinky, slimy intestines slithered out. Obviously the poor little guy had some pretty bad body trauma. Chuckles couldn't help but stare at the goo and feel vindicated. He knew he was supposed to pick up this squirrel and here was the reason. He stuck his index finger in the mess, looped an undamaged section of intestine around it and pulled.

Something snapped in his head. He had an idea. The tenuous hold on his sanity had broken—he was free!

The hours passed like minutes, Chuckles smiling ear to ear the whole while. It was tedious work removing all of the intestines and organs. It took even longer to empty them of the various (and rapidly spoiling) fluids. Finally, his squirrel meat dinner long forgotten, he stood over the pile of innards, ready to create. The trickiest one to work with was by far the heart, so tiny with all those little openings. His trained fingers worked and tied them all closed, all but one. He had a few ideas what he could make with it, but he first he had to see how it inflated.

13

He put the remaining opening to his mouth and blew. Nothing. He tried harder. Except for looking more rounded, it hadn't changed in size. On occasion he would get a bag of "bad" balloons that did the same thing. You could blow out your eardrums trying to inflate the fuckers. In those cases he took out his small bicycle pump to inflate and loosen up the balloons so they were ready for the show. He got the pump, hooked it up and started to inflate the heart. He smiled. It was working! He pumped air into the little heart balloon until...POP! He was surprised at how much blood was left in it after such a thorough washing. He had been smiling when it exploded and bits of heart and blood stuck to his teeth as well as the rest of him.

"Well," he said out loud, "guess the heart breaks too easily." And broke out into giggles.

He worked through the night. Experiment after experiment with tiny organs, all failed, except the lungs - they inflated *very* well, but the shape left much to be desired.

Chuckles finally made his way to the intestines. Here were his inspiration and his salvation all in one. He started by checking through for damage and cut sections out that had no holes in them and tied one end closed. Soon he had a small pile of intestine balloons. He took one last look at them, crossed his fingers, honked his big red nose and began. Choosing the longest from the pile, he placed the intestine on his lips and blew. It was too slippery and shot out of his mouth and half way across the room. Unfazed, he grabbed it, stuck it back between his lips and teeth and, gently squeezing, blew it again. Success! He inflated it and quickly tied the end.

"And now for the tricky part" Chuckles said quietly.

Chuckles really did have a way with balloons. He was a master and could form just about any shape you could think up. He already knew what this one was to be. He fashioned a tiny squirrel intestine balloon. Even he couldn't believe the level of detail his new medium could provide. He crawled on his knees from where he was sitting and placed the squirrel on the window, looking out at the world, just as the sun was rising in the distance. He crawled back, laid his face on the pelt and fell asleep smiling.

The squirrel was staring at the setting sun when Chuckles finally stirred. He hadn't felt so good or refreshed in ages. The squirrel meat was calling to him. He soaked it in some water, added some salt and fried it up. He hoped that, somewhere, the squirrel knew how much Chuckles owed him. Not just for the meal, but the new direction with his art. He realized that he was itching to create again and reached out towards the pile of intestine balloons. His hand grazed them.

Chuckles screamed with horror. They had dried out while he slept.

He was ruined! He could never use them to create again! He started sobbing so hard he had trouble breathing. He was trying to catch his breath and began to panic. He caught sight of the intestine squirrel on his windowsill and became calm. His breathing returned to normal. Would *that* squirrel begin bawling like a baby at a small setback? No, it would not. And neither would Chuckles.

"Suck it up, buttercup," he told himself. Chuckles had a plan.

He decided not to wear the squeaky shoes and work under cover of darkness. It wasn't that he was ashamed to admit what he was doing, it's just that he had so much to do and couldn't spare the time to talk to any nosey arsehole that got to wondering. He took a quick glance in the mirror. He looked younger! Sure, his makeup was smeared and there were bits of blood and flesh on his face, but this was a new Chuckles. He was on the right path. He reached for his bag and headed out the door.

The key was fresh animals...dead, but fresh. He certainly wasn't going to kill any himself—that would be crazy! He knew he was going to have to pound the pavement, so to speak, but he didn't mind. He had a mental list of places, near parks and ravines, which he was going to visit. The more animals, the more dead animals. He would liberate them all, even the ones that weren't fresh. He would take their pelts, preserve the memory of their struggle and then their liberation. Yes! He was their Liberator. That would make a crappy clown name though, best to stick with Chuckles.

His first stop was a local high school. He knew the science lab had various animals preserved in containers. It was easy enough to break into, main floor, large windows. He found a big pail with what looked like a shark inside it. He took the shark out and laid it on the floor. He saw several smaller containers with various animal and animal parts and carefully drained the preservative into the shark bucket until it was fairly full. He snapped the lid closed and returned back home. He quickly deposited the booty in his apartment and headed back out the door.

He spent every night for the next six nights walking the city. There were many squirrels. He had found a couple that were fresh enough to eat, but none that had intestines that were fresh enough to stretch and create with. He thought, on day three, that he had found a raccoon, but it turned out to be a badly mangled cat, useless for his art. Nevertheless, he liberated its pelt as well.

On the seventh day, Chuckles was dreaming. He no longer had to walk anywhere. All the squirrels that he had liberated in life lifted him on their backs in his dream. He was carried like a king throughout the city, his pelt cape flapping majestically in the breeze. They deposited him in front of a grey stone building. He was smiling down at them, but they were all staring past him. He looked up and read the words "City Pound".

He awoke that evening with a new plan. What could be better than liberating squirrels? Liberating the loved and forgotten, the cats and dogs that met their end at the pound. He knew there was no way he could save them all, but one per week should do it. That would keep him fed, add to his pile of pelts, and supply the fresh intestines for his balloons. The pound was only a fifteen minute walk and, as luck would have it, it was Friday and they were open until 9:00 PM. He approached the grey stone animal pound and went inside. The place was empty of humans, save one, so he knew whom to approach. The din from cats and dogs suggested a full house. He walked up to the man behind a small desk and read 'Matt' on his nametag.

"This may sound weird", Chuckles began, "but I lost my monkey. He wears a little striped vest and answers to the name "Monty." Has anyone turned him in?"

Matt looked Chuckles up and down and blinked twice, like he wasn't exactly sure what he was seeing. He cleared his throat and answered, "Uh, that would be no, sorry."

"Oh," continued Chuckles, "Can you tell me what day you put the animals down? It would break my heart to think of my Monty stuck here thinking I forgot about him and then...well, you know."

"We put them down every Monday evening," explained Matt without emotion, "if they come in on the weekend, it will be the following Monday."

"Thanks, I'll make sure to check back Monday if I don't find him."

There was no doubt about it; everything was finally coming together for Chuckles. He was even starting to look younger. He would get fresh intestines and practice and, in about a month, perfect a new act: Chuckles and his Animals. He spent the weekend sewing the squirrel pelts together to make pants.

When Monday came, he woke earlier in the afternoon than usual. He felt like a kid on Christmas morning, but decided to be productive while he waited for the animal pound to close and the after hour's extermination to begin. He used his considerable drawing talents to design a new advertising poster for Chuckles and His Animals. He drew squirrels frolicking, a cat dancing, a dog balancing on a ball, even threw in the raccoon he thought he had, honking on a shiny horn. He added his prepaid cell phone number, as his landline had long ago been cut off, and "Balloon Animal Artist Extraordinaire" just for good measure.

On the way to the pound he dropped of the flyer at a local print and copy place and ordered what the remains of his money could buy, minus $5. He then bought a $5 calling card to add minutes to his phone. He knew he wouldn't make rent next week anyway and now he had a regular source of food, he had all he needed. If the act went over the way he thought it would, he would be able to pay up the rent next month, maybe even get a case of beer. It had been so long since he'd experienced the simple pleasure of a cold beer on a hot day that his mouth watered in anticipation.

It was just before six when he got to the pound, so he headed to an alley across the street. It wasn't dark yet, but the alley was and it served as an excellent vantage point to observe the pound. There was only one truck in the lot. Chuckles bet it belonged to that douche, Matt. *He probably enjoys killing them. The humane thing would be to give the animals a chance, or at least more than a freaking week.*

After about fifteen minutes he heard a door open, followed by the sound of someone screeching open the rusty side of a dumpster. He couldn't see anyone, but he bet the area to the side of the pound, with the ten foot tall wooden fence, was where it came from. Scraping, dragging, and banging sounds carried on for another five minutes, then stopped. A couple minutes later, Matt appeared, exited, and locked the doors behind him. He got into the truck and sped away.

Chuckles checked to make sure the coast was clear, pushed a small dumpster from the alley across the road, and parked it against the fence. No one was about, so he scaled the dumpster and jumped over the fence. He landed hard, but safely and looked around. He spotted the pound's dumpster. His eyes immediately fell on a skinny leg sticking out of the small door opening on the side of the dumpster. He felt like crying. Even trash is treated with more respect. *Liberating this animal is special.* He felt his heart swell as he maneuvered the dead dog out of the dumpster. He set it down gently and rolled a smaller dumpster back over to the fence. He peeked to see no one was around, threw the dog over the fence, and into the first dumpster, following quickly behind. He popped back out, rolled the dumpster back to the darkened alley and removed the dog. The dog was still warm as Chuckles pulled the bag up around its considerable frame.

The clown rushed home with the dog in the bag and bounded up the stairs. He got him out of the bag and onto the newspapers he had spread out in advance. He decided to name the dog Bozo, the most honorable name he could think of, and gave him a kiss on his soft muzzle. "Suck it up, buttercup" he said, steeling himself. He was ready to liberate

Bozo.

The next week was a blur of intestines and fried dog meat. Once he had all the intestines cut to size and stored in the old shark pail, he worked his magic, beginning with a balloon animal in Bozo's likeness to sit next to the squirrel in the window sill.

The next Monday, he repeated the process. He started to fill out his clothes again and was looking younger still. Some of the intestine balloons were practiced on and the rest were saved. Two more Mondays passed and Chuckles felt refreshed and ready. He had a full belly and a new act. He took his new advertising posters and hit the streets.

Chuckles was out in daylight again for the first time in quite a while. In his deranged mind, he saw welcoming smiles. Those who saw him had quite a different story. Chuckles had been so busy he had completely forgotten to bathe or wash his clothes. To anyone that was unfortunate enough to get too close, the combined smells of blood, feces and fried dog meat were strong enough to bring tears. As he planned, he no longer removed his makeup, just touched it up on occasion. You could see the dementia smeared all over his face. Needless to say, no one who saw him putting up posters had dared to call his phone, let alone considered hiring him. Unfortunately, Theresa wasn't witness to the spectacle.

When Theresa was six years old, her mother had hired Chuckles to perform at her birthday party. She never forgot him. There was even a picture she still had of her holding her Statue of Liberty balloon that Chuckles had made. Seeing the poster brought back fond memories. On a whim, she decided to get Chuckles to perform at her twins' fourth birthday party on Saturday.

When Theresa phoned, Chuckles was over the moon with excitement. They made the arrangements and when he hung up, Chuckles grabbed the Squirrel and Bozo and danced around the room. He would finally have his chance to show his art again.

Step, slap squeak.

He headed up the stairs to Theresa's door. As instructed, he would let himself in. This also gave him the chance to lock the door behind him. When asked later, no one could say what first caught their attention, the squeak or the smell.

Then the screaming began. No one knew what to do. A clown from a nightmare, wearing a dog skin cape and squirrel pants, stood in the living room.

Chuckles was thrilled by the screams of excitement and was surprised that most of the adults were screaming too. He opened the intestine bucket. A little blond girl nearest to him passed out cold. He decided he would make her something special for when she awoke. He started inflating and shaping the intestines into a unicorn. Still the screaming continued. He worked quickly and, within a minute, tried to hand the mother the unicorn, which stood about twenty four inches high. She refused it.

Everyone started gathering their kids and backing away. He was not impressing them. What had he missed? His mind grasped for the answer and he found it. Of course, the intestine creations lacked sheer size, the size that impressed. He needed to make something bigger. But how? He had so carefully planned his performance and cut down the intestines.

"Wait," he cried desperately. "My next creation is sure to delight and amaze you! I will now create a man-sized reproduction of the Statue of Liberty!"

He delved into his bag and pulled out his skinning knife and seltzer bottle. The chorus of screams erupted anew. Chuckles glanced around and all he saw and heard were looks of amazement and screams of adoration. *I have them, finally*, he thought. He slashed open his own gut, ripping furiously at his intestines, pulling them out. He cut a nice long piece and was busy cleaning it with his seltzer bottle when he passed out from the blood loss.

About Tina Piney

Living on a windswept hill in Ontario, Canada, Tina spends her time doting on her four year old twins. When she has a moment to herself, she like to read, daydream, and write. She loves Clive Barker, Halloween, and just about anything spooky.

THE SULTAN OF WEIRD
John Ledger

Constructed in 1847, the Davenport mansion was a gigantic black eyesore watching over the end of Mason Lane. Andrew Davenport used it as a winter home for his family of nine. But after three years, Andrew, his wife Elizabeth, their six daughters and son had vacated the house permanently. Andrew swore the mansion was cursed and had refused to let the evil that lived there cause any harm to his family. He sold the mansion to a wealthy investor by the name of William York, warning him of the evil within those black walls. Since he planned on renting out the home or reselling it to turn a profit, Mr. York wasn't concerned about any dark paranormal activity that might or might not infest the mansion. He was practical, a businessman, not given to worrying about spooks and bumps in the night. The Davenports signed the necessary paperwork and completed their transaction and that was that. They left as quickly as they could.

Mr. York couldn't believe how quickly he was contacted about the property. A woman with an Asian accent was on the phone claiming that she needed to find a home for her brother, and that he was royalty. A Sultan from Turkey who would need a large estate for his wives and his servants. William thought it was the craziest shit he'd ever heard, but the price she offered to pay was too pretty to pass on, so they made a deal. Two days later, a group of twenty or more people moved into the mansion and it wasn't too far into the first week of their arrival when the neighbors began to express concern amongst one another. Many strange things had transpired since the Sultan's arrival, and it was only getting weirder.

All of the windows had been boarded up and painted pink, while the once blackened atrocity of a home was now a gold and pink nightmare. The neighbors had also noticed that numerous females of foreign descent entered the home but none of them ever left. A limousine would leave and bring them back to the house one or two at a time but the next time the limo left, it was only the driver. One neighbor in particular was very involved in the neighborhood watch situation and very vocal as well. Oliver

Thorn called the police when it all went down and spoke to the local news.

"It was like something from another planet. They had guards outside at all times and they were like little people, midgets, you know? And they were naked, all of them, except they had diapers on. They had swords too, weirdest shit I ever seen. That nut, he had parties or something going on. We always heard the same music, weird Indian sounding stuff, I don't know, I'm an old man. But I ain't crazy and I know what I saw today! I'm just glad it's all over. They need to burn that house down."

Oliver's statement to the police about what he'd witnessed sure sounded crazy though, completely bat shit crazy. Apparently, the Sultan was out on his front lawn, riding a donkey around in the nude. And that wasn't even the crazy part. His seven wives, also in their birthday suits, were crawling around the yard on all fours like dogs while the Sultan yelled and screamed commands at them in some foreign tongue.

The events that followed would be forever burned into Oliver Thorn's brain.

The women were ordered to defecate in the yard, then forced to sample each other's droppings. Oliver threw up in his mouth a little as he watched this, but he couldn't force himself to turn away; it was like a car accident that you just had to investigate, only much worse. The Sultan then jumped off of his donkey and retrieved a bullwhip from the porch. He continued to scream at the women as he made his rounds, lashing all of them until they were bloody and in tears. The front doors suddenly opened and out came the midgets with knives and erections, ready to strike. The women were lined up in a horizontal row, still on all fours, waiting for whatever was about to happen next. The Sultan commanded the midgets and they were eager to please as they each lined up behind the wives, mounting them from behind. The Sultan laughed triumphantly like a raving lunatic, stroking his massive erection as he watched the show that he provided for himself. He yelled out one last command and the midgets responded by slitting the wives' throats from behind and then sawing off their heads. They came, and so did the Sultan before disappearing back inside the Golden Palace with the heads.

As soon as the police arrived they noticed the stench of death in the air. Then they saw the headless bodies in the front lawn and blood oozing out from underneath the front doors of the crazy house. It was time to go in with guns drawn.

After opening the front door, several officers began blowing chunks on the spot. The few who didn't stood wide-eyed in shock, taking it all in. There were more dead women inside and many other bodies as well.

22

Parts would be a better description, considering there were arms, legs, feet, and torsos scattered about like some satanic jigsaw puzzle. It was impossible to tell how many people had been killed here. Organs, blood, shit and other fluids decorated the walls, floor and furniture, but no heads were found anywhere. Neither was the Sultan. Days later, police would determine that the midget's bodies were amongst the carnage. The mansion was cleaned up and the neighborhood was happy to see it vacated once again. They decided to paint it black again because nobody wanted to remember the "Golden Palace".

Several hundred miles away...

Andrew Davenport was sitting on the front porch in his rocking chair when he saw him. He figured the Jack he was drinking must've gotten the best of him until one of his daughters, Adelia, tapped him on the shoulder. "Daddy, who's that man?" She asked.

"I don't know baby. Just a stranger. Now go back inside and get to bed, honey."

"Okay, daddy. Goodnight." She gave her daddy a kiss and ran back inside the house. Andrew watched and waited as a tear fell from his eye. This was it, this was their end. His whole family was about to be slaughtered and there was nothing that he could do about it. The visions from the black house weren't about the house. They were about him—the stranger, the master. It didn't matter that Andrew had moved his family away to safety- because there was none. There was no escaping the evil.

Andrew had his gun in his hand, ready to end it all himself. He knew it was the coward's way out, but there was no way he could bear witness to his visions becoming a reality. Just as he was ready to pull the trigger ,the demon rode by on his donkey with a bag full of heads and kept on going down the road. Andrew let out a sigh of relief and took another shot from the bottle. He was ready to thank God when his prayers were interrupted by a female voice.

"You're not safe."

"What? Who the hell are you?" Andrew looked over to see an Asian woman dressed in all black standing on the step of his porch. She had come out of nowhere, literally.

"Who I am does not matter. My master just showed you that he knows where you are. You are not safe here and this is not your home. The mansion needs you and your family. You shall return there immediately."

"I don't think so lady. You're fucking nuts and we are not going back to that house. No way in hell."

"It's funny you mention hell, Mr. Davenport, because when you built the mansion you opened a doorway to a sort of hell. You opened a portal to another dimension which now resides in that house and it's your responsibility to take care of it."

"You can kiss my ass. Get off my property, lady. Now." Andrew pointed the gun at the woman's head and she smiled as she stepped towards him with eyes full of malice. Andrew tried to pull the trigger, but he couldn't. He couldn't move at all. The woman stared at him intently and he was frozen in place. She unbuckled his pants and took his organ in her hands as she whispered into his ear. "You can't move because I'm not letting you. I, like my master, have powers that you are incapable of understanding. As you can see, no matter how hard you resist and no matter how much you want to kill me right now, you can't stop your cock from throbbing in my hand. You will do as I say or we will devour your whole fucking family. Do you understand me, Andrew?"

"Yes." Andrew came and he cried as the woman vanished into thin air. Andrew finished his bottle of Jack and went to bed. He had a long day of moving ahead of him.

***

About John Ledger

John Ledger lives in Enola, Pennsylvania, with his angel Erica and their four children; Carson, Kaila, Logan, and Layla. He has several short stories published amongst multiple JWK Fiction and upcoming JEA anthologies. His first book, a collection titled *Abstract Island,* will be published by JEA sometime in 2015. John has co-edited the anthologies *Floppy Shoes Apocalypse* and *'Cellar Door III: Animals/Hell II: Citizens,* and is also involved with several upcoming projects such as *Under The Bridge, Fata Arcana, Doorway To Death, 13:Trashed, Drowning in Gore, Cherry Nose Nightmares, Creampie Facial, and Suburban Secrets.* John enjoys video games, serial killers, dogs, punk rock, wrestling, and Chinese food. You can find him on Facebook, talking a bunch of nonsense.

GROWING PAINS
Amanda M. Lyons

Her name was Abigail Elizabeth Kain, and she was born in the middle of a hot and balmy summer to two young parents who were just starting out themselves. While certainly not teenagers, Hailey and Ethan were relatively new to the idea of being out on their own. They'd graduated a few years before and lived with Hailey's mother for a couple of years after that. Young and feeling reckless, they'd conceived Abby on a whim about eight months after they moved into their own place, a small one bedroom at the top of some stairs in what amounted to a triplex. It wasn't much, but they were happy; and two years sounded like enough of a commitment.

The pregnancy hadn't exactly gone according to plan. First there was the false positive for cerebral palsy, which had sent Hailey into hysterics at three months. Then the ice storm a few weeks after that, which took out the power, and with it, the heat, leaving them no other choice but to stay with his brother until it was over. The final, and for Hailey, most frightening thing, was the news that a C-section would be needed, dashing all dreams for a natural birth. Despite all of these things, and all of the little disappointments that come with the idea of parenting versus the reality, they were happy to have made the choice and were learning how to be good at their new job.

Abigail was a healthy baby, tall and sturdy, with full lips and blue-grey eyes like her mother's. It took them a while to get used to waking up all night and day long, to being tired and out of sorts while she, and they, sorted out the schedule that worked best for them. It took time, but eventually they worked it through, though no less exhausted and vigilant than before.

Out in the yard, below a tree that both parents passed every day, that indeed Abigail herself passed every day in a stroller on her way to yet another desperate walk so her mother might catch a nap, there was an unusual growth. It looked like any old harmless fungus that might grow on or near the roots of a tree, and maybe that was why it never got more than

25

a passing glance from any of the people that passed it on the way to their cars. Well, that and the fact that we humans rarely see all of the details, the small changes in our lives, until they slap us in the face. It was a mottled blend of orange, brown and bits of white, lacey shapes whirling out and out from a center piece, the whole of the fungi as wide as two feet in circumference.

It was a creation most unwholesome, awful to look at and even worse to encounter if you knew what it really was. Of course, Ohio was full of ugly fungi, surely it was just more of that? Tricky, tricky little abomination, how you fooled them, bidding your time.

Abigail was two months old, a wobbly, joyful little bundle when she learned just what it was, what it could do. How could she tell them what had happened? How she was looking at it, noting the variations in color enough to look, just when the thing itself decided to spring its awful trap.

The movement was so imperceptible, so minute that no one else saw. Some small fiber popped up and into the air just as little Abigail had peered over from her cradle in the stroller, meeting her face with a tiny plop on contact. It landed on her nose, making her already cross-eyed appearance more pronounced, almost humorous. Then it drifted to her tear duct and up into that tiny space. A startled look swam across her face, and then she went back to being the small baby she was. Deep within, the tiny invader began its work.

Over the next three weeks the differences were small, little things were off about little Abby. Hailey, her mother, thought there was just a little less light about her, a softer, less invested suck in her nursing, but at her well-baby visit the nurse and the doctor both found nothing to indicate that anything was really wrong, no physical differences, certainly no fever or change in her mental state. Nevertheless, within, the fungus had begun to grow.

It was small at first, a tiny bud that had imbedded itself in the frontal lobe of the small baby and did little to affect her as it started, branching out in tiny tendrils from the base filial, a little tree which grew up and over the space around her frontal lobe, slipped small little fingers between it and her temporal lobe, and wrapped lovingly around the parietal and occipital lobes. Then it sent long cool branches into the cerebral cortex and down to the brainstem. It was a subtle and delicate process, one that did not disturb Abby much beyond a strange tickling sensation that would cause her to stop nursing and listen, attentive and alert, as it slithered along the whorls of her brain.

Hailey watched, alert for small changes, but it did not seem to be anything too important, not then. Her baby's little mouth would latch back where it had been a moment before and she would continue to nurse with abandon, lost in the sensation and the warm comfort of a full belly. Soon, she drifted off to sleep, oblivious to the slow creep of change in her small skull, the parasitic mycelium slipping into her control centers, her motor functions, and various glands that had barely begun to produce anything for her to live and thrive on.

Each day was busy, rife with new discoveries for the child: tummy time, bright objects to gaze at, and the loving comfort of her parents' arms. It also came with guests, sweet, strange faces that fascinated the small baby and that the fungi, in its small cell, noted with quiet calculation. Proximity and time, those were its weapons. It had one, but there was still so much more of the other yet to endure.

No matter, it would come, soon it would grow, soon it would branch out further, soon it would be able to build up its mass and then, oh then it would have what it sought!

You didn't think that fungi could embody the complexity of thought? That it was no more than some mindless lump for you to crush underfoot, to chop into your meals, to mash into powder for your medicines? Oh no, no, you see, arrogant as we are, we do not know all, we do not always see, and we shall always suffer for that blindness. Watch now as it grows, watch as it slowly plots its path, causes Abigail to turn her face to the light of the sun creeping into her bedroom, the better to reach its goals. Watch it and learn.

Soon she can feel it pressing out the shifting discs of her as yet unsealed skull, filling up all of the spaces in her head, pressing down on her mind, sending more and more messages, more orders for her to follow. She learns to lift her head, to roll over, to shift and to undulate to meet its demands. She seems to be growing like any normal baby, to grow and to develop, but it makes her a child who is at turns utterly quiet and colicky. A child who loses her small smiles almost as soon as she begins them, who listens and watches intently, focused on seemingly nothing at all.

"Don't you think it's strange, Ethan? How she does that? Doesn't it make you worry there's something wrong with her? Something...different?"

"Again? Jesus, Hailey, how many doctors will it take? How many clean bills of health? She's fine, she'll *be* fine, just let her be."

"But I—"

"Drop it."

A subtle distance is growing between them, an anger and frustration, a resentment growing in him as she struggles to make him see.

But, in time, he will come to see it too, to see it and to watch in horror, a horror so strong that it demands denial. So strong that he begins to give warning looks and, from time to time when she just won't let it go, he hits her, hits her and fights not to look into the crib where alien eyes look back at him from his daughter's face.

By then there is no denying that something is wrong, her eyes are wrong, her position as she lies in her crib and as she nurses at her mother's breast is wrong. Everything is wrong and there doesn't seem to be any way to make it stop.

And there isn't, not now, nor was there ever, not really. Her head is growing rounder, heavier and more unnatural, sometimes, when they look at her soft spot, the smooth indented flesh seems to pulse in a new way, as if there were something there, something awful and unknowable. They've given up on doctors now, feeding her, changing her, bathing her, all the while knowing that something must be coming.

And one day, in the middle of the afternoon, on a day her father has opted to stay home from work and her mother is resting wrapped in his arms a few feet away from her crib in their bed. It happens.

They don't know that Mrs. Jacobs, down the street, is already fruiting in her 2nd floor bedroom, her cats pissing and shitting wherever they like as they steer clear of the only human they have ever really known, vast, thick, pieces of fungus poking out of her flesh, her head, her face, one grotesque pillar of it having torn through her opened mouth and stretched it so taught that it has cracked her jaw apart in her flesh. Nor do they know about Colton Andrews, the paperboy whose body exploded with life one night as his mother attempted to give him a bath after a long bought of seeming illness, or how it took her and, shortly after that, his father too. There are many more, so many from just one horrid, beastly, little fungi at the root of a tall oak tree on one street. Dogs, cats, squirrels, men, women, children, all of them growing in ways they had never imagined they could.

Ethan and Hailey Kain did not know what was happening around them, what had already begun to happen all over town, because they were watching as their beloved six month old baby sat up at an unnatural angle in her bed. Looked at them with her wide, shining eyes and reached out her arms. For a moment, Hailey stayed in the bed, watching and waiting, and then she gave into her mothering instincts and swept the infant up in her arms. Abigail waited for her to settle into the bed with her father and then she began to turn to her mother's breast, giving the signal that she wanted to nurse. With reluctant movements, Hailey freed her breast from her oversized t-shirt and her baby latched home.

She howled in horror, the pain of those jaws wrapped tight into the flesh of her breast, an awful sensation overcome only by the sight of her daughter's skull exploding with an audible pop that sent chunks of her skull flying across the room to imbed in the wood-paneled closet. Thick, wet organic noises followed in the seconds after, the sound of the fungi unfurling in the baby's empty skull, through the grey matter, and into the air for three feet around her head, sending forth its own spawn into the parents' faces as it forced her eyes from her sockets to expand there too.

Its young did not wait, growing at a much faster rate than their progenitor, sending forth tendrils and thick fungi from the parents in seconds. So quickly that they did not so much as get a moment to cry out in horror over the loss of their baby, now little more than broken bones and burst open meat in their laps. Their lower jaws were ripped from their faces with the force of the new growth, their chests a writhing mass of new life and their soon lifeless bodies rendered terribly artful sculptures. A new silence fell over their small town, and, in time, the one after that, and then the next. A terrible wave of new life shot into life, rendering the most heavily overpopulated animal on the planet— and murderer of so many other species—a quivering sea of reclaimed nature. Mother Earth had found her solution.

***

About Amanda M. Lyons

A longtime fan of horror and fantasy, Ms. Lyons writes character driven novels that, while influenced by her darker interests, can also be heavily laced with fantasy, romance, history and magic. Amanda M. Lyons has lived her whole life in rural Ohio where she lives with her fiancee and two children. Amanda is also Lead Editor US Division with J Ellington Ashton Press and a freelance novel editor.

RAINBOW EXPULSIONS
Jorge Palacios

My story began at the age of twelve, when I was leaving home from school. It was a hot and humid day, and the van's constant shaking was becoming something of a hassle for my best friend, Stephen. Stephen was a fat kid who liked to play softball and eat nachos the way a cow eats grass. He told me when he got on board that he'd been feeling sick, worried about a ham sandwich he ate the previous night which might have been tainted or rotten. As he shook back and forth, his face became paler, and he talked less and less, as I continued the conversation about yesterday afternoon's episode of the *Mighty Morphin Power Rangers* and how I wanted the blue Ranger to be my boyfriend.

It happened as we turned onto the highway. It was only ten minutes away from the school, but whatever was inside Stephen could not hold itself any longer. He leaned over towards me and vomited, the chunky liquids falling on my face and body. You could say that the other students in the bus reacted completely normal to the situation, screaming and hollering, words like "ew" and "gross" coming out of them.

The bus driver started to laugh. My reaction was completely different, however. As I felt the warmth of the digested contents inside Stephen's stomach, I couldn't explain why, but I enjoyed it. It was warm, as I said, but it also felt electric, full of energy and life. After it happened, I looked at myself and felt fascinated with what I saw. It was an orange/yellow liquid, and in it were bits and pieces of bread, cheese, ham, nachos and pepperoni. I don't know if it was the smell, but I became nauseous as well, and I vomited all over Stephen, who had collapsed onto his seat. Like clockwork, he began to vomit again, this time onto himself. The other students kept screaming, and some also began to vomit. The bus driver wasn't laughing anymore, and he also vomited all over himself and had to pull over.

The incident was henceforth known in the annals of the school's history as the Chunkblower Catastrophe. It would have been talked about for years and years, and until my graduation, I was known as Hurling Harley, the girl who instigated an entire grade to vomiting. I became an urban legend, referred to in the same vein as the boy who got his penis stuck on the clam chowder in the school cafeteria, and the girl who had her period climbing the rope during gym class and made blood rain down on the coach.

Needless to say, I wasn't very popular.

At least not in school.

By the time I was fifteen, I had grown tits and an ass that would make most thirty year olds jealous of me. I began to hang out at the mall, and listened to rock & roll, with bands like AC/DC, Kiss and Black Sabbath ruling my world. I was into danger and wanted to be a part of it, but since I didn't have a driver's license, I could barely make it out of the multiplex. I met my first sexual encounter, Jake, right around that time. I was hanging out in front of the bookstore, when this kid in a Dracula shirt approached me. We talked about horror movies and Metallica, then he invited me to see *Wishmaster*. I was overjoyed; he wasn't. He began to freak out and, fifteen minutes into the movie, he walked out. I tried not to laugh at him. I could have followed him, but I decided to stay, since I was loving this movie too much.

After the movie was done, I saw him in front of the bookstore. I tried not to make fun of him, but it was difficult not to.

"What the hell, man?" I asked.

"Shut up, bitch!" he said.

"Don't call me bitch," I continued. "You're the fucking bitch! You're the one who couldn't handle a little latex, makeup, and Karo syrup!"

"Fuck you!"

He meant it, too. He crossed his arms and looked at the floor, clearly embarrassed. He had leather boots with a chain around them that looked pretty cool. I looked at him with pity, and I decided that I wanted him to take my virginity away. As you can imagine, he got really excited and said yes immediately.

On the way to his motorcycle (yes, I said motorcycle) I found out a couple of things. First, he was twenty-two, which made his squeamishness even more pathetic. He told me he was studying for a business major and had plans to form his own rock & roll bar which he would decorate with all sorts of Satanic-looking crap. I just nodded. I knew I was dealing with nothing but a poseur, a wannabe rock & roller who acted all badass, but was nothing but a pussy. Still, I wanted to lose my virginity, and a cock is a cock, as the saying goes. At least the motorcycle's vibrations felt good between my legs, getting me wet before we even reached his apartment.

It was the kind of place you'd expect a poseur to have. For all his talk of rock & roll, he had posters of mainstream bands like Fleetwood Mac, Aerosmith (90's Aerosmith, yeech) and haircut-era Metallica. By this time I was getting into NWOBHM bands and underground stuff, so I felt a little turned off, but I was still wet from the motorcycle. We both got naked at the same time, and I have to admit that he looked pretty good naked: his figure was nice, he had a cool demon tattoo above his crotch, and his penis was big and clean. He looked very pleased to see me, too, but I knew I looked good naked.

He approached me and began to kiss me. I felt no warmth or emotion, and as he took my virginity, I barely reacted. Then I began to remember Stephen, and our vomiting incident in the bus. The warmth of the vomit, the pain that came from doing it to him. I began to get very hot and emotional, and I realized that *that* was the moment that I truly lost my virginity. Sexuality wasn't just about penetration: it was about the exchange of energy, and what is vomit, if not half-digested energy? Stephen and I made love that day, and it was the kind of love that didn't hurt the first time you did it.

I began to gag loudly but Jake didn't seem to care about it, one way or another. He was too busy having a good fuck, and just as he came (two minutes, longer than most men) I hurled all over him. I was on top, so it fell all over his chest and face, plus his mouth was open, chunks of bile and pizza showering him. He began to scream in horror, gagging as he pushed me off of him and running into the bathroom. As he showered, screaming and cursing, I was in the throes of my first orgasm. It was explosive, and it made me shake all over. I dressed quickly and left his apartment before he got out of the shower.

I ran all the way to the coffee shop on the corner, and called my dad from my cell phone. He picked me up twenty minutes later.

I turned thirty-one this year, and every sexual experience since then had been somewhat uneventful. Sure, I had been in love with two or three men, and I had a couple of non-romantic sexual experiences. None of them were mind -blowing, most were passable, but nothing compared to the energy and passion I felt when I had my two vomiting experiences. When I masturbated, I would gag myself with my hand, sticking it deep inside until I expelled whatever was in my stomach at the time. I didn't do it the way those bulimic bitches did it, to try to get thinner or because they saw themselves fat when they were rail thin. The warmth and the energy really turned me on, and I was terrified every year that passed, as I realized I had an intense vomit fetish. I would puke on myself, letting it fall on my vagina and stomach, fingering myself harder, letting the warm, digested food go inside me, and getting hotter and hotter as I did so. Then I would take a long, hot shower, cleaning myself out. It was almost a weekly routine, and it got to the point where I could barely get hot if I *didn't* think of vomit.

I was a permanent fixture at Weston and Bros. I had been working there for eight years, selling insurance and trying my best to out-smart my co-workers, trying to steal their customers, and making sure I was making more money than the rest of them. We went from house to house, acting as if our insurance was the REAL insurance, the one that really worked and was worth sinking a ton of money into. And me? I was one of the best of the bullshit artists. Perhaps it was because I am a beautiful woman, or because I could make a good 'caring puppy' face as I listened to all their problems, but I was the most successful saleswoman at the firm. But even though I made a good living, I was lonely. My dark secrets, as well as my busy schedule, made me afraid of going out and meeting friends, and terrified of going out on a date. Other than some, well, extracurricular activities, I hadn't had sex for two years, until he showed up.

I met him at work. He was tall, dark and handsome, with nicely trimmed short hair on top of his head and a dark goatee that matched the color of his eyes. His suit was impeccable and his shoes shone. I take notice of little things like that. We were all called to the meeting room by Mr. Weston, our boss, and I sat on the front row, the top saleswoman of the firm, looking at him as he stood next to the boss.

"Ladies and gentlemen," the boss said, "I want you all to meet Robert Kingston, our newest member. Robert used to work with Stark Bros, and has come to us with years of experience back in Oregon. Now that he's with us, I'd like one of you to volunteer to give him a tour of Widow Falls, particularly the South side, where he'll be taking over the dearly departed Johnson."

Ah, yes. Johnson. I murdered him.

I found Johnson sneaking around one of my houses, trying to sneak in on my territory. I followed him home, and after I knocked him out with my car's crowbar, I disemboweled him. I loved to kill people, especially if I could take my time to play with their bodies. I opened his stomach up and bathed in the insides, pouring the contents of his stomach and intestines all over my body. He had been my thirteenth. These were the extracurricular activities I was referring to.

After I was done, I took a shower to wash all the blood and goo off, then wrapped his body in a carpet I always kept in the trunk of my car.

Dragging the corpse to my trunk is always the hardest part of disposing of the body, but you can't do anything you love without suffering a little. After that bit of unpleasantness, I went back to the house and cleaned the blood off of the floor and walls. Then I went home and cut the body up, keeping some chunks so I could eat in my spare time. The human body is similar to pork, and if you cook it well, it can be pretty tasty. After that, I stayed up all night listening to Midnight's *Satanic Royalty* and Slayer's *Reign in Blood.* All in all, it was a great fucking weekend.

Anyway, back to the meeting.

Mr. Weston patted Robert on the back, the way a proud father would, and looked at him like he had just won the lottery. Then he looked at us.

"Which one of you would like to give this man a tour of the South Side?" the boss asked.

Nobody lifted their arms, as if they were afraid of exposing any secrets to the new guy. I grinned, and raised my arm.

"Ah, excellent," the boss said the moment he noticed my arm raised. "If anybody is experienced enough to help you, Mr. Kingston, it's Harley. She is our top business-person!"

My co-workers groaned in low voices, but I paid no attention. Robert smiled at me as he went back to his desk, and the meeting went on. When it was done, he approached me as I was picking up my stuff.

"Ms. Townsend," he said. He kind of spooked me, as I was concentrated on putting all my papers in order.

"Jesus fuck!" I said, in a louder voice than I would normally allow myself.

"Oh, I'm sorry," he said, embarrassed, "I just wanted to introduce myself properly, and talk about when we can schedule that tour Mr. Weston talked about.

I nodded, looking down at his bulge.

"Well, I have a couple of things to take care of the rest of the week," I said, fixing my hair and glasses, making sure he could notice that 'nerd chic' that men are so attracted to, "but I'm free this Saturday, if you want."

"Yeah, I'd love to!" he said.

I was overjoyed. His voice was shaky and excited, it reminded me of my first fuck, Jake, and how excited he got when I told him I'd fuck him. I knew I had him hook, line and sinker, as the old saying goes. I had a good feeling about him; I felt he wouldn't judge me. Perhaps I had found the man who would not hate my, dare I say, exotic tastes.

I have always read about people having religious experiences, or epiphanies, depending on your religious orientation. I never really believed them, since I thought people were either tripping on chemicals, or having some sort of electricity being released by the brain when on their deathbed. I think I saw a documentary about it, how you hallucinated from the lack of oxygen in your brain and you saw angels and demons, and Heaven & Hell. However, last night, I had something that could only be classified as a revelation by the Gods of Puke themselves.

I had gone to sleep after having a big bowl of ice cream and puking it all over myself. I guess I passed out, because when I woke up I was completely covered in the stuff and had my fingers up my snatch. Anyway, while I slept, I had the most bizarre dream I ever had in my life. It involved me, walking down a street on a rainy day. Suddenly I ran into a ten-foot-tall Sasquatch creature with an umbrella and a bowl of spaghetti. For a couple of seconds we talked about mundane things, until he threw the bowl down onto the sidewalk, crashing into pieces that became insects.

The Sasquatch opened its mouth, stuck his fingers down his throat, and vomited all over me. But it wasn't any kind of regular food vomit, it was rainbow-colored, even the chunky stuff. It flowed and flowed in ways that no human being could ever vomit, like they do in comedy movies or SNL skits, and it all fell on me, the warmth expulsed from this creature feeling like a beautiful, intimate expression of love.

After the monster vomited on me, I walked back, and took off my clothes. The vomit had soaked me through my clothes, and my naked body was covered in it. I looked at a puddle under me and saw my reflection: a beautiful, statuesque woman, covered in rainbow-colored vomit from head to toe, looking like a walking work of art. The colors shone and seemed to move and be alive, and my entire body seemed to be tingling all over.

That's when I woke up, and knew exactly what I had to do. I picked up the phone and called Robert, telling him to meet me at Kingston Park at 11am on Saturday. I had an entire evening planned for this man, and it was going to end with him vomiting a rainbow all over my body...whether he liked it or not.

I got to the park an hour before we were supposed to meet. I couldn't really help myself; I've always been the type that shows up really early to places. If there's a metal or punk show, I go about an hour earlier than the flyer says it's going to start just so that I can get a good parking space nearby. I was also dead tired, since I wasn't able to sleep last night. I went to bed about nine, but I laid about for a couple of hours, thinking about this man vomiting all over me. I had so many plans, and I knew he'd understand.

He had to.

I gave up about one in the morning. I began to watch Beverly Hillbillies reruns until I was bored silly. I had to get out of the house; I wore my favorite leather outfit, black high heel boots and black leather gloves, got myself made up really pale, my lips as red as roses, and left. I needed to let off some steam.

There was a show still going on at The Rooster. Abominable Autopsy, the headlining act visiting from Chicago, were halfway through their set, so I got in for free. The audience was 89 and a half percent male, so I could feel all eyes on me from the moment I walked in. Metalheads, long-haired and short, tattooed or not, either looking at me, or spinning in the pit. The music was banging and amazing, heavy as fuck, old school death metal, and I got in the pit to get my ass kicked and kick some of my own in the process. It was awesome; being in a death metal mosh pit was just as good, if not better, than having a sex marathon. Or being puked on.

When the band finished, I limped to the bar. The heel on one of my boots broke, but it was okay, I got what I came for. A lot of tomorrow's nervousness had gone away, and I felt relaxed. My leather dress didn't even feel heavy, even if it was covered in sweat. I took off my boots and walked barefoot on The Rooster's dirty floor. It was full of dirt, grime, cigarettes and alcohol. I hoped not to step on a broken bottle.

I sat at the bar and ordered a Whiskey Sour. I noticed a very drunk-looking fat guy next to me on what looked like his twelfth can of Pabst Blue Ribbon. He swung to and fro, like a man on a boat, nodding his head to the Repulsion album blasting on the stereo. I felt fascinated, like I was watching an Abstract Expressionist painting gain a third dimension. His eyes looked small under the alcohol, letting out tears and mumbling about how lonely he felt. I pitied him, but only in the way you pity an animal in the zoo. I liked his WASP shirt, however, and knew that I could probably get along with him if I wanted to be his friend.

Suddenly the metalhead opened his mouth, and a wave of vomit began to flow from it. It was glorious, almost in slow motion, set to "Maggots in your Coffin" as it splashed onto the floor. It was a kind of vomit that I'd never seen before: chunky, like oatmeal that had been half-digested, with chunks of bread and chips, and colored green. When it stopped, I felt disappointed, as I knew this beautiful display was over. I wanted it to go on and on, to have a remote control for life, so that I could replay it again and again, frame by frame, look at every bit of detail, every bit of digested fluid and matter, analyze it, zoom into it! I felt hysterical inside me and wanted to cry, until the idea popped into my head...

I slid from the bar's seat and fell on my knees to the floor. I crawled towards the vomit, just as the last few spits were being released by the fat metalhead. The fat metalhead soon collapsed, falling back at the bar so that he wouldn't fall over or to the side. I could hear people complain about the smell and the bartender screaming about how he wasn't going to "clean that shit up."

I didn't care for any of them; I knew what I wanted. I began to lick the vomit slowly, it felt orgasmic as it went into my mouth, still warm and full of energy, and I swallowed it little by little. I heard everybody gasping and screaming around me. Some tough motherfuckers these turned out to be, dressing the part, only to be a little freaked out by a bit of vomit eating. I brushed it off and continued, enjoying every bit, especially if I happened to grab a chunk of solid food in my mouth. I continued until I was picked up by my shoulders by two tall, muscular men. They were gagging and calling me a 'sick bitch' as they dragged me away, but I was possessed, fighting to make my way to the vomit, to bury my face in it. I spit and spewed vomit of my own at them, screaming, calling them "faggots'" and "weaklings" until I was tossed out on my ass.

I fell on the hard concrete, hurting my back in the process. I still heard them screaming as I slowly got up, ignoring the pain. I walked to the car, metalheads and passers-by staring at me like the curiosity that I was: a leather-clad woman with a mouth covered in green vomit. I drove home, showered slowly, then went back to the TV.

When I got to the park, I sat down at the first bench I saw, the one next to the famous "Iraq War Tree," a big tree decorated with ribbons & shit that were already starting to rot. I was full of painkillers, my back still hurting from last night's excursion. I don't know if I'll ever be allowed back to The Rooster, or any other metal show, ever again. I guess I've gone back to high school status, and will forever be known as "Hurling Harley" among my brethren.

It was 11am when I felt a hand touch my shoulder. I dressed pretty conservative for the meeting: a blue sweater with jeans, nice walking shoes. I was half awake from the painkillers when I looked up at the man shaking my shoulder. It was Robert, standing neat and confident in a grey suit. I smiled; he looked so handsome.

"Well, look at you..." I said, trying not to drool.

"Sorry, I thought you were going to fall over."

I got up and gave him a kiss on the cheek. He seemed nervous, and hyperventilating. I pointed at his suit.

"Why are you wearing a suit?" I asked.

"You don't like it?"

"No, I like it, you look very handsome, I was wondering why you were wearing it, though."   "Isn't this a work-related thing?"

"Well, yeah, but you don't have to act like it is. We're going to be driving around the city, not meeting with customers."

He smiled and looked down to the ground, awkwardly adjusting his tie. For a few seconds there, he looked like a little kid. It was adorable and incredibly attractive.

"Whatever," I said, "Let's get going. We have a long day ahead of us."

I took him to all the primary real-estate locations. Yorkville Square, The Tennant area, some of the suburbs. He was very kind and funny, and even paid for some of the gas. His conversation skills were a little rusty, so I had to do most of the talking. Almost all of it was business-related; I really had to take him, sit him down, if I wanted to get to know him. I drove him to one of the houses, Rickenback 115 on Crimsong Avenue, and ordered Chinese food. I bought noodles, he bought Mandarin chicken and rice, along with two bottles of water. I ate with chopsticks, he ate with his fork. I kept looking at him as he ate; he was very concentrated on his food, like he hadn't had any in a while. He liked to suck on the chicken, and I have to admit, it kind of turned me on.

"So," I said, swallowing a gulp of noodles, "what exactly brought you to this city?"

He grabbed his water and took a big gulp, swallowing his food, then looked at me.

"Well, I graduated, and worked all sorts of crap, from dishwasher to busboy to bus driver, I even modeled nude for some artsy fartsy photographer in Portland..."

I perked up when I heard this. I was definitely going to Google that shit when I got home.

"Then my cousin Jerry asked me to come to the city, something about a good place for opportunities because of the good economy over here. I took the risk, flew here, and now I'm selling houses. It's ironic, walking into these big houses, while I myself live in an apartment no bigger than half this living room."

"Don't worry about that," I said. "If you become good at this job, you'll be able to live in a place like this. Real estate is a really good way to make an income."

"That's what I heard. Your place must be as big as this."

"Yeah," I said. I sucked on some noodles, swallowed them, and continued, "I have a big place, but I don't decorate this obnoxiously. I'm much more of a minimalist."

"Minimalist?"

"Yeah, minimalist."

"What's a minimalist?"

What a turn-off.

"It's somebody who can live well with little."

Robert went 'Oh', sounding surprised, then returned to his food. It's a good thing I only wanted him for the fucking, because if there's one thing that I can't stand in a man, it's stupidity. Sometimes I envy lesbians; women are always smarter than men, and it must be refreshing going out with someone who isn't a complete idiot, or knows more about literature and politics than sports and cereal box mascots.

I looked out the window. The sun was beginning to go down. It was time for the ultimate test.

"So," he said, "What now?"

Robert put down his foam box and closed it, then grabbed the hand sanitizer patches that came with the bag, cleaning himself up. I kind of wanted to scream 'don't', as I wanted him to keep his mouth dirty.

"Well," I said, "There's only one place we haven't gone to. Do you like the carnival?"

His eyes and ears perked up.

The carnival was fun, in a bland, romance movie kind of way, but still fun. We went to the world's least scary spook house, rode on bumper cars, ate cotton candy, and took a couple of photos together at the booth. I don't know what it was about this guy, but when we got to the carnival, he seemed to light up, like a child having fun.

He talked and talked about himself in a way that I couldn't get him to when we were working, and he told me about his Russian parents who came to the US in the Eighties; his father a street worker, his mother a housewife. He told me about his education and old odd jobs in detail, giving me his best and worst experiences. My favorite of them was when he told me how a former porn star had come to the establishment with his boyfriend/suitcase pimp and he threw coffee all over her, disfiguring her and forcing her later to become a 'fetish porn star' for people who are sexually attracted to burn victims. It sounded like something out of a Jim Thompson novel.

My favorite moment of the night was when we got into the Ferris wheel. We had drunk a couple of hard lemonades, and I don't think it was sitting well with his stomach. I rocked the cart on purpose, back and forth, laughing in my drunken haze as he begged me to stop. I saw him rock back into the cart, gagging and heaving, expecting the vomit that contained yellow lemonade and pink cotton candies to expulse from his mouth, all over the people down the street. I looked in anticipation, almost wet, but sadly, it didn't happen. His stomach was stronger than I had hoped.

After this, I invited him to my house. He said yes.

I hoped he wouldn't feel intimidated by my house as we drove down Rico Ave. to my place. It was decorated with a lot of heavy metal and punk rock posters. I pulled up and he clumsily stumbled out of the car; he couldn't handle his liquor very well. I opened the door and let him in.

"Wow," he said, "This place is like a dungeon... full of dark and evil shit."

"If you say so."

I laughed as I threw my keys on the counter next to the door and took off my coat.

"I need to use the bathroom." he said. His body was rocking back and forth, and giving out small burps.

I nodded, and pointed him to it. Robert walked towards it and slammed the door; I could hear the lock being closed. I walked up to it slowly, making sure he couldn't hear my steps, and placed my head to the door. I heard him vomit, and I cursed myself that I couldn't be there with him. He puked and puked, and as he did so, I played with my clit. I could feel it wet my pants. Imagining his vomit, which was probably pink, turning into the rainbow colors from my dream, I let out small moans. I was pretty much ready to cum, but I heard the flush. I composed myself and walked away, feeling the wetness between my legs as I walked away.

He opened the door, and stared at me. He was wiping his mouth. He felt embarrassed, and walked slowly towards me. I smiled, showing my teeth, making sure I felt cool and comfortable. Robert stood in front of me, tall and good-looking, but sick as well. I looked up to him, wet to the bone, trying not to shake.

"I'm sorry," he said, "I guess I don't have much of a stomach for alcohol."

You poor baby.

I nodded, and began to kiss him. He tried backing away, but I placed my arms behind his head, making sure to keep him close. I could still taste the vomit in his mouth, warm and vile, just how I liked it. I opened my eyes and saw his: they were wide, either from being nervous, in shock, or terrified.

41

Finally he found the strength to back away, and he laughed awkwardly.

"I'm sorry, I just vomited..."

"I know." I said. I looked down, but raised my eyes toward him, looking coy and innocent. His smile went away, as he looked down on me.

"What?" he asked.

"I said, I know. And I like it."

He paused, didn't seem to know how to answer. I walked up towards him, placing my hands on his stomach.

"I'm going to get right to the point," I said, "You and I are going to have sex tonight, there's no denying it, we're almost there. I've never enjoyed real sex. The idea of getting penetrated is fun, but not as fun as some of my..." I paused for a few seconds, trying not to laugh, as I searched for the right words. "Well, I have a severe case of Emetophilia."

He gulped, and asked "What is Emetophilia?"

"Emetophilia... is the act of becoming aroused with vomit, or seeing somebody vomit."

He became completely pale, and his breathing became quicker.

"I want you to vomit all over me!"

He began to shake his head, and pushed me away. He began to walk towards the door.

"I'm sorry, I have to go," he said.

"Where will you go?" I asked, "I gave you a ride."

"I have to go!"

I looked at my Venus De Milo porcelain doll, and slowly picked it up. Robert walked up towards the door and fidgeted with it; he didn't notice I had locked it.

"Hey," he said, "Why is this door locked?"

I didn't give him the benefit of an answer, just knocked him over the head with the doll. It was crushed into a dozen pieces the minute it hit him, as I used all the strength I could muster to knock him out, and knock him out it did. He fell backwards and collapsed in front of me so quickly that I had to get out of the way or he'd collapse on me. When he fell to the floor, he grumbled for a couple of seconds, shaking his head. I grinned.

The next hour was quite a workout. Robert was a tall, strong man and he weighed easy, *easy*, two hundred and ten pounds, all muscle. Dragging him from the living room to my basement knocked the wind out of me, but I was able to do it eventually, making sure not to bruise him too much as I led him down the basement stairs. I placed him on a chair and taped him up, then used the tape to keep his head forward and immobile.

Then I went up, took my clothes off, had a quick shower and drank about three glasses of water. I changed into jeans and a t-shirt, then drove to the convenience store. There, I bought five boxes of Fruity Pellets, my favorite multi-colored cereal, and two big jugs of milk.

When I got back home, he was still knocked out. I went to my room and grabbed my dental mouth gag. I had stolen it a couple of years ago in a dentist visit, and had used it plenty of times on myself for my solo sexual escapades. I was ecstatic that I'd be able to use it on somebody else, finally! I opened Robert's mouth and placed it on him, opening it as wide as it could. Sweet, it fits! Then I grabbed my enema tube and plastic funnel, grabbed the bucket, and mixed the cereal with the milk, leaving everything ready for when he woke up.

Then I sat down, and waited.

I was completely nude by the time he started regaining consciousness. As I stared at him, I was worried that I might have given him a concussion and accidentally murdered him, but thankfully his constant farting made me think differently. His head seemed to weigh about a hundred pounds as he slowly raised it, his eyes blinking rapidly. He looked at me first, sitting across from him in a chair I had pulled close to me, and smiled briefly. He had obviously thought about my naked body before, so I guess seeing me nude and meeting his expectations made him more than happy. His happiness went away the moment he realized he couldn't move any of his extremities or neck. He began to hyperventilate and struggle, trying to set himself loose from the black tape that covered his body and stuck him to the chair.

"What the fuck is going on?"

I smiled, and opened my legs.

"Finally," I said, "You're awake. I've been waiting for three hours."

"What is this?" he screamed.

"Look, don't get uptight. I had to stop you, after you got so damn rowdy after I told you of my sexual fetish."

He paused for a few seconds; it seems the memory of my confession was returning to him, and he began to look freaked out, at least more than before. He lowered his head, thinking of God-knows-what, then raised it, eyes wide open.

"What are you going to do?"

I smiled.

"I'm going to feed you a special blend I've created for you and only you, my dear. I am going to feed it to you, and then I'm going to force you to vomit it onto me."

After a few seconds speechless, he opened his mouth and said "Oh."

I got up from my chair and grabbed the dental mouth gag.

"Open wide."

He hesitated.

"Open wide," I said, "Or I'll open your stomach and spill your intestines all over the floor, Robert."

He opened his mouth, and allowed me to place the dental gag, making his mouth as wide as my fist. I attached the enema tube onto the funnel's bottom, and dangled it from the wall. I lubed up the tube, and slowly inserted it down Robert's throat, delicately, so that it wouldn't puncture his esophagus. After it was over, I wiped the sweat from my forehead. I picked up the bucket and began to slowly pour it into the funnel. I would pour a big chunk, and let his body digest it. It was a fun process, as I saw the cereal go down the tube, and his stomach and chest heave up and down as it filled his stomach. He made icky sounds in the process, like "ack" and "ukg".

I let it go on for an hour and a half. His belly was swollen, and in his face I could see that he was ill, the process leaving him almost ready to heave. I walked towards my basement table and grabbed a pair of latex gloves that I had been saving for special occasions, and slowly put them on. Then I walked towards Robert.

"OK, Robert, here's what's up. I'm going to slowly pull out the tube, but you're not going to vomit or do anything like that until I say so, understood?"

He nodded, slowly.

"If you vomit before I tell you too, I'll grab my hammer and smash your face until it looks like mashed potatoes, understood?"

His eyes opened wide and he nodded, again. I placed my fingers on the tube and slowly pulled it out. He gagged once in a while, something which he sadly couldn't control, but considering what I just told him, he made sure he wasn't going to let anything come out of him without my say-so. After a slow process that must have felt like a million years to him, I pulled out the end of the tube. His stomach was so full of rainbow-colored milk and cereal that almost half the tube was covered in it. I licked it slowly, enjoying the warm sensation and already my vagina was tingling from the heat it released.

I looked down at Robert after I finished, and he was heaving, letting out burps and gags. I tried not to laugh, as he simply looked adorable. I got on my knees, and stuck two gloved fingers down his throat. He began to gag loudly, and the more he did it, the wetter I became, shoving my fingers deeper until, after about twelve seconds, he began to vomit on me.

It felt as glorious as I imagined it to be. It was like hot water, and as it fell, my entire body seemed to be transforming, changing into different colors. I kept shoving my fingers, and he kept vomiting. It went on and on until everything in his stomach had been expulsed, even the stuff that was there before I started feeding him. When I was done, he let out a loud groan and collapsed his entire body. I don't know if he had an aneurism, a heart attack, or perhaps his empty stomach and constant heaving made his body run out of energy, but the man who had just given me his all was dead.

For a few seconds, I felt regret. I didn't mean to kill him; I saved that for lower forms of life, but there he was, dead, evacuating and the last of his vomit dripping from his mouth. But I shrugged, the guilt not staying on me for long. I walked upstairs, feeling bits of vomit fall onto the floor with each step, but I didn't look, not wanting to spoil the surprise. I finally reached my bedroom, and placed myself in front of my full-body mirror. I looked as beautiful as I imagined I would: every inch of my body was covered in steaming, multi-colored vomit. I had become what I always wanted since my dream, a living rainbow. I stared at myself for hours, crying in happiness.

I let it dry on my body, and kept it on for a couple more hours until I inevitably had to shower. Thankfully, there was enough time to masturbate in between. After that, I disposed of Robert's body, then showered. Nobody ever talked or asked about him after that, even though the police had gone to his house a couple of times. I was even summoned to be questioned, being the last person to see him alive, but no evidence equals no crime. He was just another tool that went away.

I never got the urge to murder or practice my Emetophilia after that, as I felt I had reached the pinnacle of its expression, but what an expression, what an art, it had been! It was the happiest moment of my life.

* * *

About Jorge Palacios

Jorge Palacios is a failed exploitation filmmaker turned horror writer. He lives and writes in Puerto Rico, where he watches extreme horror, exploitation and porn movies, reads fucked up books and publishes zines full of his own writing. He also goes to punk shows and hits on chicks with weird hair.

MOMMA BIRD THE NEW GUY
Essel Pratt

"I've never been to a forbidden dinner party before," said a twenty-something man. He adjusted his black silk tie and wiped a few specks of dandruff from his lapel.

"Quiet down, Steven," said an older gentleman in a matching suit. "I told you that no one can know about this. This is not exactly an event that is publicized. If word got out about this sort of thing, we could be blacklisted from other important social functions and demonized by the media."

"Isn't this just dinner, Mr. Jacobs?" asked the younger man. "How can it be that bad?"

"I told you to be quiet. Now, let's get to the car. You will see when we get there."

"Yes sir," responded Steven.

"And, when we get there, call me Marvin," he replied. "If you are to be a part of my inner circle, I cannot have you speaking to me like I am so high and mighty."

"Yes, sir. I mean, Marvin."

Both men approached a jet black stretched limousine. Standing next to it, with the door held open, was a large man dressed in a typical chauffer uniform, complete with his fancy hat.

"Good evening, gentlemen," he greeted them. "There is chilled champagne in the ice bucket and cheese and crackers ready for you to snack on. Your destination is approximately a three hour drive from here, as I will be taking the less conspicuous routes. Please, let me know if there is anything you need."

Steven attempted to shake the man's hand and thank him, but Marvin shoved him into the vehicle and forced him into his seat.

"Steven," said Marvin. "As a partner of the firm, you will be exposed to some unorthodox privileges and exotic treats. Tonight, you will be introduced to a dinner like no other you have ever experienced. Whether you enjoy it or not, I expect you to smile and clean your plate. Failing to do so will result in the worst possible insult to our esteemed chef and host. Now, drink some champagne and get your fill of crackers. It will help to curb any unnerving feelings within your gut as we prepare to eat."

The limo's engine cranked and the car jerked forward as they began the drive toward the mysterious destination. Not even Marvin was aware of the end point of the journey, nor did he care. He was only interested in the exotic dishes that were sure to please and tease his palate.

***

Sterile white place settings of pristine bone china and the finest crystal drinkware were lined upon an exquisitely set table of fine red linens and illuminated by beeswax candles. Clinking and clanking of silverware and cookware echoed from the adjoining kitchen, where the master chef finished his rare treats.

He took great care to ensure perfection was personified within each entrée. His guests deserved only the best of what he had to offer despite the eccentric methods by which he opted to serve them.

In the background, Tchaikovsky provided the soundtrack during preparation. The melodic composition of Russian intensity motivated Master Chef Stanislav to create unique dishes that would make Mother Russia proud that he was her son. Each pinch of spice sprinkled upon the delicate cuts of rare meats layered with the already delicate flavors, creating a vortex of piquancy that was bound to titillate the senses beyond customary comprehension.

Final provisions were being conducted as Stanislav's meager staff of his most trusted comrades moved the plated dishes out into the exquisite dining area, where state of the art warming and cooling areas lined the back wall.

The three employees spoke only Russian. They were once abandoned children who lived hidden behind his home town's open market, scrounging any bits of food that were available. They were his inspiration and the genius behind his presentations.

"Pozhaluysta , zakonchit' prinimat' posudu v stolovoy," he directed their work. "YA sobirayus' izmenit' v nechto boleye presntable . Togda my budem zhdat' prikhoda nashikh gostey.

His comrades began to transfer the plated dishes to the holding area, careful that none of the garnishments or sauces were displaced during the journey. Their steps were set into the plush carpet with precision, following the path that had been worn over time, like disciplined soldiers in the Red Army.

Stanislav left them to their work as he proceeded to make his way upstairs to change out of his chef's gear and into a custom suit. His hand traced the zebra wood banister as he traversed each step, the sound of Tchaikovsky fading as he reached the top. Prior to entering his wardrobe room, he opened a dark red door, majestically carved with an inspirational scene featuring Noah's ark.

Inside the room, he was greeted by a symphony of animal noises. He did not step inside, but rather flipped on the light switch and surveyed the majestic animals within. A large lion rested his hand upon his front paws near the back of the room. He seemed rather uninterested in the noise around him as he licked his toes while purring loudly. A gorilla rattled his cage bars while propelling spittle from his vibrating lips. A small fox paced his cell nervously, averting his glimpse from the direction of every new noise. A vibrant sirocco squawked loudly, asserting his dominance over the other creatures in his presence, frightening the armadillo that scurried within the cage below.

Stanislav closed his eyes and sorted the noises in his mind, placing each pitch and melody in perfect harmony. He smiled and closed the door, saving the composition in his memory banks for later reference. Music was his motivation, his inspiration, and how he focused on his creations, even if it was unconventional in nature.

"Chisto krasivaya," he said in his native tongue.

It did not take him long to shower and change into his favorite navy blue three piece suit. He finished his ensemble by affixing his signature Russian red bow tie, careful to ensure it did not tilt to the side. Perfection in appearance was important to him.

As he finished his personal final touches, applying a light fragrance and unscented moisturizer, he could see car lights glare through the window. His guests had arrived and school boy giddiness flowed through his nerves. He waited a few minutes before making his way downstairs, it was his method to allow his guests to know he was in charge.

The melodic doorbell signaled the appearance, each arriving at the same time, just as he had planned. Stanislav took the side staircase down to the room that each was ushered into. He approached them from behind, admiring their chatter for a few moments before clearing his throat and welcoming them.

He shook each guest's hand, welcoming them to his majestic home.

"Ah, I see we have a new guest of honor tonight, welcome," he said while shaking Steven's hand.

"I am happy to be invited. My name is..." Steven was cut off.

"Oh, my dear sir, I apologize," said Stanislav. "I do not require your name, as it is best that you remain anonymous to the group. We are a secret society, and although you may meet during business ventures, here we are nameless connoisseurs of forbidden feasts. You may know me as Stanislav, as I do not care to hide my artistry behind a farce. But my business is secrecy and it pays me well. Your business demands the secrecy that I provide. Now, drink your bloody Mary—it has real pig blood inside—and prepare your palate for the unusual dishes that I am preparing for you tonight."

"Yes, sir," replied Steven.

"Please, relax," replied Stanislav. "You are the guest tonight, and I have a particularly special treat for you during dessert."

Stanislav left the room while the men mingled. There were five men present, all American in nationality, all leaders of the most prestigious companies, and each putting their careers at risk for belonging to such a forbidden club. They tended to stray from current situation during their chatter, instead focusing on stock trades, hostile takeovers, and random gossip regarding competing companies.

Steven stood in the circle, nodding his head and providing just enough content to remain relevant in the group. He was much younger than the rest, almost half their age, and felt a tad out of place. Still, he was proud to be invited to such a prestigious event and careful not to screw up future opportunities by revealing his opinions too soon.

After about twenty minutes, a bell sounded from the dining area and one of the Russian comrades appeared to escort the men to dinner. He did not say a word, instead bowing to the men and pointing in the direction of the feast.

One by one, the business men made their way to their seats. Marvin Jacobs went last, pushing Steven in front of him. Steven surveyed the bland hallway, lined with paintings of various animals, many of which he had never seen before. The artist was unknown to him, but had a way of creating realism out of the paints that he used.

Within the dining room, Steven was escorted to the seat opposite the head of the table, with the other men flanking the side. He noticed that there were no articles of silverware present, and wondered if the meal would be eaten with their hands. He had no idea what to expect and was a little nervous as to whether he would embarrass himself in front of the other men.

He nervously played with his napkin, twisting it between his fingers. It was very soft and dissimilar to the paper napkins that he used at home. He tried to focus on the conversation at the table, but found himself lost to his own thoughts.

Forcing himself to snap out of his weird funk, he placed the napkin in his lap and grabbed for the crystal chalice of water that was before him. The chilled vessel fit perfectly into his shaking hands. He took a sip and recognized a hint of lemon in the drink, along with an unknown ingredient that he had never tasted before. He took another sip and found it quite pleasing to his taste buds. Swirling the glass, he took a whiff to see if he could pinpoint what it was.

"Ah, I see you enjoy the beverage," said Stanislav as he entered the room. "Care to guess the secret ingredient?"

"I cannot recognize it," said Steven.

"I wouldn't think so," replied Stanislav. "It is quite rare and unobtainable in the United States."

"Care to share the secret?" asked Steven.

"But of course," he replied. "The secret ingredients will be revealed after every sample. The lemon water, that you have sampled, is simply water from the tap, two drops of freshly squeezed lemon, and an ounce of filtered urine extracted directly from the bladder of a pregnant aboriginal woman."

Steven chuckled. "Seriously, what is it? It kind of numbs my mouth."

"Sir, I am not a comedian. I only share the true nature of my ingredients," replied Stanislav.

Steven grabbed his napkin and wiped his tongue. The men at the table chuckled at him as they each sipped the beverage and applauded Stanislav for the thirst-quenching beverage. Stanislav responded by seating himself at the head of the table and summoning the first dish.

The comrades placed a dish in front of each of the guests, pulling the covers off to reveal what appeared to be a simple salad. The greens were nothing more than garden lettuce and the other veggies appeared common as well. A glob of juicy scrambled eggs were piled on top; the aroma was enticing.

"Dig in, gentlemen," said Stanislav.

The men each grabbed the gold fork that was stuck into the salad, taking careful bites and swirling the contents into their mouths to savor the flavor. Steven stared at the others before taking a bite. He slowly lifted his forkful to his lips, smelling it before putting it into his mouth. The aroma was fantastic, as was the taste. The egg was unique, fluffy, and the texture was pleasing to his tongue. The small salad was consumed rather quickly by the men.

"So, how was it?" asked Stanislav.

Each of the men nodded their head yes as they swallowed the last bite, clapping their hands. Steven mimicked their praise, awaiting the secret ingredient.

"So, young man, what is the ingredient in this dish?" asked Stanislav.

"It seems like the best scrambled chicken egg I have ever eaten," replied Steven. "But it cannot be chicken, can it?"

"Well, you are correct. It is simply a common chicken egg. However, the preparation is what makes it special. That will be revealed later. Now, let us eat soup."

The comrades took away the empty dishes and replaced them with bowls of soup. The broth appeared to be beef in nature, as did the chunks of meat within. Each guest grabbed the gold spoon and sipped the broth. Steven followed along, and sampled the chunky meat. The cup size bowl did not last long as the men sipped it down. There was a hint of spice in the broth, possible jalapeno peppers and black pepper intermixed within the simple beef stock broth. The meat was tender and melted in their mouths. It had a slightly acidic flavor that complimented the broth well.

"I won't force a guess out of this one," said Stanislav. "The beef soup that you are eating has been flavored with chunks of prepared dingo loin. It is a dish that I have enjoyed for quite a few years. Again, the preparations are what makes it special. The prep of each dish shares a common theme, which will be revealed prior to the dessert."

While he was speaking, the soup cups were replaced with gold plates topped with noodles and meat gravy.

"This is a dish that I am especially proud of, and was quite difficult to obtain," said Stanislav. "Please, enjoy."

Once again, the older men anxiously dug in and savored the serving. The noodles were cooked in a slurry of boiling water, spices, and lime juice. The flavor soaked all the way through each strand. The meat sauce on top contained chunks of meat that was a little tough to chew. The taste was unlike anything Steven had ever tasted before. He savored each bite and tried to identify the flavor. It was a little gamey, but pleasurable to the taste buds and mingling perfectly with the sourness of the noodles.

"So, how was it?" asked Stanislav, directing his query to Steven.

"That was the best dish that I have ever tasted. What was that meat?"

"I'm so happy you asked. That, my friend, was lion."

"Well, that is something I will probably never eat again, it was delicious," replied Steven.

"Oh, maybe not," said Stanislav. "I actually serve it every year, in one form or another. The meat was boiled in turkey broth and a dash of spices. The consistency is the product of our secret preparation method. Now for the next dish."

Once again the comrades cleared the table and placed the next dish before each guest. The morsel was prepared on a salad plate. Inside a folded tortilla, like a taco, was melted goat cheese, diced black olives, a bit of fresh spinach, and a red meat that appeared to be basted with sauce.

Steven didn't bother to guess the type of meat, instead he took a bite. The juices dribbled down his chin and he quickly wiped them with his napkin. He didn't want to appear to be a slob in front of everyone. He finished the rest of his unusual taco with more care, savoring the flavor prior to swallowing it down. It was the best dish he had ever tasted, although he could have said that for each of the previous dishes.

"Dear, Lord," said Steven. "That is just fantastic; I could eat it once a week and never grow tired of it!"

"Your enthusiasm is well received and I thank you," said Stanislav. "However, I am afraid it would be quite difficult for you to find pachyderm in your local grocery market."

"Pachyderm?" asked Steven with his head cocked to the side.

"Yes, my dear boy. You just consumed elephant," said Stanislav. "It is quite delicious, but really is only good in moderation. Eating too much tends to give the consumer a tragic pain in the abdomen. I am not sure why, alas. And now let us move on to the final entrée before dessert."

The comrades had the new dish in front of the gentlemen faster than they could say thank you. The lid remained on for the guests to remove. It was cold to the touch and made of pure silver. The metal almost burned the skin it was so frigid. Steven was the first to remove the lid and get a glimpse of the morsels inside.

There were three cubes of raw meat. One was bright pink, another near white, and the third was similar to dark meat chicken. A chunky sauce was drizzled over each. Every piece had a different sauce on top with chunks that seemed to match the cube.

The pink one had a salty taste, and was difficult to chew and swallow. It was as if his gag reflex would not accept it to be ingested, but he managed. The white meat was fishy and melted in his mouth rather easily. The darker meat was very tasty and included a spice that tingled his throat as he swallowed. It was an odd mixture of flavors and he was curious as to their origins.

"I see that you had difficulty with this dish," said Stanislav. "Not to worry, that is to be expected for a first time connoisseur of rare delicacies. The white cube was actually whale meat, not an easy cut to acquire, but I know a few people. The pink meat, well, let's just say that a tradition around here is that the members donate their bodies to me after they expire. To be Frank with you, that was Frank, the man you replaced."

Steven could feel himself begin to gag. "That was a person?"

"Yes," said Stanislav. "A favorite treat amongst our members. Now, the final piece, the darker meat. That was your dog, Finn."

"Wait, what?" said Steven.

"You see, the entrees we serve here are quite rare and not exactly legal. Therefore, I need to ensure you are aware of the seriousness of our secrecy. Your poor pooch was a simple sacrifice for the cause. If you decide to share this experience with anyone, you will join your friend Finn as a dish. Do I have your understanding?"

"Yes, sir," replied Steven. He was unaware what to say other than yes, so he asked what the secret preparation technique was, without realizing he had asked.

"Ah yes, well, it is quite genius, if I do say so myself. " Replied Stanislav. "Before I share, there is something else we must do."

Stanislav waved his hand toward the three comrades. They grabbed a gold velvet rope from a nearby draw and rushed over to Steven. Within moments, he was tied to his chair, unable to move anything but his head.

"What is the meaning of this?"

"Don't fret, I just do not want you to run from the final course of the night," said Stanislav. "It is rather gut churning, even for us, but an appropriate ending to such a great meal. We will untie you as soon as we are finished."

The gentlemen on either side of the table received a domed tray. The comrades removed the lid to reveal a brown gelato that smelled absolutely horrendous.

"Please, we will eat one at a time, in a clockwise motion. You all know what to do."

Marvin was the first to eat. He quickly swallowed two spoonfuls of the dessert, forcing himself not to gag as it settled. He stood quickly and rushed over to Steven. As he did so, the comrades held Steven's head back and forced his mouth open. He tried to struggle, but to no avail. He looked up into Marvin's apologetic eyes, just as the old man regurgitated the meal into Steven's mouth.

Steven tried to move his head to the side, but he could not. The warm acidic entrees and the cold gelato created a strange sensation as it overflowed from his mouth and oozed down his cheeks and chin. Before he could begin vomiting, the others approached him one by one and regurgitated their meal into his mouth as well.

Steven's stomach began to churn as his own vomit exploded from his throat, all over the men standing around him. He felt nauseous and his throat burned with the combination of acidic flavorings and his own vomitus excretions. He was exhausted and ready to leave.

Stanislav walked over and untied Steven as the men started to clap.

"Before you respond to what just happened, I feel I must say a few words," said Stanislav. "The secret preparation method, as you may have guessed, uses regurgitation as an essential step. Each piece of meat that you tasted was fed to the same species and regurgitated by that animal. Therefore, you not only sample the meat of the rare animals, but also the stomach acids as well, something that is not easily attained by normal means."

"That is disgusting," responded Steven.

"Yes, but tasty, for the most part. Wouldn't you agree?" asked Stanislav.

"I guess most of it was," replied Steven.

"Our club aims to provide only the rarest dishes to the guests. I hold four of these samplings a year, and only one in the United States. There are twenty seven people that I serve, in total, and you are now one of them. Congratulations on becoming a member."

"Wait, you have not told us what was in the last dish. Was it simply gelato? It smelled atrocious, yet familiar," said Steven.

"Ah, well, that is something that I am not necessarily proud of. You see prior to leaving for my party, I instructed your driver to exhume your feces from the toilet," said Stanislav. "He had to circumvent the drainage system and collect your excrement, then place it in an ice cream maker on the way to ensure it remained fresh. The flavor was rather nutty and contained hints of peppermint and caramel. Very good, I must say. However, even these gentlemen could not stomach it, so I instructed them to mother bird it into your gullet."

Steven dry heaved a few times and began to sweat. The comrades took him by the arm and escorted him to a room where he could clean up and put on a clean suit. Each of the other men made their way to separate rooms and did the same.

* * *

When Steven exited his dressing room, the other men were seated in front of a fireplace, discussing the meal and complimenting Stanislav on another great year. He was explaining how difficult it was to feed the wale chunks to another whale and collect the vomit from the open waters. He was quite animated in his explanation.

He noticed Steven standing in the doorway and motioned for him to enter. Marvin handed him a glass of red wine and offered him a seat. Steven sat down and nervously sniffed the liquid.

"Young man, do not fret," said Stanislav. "The dinner is over; there is no need to worry about the drink. It is just wine, from normal grapes, made in a small town in the east of France. There is no need to hurl your thoughts toward a Technicolor yawn."

The men all laughed rowdily at the joke and raised their glasses toward the chef. Steven copied their gesture and sipped his wine. He soon became lost in conversation, wondering what delicacies would be served the following year.

***

About Essel Pratt

Essel Pratt is the author of *Final Reverie* and *ABC's of Zombie Friendship*. He has appeared on over 35 anthologies and doesn't plan on stopping anytime soon. Essel lives in Mishawaka, Indiana with his wife, kids, dogs, and cats. When he isn't writing short stories or novels, he is usually working on edits for other writers, working his day job, or writing for the Inquisitr. Essel focuses his writing in the horror and fantasy genres, but is not beyond stretching his fingers into other territories.

PRETTY POLLY PUKING
Magan Rodriguez

Plain and vacant stares across
The table that remains a
Chasm;
An inevitable ending.

Sloppy seconds,
A black spiral of emotion
And food that goes back longer
Than history
Or time.

Metal *plink, plink,*
Plonk, plonk
Of silverware through inedible,
Indestructible...what they may or may not
Call food? Is there a question?

Shoe leather liver
And indistinguishable green things
called 'peas'
and inedible.

Everything is inedible.
It's a hospital, for Christ's sake.
Two girls, not enemies,
Not best friends, but ward mates;
Two girls far, far away from home
And across the table.

She reaches for her fork

And notices the girl
Eating...eating...eating...
Here it comes: secret assassination.

Her stomach rumbles,
Grumbles incessant,
Gross fascination
Across the table.

It comes,
Exorcist like
And nearly pea green.

Two girls do not sit together.
Never, ever again.

THE TROUBLE WITH KEVIN'S COLON

Tristann Jones

You could set your watch by Kevin's colon. Everyday. Every day he went to the bathroom at precisely 9:17 a.m. It was the perfect time of day to take a shit at work. Everyone was expected to report to work promptly at 9:00 am. So, by 9:00am they'd started up their computers, gotten their coffee, used the bathroom, and gabbed at the water cooler. Which was exactly how Kevin liked it.

He didn't drink coffee or engage in small talk; he was able to check through all his emails by the time his co-workers finally got down to business. This worked out perfectly; no one was paying attention to him or the fact that he got up from his desk and went to the bathroom at the same time every morning.

He preferred shitting at work because then he could prolong cleaning the toilet at his own place. It also meant he could make a roll of toilet paper last for months. Tiffany used to be in charge of cleaning and shopping; now that he was on his own again, he tried to avoid them at all costs.

Actually, Kevin tried to avoid all "adult" responsibilities at all costs. He wished he was more than a low-level computer programmer. Then, he could afford a maid and a chef and a driver. All he really wanted to be responsible for was eating, sleeping, masturbating, and the most basic levels of self-cleaning. If he could pay a sexy nurse to sponge bathe him, he would. Gladly. Actually, that would probably come before the maid, chef, and driver.

Tiffany moved out 9 months ago, and no woman had touched him since. It had really been months since she *touched* him, but she did hug him good-bye and that certainly fucking counted.

Kevin's life was sad and he knew it. He was overweight, unhappy, and alone. But, if there was one thing he could count on, it was his colon, and come 10:17, they were the best of friends.

Kevin tried to act nonchalant as he pushed back his chair, stood up, and strode down the long row of cubicles. Whoever invented cubicles had to have been a sadist. They were the legal and socially acceptable way to cage human beings for eight hours a day. Every time he walked out of them, Kevin felt like he was escaping. Escaping just to go sit in another tiny box for a few moments of privacy during the long workday.

In the six years Kevin had worked at Sitco, no one had ever come into the bathroom while he was partaking in his daily ritual. He knew one day his luck would run out, but he wasn't expecting it to be today. So, he was completely unprepared when he heard the bathroom door creak open just as a giant load was about to exit his body. There was no stopping it.

It sank into the water with a loud plop just as the door closed. No one was supposed to be in the bathroom, and certainly he didn't want anyone to hear him taking a shit. This was private business.

As he willed himself invisible, Kevin heard the clacking footsteps of heels against the bathroom tile. It was a woman. It was a woman, and Kevin was mortified. She must be new; she must have just come into the wrong room. Surely, once she saw the urinals, she would quickly exit. But she didn't. She kept walking, kept walking. Right up to Kevin's stall.

Kevin held his breath; surely she could tell it was occupied. Then, he realized that was the point. As he lowered his head in shame, he looked down and saw her pointy-toed black dress shoes peek under the stall door. Reflexes made him look up, and he saw her eye peering at him through the crack in the door. Under any other circumstance, it would have been a gorgeous eye to have staring at him. An icy blue. But under the current circumstances, it was terrifying.

The shock of looking up to see this woman looking back at him made Kevin jump and release. There was another plop in the toilet, followed by the most adorable giggle he'd ever heard. Between her eye, her shoes, and her laugh, Kevin knew this girl must be stunning.

There was a soft rustling, and Kevin looked down to see silky pink panties glide down the woman's calf and around her ankles. She stepped out of them and kicked them to him under the stall. She pressed her plump rosy lips against the crack in the door and whispered "again."

Kevin had no idea what was happening. It was taking all his restraint to keep his ass clenched to stop from doing it again, but apparently that was what she wanted. There was no way out of this situation. He couldn't just get up and leave; he still needed to wipe. And the only thing more mortifying than letting this woman watch him shit would be letting her see him wipe. He didn't want to speak to her, which would acknowledge that she was there, that she was watching him.

Kevin couldn't hold it back anymore; he had eaten Chinese for dinner the night before. His colon was very demanding, and it was time, whether he wanted it to be or not.

He closed his eyes and pushed, hoping to end this as quickly as possible. Another loud splash echoed through the bathroom. Until the day he died, Kevin would never forget what happened next.

She started moaning.

He leaned slightly so he could see her better, while delicately maintaining his balance. There she was, in all her glory, skirt hiked up around her hips, grasping at her breasts with one hand, rubbing her clit with the other, headed tossed back in ecstasy. He could hear the slippery sound of her fingers working furiously at her wet pussy. The more he relaxed and let nature take its course, the louder she got. Louder. And louder. Just as he finished dropping his load, she finished too.

She delicately cleared her throat, pulled her skirt down, and flipped her hair as she turned and walked to the sink. She was everything Kevin had ever hoped or dreamed for in a woman, but he didn't recognize her. Maybe she was a temp.

He didn't know if he should hurry to wipe so he could go out and see her. Or if he should cower in the stall until she left. She was his dream woman, but he was too embarrassed to greet the woman who had just masturbated while watching him take a giant shit. So, he cowered.

Kevin finished with his business, washed his hands, and was about to head back to his desk when he remembered her panties were still in the stall—a token of their love. He swooped down, scooped them up, and rammed them into his pocket before he left his sanctuary.

That Tuesday was an unbearable painful one; each minute ticked by so slowly. But whenever he needed a little boost, he reached into his pocket to finger her wet panties. Next time. Next time, he would be ready for her.

***

Something about being a temp makes you completely invisible. The day Eden went in for her interview at Sitco, she turned the heads of every man she walked past. She was stunning and she knew it. Icy blue eyes. Plump, rosy lips. Long brown hair. Legs for days. She was used to a lot of attention. But the second she was hired on as a temp, no one noticed her again. Temps and ninjas should compete to see who is stealthier.

It's not like Eden tried to hide. But people, the men at work, just started looking through her, beyond her. Women purposely didn't look at her. It made her incredibly lonely.

She knew making copies and mailing packages wasn't going to give her life some grand purpose, but she had such a good feeling when she got the job. She hoped to make some friends, meet her future husband, and finally get where she wanted to be in life.

Eden's life had fallen apart a few months before she went in for the interview. Her boyfriend, the love of her life, the man she planned on marrying and having babies with, became just too much to take. Throughout their entire relationship, he never treated her that well. She was his last priority, but at least she was a priority, right? But after two years, it escalated to the level of emotional abuse. She knew she had to get out.

As a last ditch-effort to keep her, Fred planned an impromptu vacation, but it completely backfired and cost Eden just about everything. So, she left. And, within the course of a few weeks, she found herself alone, living in a new town, and searching for a new job.

She thought landing the gig at Sitco would solve all her problems. But that didn't happen. Instead, she became even more isolated and unhappy. This went on for days. And weeks. And months.

And then, one day, she noticed Kevin. Normally, Eden went for the clean-cut, six-pack abs kind of guy. She liked chiseled features, perfectly-shaved, strong chins, and Greek gods. Kevin was nothing like that. He was heavy. Let's be honest— he was fat. He was bald too; well, he was balding, so he shaved his head to hide this fact. And he had a thick, full beard. It was brown, but had a red hint to it. By the end of the day, there were almost always food stains on his shirt and sweat stains too. He was nothing like her typical type, but since they had all treated her horribly so far, maybe it was time for a change.

There was something endearing about Kevin, something familiar and safe. She knew he would worship her; he just had to see her first.

Eden started watching Kevin. Watching pretty aggressively. Stalking might be a bit extreme, but she wasn't far off. She noticed that he never drank coffee. And he never set foot in the break room if there were other people in it. She noticed that he always brought pizza for lunch on Mondays. She noticed he owned exactly four ties. He didn't wear them in a particular rotation, but he never wore the same one two days in a row. And he went to the restroom at the same exact time each morning.

It must have been a requirement to be self-centered if you wanted to work at Sitco. People talked to each other, but only about themselves. No one listened when anyone talked. They just waited for the jabbering to stop so they could start talking. So Eden wasn't surprised that she was the only one who seemed to notice Kevin's morning routine. He would stand up and look around to see if anyone was watching him. Eden always was, but he never saw her. He would make his best attempt at a stroll as he headed to the restroom. He could have skipped there each morning and his co-workers still wouldn't have bothered with him.

The amount of time Kevin spent away from his desk varied from day to day, but when he'd return, there was always such a lightness about him, an ease, a happiness. Whatever he did in the bathroom each morning seemed to greatly alleviate his mood. And Eden wanted some of it.

The first time she followed him, she just stood around the corner from the restroom and waited. She meant to sneak off before he came out. But it was a quick trip for him that morning. It didn't matter though; he didn't see her when he walked by.

The next time, she got much closer to the door. She could hear when he locked the stall, when he flushed the toilet, and when he washed his hands. Then, she quickly ducked into the women's restroom so he wouldn't open the door and run into her.

After a few more visits, she worked up the nerve to lean against the door enough to hear what he was doing inside. She knew it had to be one of just a few options. But part of her really thought he went in there to jerk one out each morning. It would certainly make the day more bearable to start it with a good orgasm. It would certainly explain why he was in such a good mood when he came back to his desk.

One morning, Eden slowly, oh, so slowly, creaked open the door and put her ear into the crack. He wasn't masturbating. He was taking a shit. But that was also a great way of relieving some tension to get through the day.

So, the mystery was solved. Promptly, at the same time each morning, he took a shit. Eden found something really appealing about this, though. He was predictable and safe. No surprises. He wouldn't try to whisk her away on a surprise trip that would end up costing her a dream job. Not like the last one; Kevin wasn't spontaneous and adventurous. That just wasn't his style, and she liked that.

After he finished that morning, she hid in the women's restroom, and as soon as he walked past, she darted into the men's restroom. She checked the stalls until she found the one housing the toilet still refilling itself with fresh water. Eden went into "Kevin's" stall. She hiked up her skirt and sat down. The seat was still warm from his flesh, and the warmth spread through her whole body as she relaxed on the hard plastic. The room still smelled of him, his stench. The sights, the smells, the sounds and feelings, overcame her. *This must be love*, she thought.

The next day she followed him, she just wanted to listen again. And the next. And the next. Each day, she would listen intently as he relieved his colon. And then, she would sit in his stall to take it all in. After a few weeks, she felt so close to him. It became her everything. Without meaning to or realizing it, she started touching herself as she sat in the stall, basking in his shit.

The first time it happened, Eden was shocked and mortified that she had masturbated at work. But it was the most intense orgasm she had ever experienced. She needed more. Kevin needed to give her more.

It was a Tuesday like any other. Kevin discretely made his way to the restroom, and Eden followed behind. She had mastered opening the door without being heard. It was a slow process, but worth every second. Just as she finally opened the door enough to listen, a woman turned the corner, heading to the women's restroom. Eden was going to be caught and labeled a creep if she didn't think fast. So, she quickly leapt into the men's restroom. Just as the door closed behind her, she heard a loud plop.

The sound of her heels echoed throughout the restroom. He must have known she was there. Now was the time. Her time.

She walked directly up to his stall and positioned her right eye to see through the gap between the door and the wall. He was breathtaking, sitting there, completely vulnerable, but without losing his air of masculinity. She wanted to bust open the door then ride his cock right then and there.

She must have startled him because she heard a sharp intake of breath and then a quick exhale, which also released the tension in his body. There was another loud plop in the bowl. Eden couldn't help herself; she giggled. She'd dreamed of being this close to him for so long, and now it was finally happening.

With the upmost sense of urgency, she hiked up her skirt and slid her panties off. She kicked them to him under the stall. Every muscle in her body ached for him, yearned for him. If she didn't touch herself now, she felt like she might explode. The desire completely overtook every nerve in her body. She leaned forward with her plump lips and begged "again."

And then it began. She started passionately groping at herself. Her neck, her breasts, her pussy. Eden worked furiously, trying to satisfy every inch of her body that direly needed to be touched. She heard Kevin continue his business on the other side of the stall, but her mind was miles above the here and now.

Eden imagined herself on the other side of the door, Kevin's fat cock grinding deep into her ass as he relieved himself on the other end. Both of their assholes gaping wide.

She imagined herself standing in front of him, spread wide as he licked her innermost regions. She wanted his tongue, circling around her rim and plunging deep inside.

She imagined herself kneeling in front of him on the throne, sucking him and taking his entire length deep into her throat, and his body continuing to clench and relax as he emptied himself.

She imagined him scooping his matter from the toilet and smearing it across her naked chest, her nipples so hard they begged to be bitten. He would rub it across her breasts, cupping them in his hands as he worked, rubbing it down her body as he made his way to her eager, awaiting pussy.

She imagined climbing on his lap as he sat on the toilet, ramming his dick into her juicy, wet pussy and riding him so hard they broke the toilet. They would collapse onto the floor in a mess of toilet water and waste and continue fucking. Eden knew he would fuck her so good her screams would drag the attention of everyone else that worked on the floor. But they would continue on as a crowd gathered to watch.

All of these images flashed through her brain in rapid succession, and she furiously fingered her wet pussy. It was exquisite. The release that came as she came was overpowering. Her entire body tremored as she felt herself clench and relax, more and more juices rushing forward. In her head, she begged for Kevin to make eye contact with her. She knew if he did, her orgasm would only intensify, and she would squirt her satisfaction all over the stall door.

But he didn't. He cowered within the stall. When Eden's eyes finally rolled forward in her head, she looked at Kevin and realized he was mortified. He had no idea what was going on, and he certainly couldn't comprehend her feelings for him.

And this realization horrified Eden. She loved him, but he was scared of her now. She cleared her throat, composed herself, and walked to the sink to clean up. There was no motion from Kevin on the other side of the stall. She hurriedly departed the restroom, hoping today wouldn't be the day he finally saw her. She was so sure she had ruined everything.

Eden calmly returned to her desk. Kevin returned to his a few minutes later. She wanted to spend the remainder of the day smacking her forehead against her keyboard. Stupid. Stupid. Stupid.

Just as she was about to melt into her chair and sink under the desk in shame, Eden saw Kevin reach into his pocket. A smile spread across his face as he fingered the contents, and as he pulled his fingers back out, she caught a brief glimpse of her pink panties.

He lifted his fingers up to his nose and inhaled deeply. Then, he slipped his index finger into his mouth and tenderly bit at the tip.

Maybe, just maybe, all hope wasn't lost. Maybe, next time, he would want her too.

***

About Tristann Jones

Tristann is a writer, though she spends her days working as a media editor. Something has to pay for her Mr. Potato Head addiction. She had poetry, short stories, and photography published in the 2009, 2010, and 2011 editions of the Woodhouse Literary Magazine. She also placed second in the 2009 Seth J. Kittay Poetry Contest for her poem, *Each Morning*. She enjoys working with her community theatre, watching any and every scary movie she can get her hands on, and playing bar trivia.

CONDOM-LEECHES
Zoltan Komor

The smoke of a train churns above the jungle. Old alarm clocks crack into pieces under the heavy feet of hippopotami. The hour and the minute hands wriggle out of the broken instruments, crawl under the skin of parrots. The birds begin to tick. On the riverbank, a young lady is getting sicker and sicker every minute. Her skin is whiter than ever. She slowly massages her belly, and leans over the rolling water, making terrible sounds and vomiting used condoms into the waves.

"I'll be better soon" she vows to her fiancé, who cuddles her from behind, not letting his dear bride fall into the water. But as soon as she finishes the sentence, another condom, like a giant pink worm, slips out of her thin lips. It plops into the river.

"Damn this ugly jungle!" mutters the man wearing a safari hat behind him. Swatted mosquitoes fall out of his mustache as he talks. "Visiting this rotten place sure means catching a darn disease! Touching a liana or stepping over a puddle is enough! Even the sight of this river is infectious! These backwoods are much worse than a French shit-house! We need to find a doctor, my love!"

Of course where would they find a doctor at a place like this? The bloom of the heart is dropping its petals. Dirty water arises from the lifeline in a palm. The only available medicine is the fog, poised on an old silver spoon.

Further, deep in the jungle, a train falls into the native tribe's trap. The ground crashes in under its wheels, and the iron horse falls into a pit filled with sharp lances. The train hoots in pain, even the distant mountains shattered by its voice. On the brink of the trap, black hunters watch the suffering machine. Their faces are painted red with blood. A tribal song like poison oozes from their mouths. The sound flushes into the sky. Birds fly by and explode like they were thrown hand grenades.

There are small wounds on the side of the hippopotami.

Nightmares wreathe from them, like evil djinns. Crocodile masks. Somewhere nearby a gun fires colorful parrots to the sky. Next to the village is a small black boy who hunts for catfish in the river with his bare hands. With his small fingers, he feels out the caves of these animals in the shallow rill, and tempts them to bite on them. This is a dangerous task, as sometimes snakes or alligator turtles take up the fish's quarters. And there are even giant catfish, sometimes six or seven feet long, which can swallow the boy in one piece. The child knows this, but his hunger forces him to take the risk. He stumbles up and down in the water, walking the same path over and over again. As he doubles over, his spine chambers out from his dark skin like a snake hiding under the sand. His slats are clearly visible; the small chest looks like a bird's-cage.

All of a sudden, someone yells his name. His mother waves from the riverbank. She calls him to come home. There will be a big feast soon; his father and the fellow hunters captured something enormous in the jungle. The child runs out to the bank, but his mother screams when she sees the pink, transparent worms on her son's skinny body. The condom-leeches keep swelling as they suck the boy's blood. The child looks down at them with rounded eyes. The worms are getting bigger and bigger, a few so full now that they pop out with a snappy sound. Blood splashes onto the boy's face and to the mother who tries to pluck off the leeches.

Soon the dangled wick in the sky burns away. Matchsticks impregnate the night. On the bank, the tribe is burying the small catfisher boy. The sound of clashing lanceheads like the noise of old rocks rolling on each other in the river. They put wet slab on to the dead boy's body. The mother gives a last kiss on his forehead.

People wearing crocodile-masks huddle around a fire. They pass around train driblets at the feast, held in remembrance of the child. On the riverbank, catfish squirm in the puddle, trying to get rid of the pink worms that cling on their abdomens and gills. The sound of their squirming is just like the sound of flapping wings. A parrot-winged angel barges against the cape of heaven again and again.

***

About Zoltán Komor

Zoltán Komor was born in June 14, 1986. He lives in Hungary. He writes surreal short stories and ispublished in several literary magazines (*Horror, Sleaze and Trash*; *Drabblecast*; *The Phantom Drift*; *Gone Lawn*; *Bizarro Central*; *Bizarrocast*; *Thrice Fiction Magazine*; *The Missing Slate*; *The*

Gap-Toothed Madness; *Wilderness House Literary Review*; etc.) His first English book, titled *Flamingos in the Ashtray: 25 Bizarro Short Stories*, was released by Burning Bulb Publishing in 2014. His second English book, titled *Tumour-djinn*, was released by MorbidbookS in the same year.

TEMPER, TEMPER
Doug Rinaldi

This is how it all happened, as true as I can recall, anyway. I committed a random act of senseless violence. Senseless. Violence. Not sure which word is more of an understatement at this point. Though I say *a* random act, it was definitely more than one, but who's counting, right?

Who would've thought that I, of all people, would be capable of such heinousness? In all honesty, I'd be the last to believe it. Reflecting back, I find it strange, yet surprisingly invigorating, how things happen sometimes. Don't you?

Why I'm admitting any of this, I don't rightly know. To clear my conscience, perhaps? Maybe I'm just bored. Or, maybe I am just out-of-my-fucking-gourd loony tunes. Nevertheless, what I'm about to tell you is true . . . as true as I can recall, anyway.

***

It was cold and rainy, a completely miserable day, all around. Gray clouds clung to the sky like pajamas to skin after a wet dream, while the wind whistled through the treetops and attic window. Old shingles, hanging onto the roof for dear life, rattled in the breeze. It was the kind of day where all you wanted to do was sit on your ass. Maybe watch some talk shows.

You know the ones I'm talking about, right? *You are NOT the father!* Those shows crack me up. Nothing but ridiculous hours chock full of ignorant assholes beating each other up because some bitch 'stole my man.' Sometimes you might get lucky enough to catch an episode on pregnant teenage lesbian witch doctors on crack. That's always good for a laugh. Can't say they're not entertaining.

Yet, all I really wanted to do that day was plop on the couch in my underwear and scratch my balls. It certainly wasn't the kind of day you

71

wanted to be driving, never mind being bothered with a job interview. As luck would have it, I was stuck doing both.

As it goes, I got a call on the previous Friday for job testing at New England Telephone Service, NETS for short. They wanted me to drive on down to North Haven and test for a highly technical position for which I was highly under qualified. I knew it was a stretch, but what the hell, right? It wasn't as if my current job was paying me enough to keep me nipple-deep in hookers and blow or anything. So, we set up the time for the testing: Thursday at eleven A.M. Any earlier and it would've disturbed my beauty sleep.

***

The fog was a real pisser. Fundamentally, I'm a shitty driver. Throw in various weather anomalies—like heavy rain and wind—and, boy, do I suck. But, I digress. I finally made it there, unscathed. After I found a primo parking spot, I strolled up to the fourth floor, ready to flunk this test.

The room was full of other applicants, all of them there for the same reason. If I'm being honest, they all looked pathetic wearing their three-piece suits, as if dressing in your Sunday's best will cause a dramatic effect on how well you perform on a standardized test. *Anyway*, I took my seat and patiently waited for someone to herd us into a cramped little room to prod and probe our brains.

Overall, I think I had done all right. I didn't ace it . . . of that, I'm positive. Timed tests don't reveal how smart you actually might be, in my opinion; they just add that extra stress you really don't need when taking it. You have ten minutes to answer fifty questions on things you've never even thought about let alone know.

Pick up your unsharpened number two pencils.

Ready . . . set . . . okay, time's up.

When all was said and done, I don't think I did horribly—not that I'd ever know now. I blew that chance a long time ago. Wouldn't be too kosher if I called them up out of the blue and asked, "Hey, remember me? Did I pass that test?" It might be good for a few chuckles on my end, but it just wouldn't be right. Some cultures might consider such behavior rude. At any rate, I'm too busy right now for could've beens. I have bigger fish to fry, as they say.

In the waiting room, I sat gazing out the window with the rest of the genetic defectives, drool collecting in the corner of our mouths as we anticipated the call of our names. Did I mention what a crappy day it was?

I could've been home organizing my underwear drawer and derived more pleasure and excitement.

I didn't notice at first, but out of the corner of my eye, I caught sight of one of my fellow test-takers giving me the stink-eye. Perhaps I was just imagining it at first. It's happened before. Sometimes my imagination gets the best of me. Just to confirm what I thought I saw, I did one of those sneak peeks. One of those kinds of looks you do when you're checking out someone that's not too hard on the eyes. You know, the one where you look first over one shoulder and then rotate your head all the way to the other side while pretending to be enthralled by the decorating job someone did, when, in fact, the vomit-inducing yellowish green wallpaper pattern was enough to make your eyes bleed. You instead focus on that one object of desire—or in my case, object of unease. Nonchalantly, I performed the maneuver. I didn't want it to look obvious, but, with years of practice at ogling the opposite sex, it worked like a charm.

Yup. He was looking at me and it was creeping me the fuck out! I wasn't quite at the uncomfortable phase, yet, but I would be well on my way if he planned to keep it up. Over the years, I've had many a person stare at me for one odd reason or another. Nothing too new. Before I knew it, he looked away.

As I sat there, my ass cheeks falling asleep on the stony couch cushion, an idea for a story popped into my noggin. I imagined sitting here at the NETS building for testing and this weirdo is giving everyone dirty looks. They call his name to get his test scores and when he comes out the fellow flips his lid.

Out comes the pickaxe—nope, too big.

Out comes the machete—too cliché.

Out comes a particle beam modulator, for all I care! The point of the idea is that the guy freaks and goes ape shit on the others in the waiting room. Excluding me, of course. I would be at home getting a blowjob or something when *that* shit hit the fan. I'll just write about it, thank you muchly. Well, it sounded like it would make an interesting story at the time. I should realize that whenever I get a good idea I should forget about it immediately because it's more or less gonna suck.

So, without further ado, streaming video memories in the form of the porn I watched the night before clogged up my thought pipes. The nubile starlet just happened to be rubbing her naked form down with body oil. It felt a bit awkward, considering my surroundings, to be thinking of such business, so I blinked my eyes and the vision departed.

Not quick enough, though—she got me.

That familiar rising sensation filled my pants like yeast in a bread machine. How fucking convenient, right? Sitting there with a bunch of other dudes, at a job interview no less, and I pitched a tent. Inopportune timing, to say the least. As I shifted uncomfortably in my seat, I tried to conceal my sprouting dilemma. Visions of me strangling the blood out of the damn thing so it would disappear danced in my mind's eye, but I rethought that notion. The others might not have looked on it too kindly.

Some stuck up receptionist who looked like she applied makeup to her ugly face with a spatula called the first name. Up the loser went as he followed some other pencil pusher down the hall. When I looked back, I realized that the fellow was staring at me again with this scowl scrawled across his face. I mean, he looked like he wanted to kill me without giving it a second thought. If looks could kill . . . .

Anyway, I turned my head, trying not to meet his stare, but, like a magnet, my eyes returned to his hateful gaze. Now this was growing unpleasant. This asshole and my public hard-on were damn near giving me a complex. What the hell was his problem? I didn't know him from a hole in the wall, but he was eyeing me as if I just fucked his wife.

It took all I had not to say something. Keep your mouth shut, I told myself. *Not worth it.* I tried my damnedest to ignore him and just concentrate on getting rid of my raging boner, but his gaze was unwavering; I don't think he even blinked once. The skin of his forehead crinkled while taut lips curved around his snarling mouth.

That was it! I couldn't keep quiet anymore. "Is there something I could help you with?" I said, painting the sentence with a roller covered in sarcasm.

He said nothing.

"Would you please stop gawking at me then?" I snapped. "It's freakin' me out, man."

Again, nothing but his persistent staring. The others in the room looked back and forth at us as if we were John McEnroe and Ivan Lendl in the '84 French Open. I looked away as they called another applicant to that fateful place down the hall. *What the fuck is going on?* He still glared at me. I shifted awkwardly on the concrete couch, straightening my tie.

Finally, I broke down and asked him what the fuck his problem was. Now, I'm not one for violence, especially when it involves me personally, so I knew I was stepping into relatively uncertain waters, being all confrontational and shit. If two *other* people felt like pounding each other into mulch, more power to them. Still, to this day, I have a natural aversion to pain.

My question didn't even faze him; the scowl just sat parked on his pockmarked face. Not even a flinch, for crissakes. From him to me, our audience continued to watch on, uncertain where it was headed, but positive that it would probably get exciting.

I got a little bold, felt a little jaunty, and wanted to get a rise out of the chap, so I winked at him. Got zilch, except for a few chuckles from the gallery. My face burned hot as if all my blood had squeezed into my head. With my hard-on still aching, I knew that couldn't be true. It was throbbing like mad, oblivious to the current quandary.

"Stop looking at me!" I blurted, clenching my teeth so hard they hurt. Everyone shut up at the same time, while the dork next to me practically jumped out of his skin. The vein in my forehead bulged and thumped.

The lips of his twisted mouth began to move. Finally, a bona fide reaction. They parted as he began to speak. "Temper, temper . . ."

That's when, I surmise, my day might've taken an unexpected turn or, as I like to refer to it, got interesting. As I told you before, I had a sense that this day could only get worse, but this was a complete surprise, even by surprise standards.

Temper, temper? Are you fucking serious?

Wow. I snapped. I mean, damn, talk about going from zero to homicidal in no time flat.

I jumped from my seat, almost crosschecking the guy seated next to me by accident. Well, he shouldn't have been in my way. I leapt over the atrocious floral-painted table in front of me, my foot catching on the lip. The loud crash was enough to bring the army of office zombies out from the solitary confinement of their claustrophobic cubicles. Paying no attention to the noise or mess I was making, I carried on through the waiting room, eyes focused with furious intent. A man on a mission, I was. Even with my pulsating cock, as inadequate as it may be, pushing painfully against the insides of my pants, my resolve had the pinpoint accuracy of a Stinger missile. I had just had enough and there was no way to stop me. A metamorphosis took place and I was no longer in my right mind—or in any mind, for that fact.

Seeing through eyes of burning wrath, I finally reached my objective, the target of my newfound fury. Time seemed to ooze forward. My senses heightened, I could almost smell my prey. He smelled how he looked, like a piece of shit, but that's neither here nor there as my mouth watered with the anticipation of the kill.

With gaping mouths and wide eyes, my audience stood

dumbfounded in their positions, unable to do anything but watch. My "friend" with the staring problem didn't budge. I don't know if it was from fright or if he just didn't give a flying fuck that he was about to get the worst, and possibly the last, beating of his life.

Usually, there is an urge not to upset the herd when it comes to violence. Some fights don't make it past a punch or two before someone intervenes to suppress the action. Right then, though, no one seemed capable of doing anything to prevent the havoc I was gearing up to unleash.

It must have looked like a panel out of a superhero comic book with my mouth open, a bellow of rage piercing the palpable silence. With my fist raised above my head, I must've resembled some raving lunatic . . . but I didn't care. All that mattered was planting my fist into that fucker's face. My erectile concern was now a thing of the past, not even a blip on the radar, as it now actually felt appropriate for the mood at the time. Hey, different strokes for different folks, right?

With an uncharacteristic deftness, my fist connected with flesh and bone. A resounding crack filled the air as the man's nose exploded, spraying blood on my shirt and tie. That only infuriated me more—I really liked that tie. Repeatedly, my hammer-fist smashed down, a continuous barrage of blows about his head and ear, each punch in unison with the jolt of my manhood. I felt my arm and hand growing sore, but I was unable to contain myself. It was almost like masturbating without touching myself, but a little more work when it came to clean up. This insistent need to continue punishing this man, this total stranger, wouldn't let me stop. I needed to see his blood, needed to see it covering *everything*. Even though I couldn't fathom why, I ached to see him bleed from every orifice of his body.

Leave it to one of the talking monkeys in the room, watching my horrific display of anger and frenzy, to decide to play hero. He grabbed my shirt, attempting to pry me away from the bloody mess.

That was his first *and* last mistake.

It was just a genuine reflex, that's all. Honest Abe. I mean, he shouldn't have touched me in the first place, but in doing so, he forfeited his life. With one swift motion, my palm made purchase with the Samaritan's nose, instantly shattering it—more blood staining my shirt. Shards of bone ripped through tender brain tissue as if it were a rotten banana. He was dead before he hit the ground. Instant death. That's that. He didn't know what hit him. Well, he might've; I'm not a doctor.

I don't think anybody else stepped an inch closer after that. Who could blame them? How often do you get to see a man snap and beat someone to hamburger? With as much lack of faith I have in my fellow human beings, if I didn't know any better, I would think that they had been enjoying themselves. Their primal instincts took over, reduced to nothing but a drooling horde of primates. They might as well have been wearing animal skin loincloths and picking bugs off each other.

My human punching bag began to moan incoherently, wet gurgling sounds rumbled in his partially collapsed throat. I couldn't help but chuckle when I saw blood streaming from his mouth like a loose faucet head. It just struck me as funny, little foamy blood bubbles forming in the corner of his almost toothless mouth.

I wasn't quite finished.

"How's this for temper?" With both hands clenched into fists, I began raining blows down upon the sorry excuse of a human, one fist at a time. When I got tired of that, I wove both fists together—a double ax handle. I wasn't drawing any satisfaction from that method anymore. I needed something new, something that would liven things up. With unquenchable need, my fingers tore into his flesh. My balls tightened in delight. Starting at his face, I peeled skin and muscle from the bone as if peeling an orange (or a grapefruit—it's a matter of preference I find). I might have been giggling, too. Some parts are just a reddish haze.

That's when I detected, barely at first, the familiar strain burning down below in the pit of my manly being. I started pulling veins from his neck as if I was restringing a ukulele. Sheets of blood spurted out onto me, painting over the horrid wallpaper of the waiting area. The taste was intense; blood filled my mouth and drenched my skin. I was a vicious crimson mess. The others were too far away to relish in the glorious rapture of the blood bath. *More for me.*

In my blissful state, I found digging and gouging through ripe flesh easier than I expected it to be. The flow of adrenalin coursing through me was invigorating, empowering me to do these things. It was like a drug and I was addicted—a certified blood junkie.

As I ripped muscle from bone, it brought me back to a familiar, simpler time when I was younger. My mother would give me treats in my lunch box or when I was sitting on the porch watching the cars go by. A treat that had always made me smile. Back then, Fruit Roll-ups were the best invention ever created on God's green Earth. I enjoyed the shit outta them! Now they held a different meaning, but they still make me smile. Pealing a Fruit Roll-up from its plastic wrapper made a sound not too far removed from the noise made by ripping this douche's face off. Except this sound was wetter and a wee bit messier. Yet, it's still interesting how some things stick with you through the years. Ah, memories. . . .

By the time I completed my punishment, the man was deader than dog shit. I mean, there could be no doubt about it, no challenge from the opposing team. You didn't need to stick him with a fork to tell that he was done. Half his skull was showing; flaps of muscle hung flaccidly from the skull. In the onslaught, I had crushed his windpipe and yanked it out through a breach in his throat, where it swung like a morbid pendulum. His severed jugular vein was nothing short of a bloody volcano spewing sanguine lava. Yet, I was still brimming with vim and vigor, especially my cock, which, as luck would have it, felt about ready to detonate.

It didn't initially register that I was perched on the gentleman's lap while I was dissecting his face until tears filled my eyes and my ears popped. A hot surge streamed out of my dick, plastering the insides of my nicely ironed pants to my leg. With a deep sigh and a gratifying nod, I stood up to admire my work, wiping my hands together for a job well done. As I turned around, everyone stumbled a step back.

Ha ha! I must've been a sight to behold, all covered in blood and pieces of face and such. Either that or I had a booger hanging out of my nose. As I smiled at the goofy looking throng, my teeth dripped with the sweet red elixir of life. Someone puked into a fake potted plant. *Fuckin' pussy.*

To this day, I still don't know why the asshole didn't fight back. He barely even moved while I took his face apart. I mean, one way or the other, he hadn't stood a chance. The entire foray must have only taken less than a minute, but to me (and possibly the recently dead guy) it felt like hours. Though spent, I savored every bit of it. The phenomenal orgasm was just an extra-added bonus.

One thing's for sure, I never knew I had it in me. True talk. Why would I lie about such a thing? If I were going to make something up, I would say I banged two supermodel pornstars at the same time. Well, in reality, if you saw me, you'd know right off the bat that would definitely be a lie, a falsehood, and an untruth.

Nevertheless, it happened (the murder—not the super model thing. That would be a whole other tale of awesomeness). I brutally killed a man in cold blood. I fucked him up right good and it happened to be the most sexually arousing—and satisfying—act I had ever committed.

As I gazed upon the results of my carnage, and the vibrant redecorating job I had done, I straightened my tie and brushed off my soggy pants. The grin on my face made my cheeks hurt, but I didn't care. I had thoroughly enjoyed myself. If I smoked, I would've lit up.

Never had I seen so many people jump so high and in such unison as I did when I finally moved to leave. There was no reason to stay. I was pretty Goddamn sure they weren't gonna hire me now. Better to hightail it out of there before the fuzz showed up. I had important things to tend to now, and going to prison wasn't on that list.

There was so much more killing to be done, I then realized. Oh, no. I wasn't done by a long shot. With my newfound taste for bloodshed and a vision of a better world, I was going places. And if I came like that every time I killed, I'd be stupid to give it up. Especially since nothing had ever made me feel that damn good.

***

Please, don't consider me mad. I truly believe I am the farthest thing from it. Sanity and I are good ole pals. If I were insane, wouldn't I have a modus operandi, a trusty old M.O? You know, those pointless things murderers have that get them caught all the time. I see them all on *America's Most Wanted*. To me, *that's* what's crazy. Soon they would be on to my pattern, then—BAM—off to the pokey I go. No, not for me, thanks. Gotta keep them guessing. That's the fun, no motive. Keep 'em guessin' till the end. They already know who I am. I'm no fool. They just can't find me . . . and they never will.

By now, I have quite a few notches on my bedpost, so to say. Shit, I had killed two more jerk-offs before I even made it out of the NETS building that day. No sweet, creamy release then, though. A man needs some time to rest and recharge, refill the spank-bank. Nevertheless, those looks of utter surprise in their eyes right before they board that train to cloud-land is priceless. It's the bee's knees. And isn't that what it's all about in the end, really? The spectacular uninhibited joy of it all.

THE DARKNESS CONSUMES
Michael Noe

There was something about the way the woman lay on the piss-stained mattress that made him want to fuck her. Maybe it was the way her blonde hair fell over her tiny but perky breasts, or how her blue, sightless eyes fixed on him in the dim light of the cheap motel that smelled of feet and stale sweat. As he looked at the nude dead woman he felt his dick grow hard. If he was going to do it, he needed to hurry up, before she grew cold. He wanted to feel her dwindling heat, feel her dead cunt wrap itself around his cock. The fact that she was dead didn't bother him in the slightest and actually made it easier for him to have sex with her. As a junkie, he had found that his morals had already gone to hell anyway, so why not stoop to a new low?

Rick's life was already on a slight decline, so why not ensure that it kept sliding into new depths? Her being dead was a plus—after he fucked her she couldn't take his drugs or his money. All he needed to do was get his nut and slip out of the cheap motel undetected. It was a poor neighborhood, so slipping out wasn't all that difficult. The motel was a haven for junkies like himself, and the management usually looked the other way unless interference became necessary. That was the nice thing about being a junkie. No one noticed you. You were at the bottom rung of life's ladder and there was no hope of climbing up.

He looked at the woman laying there and he tried to remember her name. Laura? Jennifer? He couldn't remember it and he could only vaguely remember meeting her. Rick had noticed that all junkies had some sort of radar that found other junkies. It was foolproof and, no matter where he was, his junkie radar was never wrong. Spider Man had his spidey senses and Rick had his junkie senses. He had found more drugs through his radar than he did anything else. His radar honed in on functioning junkies like himself, who had their shit together and could offer him a couch to crash on or something to eat. Up until this evening he had thought he had

81

been a functioning junkie, but as he looked at the dead girl next to him, he realized that it was all bullshit. There were no functioning junkies, just different levels of addiction and right now Rick saw that he was at the final level. It could have been *him* laying there, staring blankly at the ceiling. It could have been him, dead in some cheap motel while some other junkie stared at him indifferently. There was no dignity in an overdose. The more he stared at her, the more he saw just how sad the situation had suddenly become. This woman was dead and there was nothing he could do about it. *Fuck her*, he thought stroking his penis. She was gone and there was nothing he could do to bring her back.

Instead of doing the right and moral thing, he closed her eyes and slid himself inside of her. He knew they had the rest of the night before they had to check out, so he hit another level of immorality and defiled her naked corpse. Later, he would take her money and drugs and he would head off into the sunset. For now, he was content to fuck this lifeless corpse.

Once he'd discovered drugs, nothing was ever the same. Time didn't mean anything and, while meeting up with this woman was nice, the fact that she had drugs was much nicer and now he was balls deep in her dead vagina. It was the junkie's version of the circle of life. Hakuna Matata and all that bullshit meant nothing because there were always worries. Where was the next fix coming from? Would the next fix be just enough to kill him? Death was real and tangible. It was something he knew a lot about. All junkies eventually died. It was just a matter of time.

He thrust himself deeper inside the dead woman and felt the sudden release as the orgasm overtook him. It allowed him to forget about everything for a moment and as he pulled out he wondered if he would be able to fuck her again. She was dead, after all, and at some point wouldn't she begin to stiffen up? Did he really want to break one of her legs so he could stick his dick in her one last time? Fuck that noise. He grabbed her legs and spread them just enough so he could fuck her later. While he smoked, he went through her wallet and found a twenty and enough drugs to get him through the night. He patted her on the ass and thought about kissing her before taking a shower, but decided against it.

He had to draw the line somewhere, didn't he? Kissing her seemed a bit too intimate, whereas just fucking her somehow wasn't. It was all about perspective, and while Rick may have been just another junkie without a moral compass he had limits. He needed the shower. He needed to wipe away her stench, which clung to him like a blanket. It smelled of rotten cheese and a freshly opened can of tuna. It intermingled with the smell of his onion-scented sweat and made him a little nauseous in ways fucking a dead woman couldn't.

The shower felt good and washed away the dirt that had accumulated over the last few days. He had no other clothes, so he had no choice but to wear them again. His thoughts drifted to the past and how his life used to be before he became a junkie. He was married to a successful attorney and had himself been a successful real estate agent who owned a variety of stocks. He had become rich by twenty five and he had been happy. He and his wife lived in a gated community on the outskirts of town, among Akron, Ohio's elite. It was a good life but then he had discovered his one true weakness and it was all downhill from there.

He lost the wife, the money, and the cars and suddenly he was just another bum looking for his next fix. His wife had made sure that he was left with nothing as long as he used and, while he hated her for it, he could see that it made a great deal of sense. He had left the marriage with a sizeable income. And now? It was ingested in his veins and up his nose. Rick floated along for awhile, but the money soon disappeared and his ex-wife had stopped talking to him. Everyone, it seemed, stopped talking to him. But who needed them, anyway? They couldn't help him and no matter how much he begged they refused to give him any money, so fuck them. They had gotten smart real quick, and he hated them for it.

He had lost everything and, while it was sad to see it all go, he wasn't really surprised. His downward spiral had started spinning out of control and everyone wondered when he would hit rock bottom. The problem with hitting rock bottom was that it hurt a great deal and Rick wondered when his hit would happen. Losing everything already seemed like a pretty solid low already, so hitting bottom now seemed like a welcome relief. He was now fucking a corpse—that seemed like a pretty direct hit to the bottom. All he really needed to complete his journey was death or maybe a really bad overdose that didn't kill him, but took away a part of his body. An arm would fuck him up. If he lost an arm it would make shooting up a little difficult. Of course, the alternative would be to snort more, but the feeling of drugs coursing through his veins made him feel almost invincible.

He turned off the shower and stepped out, hating the old air that made his bones ache. Rick dried quickly and stepped back into his clothes, hating the way they made him feel dirty. He could smell the sweat that had absorbed into the fabric and there were a variety of stains on the black t-shirt that he couldn't see but smelled. Now that he had some money, he could get a decent meal and make a call to his dealer, who happened to be the closest thing to a friend he had at the moment.

Rick had lost a lot of friends over the last few months and even gained a few enemies. He tried not to think about the money he had lost to a particular dealer or how he knew that if he was ever caught dying from an overdose would seem almost pleasant. Rick tried to shift his thoughts to the dead girl and what he planned to do about her. As far as he knew no one had seen her enter the room with him. No one had been following him, so leaving wouldn't prove too difficult. All he had to do was throw on his shoes and get the hell out. Except the door had just opened and a familiar voice spoke.

"Hello, Rick. Nice to see you. What in the fuck did you do? Please tell me you didn't kill that poor woman." The voice was cheerful and way too pleasant. It filled Rick with dread because he knew that his leaving was now going to be a lot more interesting.

"Of course not. Look, I know why you're here, so let's get this over with. You wanna kill me now? You'd be doing me a favor you know."

"You still have a sense of humor. I like that. Nice to see a junkie with a knack for chuckles. Why would we kill you?" The man frowned and looked at Rick with such intensity that it would probably make most people shit in their pants. Rick wasn't most people and, while he may have been scared, he needed to play it cool and not let them know just how scared he was.

"Jimmy didn't send you? How did you even get in here? " Rick was suddenly confused and scared to the point where shitting his pants was now a very strong possibility. The dread crawled slowly up his back and left wet kisses on his neck. This wasn't going to end well. He eyed the girl and wondered what kind of bad voodoo she had brought down on him.

"No, and thank God. You realize that if Jimmy had sent us you'd not only be dead, but my associate here would be butt-fucking your lifeless corpse right about now. You're a popular man, Rick. Now, let's go for a ride. How we got in doesn't really matter."

A large black man walked into the room and pointed a gun at Rick's stomach while the other man grabbed his elbows and roughly pushed him out of the room.

It was a silent moonless night that reeked of stale garbage and cigarette smoke. For a second he thought about making a run for it, but he knew he wouldn't make it far. They'd pump him full of bullets and stuff his corpse into the car; or worse yet, they'd just take his head to prove that there was one less junkie piece of trash littering the streets. The thing that scared him was that he had no value anymore. There were people all over that contributed to society, yet here he was with nothing to offer anyone. Not anymore. He could remember a time when his life had some value to it, but now he was just another junkie and all of his real friends stepped aside and vanished like roaches when bathed in light. He tried to think of some profound words of wisdom that would grant him some type of reprieve, yet there was nothing to say. Who would miss him or even notice that he was gone? No one.

Was it sad? Sure, but when you're being shoved head first into a car there isn't really a whole lot of time to reflect or even think about your life or what it had meant at some point. There was some meaning somewhere wasn't there? Rick hadn't always been a junkie. At one point someone would have missed him, but now it was all gone. There were memories of a life before drugs, but when he tried to remember them it was like looking through a sheet of dense ice.

He didn't want them just tossing him, so he calmly got inside and tried to smile, but it was far too difficult. It was a bit funny that while he had assumed that he would die of an overdose he never thought that he would die a violent death. Rick had a vision that he would die screaming, and he would probably die shitting his pants in terror. It was a bit undignified, but fitting for someone like himself. A lesson you never learned in school. You always heard about how bad drugs were in theory, but you never got to hear just how bad they actually were.

Forget just the addictive nature of them and focus on the long term effects that no one spoke about. Everyone knew that at some point you lose everything, but what no one talked about was that sometimes you make stupid decisions. You get sent on a run and instead of delivering all the drugs you just deliver some of them, and since you've already fucked up, why not dig the hole a little deeper and keep some of the money too? Rick saw it as a fair trade for risking his life, but no one else did. And that was why he was in the back seat of a car heading toward his death. Of all the ways he imagined death to be, this wasn't on the list.

"Where are we going?" Rick asked with just small amount of bravery.

The big back man smiled as if Rick had just told a funny joke or ripped a juicy fart. "It's a surprise, my man. Just try and relax, man. You have nothing to fear...yet."

Yet? The man kept smiling and it made Rick wish he could take some of the edge off, but he doubted if these two would allow him to do any drugs en-route. All he could do was sit and wonder what these two had in store for him. If he wasn't being taken to see someone who would probably kill him. The life of a junkie was short.

"What happens if I try and make a run for it?"

The white guy chuckled. "I shoot you in the back of the knee, and he plucks out one of your eyes like an olive and fucks the empty, bloody socket. I've seen his dick. Before you die you'll get to experience a true mind fuck. Best to be compliant. You don't want his big black cock shoved in your empty eye socket."

"I'd nut so much your other eye would pop right out and cum would shoot through your nostrils." The black man winked at him and went back to looking out the window.

Rick felt sick to his stomach and wished he had some drugs. They would not only take the edge off, but make him feel less like he was going to shit his pants. He had never been this frightened, but these two acted as if everything was perfectly normal.

The big black gentleman looked like the sort of fellow that would socket fuck someone. He had no doubt that if he ran they would do exactly what they promised without any warning whatsoever. His muscles bulged under his powder blue suit, while the white guy looked scrawny and almost unhealthy next to him. There was a hardness in each of their eyes that he had seen in other people but, thankfully, he had never encountered it until now. These were the types of guys that would anally rape your grandmother and then punt your puppy into traffic for shits and giggles. If this had been a movie they would be walking clichés. But this wasn't a movie. These guys actually existed and they were hired to hurt people. To kill people.

What he needed was someone to walk with him to announce that he was in fact a dead man walking. He wasn't a religious man, but he could sure use a priest to administer his last rites.

There's no way you're going to survive this.

He probably wouldn't, but he would refuse to cry or make himself look weak.

You're going to cry like a bitch.

The car rolled into a concrete parking deck. Graffiti about the clearance sign told him that Andy loved Jessica. He wondered if she still did. It saddened him to realize that his own chances of ever finding love were somewhere between slim and nonexistent. He had made a vow that if he did make it out alive he would quit drugs, try and rebuild his life. This was like a thug version of *Scared Straight,* but without the prison and screaming convicts.

They drove into downtown Akron. He knew each building they

86

passed. Lock 3, Rubber Ducks Stadium. Once upon a time and in another life, this had all been a part of his life, but had all gone away in a haze of drugs. Rick wanted to point fingers and blame everyone else for his addiction, but no one forced those drugs into his system. Sure, he could blame his ex-wife for abandoning their marriage, but she had grown tired of being married to a junkie. He had hated her for that of course, but as he walked away, he knew deep down that he had caused his downfall. No one else. It was safer to point fingers than to be an adult and put on his big boy britches and take responsibility for the mess that he himself had created.

He had allowed his life to turn to shit and now? Now, it was time to die. It brought out all sorts of questions about God, the Devil, and mortality. There had been countless mornings that he had woken up and he should have been dead. Somehow he had beat the odds and it would make sense to stop, but no, he kept right on going.

They turned into a concrete parking deck and Rick felt his stomach drop. They were getting close to their destination and he fought back the urge to beg them to let him go. They would just laugh and mock him. It was better to stay silent and try and figure out where they were. To the right was a skywalk that connected the parking deck to the building across the street. It wasn't foreboding and looked like every other building he had ever been in, except now he was wearing dirt encrusted blue jeans and a loose fitting black t-shirt.

He hadn't shaved in months and with all of his money going toward his habit he hadn't had any extra funds to get a hair cut either. Despite his shower, he looked like a hobo. Rick was the guy that people turned away from when he got too close to them on the street. He stuck out here, but, thankfully, it was after five in the evening and most if not all of the businesses were closed for the day. They at least allowed him to walk on his own. He had expected them to guide him by his elbows again. They entered an elevator and the black man pressed eight.

When the doors opened he could see that they were in a hallway that only allowed them to go right or left. A sign listed the various buildings, but none of them gave him a clue as to where they were going. The doors were all wooden with little placards announcing what was they were, but the door they entered had no placard.

The door opened onto a waiting room with a leather couch and potted plants. A flat screen mounted on the wall was playing that afternoon's episode of CNN. A large registration desk sat empty, a door leading to the office just beyond it. Now Rick was starting to become a little afraid. The saliva dried up in his mouth and his knees shook as if all the muscles and ligaments had been replaced by thin strips of Laffy Taffy. The office didn't appear to belong to a doctor, which left too many options for his drug addicted brain to figure out. Rick knew that he would find out soon enough.

He was led into a spacious office with a large mahogany desk. The carpet was a dark blue and the walls were a light gray that darkened the room a little despite the lamps that had been placed in various corners. It was an office designed to instill comfort, but Rick had never felt so *uncomfortable* in his entire life. It was unnerving, and the wait prolonged the tension a hundred fold.

When the door finally opened the fear that Rick felt drained away. In its place was a dull fury. If it hadn't been for the two gentleman beside him he would have jumped up and left the room. "You've got to be kidding me." He said with a frown.

The man smiled and held his arms out. "No hug for your big brother? Oh how the mighty have fallen. You look like shit, man. If mom could see you now it would break her heart. "

"Like you give you a shit about me. Why exactly am I here? I don't like family reunions, Adam."

"You've always been direct and to the point. I've always admired that about you," Adam lit a cigarette and pushed the pack to Rick. "I always thought you were the smart one. You had a wife, nice business, and now look at you. You smell like shit. I know what you did to Jimmy McAllister and I have to say that was pretty stupid."

Rick shrugged and tried to figure out what he could say. No matter what he said, the truth was that he was a junkie and hadn't really thought about what would happen once Jimmy realized he was missing some cash and product. "Not one of my finer moments. If you're going to lecture me, can we speed it along? I have shit to do."

"You and I both know that once you leave here you're going to get high and sleep in a dumpster somewhere. The fact is that once you leave here you're a dead man. You've been smart so far, but you're going to fuck up, and once Jimmy finds you he is going to rip you apart. You're lucky I found you instead of him."

"How did you find me?"

"Wasn't easy. You move around a lot. I have people around that owe me favors. Just so happens the desk clerk and I go way back. As soon as you checked in, he called me."

Rick frowned and reached for another cigarette. The nicotine helped keep his thoughts focused. "What's the point? Why? You and I have never been close. So why all of a sudden are you looking for me?"

"Despite our differences we're brothers. This may come as a shock, but I love you and when I heard about what you did, I called Jimmy and paid off your debt. Now you owe me."

"What do you mean I owe you? You're going to hang this over my head, aren't you? What do you want?"

Adam smiled. "Simple. I want you to take out three people that owe me money. Jimmy and I are businessmen. He runs mainly drugs, but I run a lot more. I have been successful because people know what happens when you fuck me over. See, if you had pulled that shit with me, you would already have been dead. I would have found you and blew your teeth through your asshole." The smile was gone as Adam glared at his brother.

"You want me to kill for you?" The shock was evident in his voice. This was insane! Rick wasn't a killer. There was no way he was going to do this. "What if I refuse?"

Adam snapped his fingers, "Bring in Walter. You're gonna love this, Rick." Walter was obviously a tweaker. He walked with a zombie lurch and his eyes were wide and glassy. Without a word, Adam pulled out a Glock. Walter's head exploded like an overripe watermelon.

"Jesus Christ! What the fuck?" Rick screamed. Hot piss exploded from his flaccid penis and now the fear was screaming at him. He had never been this terrified.

"Pretty cool, wasn't it? You refuse or try and fuck me over you'll end up just like Walter here. You owe me and I swear to Christ I am not one to be fucked with. Understand?"

Rick nodded. His brain had disconnected the wires to his mouth. There were million of thoughts but words eluded him. What was he going to say? No wasn't exactly an option. When the wires *did* uncross, he was able to stammer, but nothing logical came out. It was all nonsense.

"You'll be fine, Rick. Just do what I ask and we can go our separate ways and we'll never have to speak to each other again."

"You're fucking crazy! You can't make me do this." Rick stammered.

"Walter's brain slushy says I can. It's quite brilliant. You're a junkie and once people hear that you're offing people that owe me money, it'll strike fear into everyone's heart. On top of your being my brother. It's fucking genius."

"I can't do this. There's no way."

"You can and will. You can't say no. Now, I want you to shower and get to work. You won't get a gun until you arrive to each location. If you even try and pull a fast one, that big black gentleman will not only blow your brains out, but he will parade your corpse around like those assholes did in that shitty movie *Weekend At Bernie's*. God, I hated that movie. You'll also find clean clothes. And *please,* fix yourself something to eat."

They were ushered out and Rick felt as if he had been thrust into a nightmare. There's no way he could do this. It was crazy. He would have rather dealt with Jimmy than be forced to do this. Then he had a brilliant idea, but wondered if he could actually pull it off. If he killed himself it was all over, wasn't it? He would be saving three lives, and Adam couldn't have his goons kill him if he blew his own brains out. The more he thought about it though, the less sense it made. These were junkies after all. Why should he spare their life? The one good thing that had come out of this was that he would no longer be doing drugs. The desire was gone. He needed a wake up call and this was it.

"Call Adam for me. I want to talk to him." Rick had stopped walking and waited while the white guy frowned at him.

"Why should I do that? That wasn't part of the rules."

"Fuck the rules. Just do it."

He punched in a number and handed the phone to Rick. "I need your help, Adam. If I'm going to do this I need your help."

Adam sighed and remained silent. Rick knew what he was thinking. His junkie brother wanted some kind of payment so he could get high after this. "What could you possibly want? Money?"

"After this I want you to help me get my life in order. This shit is crazy and after tonight I doubt very much that I'll ever get high again. I just need a place to stay and maybe a job. I'm sure you can handle that right?"

"You know I can, but I'll be watching you very closely. You screw up once and you'll be out on your ass. Just get through tonight and we'll deal with tomorrow later." Adam hung up and Rick handed the phone back.

"We're going to be spending a lot of time together, so, can I at least get your names?" Rick asked casually.

The white guy shrugged. The black guy just glared through him. "Steve, and that big black bastard over there is Elliot. He looks mean as hell, but he's probably the nicest guy you'll ever meet. A good dude to have on your side."

They lapsed into silence and headed to Adam's house. After showering and changing into fresh clothes, Rick felt more like his old self. For the first time in a long while he felt clear headed and focused. If it hadn't been for the murders he was about to commit, he would be euphoric. *Just get through this,* he thought as he walked back into the living room. *These are people who are just like you were.* It was odd thinking of himself as a former junkie already, and it had only been a couple hours since he had been in that motel room, balls deep in that dead chick. He was still angry over all of the shit he had done and he saw this as a chance to purge himself of all of his demons. These were junkies who had no desire to clean up their lives, so why not sacrifice them? It made perfect sense. This was an opportunity to rectify all of his mistakes.

"Let's get this over with. What happens if they try and kill me?" Rick asked casually.

"Simple. We kill them. We're supposed to watch you, but if shit goes down we'll have your back. I heard what you said to your brother. Hell of wake up call, isn't it? Despite what you might think, your brother was just looking out for you."

"No need to explain. The more I think about it these are just junkies like me and they owe my brother money, so they need to be taken out. Right? Just business for Adam, right?"

Steve nodded and they all climbed into Elliot's '86 Buick Skylark. The car smelled of Patchouli, which struck Rick as funny because Elliot didn't look at all like a hippy. They drove toward Summit Lake and Rick was surprised by how run down and neglected this part of Akron was. When they approached Summit Lake Apartments, Rick perked up a little. He had been here before. Even in the darkness he knew where they were headed and it scared him a little. Once upon a time this area had been an amusement park, but was now one of the poorest neighborhoods in Akron. It also had quite a nasty reputation.

You were fine driving through in the daytime, but it wasn't the type of place you wanted to get a flat tire at night. A majority of the houses they passed were boarded up, waist high weeds grew wild in the yards. It made him sad to be around such decay and he wondered what these neighborhoods looked like before they became victims of neglect. There was nothing to keep people living there. Crime was high, no one felt safe enough to stay. It not only brought down property values, but the only people willing to stay were the gang bangers and criminals.

"You okay, Rick?" Steve asked.

Rick nodded and smiled. "Of course. Just another day at work for you guys, isn't it? Which apartment is it?" Rick asked

"Thirty Two Cicero. Hopefully we come out without losing any blood. You sure you're okay?" Steve asked again. He handed Rick a Glock 19 equipped with a silencer. The gun felt good in his hand, almost as if it were created just for him. He had never shot a gun before, but how hard could it be? You just point, shoot, and your target went home in a body bag. He had seen plenty of action movies, so he had some knowledge of how guns worked. Instead of answering, he just nodded. It was easier than talking.

They didn't need to knock, the front door was unlocked. Inside the apartment there was a mound of dirty dishes piled onto a nicked coffee table, the couch was threadbare and had a multitude of cigarette burns. A television was tuned to some religious show that featured a sweating preacher denouncing sin. On one end sat a man wearing only a pair of boxers, his hair was thinning and stood up in dirty spikes. Rick's attention was drawn to the woman that sat next to him. She was dressed in a sports bra and a tattered pair of shorts that hadn't seen a washer in a long time. Her dirty blond hair was tied back in a loose ponytail that exposed her long slender neck. Neither one of them acknowledged them as they stood at the end of the couch. Rick watched the woman and felt an erection growing. He brought the gun out quickly and pointed it at the man's head.

"Goddamn, baby, you got some dick sucking lips. Get your sweet ass over here and put those lips to use!"

That got their attention. The man raised his arms in surrender while the woman just stared at him in horror. Rick pulled the trigger and giggled as the man's brain's turned the wall into a Rorschach blot. "You got brains on my shoes, you stupid fuck!" Rick swung his pistol into the man's ruined head, forcing more flecks of brain and blood to explode in a chunky mist. Peeled back and opened up, the skull looked like a half-eaten orange. Brains and blood mixed together in a runny soup; the woman had bits of skull in her hair.

"All right, bitch. You better get that sweet ass over here before I count to three. Don't make me kill me you." He undid his belt,, his erect penis wobbling like a Bobble Head. She walked slowly toward him and tentatively got down her knees, her mouth swallowing his cock.

"Suck it, bitch!" He shoved her head closer, impaling her throat on his erection. She gagged and once again he brought up the pistol. Her head erupted in a shower of gore, her mouth convulsions causing him to ejaculate. He worked her head like a puppet, his gore covered hands slick with her blood and brain matter. He handed the gun to Steve and pulled his pants up. "The bitch used her teeth."

Outside, Rick felt exhilarated. Elliot was on the phone talking to Adam. "How'd I do?" He asked.

"You are one sick son of a bitch. Did you have to do that?"

Rick laughed and slid into the backseat. "Look, I did what you asked, didn't I? That bitch was a liability. Oh, wait, you mean making her suck my dick? No, I didn't, but those lips were built for cock. You wouldn't have done that?"

Elliot had now joined them. He looked just as disgusted as Steve. "Your brother says hello. I didn't tell him what you did to that woman before you killed her. He would have been pissed."

"So what! She was a useless whore. You know, before you showed up at my hotel room I fucked that dead woman you saw in my bed. I didn't kill her, but I sure did fuck her. You guys have no idea how sick I am. I'm just a junkie, remember? You guys said it yourself. You have no respect for me, so why should I behave?"

"Look, we have two more stops and you need to be cool, man. If Adam hears about that shit you pulled, we're all dead, you hear me? Did you really fuck that girl?"

Rick nodded and stared out the window. Something had awakened inside of him and it scared him. At the motel the same thing had happened. It was like he had stepped outside of himself only to have a darker part take over. He enjoyed killing those two more than he wanted to admit. The feel of the dead girl's lips around his dick made him stiffen up again. What would happen at the next stop? Would the dark part of him take over or would he remain in control? The thing that scared him the most was his lack of remorse. He felt nothing. There was no hint of any emotion at all. There should be some type of shock, shouldn't there? Not only had he killed the man, but he had forced a woman to perform oral sex on him before shooting her. There were bits of brains and blood on his shirt, his cock was sticky with her blood and saliva, yet he felt nothing. He wondered what would happen after the night had ended. What did the future hold for him? To everyone who knew him now he was just a junkie, but he had been so much more. His brother was giving him his life back, he just didn't know it.

The neighborhood grew more depressing the farther they went. It was easy to see why these people owed Adam money. They were poor people who lived in neighborhoods that featured a store on just about every corner. He was happy to see the bright lights of Kenmore Boulevard, even though it wasn't any safer than the neighborhood they just left, it looked more alive than dead. Past the Boulevard, they headed toward Barberton, which was safer depending on where you lived. It seemed strange to be driving into the Magic City just to kill someone. After nine in the evening the town was desolate. No cars drove past, the sidewalks were empty. It unnerved Rick a little that no one was out.

"Where are we headed?"

"Lake Anna. Our guy lives in a house close by, but Adam says he spends a lot of time at the lake, feeding ducks and shit."

"You're kidding, right? He a user?"

Elliot shook his head and decided to join the conversation. "He wasn't. He was a seller for awhile, but you never know with these guys. He may try and run, so you need to hobble him."

"Hobble him?"

"Yeah, hobble him," Steve added his thoughts to the conversation. Rick could see a slight smile spread across his face. "Shoot him in the knee so he can't run. When he's down, you can do whatever you want to him. He ain't going nowhere."

Rick could see himself using this method of torture. That was exactly was it was. You shot some poor defenseless bastard in the knee cap and while he crawled around screaming you took potshots at other parts of their anatomy. It was sick and cruel, but it was effective. If you took out a knee, there would be a great deal of blood and the pain would drive a person to madness. What was the human threshold to pain? Rick had no idea, but he wanted to find out. He wanted to bring someone to the threshold of death and bring them screaming back to life. There were so many possibilities it made him giddy. Everyone had different thresholds and what made one person whimper would push another into death.

Torture was unique because it made the person submissive. Apply enough pain and even the most strong-willed person will bawl like a baby. He assumed that these two goons he was riding with did it all the time. Sure, his brother might be an intelligent man, but when you were dealing with society's lowest common denominator you had to speak a language they understood. Pain was a universal language. It said; "No more fucking around, buddy. Shit's about to get ugly." Torture was how you twisted the odds in your favor. It was an unfair advantage, but life was an unfair mistress that teased you and taunted you. So why not stack the odds in your favor? These two goons would use every advantage they could. Take a man's knees out and he was your bitch. Even the strongest person couldn't function with one or two broken knees.

"Do you see him, Elliot?" Steve asked, slowing the car down so they could look across the circular pool that wasn't really a lake, but had always been referred to as Lake Anna.

"Nope. Shall we try his house?"

They took a right, headed down Third Sreet, and stopped in front of a light blue duplex. Across the street, the lights of Lake Anna YMCA shone brightly despite being closed. Rick looked around and saw that there was only one other house on the street. No lights were on, so the odds of them being disturbed were pretty slim. This was another house he had been to. He suddenly realized what was going on. "These are all houses I've been to. Why am I taking out people that have sold me drugs?"

"I have no idea what's going on. I was told to take you to pay off your debt to your brother. Elliot and I were paid to be your babysitters and to make sure shit didn't get out of hand. On that count, so far, we've failed. If you have some beef with any of these assholes, it's news to me." Elliot parked close to the house and opened his door. Rick couldn't help but feel that something was going on. Some plan had been put into motion as if his brother somehow knew that he would smarten up.

"This mother fucker is a serious scumbag. Instead of wasting bullets on him, let me have a tire iron."

Elliot shook his head. "We have direct orders. No way."

"You're kidding me, right? You always listen to your boss? Here's the deal. Either you hand me the tire iron or I walk. You'll have to kill me then, because Adam said if I failed to comply you were supposed to take me out."

"You can't be serious."

"*Dead* fucking serious. Better yet, here, kill me." Rick dropped to his knees and raised his arms. Neither man made a move to shoot him. They had dealt with all sorts of crazy people, but Rick wondered if they had dealt with anyone who had nothing to lose. If they killed him, so what? In a way they would be doing him a favor.

"Get the fuck up, man. Elliot, just get him the tire iron. I don't know what you have planned, but it's on your head. I wash my hands of this shit, right now."

"Fine with me. This asshole was supposed to sell me some drugs, but instead he took my money and failed to deliver his end of the bargain. This shit is personal, and if Adam has a problem with that, he can see me." Rick took the tire iron and walked with purpose to the house. He looked at the windows of the opposite duplex and thought about how he wanted to play it. Either way, it was going to be messy. But what about the neighbors? If this cocksucker screamed then things would get ugly real fast. He looked behind him and saw that only Elliot was following him. He smiled and wondered what Elliot was thinking.

He opened the screen door, tried the handle, and was disappointed to find it locked. It would have been easier if it had been unlocked. He could just walk in and do what he had to do. Now he had to wait until someone opened the door. It made him even angrier that he had to stand out here like an asshole. When the door finally opened a crack, he smiled and pushed his way in. His target squealed like a girl as he teetered off balance and landed firmly on his ass.

"How are ya, fuck face? Remember me?" Rick snarled. He smiled and raised the tire iron.

There was a whimper as the cold steel met the dealer's head. The first blow shattered his shoulders. Another blow sent his teeth flying, his jaw not only broken, but disintegrated. Blood squirted into Rick's eyes, temporarily blinding him. The man's head had become a lumpy mess that resembled a pile of mashed potatoes doused with ketchup. He could hear Elliot retch as the tire iron thumped against the dealer's torso. A pool of blood spread out underneath the ruined body, Rick could smell shit mixing in with the warm coppery stench.

Rick could feel himself being led outside to the waiting car. He struggled under Elliot's grasp. He wanted to go back in, but the grip on his elbow was too strong.

"Get in the goddamn car." Elliot growled. Rick obeyed and dropped the blood-splattered tire iron onto the street. He shrugged in compliance and climbed in. He was out of breath and suddenly very tired. Everything that had just transpired was a blur. The sound of the tire iron striking flesh had been like a broom handle hitting a bag of flour.

They sped off into the night, Rick closed his eyes and tried to slow his breathing. He was growing tired and wished that this was all over. It had been a long night, one that some would say only existed in nightmares. How many people in Rick's situation would have actually survived this? He doubted anyone would. It tested a person, showed them what they were truly capable of. He had committed murder, yet he was strangely calm, almost at peace with it. This was just one step closer to a new beginning and one that closed the past for good. There had been no other option. He was stuck on this weird ride that seemed close to be spinning out of control.

As they drove, he dozed. His mind was a kaleidoscope of images. He saw everything through a haze of blood and in his dreams he saw demons with blackened skin and eyes the color of stop lights. They beckoned to him as if they had been waiting for him, the smell of sulfur so pungent it stung his nostrils.

"Wake up, sleeping beauty. Last stop." Elliot shook him one last time and attempted a smile, but it looked forced. There was something in his eyes that shone for just a second and winked out like the flame of a candle. It was revulsion. Rick got the feeling that if Elliot had his way, he'd already have a bullet in his head. But he was too afraid of his brother to try anything stupid.

"Where are we?" He asked, stifling a yawn. They were at a storage facility of some sort. There was an army of U-Haul trucks in the parking lot, and beyond a locked gate, storage units. Steve punched in a code on a small steel keypad and the gate squeaked open on rusty wheels.

"You'll see." They parked in front of an office and they all climbed out. Rick felt a twinge of fear as they got close to the office doors. Despite the late hour, the lights were on; but he couldn't see anyone inside.

Rick stopped walking and looked around, hoping to see something, or someone. The office was tomb silent as they walked toward a door marked "Employees Only." It was decorated to appear warm and inviting, but to Rick it just felt foreboding, more like a prop. It was almost as if the fake flowers and light beige walls were an illusion. Rick had a feeling that he was about to see something no one else would ever get to see, and it filled him with dread.

They walked into a spacious office and both men looked at Rick. "Don't look so scared. Everything's going to be just fine." Steve's voice rang with hollow confidence. Rick's eyes remained fixed on the door. Elliot rocked back on his feet and remained silent.

Rick felt something cold and heavy being pressed into his wrist and for a brief second a knot of fear crawled up his spine, until he realized that Steve was discreetly handing him the Glock. He opened his hand and, as smoothly as possible, stuffed the gun into the waistband of his jeans. All they could do now was wait. That was the hardest part. His senses were in overdrive as the nerves gave way to anxiety. He had a ton of questions but doubted very much if Steve or Elliot would give him any answers.

A man walked in and smiled forcefully. He was a short squat man with thinning greasy hair that stood up in little spikes. He was dressed in a pink polo shirt and baggy blue jeans. His eyes bounced off of all them as if they weren't really looking at him but playing ping pong with an invisible opponent. "This is an unexpected surprise. I already paid Adam. We're square. You come to thank me? Who's your friend?" His voice was whiny and nasal. It made Rick want to throat punch him just so he wouldn't have to hear it anymore.

"Doesn't matter. The thing is, you were a bit short. We came here to collect." Elliot's smile was sinister and made him look certifiable. It was the kind of look that instilled fear in most people, but obviously this guy wasn't most people. He smiled right back with the same intensity.

"What the fuck are talking about? I wasn't short. I swear." Now there was a bit of fear in his voice, the smile was replaced by a look of shock.

"Rick, talk to this asshole." Steve backed up a step as Rick brought out the Glock. Instead of pointing it at him and firing, he smacked him in the jaw. There was a dull crack as the gun shattered his jaw. Blood and teeth flooded the carpet, a look of pain and fear exploded in the man's eyes as Rick grabbed him by his shirt and pulled him so close they were eye to eye.

"You calling my friends liars? Do you have any idea what I'm going to do you?" Rick shook him like a rag doll. More blood leaked from his ruined mouth. "I'm going to fuck you in the ass. You fucked my brother, and now I'm going to fuck you. Literally." Rick yanked the man's pants down, turned him around, and shoved him face first onto the desk. The man whimpered like a puppy as realization sank in. He tried to move but Rick bounced his forehead of off the wooden desk. He heard Elliot wince and Steve began laughing as the man's pockmarked ass bounced up in the air.

Rick smiled as he forced the man's ass cheeks apart. The smell of shit permeated the office. He could hear his cohorts gagging. The ass bucked wildly as Rick opened it wider. The whimpers were now muffled screams. "What a sweet, sweet ass. I'm gonna go balls deep, Harry, and maybe if you're lucky you'll pass it out. You *do* realize it's not rape if I yell surprise? Surprise!" The bucking became more frantic as Rick playfully rubbed his flabby butt cheek. Without warning, Rick began swatting his naked ass if Harry were a naughty, unruly child. The screams turned into wailing sobs, the pink flesh became bright red.

Rick smiled as he grabbed the keyboard and smashed it into Harry's head. The cord flapped wildly as keys from the keyboard sprinkled onto the desk like loose change. He fell over onto his back, piss flooding from his penis like water from a garden hose. Tears fell down his puffy cheeks, mixing with the blood from his ruined mouth. "Where's the money, Harry?"

Harry violently shook his head in response. Mewling sounds came from his mouth. Rick stepped onto his testicles, grinding them under his foot as if he were suddenly squishing grapes to make wine. The keyboard came down three times, eradicating Harry's nose. They could hear him choking as blood and the remainder of the man's teeth went down his throat, choking him. The keyboard cracked and keys littered Harry's convulsing body. Tossing away the keyboard, Rick delivered short soccer kicks to the man's body. Elliot visibly winced each time Rick's foot connected. Growing bored, he once again pulled out the Glock and took potshots at Harry. One bullet went into his ankle and another removed three fingers on his left hand.

"All you had to do was play nice, you fuck. Now look at you." Rick aimed the gun one final time. The bullet turned his right eye to pulp, fresh blood seeped from the gaping wound. He tossed the gun back to Steve and walked out without a word. Now free, he wondered what his future held. He felt a bit queasy as he climbed into the car. Steve and Elliot followed shortly after. None of them spoke as they roared off into the coming dawn.

What would happen now? Rick had no idea, but he knew he would be forever changed. He had done things he had never thought he was capable of doing; yet, as he drifted off to sleep, he knew he would do them again if he had to. Part of him actually enjoyed it. The smell of blood filtered into his dreams, he saw visions of Harry with his ass up in the air, the woman with her mouth open wide as he rammed his cock down her throat. The events of the evening replayed themselves in his dreams and he couldn't help but smile.

GO FUCK YOURSELF
Dani Brown

Baldassare was a man who loved his reflection too much to share. In Baldassare's life there was no one except Baldassare.

A bottle of luxury hand cream, naked in front of the mirror, was not the same as fucking himself in the literal sense. It was unfortunate that he couldn't bring the mirror home to meet his parents. His mother was always going on at him to bring home a nice girl and settle down. There were no girls nice enough for Baldassare.

His attempts at cloning failed in a spectacular mess of tentacles and pus-filled boils that exploded all over his ceiling and flaked down over the course of six months in a yellow snow. Yet he kept trying. His latest attempt only resulted in small, non-explosive zits.

When he wasn't tinkering with bio-engineering he would stare at the mirror for hours on end while waiting for his welfare cheque. Baldassare was the type of person who gave those who really were reliant upon state assistance a bad name. He was capable of applying for and getting any job available.

Baldassare was a firm believer in being paid just for his existence. His good looks brought smiles to the faces of women and murderous envy to the minds of men; he should be paid extra for looking too damn fine. He didn't realize that no one agreed with his self-assessment.

His looks were natural – he never required hair gel or rub-on tan. He never needed a shower either. He saved lots of money that way—extra money for luxury hand cream.

He had considered spreading his seed around, but that would equate to less time admiring his reflection. It might include child support payments, which would give him less money for luxury hand cream. Not to mention the entire messy affair of sticking his cock in a specimen that was less than perfection. He wouldn't be able to get it up unless he could fuck her from behind while watching in the mirror.

Baldassare only had eyes for himself. If his parents had given him a sister, he might have had eyes for her, assuming he hadn't hogged all the good genes. But they didn't give him a sister or a brother. Or even a pedigree dog.

Sex was a disappointment, the few times he was drunk enough to find someone else remotely good looking. No woman, man, or animal could match his glorious beauty. The few people he fucked were left blinded by the golden sun shining out of his arse.

If only his cock was long enough to twist around and fuck himself, but luxury lotion only kept it, and his hands, silky smooth. Lotions couldn't add length, but then, if it was any bigger, he would pass out each time he had an erection, so he didn't want any extra length or girth. He just wished his arsehole was in a more fuckable place.

Baldassare convinced himself that most women would die to be caressed by his hands – hands which had never seen a day's work, unless masturbation counted (and it should). Baldassare could masturbate for England or, for that matter, the entire United Kingdom, Ireland, and Scandinavia as well. It was his only hobby, conducted to thoughts of fucking himself. He didn't need porn, unless he was in it, but he didn't know how to go about becoming a porn star and he would have to stick his cock in people beneath him. That thought was enough to illicit protests from his balls.

The government should provide him with a maid. That way he wouldn't be in a constant battle with the slugs. He despised slugs, but cleaning took away from vital hours of blowing kisses to his own reflection. Sometimes the slugs offered a tasty little snack on the rare occasion he felt peckish. He would add salt by dipping them in jizz.

There wasn't much space to move inside his bedsit, except by the mirror. He kept that pristine and wiped away streaks and smears and stray bits of flying jizz with more regularity than his bowels. He didn't own a hoover to vacuum all the dry skin and jizz-flakes away from the rug in front, but that didn't matter. He used a straw to suck them up every other day.

Baldassare's shit had the gleam of perfection. He crapped thornless long stem roses. The piles of turds, wrapped in old newspapers, were like vases of cut flowers beneath the kitchen counter, where a washing machine might reside if he didn't lack the desire to use it. He had no reason to wash his few items of clothing; Baldassare's sweat acted as a natural cleanser and his urine was a natural aphrodisiac.

He considered bottling his piss and auctioning it off on the internet, but that would take time away from whispering sweet nothings to the mirror. When his thirst needed quenching, it offered more refreshment than what came out of the tap. Selling it as a sex aide would leave him with nothing to drink. Baldassare was too smart to allow that.

Each day started the same. Baldassare would drag himself out of bed when his bladder woke him up, sometime after the sun had finished its climb up the sky. He only woke each day to look at himself. That's what he lived for.

Most people make a trip to the toilet to empty their bladder shortly after waking. Not Baldassare. He would have to climb over too many festering piles of rubbish and decaying boxes to reach it. That wasted too much energy better spent in front of the mirror. And he didn't want to ruin his perfect feet by stepping in toxic mold or that puddle of vomit from two weeks ago.

He would pee into the nearest glass or bottle. If one wasn't available, he would let it flow without aiming. Baldassare didn't care if urine went all over his bedsit. He didn't want to sleep in a puddle so he always made sure he was facing away from his bed. The festering boxes blocking the way to the bathroom were his usual target. He had forgotten what was stored in them. His pee, as well as having aphrodisiac properties, also left a nice perfume to disguise the apartment's stagnant air.

Once he had relieved himself, he would look for something to eat. Baldassare kept food under the bed for convenience. He didn't like to navigate around the boxes and general waste if it could be avoided. His stomach would rumble upon waking each late afternoon as his cock bobbed up and down, pulsing for attention. It was good to have some energy for the inevitable jerking off.

Today, he rummaged under the metal frame and produced a jar of mayonnaise. He dug around more, batting away something with fur and something else with slime and located half a loaf of bread with only a little mould, which was rather good as his flat was such a mouldy festering place. And it was normal little green dots of mould, not the mould with more fur than a Maine Coon that grew on half his possessions.

He required a spoon, or a knife, or something – he wasn't about to stick his pristine nails into the jar. (Maybe he wouldn't cut himself anymore when fingering his arse if he filed them down a bit.) He wouldn't even stick them in to remove the egg-crust that formed on the top of it, even though crusty mayonnaise on his fingertips might prove a good anal lubricant.

His supplies of plastic cutlery were running low. Washing dishes was beneath him. Lack of eating utensils would require a trip to the local service station in the upcoming days – an opportunity for people to stare and mentally undress him. It would take him away from his mirror, which was why he kept putting it off. He refused to shop online as he didn't like paying for anything other than luxury hand cream. Plus, the delivery man would get a good look at Baldassare in his naked glory (his dressing gown had been sucked into the boxes six months ago), which wouldn't be fair to everyone else.

He rummaged around, feeling for something he could scoop mayonnaise with. His stomach rumbled. He wanted the slimy, slightly-off goodness down his throat. He wanted to jerk off over his reflection. He couldn't do that until after he ate something, otherwise he risked passing out.

His tongue wasn't long enough to reach into the jar. It wasn't strong enough to penetrate the crust. He couldn't exercise it by sticking it up someone's arse, because only his arsehole was good enough for licking. Baldassare wasn't that flexible. There wasn't enough floor space for yogic stretches.

The most stretching he did was reaching under the bed each late afternoon in his quest for food and plastic cutlery. He really needed to stop throwing forks and knives on top of the festering boxes. They got sucked in, never to be seen again, unless a box shit one out; but that was a rare occurrence. The box-digestion broke them down too much to be used as cutlery again. He had a little collection he planned to melt together as the ultimate butt-plug, but that still didn't get the mayonnaise out of the jar.

Baldassare held the bag of bread in his lap in despair. Tears welled in his eyes. He was hungry. Each minute he sat on the bed was a minute he wasn't jerking off. His load might spontaneously blow.

If he did cum himself, he would have a topper for his bread. Cum wasn't as good as mayonnaise first thing in the late afternoon. Baldassare was a big fan of drinking his own jizz because it was the best tasting spunk in existence. Not like he had much experience of mouthfuls of other people's jizz, but he would sometimes ejaculate in a plastic cup and drink it down while still warm and fresh, like a nice creamy mug of milk.

He opened the plastic bag protecting the bread and shoved his cock in. It was like an oversized mouldy condom that exhaled a warm cloud up his piss-hole. Tingles coursed through his body, making his peach fuzz stand on end.

Baldassare didn't need to do any rubbing; he let the bag do all the work while he thought of himself. He never realized that fucking something other than his hand could bring pleasure. Perhaps it was time he started experimenting with other household objects and foodstuffs.

There wasn't even that much mould spotted on the bread. What there was seemed to have reproduced during the brief exposure to the festering air of the flat as Baldassare checked its edibility.

The warm air cupped his balls and squeezed with a delicacy his hands have never been able to master. He wished he thought to stick a bread slice up his arse before the bag took hold of his cock, but it was too late for regrets.

Far too late for regrets. His cock didn't ooze jizz, it exploded— out of him and onto the bread. The air in the bag squeezed to milk him and provide a nutritious supplemental bread topper. The perfect breakfast for the perfect man.

He wanted it while it was still warm, but his cock was still leaking. A little spunk on his sheets wouldn't hurt; it would land on top of jizz-flakes two months old. He could lick it up if he was still hungry.

But the bag didn't want to let him go.

It felt humid in there. The pleasure was gone as Baldassare's balls were sucked dry. Skin was torn off and eaten by the mould. He could feel it being dissolved in the acid exhaled by the new species created when the mould in the bag met the mould carried on the air for the first time. His deflated balls were next on the mould's menu –they would fit through his piss-hole now that they lacked their contents.

Being castrated through his dick was not an experience Baldassare could clock as one worthy of remembrance, but if his balls grew back better than before, with just the right amount of hair, people would die just thinking of how perfect he is, and how lacking their lives were. He tried to focus on that. He succeeded until his stomach started to rumble.

His stomach didn't send up a reminder of its hunger; it sent up stomach bile and the remains of a defrosted, yet uncooked, microwavable meal he'd eaten before passing out on his bed in the early hours. The empty plastic tray sat on top of the festering boxes. It now had a healthy coating of fur.

Baldassare's arse didn't escape the rapid decompression. His intestines were squeezed by an invisible steamroller until every last scraping of shit exploded out of his anus in liquefied form. The force was strong enough to push him off his saggy mattress and onto the floor. The bread bag dangled between his legs.

Chunks of partially digested mystery meat cascaded out of his mouth with peas that were like pellets going down and no better coming back up in a gravy much thicker than what he had eaten. They bounced out of the vomit pool and rolled away to join the boxes as his balls were sucked out of his piss-hole and onto his breakfast.

The bag became heavier with the addition of his intestines, pulling him face-first into the vomit. The carpet had a super absorbency level, so he didn't risk drowning. If only he could stop vomiting. Even sponges become saturated at some point.

The steamy diarrhea (with peas) was set to join the vomit and form a treacherous estuary unless Baldassare plugged the violence from his arse. He never had a girlfriend or even brought a girl back to his flat, so the possibility of a tampon lying around was remote. He would have to use his fingers. It was either that or his teddy bear. He didn't want to use his only relic of childhood.

He reached a hand around. His wrist creaked with the early onset of arthritis caused by incessant masturbation. He lacked the time to exercise it. His anus was flowing heavy with the brown tide. The peas were like small crabs littering the shore.

Baldassare had to fight against fast-moving diarrhea to get a finger close. His arthritis didn't like it, but it was either that or drown in his own filth. As perfect as his diarrhea was, that was not the way he wanted to go. Already, his rug was in the early stages of becoming vomit-logged. The eruption from his arse was meeting with the puke and forming a deep lake.

In normal circumstances his arsehole embraced his fingertips in a warm hug and pulled them in for a kiss. But the shit deluge was not a normal circumstance. He wouldn't be able to wrap it up in little parcels to preserve for his future self. He might be able to use a straw and siphon it into a jar. If the carpet didn't drink it all first and rain it down onto the flat below.

The diarrhea acted as a lubricant. He needed his entire fist to stem the flow. He didn't feel it, except on his protesting wrist. He wanted the deodorant sample he threw into the festering boxes sometime last week. Cans of deodorant were great for those pesky liquidity days as their diameter made them a perfect arse-tampon. He didn't even have toilet paper. He viewed it as a waste of money. Why use toilet paper when you have hands that you can then lick and save on the food bill?

The texture of the shit escaping beyond his clenched fist changed. It oozed mucus. The bag mould didn't want the mucus added to his breakfast; it was a waste product with nowhere to go except into Baldassare's pores. It felt softer and more luxurious than his expensive hand cream. If he trusted he wouldn't erupt again, he would smear it all over his body, but that would have to wait until his stomach stopped rumbling.

Meanwhile, back in the bread bag, his balls were successfully pulled out through his dick without any damage to his urethra. The bag wanted to pull his stomach out through his piss-hole next, but had to suck in the last of his intestines first. The intestinal pull wasn't as painful as losing his balls.

Baldassare could feel mould spores escaping out of the bag and onto his lower body. The fur might serve to plug his arse while he rubbed mucus all over himself, but he needed to allow it a few more seconds to spread. During those precious seconds, his wrist swelled up to the size of a mutant grapefruit, rendering Baldassare imperfect.

He pulled away his swollen wrist and let the fur enter his anus and crack. If the swelling didn't decrease within an hour, he would be forced to cut off his hand with a rusty machete. He didn't want to risk living the rest of his life with a swollen wrist when there were perfect hooks to be had— some with LED lights for a bit of bling.

He heaved. More vomit poured out of him. It didn't seem possible. It wasn't possible. Baldassare wasn't a big eater. His stomach was a shriveled thing. There was no explanation for where the vomit was coming from. He didn't have time to ponder it before his body was rocked by a violent tummy rumble and a shit explosion large enough to cut through the fur and splash back against the ceiling.

The bag, growing heavier, swung between his legs. The mould formed suction cups to keep it stuck to his body.

The swelling had spread to his fingers. He couldn't make a fist again. He would need to find that deodorant or something else to plug himself with. It didn't occur to him to use his other fist.

He pulled himself the twelve inches to the boxes and kept his chin out of the vomit while not putting any weight on his wrist. Baldassare prided himself on being perfect. This swollen wrist was becoming a threat to his perfection.

The bag stayed latched on. That wouldn't lose suction until his breakfast was ready. He wasn't sure whether he should be grateful. He needed some energy to see him through a busy evening of jerking off once he grew new balls (he was confident he would, too perfect not to be able to reproduce if he met someone worthy of his seed, and the bag knew this).

His arse spewed liquidified shit and pea pellets into the air. He imagined the peas piercing through the ceiling and hitting the feet of the man above. He didn't turn his head up to find out – more important tasks were at hand.

His fingers looked like sausages about to burst in the pan. Somewhere behind all the filth he owned a freezer. This freezer had never once been defrosted. It was a waste of electricity to keep it plugged in, but he kept it up and running for when his arthritis interrupted a night of jerking off. He would chisel pieces of ice into the washing up bucket and shove his hand in until the swelling went down.

Baldassare was dizzy. It was possible the bag had sucked in some of his blood with each body part. But it felt more like his lifeforce was draining through his arse.

He crashed into the festering boxes and toppled them onto himself, spilling mouldy contents everywhere. The bread bag didn't lose its suction. It didn't stop pulling his insides out through his piss-hole either.

No one would be able to tell what the objects from the boxes once were. They were too mouldy. Not even Baldassare knew, and it was his stuff, covered in his filth and mould, although he wasn't really in a position to examine it.

Slugs oozed out of something that had cracked open. It was hard to say what that something was; or indeed where the slugs had come from. They were green mutant monsters as lazy as Baldassare. They wouldn't know how to get pregnant and, if they did, it would require too much effort.

They oozed and slimed around him. The vomit and diarrhea pool was a good feeding ground. They also loved his eyes. He blinked against them, but that didn't seem to do any good. He didn't have a hand spare to flick them away.

He remembered throwing the deodorant sample on top of the fester. Deodorant was for those who weren't blessed with smelling as good as Baldassare. He only kept it so he could spray it on those whose odor he found offensive during his rare trip into the supermarket to raid the reduced section.

It could have been swallowed by the boxes and sucked into a black hole or eaten by the slugs by now. He didn't know how many slugs there were. They could have inhabited long ago and mutated so they could eat deodorant cans. He hoped so. Slugs were a tasty snack when he felt peckish and free. More money to spend on luxury hand cream.

He really needed something to plug his anus before anything else passed through his mouth. He wouldn't even risk swallowing his vomit for fear of how quick it would burn through his insides and erupt out of his arse.

Everything he touched while searching was former bio-engineering equipment covered in mould. It would have felt like sitting on a cactus. Mould contributed to the failure of his cloning attempts.

He came across the corpse of a giant rat. It must have crawled out of the toilet and into the fester to die. It was too decomposed to eat. He threw it aside and there, beneath it, was the deodorant sample he so badly required.

His arse only oozed thick mucus now that his intestines were gone. The mucus was the best lubricant he could ask for. He made a mental note to save some for later, after he had his breakfast.

His stomach felt like it was being flattened, but nothing else came out of his mouth. He tested the theory by plucking a plump slug from the rat and swallowing.

Baldassare waited. And waited some more. Nothing came out of either end, but the bag dropped off. He felt the familiar rub of his balls, all shiny and new.

He opened it with trepidation. He wasn't sure what to expect, but knew he needed some breakfast. The smell filled the flat and covered the decay. He peeked in.

Sausages, plump with mould, had formed from his intestines in the bag. His stomach became bacon. A maggot burst out of a turd sausage. That made it appetizing. Baldassare didn't waste time with things such as cutlery. The bag was big enough to reach in without the assistance of a knife.

He ate the contents and wished for more. This was the best meal he had ever eaten. It had to be; apart from the bread, it had come out of him. It had the taste of perfection.

His post-meal farts displaced the deodorant. They took the chill out of the air and left a lingering scent of partially digested recycled sausage and mould. Baldassare filled his lungs and held his breath. This scent needed to penetrate every cell. It was his version of a shower.

His cock was growing erect—it was time. He needed to be in front of the mirror, where fantasies of riding himself were easier to come by. Sometimes he licked the mirror to imagine a French kiss.

But he had to get there first. The mould covered bio-engineering equipment had sprouted tentacles in places, to suck him into a different dimension – one where Baldassare would be considered ugly. It was growing fast. It had already swallowed the decomposed remains of the rat. Like a frog's tongue, it pulled in the slugs too.

He had to cross that to reach his destination. The tentacles pulsed, grew boils, and burst. The holes left by the eruptions spouted new tentacles. The cycle repeated.

The clockwork equipment jangled, spewing out more mould, like diarrhea out of Baldassare's eruptive arse. He felt the green stab of jealousy. His attempts at cloning always ended with jizz over everything and his arthritis playing up. Everything that came out of the machine had to be put down and buried in plastic bags under the floorboards (he didn't want fluids seeping into downstairs). This mould was better than before it was cloned.

It didn't seem fair. Sometimes his life was so unfair. It was a kick up the arse, straight from the Gods, being so perfect. They were jealous of the light shining out of his arse.

He needed a bridge. He didn't trust the mould to not suck him up and he certainly didn't want it sucking him off. It might leave scars. For all he knew, the bursting boils could be as hot as bubbling lava.

Clear and sticky pre-cum leaked out of him. He needed to figure out a way to reach his mirror before he lost his load down his leg.

As he was thinking about how unfair life was treating him, the cloned mould cleared a path. Baldassare wasn't sure of its motive. For all he knew, it might have wanted to suck up that pre-ejaculation and make a perfect copy of him. Or it could have planned to lure him into a false sense of security by pretending friendliness, then overwhelm him and suck him into it a forever mutation.

Each tiptoe into the festering shag carpet sent a shiver of anxiety coursing through his body. The shaking made the pre-cum drip from his cock. He might impregnate mould. The carpet was damp with vomit and diarrhea. His eyes darted through the steam. He needed to be aware of the mould and its ever-evolving form.

The tinkering clockwork cloning machine indicated it was still spewing out new mould. It was certainly spewing something, something Baldassare could only assume was cloned mould. For all he knew, the maggots freshly laid in ceiling diarrhea could have fallen in. If that was the case, the mould could grow wings, which, he had to admit, would be kind of cool.

Evolution didn't make much sense in his flat. It was like time had sped up. That didn't bode well for Baldassare. The last time he blew kisses to his mirror-self, he looked ten years younger than his actual age. If evolution or time had sped up, he might be jerking off over someone he wouldn't recognize. Yet, no matter how much he aged, he was certain he would remain perfect.

Something wet and sticky hit his thigh. He breathed a sigh of relief when he didn't feel the expected tentacles wrap around him. It was just an eruption from a boil. It dripped down his leg without burning.

To keep his mirror squeaky clean and dust free, he covered it with a silk cloth before going to bed and rubbed it down with window cleaner before starting his busy day of blowing kisses and whispering sweet nothings. The mould hadn't made it to the mirror yet.

Relief washed over him when he pulled away the silk; he hadn't aged overnight. He discarded it on the floor, the mould forgotten when he became lost in the watery blue of his eyes.

Baldassare watched a tentacle creep out of the bubbling amoeba the mould formed itself into beyond his reflection. He thought it was coming for him. His bladder would have released, but it was empty, as were his bowels. It reached not for his ankle, but for the window cleaner on the floor.

Mould swallowed the bottle of window cleaner before his eyes. He didn't have a spare one. His saliva would have to make the mirror gleam. His spit, like the rest of him, was pure perfection. He smeared it about and wiped it with the silken cloth. He didn't know why he bothered with window cleaner or how he came about it. The mould sent up a little burp of appreciation.

Baldassare was confident the mould wanted to watch him, maybe sample his jizz, but nothing else. It wanted sexual thrills, but couldn't have sex. It could only look on until it exploded or the cloning machine pumped out penises. He wasn't sure which was more likely of the two scenarios. Baldassare wanted to witness exploding mould cock, but only after he jerked off over his reflection.

He had something of a ritual connected to how he spent his days. First, he flexed his muscles and winked. The mould pulsed. The slow warm up was turning it on. The clock-worked equipment spewed out more perfect mould to join the blob. He wished there was mould every day. Mould appreciated his routine. No one else understood.

He met with the same disappointment he met with every day, realizing he couldn't see his back, no matter what way he turned his head. There wasn't space to put up a mirror on the opposite wall, or any floor space for a free-standing mirror. The floor space was occupied by Tupperware containers of Baldassare's runny excrement (only solid pieces could be wrapped into newspaper parcels).

The mould could see his arse. He half expected its furry touch. Maybe a little squeeze. It would save the penetration for later. The mould was counting on the clockwork machinery sending out penises made of fly and slug DNA.

The government really should provide Baldassare with a maid. Then she could stack his Tupperware containers and dust them off. A mirror could be put in front of them so Baldassare could view his back, which was just as perfect as the rest of him. She might be tempted to steal some to freeze in ice cube trays and use as a masturbation aide. Baldassare would insist CCTV be provided to keep a watch on her.

With his non-existent muscles checked, he moved onto his next task: blowing kisses. Baldassare would do this all day, every day if he didn't need to splice the time with relieving his erections. He never became bored.

But that day he wanted something different. Maybe Baldassare had experienced a wet dream. Or maybe he wanted to impress the mould. Perhaps the spores had violated his nerves and now had him under the mould's control. He inhaled. He expected the latter was true. He had no objections to becoming a slave to the mould. The mould was nearly as perfect as he was.

He wanted sex. He wanted it with himself. No one capable of matching his beauty; he'd given up on dating before he really gave it a chance. He didn't like sticking his cock in warm slimy holes belonging to something that should have a paper bag over its head at all times, except to pull food out of stainless steel orthodontic equipment.

He didn't waste time thinking about what might have been if only he had an identical twin. It took away precious moments of admiring himself. He had a twin of sorts staring back at him and copying his every perfect move. He could fuck that gorgeous person staring back at him, if only he could work out a way.

It would nearly be like fucking himself, but not quite, because the movements of the man in the mirror were exactly opposite those of Baldassare. If Baldassare blew a kiss with his right hand, mirror-Baldassare did it with his left.

His erection bobbed up and down with his movements; mould grew around his ankles, releasing a festering green mist. He was unusually randy that morning. The mould must have been releasing something into the atmosphere of his bedsit to make him think of sex for the first time in years.

Spanking it wouldn't do, even if he stuck his thumb up his arse. He'd just have an erection and be ready to go again before he even finished wiping away his half-children from mirror-Baldassare's thigh.

He needed to physically have sex with someone – fantasies about pumping his own arse wouldn't do. There must be a way for Baldassare to actually fuck himself. He looked into the mirror, into his reflected eyes.

He leaned against his mirror, placing his hands up high so his body was pressed against mirror-Baldassare. Their hands touched. Baldassare puckered his lips and went in for a kiss. It was returned.

He twisted mirror-Baldassare's nipple. The flesh felt warm and hard beneath his finger and thumb. His balls felt ready to burst. Warm air exhaled by the mould caressed his body, heightening the illusion and heating up the mirror.

Mirror-Baldassare was capable of moving his lips, but sound never came out. Lip moving soundless pleasure was consent to anything and everything. It couldn't possibly mean the opposite. A safe word would be pointless without vocal cords. Due to Baldassare's perfection, one wasn't needed.

He moved his tongue down mirror-Baldassare's body, tasting salty flesh instead of polished glass. He stopped at the nipple his fingers had so recently squeezed and sunk his teeth in. The first beads of blood left a cooper taste on this tongue as he released it and travelled downward.

He didn't have a happy trail. He had peach fuzz. Mirror-Baldassare appeared smooth, but he could feel the gentle fur against his rough tongue. The illusion didn't run a tongue down Baldassare's happy trail. With a tentacle that once might have been a slug, the mould was left to do that.

Soon his tongue would meet with the sparse pubes that sprouted from random places like stunted trees on the edge of an ever-expanding desert. Baldassare didn't wax, trim or shave. It seemed like a waste of time and money. He once plucked the few thin hairs that grew there in the days when he thought he might find someone as perfect as he was, but didn't repeat the experience. He didn't need too. Baldassare was the very image of perfection. Mirror-Baldassare was just as beautiful.

Baldassare lapped up pre-cum like a kitten with a saucer of milk. The mould went to work on his dick. He no longer cared about mating with what the cloning machine was spewing out. The can of deodorant was pulled out of his arse. It was replaced with a pulsing tentacle of goo.

This was Baldassare's first experience of a cock in his mouth. Random men in vomit-strewn alleys had tasted his jizz when he was still at a stage where he believed someone out there would be good enough for him. He refused offers of snowballing. He didn't want these men to stick their tongues near his tonsils.

The velvet soft cock skin was topped with dick-cheese. Baldassare's taste-buds celebrated. The mould was less impressed with this and sent another tentacle up his arse as punishment.

He cupped mirror-Baldassare's balls and was rewarded by drool to soothe his arthritis. Mould squeezed his. His hand wasn't covered in slime. He couldn't even pretend it was mirror-Baldassare. He still needed to blow his load and he couldn't pry himself away from the mirror.

He shoved the index finger of the other hand up mirror-Baldassare's tight arse. Another tentacle was added to his. His arse had never received such a stretching before – he lacked household objects wide enough.

He lost all track of time, but, somewhere along the line, he thought it would be fun to fuck mirror-Baldassare while the mould had its way with his anus. He didn't waste money on masturbation aides so had none in his bedsit. He was so intent upon making sweet love to his reflection he didn't want to go all the way to the sex shop in hopes they had one with a price he was willing to pay, if the mould would let him leave.

At some point, Baldassare took the mirror off the wall and moved it to his bed. The mirror lacked a hole, but mirror-Baldassare didn't. That was good enough for Baldassare. He mounted it on his festering bed, then mounted the squeaking-clean mirror.

The mould mounted him. Not all of it at once. It would crush Baldassare beneath its weight. It was enough to press his body into mirror-Baldassare with a quick thrust that met against glass. The mould controlled Baldassare's actions via his arsehole.

Hour after hour of humping created a hole where mirror-Baldassare's anus was to be found. Baldassare didn't notice until his cock was sucked in during one hard thrust.

It wasn't jagged. It didn't cut as expected of broken glass. The mirror wasn't even broken. His cock had entered the anus of his reflection. The mould penetrated deeper and looped around his bowels in search of his breakfast.

Mirror-Baldassare's arsehole was warm and tight, but not too tight. It was inviting. It hadn't so recently lost its virginity to mould tentacles. The two of them weren't as alike as the appearance might suggest.

He pumped away for no longer than thirty seconds. controlled by the tentacles inside him, before he was sucked further into mirror-Baldassare's arse. The mould wasn't only in him, searching for his breakfast; it wrapped itself around him in a protective coating. He sunk through the mirror.

Baldassare woke up. He didn't remember falling asleep. The last thing he remembered was gaining entry into mirror-Baldassare's arse, while mould tentacles fucked him. He wanted to wake up next to his reflection, but even the mould left him.

He was somewhere warm and dark. It stank of shit. His hand felt for his light switch, but didn't find it. Instead, it was slashed by what could have been broken glass. Wherever he was lacked the underlying scent of fester and decay that rode the airwaves of his bedsit and penetrated every pore.

He was surrounded by darkness. Not even an orange street lamp flickered on and off with the austerity the government was constantly droning on and on about. Orange was not his color. The light from those awful things disguised his perfections from the night-time world.

Something pressed down on him. It was warm and wet and covered in fur. He was covered in slime. Baldassare wondered if this is what it felt like to be born.

His ears picked up the sound of hushed sobbing. He didn't know who was making it or how far away they were. He tried to call out, but something was blocking his throat. Something of equal size was blocking his anus. He shouldn't be associating the two, but his mind couldn't help it. There was some distant memory relating to his throat and arsehole, but that was all he had.

Something wrapped around his wrists and ankles in one sudden movement. It lacked suction cups. It went for a cutting feel to prevent movement. A normal person might panic, but Baldassare wasn't normal. He was perfect.

A dull light shone on the horizon. As dull as it was, Baldassare had to shut his eyes against it. His head hurt. The light made it worse and made his eyes feel like they might boil away.

Warm air lifted whatever pressed down on him. The slime dried into a thick crust. He couldn't scratch at it. Struggling only cut his wrists and ankles deeper.

Moaning and a metallic rattle joined the sobbing in a chorus of debauchery. The erratic rhythm did nothing to help his head.

He found the sounds curious. He opened his eyes a little slit to a brightening world. Everything was cast in shadow, making objects hazy. It was impossible to tell what anything was. He could lift his neck and move it to each side, but he couldn't sit up and squint for a proper look.

The sobbing drew closer. An icy chill engulfed Baldassare's slime-crust coated body. He thought someone was at his feet, but where there should have been body heat, there was cold. The sobbing stopped there. He lifted his head to see a shadow in the shape of a hunchback or a person without a head – he couldn't tell which.

A gentle rain fell. It stank of sour shit with slight undertones of soap. It burnt through the slime crust. The sobbing continued. Frozen fingers touched his toes. Frostbite would ruin his perfection.

Light shone grey and brown through the gentle rain. A fog rolled across the flat land. It looked and smelt like a sewer had exploded. Baldassare couldn't explain the grey tint to some of the drops, but that would account for the brown.

The sound of laughter and grunting drowned out the unhappy rhythm of moaning and the metallic rattle. It mixed with the sound of a pig squealing; or maybe it was a goat. Either way, the sound was from a farmyard animal. A woman joined in, shouting "harder". The sobbing at his feet continued, never changing pitch.

He turned his head towards this new series of sounds. They were familiar, but not in that combination. He was able to block out the unsteady rhythm. These noises were closer. The sobbing at his feet was forgotten as a black chill made a slow navigation up his legs.

Baldassare thought his eyes were in conspiracy with his ears to deceive him. Or maybe it was a trick of the gentle shit and sludge rain. People couldn't seriously participate in what was burning his vision

Baldassare wasn't fond of computers. He didn't trust the government wasn't spying on people via webcams, so he didn't own one. He didn't have access to the world wide supply of bestiality porn, except on his phone, but that was expensive. He didn't realize that sometimes people like to sneak into farmyards and petting zoos and pleasure themselves with the pigs and goats for the pleasure of a viewing audience reaching into the millions.

The last thing he wanted to see was staring right at him and he couldn't look away. A natural part of being human was the instinct to gawp at train wrecks; Baldassare was no exception to this universal law. It looked like the two involved in the act and the pig itself were in a train wreck, or maybe the tractor on the floor beside them had fallen on top and then shifted to allow them to continue.

Guts leaked out of twisted and broken ribs and down the woman's naked torso. Her breasts sagged to her belly button in a way that suggested they were much higher when she woke up with the sun that morning. A rib poked through one and held it close while the other flapped about with her excitement. She was impaled by the horn of a riding saddle. The stirrups bounced up and down. There wasn't a horse in sight, but there was a pig.

The pig and man didn't look much better, even without a riding saddle trailing out of his arse. Baldassare had never been on a farm. He didn't realize that the pig was actually a piglet. A full-grown pig would have escaped. The piglet struggled, but the man held its legs as he thrust in and out like his skull hadn't caved in. His vocal cords were still intact enough to moan with pleasure.

The pig wouldn't make good bacon or even reformed ham. The stress would make it all stringy, preventing its meat from being glued back together.

He wished his eyesight wasn't as perfect as he was. That scene could never be unseen. The brightening sky didn't cast these two plus the pig in shadow. He could see the congealed blood at their feet and the green of the tractor behind them. He preferred the hazy shadows obscuring everything.

The rain fell on them too, but the sky was brighter – unless it was a leaking high ceiling with dimmer switches, Baldassare didn't know. The rain didn't change consistency, color, or smell. It didn't wash away the crust that coated him. It burnt through it in places, but most of the moisture rested on top. If he laid here he might slowly end up looking like those three.

It was time he looked somewhere else. He was convinced nothing could be worse than live action pig porn, not even the women who would throw themselves at him after a night of clubbing and puking down themselves while he was on his way back from the service station with plastic cutlery. He changed his habits to avoid them. The pig, on the other hand, would forever haunt his dreams.

His eyes met the source of the sobbing. An old lady with a hunched back stood by his feet. The squeal of the pig was louder. She clutched a porcelain doll with one missing eye and a moth eaten dress in a liver spotted hand. Much to Baldassare's distaste, the granny's dress was transparent. It decayed to nothing before his eyes. Her skin peeled and was carried away on the warm wind. A skeleton in a tattered dress stood before him. Her head stayed attached to the long neck. It looked more painful than the undetermined things cutting in Baldassare's wrists and ankles. Yet, still she sobbed, never changing in pitch and never looking up from his feet.

The bones of a fetus fell out of her pelvis. He cringed at the sound of the bones hitting the floor. A shatter that loud could only be made on a floor and not dirt. She didn't notice. Or maybe she did. Baldassare couldn't tell for certain. He was more concerned with his legs.

The air was warm and humid, but his legs felt like they had been stuck below the arctic ice cap for a week. They were turning black. It started at his toes and made its way towards his knees. He watched it inch forward. The pain was like nothing within his range of experience –

Baldassare sheltered his life from pain.

He did not want to watch his perfect body become an ice mummy. Even pig porn was preferable to that. He still hadn't exploded what lay to his other side. The things binding his wrists and ankles remained unseen.

His legs wouldn't work anymore, but perhaps he could drag himself away and defrost his legs in a man-size microwave. If only he could escape.

Light glittered to his side when he looked at his wrist. It was reflecting off a million tiny pieces. The glare wouldn't allow him to look at his bindings. He thought he might be raised off the floor by about two feet, based on how the bone-granny stood over him, but that did nothing to sort out his problem of being tied down to whatever he was on. It wasn't a bed. His bed was comfortable and smelt of stale semen. It didn't occur to Baldassare that his bed wasn't the only one in existence.

He turned his head in the other direction while he thought of ways to shield his eyes from the glittering light. The gentle rain should have subdued the light, but it didn't.

A four poster bed with the curtains thrown open was occupied by three people. It was at a distance equal to the pig and its companions, but didn't create as much noise and no one was leaking their insides. Which didn't mean the sight was any less disturbing.

A woman was sandwiched between two men, a cock in her mouth and one from behind; Baldassare couldn't tell what hole and didn't want to. The three of them were covered in crusty vomit, as was every other surface nearby. They didn't stop their threesome long enough to wipe it away.

The duvet half hung off the bed. Cans of deodorant and sex toys lay around them. It was pretty obvious they had been using the spray to get high. Maggots fell from the curtains. They were oblivious to everything except their pleasure.

They were in a fresher state than the cold granny and didn't have guts falling out of them like the pig-fucking duo. But, sooner or later, one or two or all three of them will start to fall to pieces. If he was a gambling man, Baldassare would have placed money on the woman in the center .She had two cocks to rip her apart. The men only had their own momentum.

Realization hit Baldassare like a tidal wave of diarrhea after a bad curry. He could no longer hear the clockwork bio-engineering equipment and whatever he was on top of didn't feel like his bed. The various states of decay of his fellow inhabitants of this place and the fact that his bed sit was only slightly larger than a tractor indicated that he had entered into some sort state between life and death. He did not want to be entering the afterlife with these people and the pig. They would make his skin crawl if it hadn't entered the mummification process encased in his own atmosphere, separate from the warm breeze and humidity.

He didn't want to have eyes anymore; he wanted them to

decompose. But had a feeling he was going to be stuck with them and the images ingrained in his mind forever.

The recent eye-rape pointed to why he hated sex so much— unless it was a date with his hand and a bottle of luxury cream. His only regret was not working out a way to fuck himself sooner.

He turned his attention back to his bindings and nearly had his blindness granted when a beam of light reflected directly into his pupil. But he wasn't that lucky. If his balls weren't frozen, they would have crawled inside him.

He wished his hands weren't tied down. Then he would be able to gouge out his eyes with the light reflecting objects. He would never be able to rid himself of the sounds of live action pig porn. That was sure to haunt him no matter how many lives he lived.

The rain never stopped, but the light grew brighter as time progressed. It was hot; a dry sort of hot and getting hotter. There was no escape. His frozen body entered the rapid defrost zone of a high power microwave. No trusty mould to protect his perfect body from burning up as a spontaneous fire engulfed his perfect body.

***

About Dani Brown

Dani Brown is a rather boring person and spends far too much time knitting and trying to get cat fur off her clothing. Her novellas *My Lovely Wife* and *Middle Age Rae of Fucking Sunshine* are out now from Morbidbooks. You can check out her art at facebook.com/doomsdayliverpool. She dreams of moving to Iceland.

FENG'S

Gregor Cole

So, my friend Brogan tells me of this place, okay, where the food is like the greatest thing anyone has ever stuffed into their head.

He tells me that it's an all you can eat place where they don't hurry you to leave, the drinks aren't stupidly overpriced, and the waiting staff actually wait your table. The staff actually bring the right orders and everything.

There's this buffet area where you can help yourself and a select menu that's a little extra but not by much. He even told me that there was a chef's special menu that is meant to be some kind of big secret; a 'those that know ask' kind of deal.

Now I'm a bit of a foodie, so the idea sounded like my kind of deal.

Brogan didn't order off of the special menu. He was on a date and didn't want to spend too much on food. He just wanted to get the girl drunk and get her back to his place. So he tells me he's free one day in the week and we make some plans to meet up. You know, grab a few drinks, get something to eat, and see where the night takes us. Brogan tells me he knows this club that's just bulging with student pussy that's really close to this restaurant he's been raving about.

I've got next to fuck all to do during that week, so I tell him I'm down and we arrange to meet in the afternoon.

That morning I take a bath, shave my balls, and splash on some cologne (on my face not my balls. I did that once in college and I nearly passed out screaming). I dig out and iron my favourite Fred Perry and lace up my newest, whitest trainers.

If I'm going out, I'm making the effort, right?

So I'm looking sharp when I'm walking to the spot where I said that I'd meet Brogan, some dive bar on the other side of town, but it's a nice day so I'm strolling.

The town was alive, all the coffee shops and bars were crammed with people that spilled onto the street with their lattes and wine. For a weekday it was great; the summer really brings the people out.

I lit a cigarette, crossed the street, and headed towards the bar. The place was a real dump. It used to be a biker place until there was a killing or gun fight or something involving armed police and a car on fire. Whatever the story was, it was a cheap place to start the night and sink a few with little to no crowd, and the pool table was free during the day.

The floor of the bar was sticky with a layer of grime from dirty boots and spilt booze and the place had a heavy stink of stale cigarettes and disinfectant. The jukebox flashed and honked out some 80's cock rock rubbish while the pinball machine next to it blinked and rattled.

The bar was as good as empty with only a couple of people in one of the booths; a pile of glasses had stacked up on their table and I guessed they had been there some time.

I rolled up to the bar, which looked empty until something caught my eye down on the floor behind it; the barman's arse crack. He was re-stocking one of the fridges with bottles of some cheap American beer with a beaver on the label. His jeans were riding a little low.

Without staring at the vast expanse of his vertical smile, I coughed into my hand to get his attention. His head snapped around to see me standing there and he made his way to his feet with a few grunts and groans.

The barman was a biker looking dude with an oversized beard and black bandana printed with tiny ganja leaves. He struggled with the belt on his jeans to rearrange his balls and get comfortable, his beer belly spilling out from under his 'fuck-you' t-shirt.

"Yes, mate?" He stroked his beard as he spoke while still fidgeting with his trousers. "What can I get you?"

I scanned the selection behind the bar. "I'll have a pint of that," pointing to a tap labelled Wolf Trap, "and a shot of that Tar-Pitt whiskey." I was fully intent on getting trashed that evening.

The biker dude nodded "No problem." pulled a glass from under the bar, and started to pour from the tap with the label of a cartoon wolf with its throat cut on it.

The barman dumped the glass of foamy beer on the bar, turned to fetch down the bottle of dark brown liquid, and proceeded to tip some into a shot glass with a skull etched onto it. As soon as the spirit came flooding out I could smell it. The stuff splashed into and over the glass leaving a little puddle.

The beer was good, but the shot was not.

It wasn't what you would call smooth and it felt like the worst acid reflux I had ever had, but I necked the drink and waved for another. "And again." I winced and wiped my lips as the barman poured another. A glug of the beer did little to cool the fire that was rolling its way down to my stomach.

Another shot on the bar and the puddle of spirit got a little bigger. "Not seen you in here before." The barman's voice was that of a forty a day smoker. "Business or pleasure?" He chuckled to himself.

"Just meeting a mate, as good a place as any to start a night out I guess." I slammed the shot back and the fire in my gullet returned. The barman raised an eyebrow and wiped the bar clean with a dirty dishcloth that he slapped over his shoulder.

"Looking for a party, eh?" He rubbed his massive tattooed hands together. "If there's anything you need, give us a shout." He fired the 'six shooters' at me and winked, poured another shot, then crawled back down to finish the bottling up.

His butt-crack was back on display as he once again fidgeted with his belt.

I tried to forget about the pain in my throat from the harsh shots and started on the third one. Now that the barman had gone back to playing with his jeans on the floor, I found the pressure off me to smash it.

Taking a moment to build up the courage to down the last shot, I looked around, honing in on the pool table. Its green baize was inviting. The cues looked solid and new, lined up in the rack on the wall like a row of thin, polished soldiers.

Scooping up my beer and shot of horrid brown shit, I made my way to the table, the effect of the heavy whiskey had already taken hold and I tripped over my own foot as I turned, splashing some of the beer on the floor and whiskey up my shirt. Great, now I stank like a homeless person.

I steadied myself and continued to the table.

It was one of those bars that had bands on at the weekends and the walls around the pool table were covered with flyers and posters promoting various acts. A psychobilly band called Dead and the Cameramen caught my eye. The poster had a half-naked woman with a 50's hair-do bent over a coffin; frilly panties and big tits. I wondered whether she was in the band. Might have to pop along and check them out.

For a dump of a bar the table was in great condition and the balls had a high sheen, as good as brand new. The cushions were firm and there were no traces of spilt beer or crisp crumbs on the green covering. There was not one chip in the white ball, they had to be new.

I took a cue down from the rack and bounced it gently on the floor by its rubber stopper. It was smooth and weighty. The tip was in good condition too, not too big, not too small and nice and round. I was even surprised to see that there was a pot on the rack filled with chalk and I took one of the blue squares and dusted the tip of the cue with a squeak.

Bloody hell, a pub with a proper table, I could get used to this. I rounded the table to set the balls up.

As I was kneeling down to retrieve the triangle and the rest of the balls from inside the table, I heard a familiar voice.

"OI, YOU FUCKING WANKER!"

Both the barman and I popped up from where we were crouching like meerkats sensing danger. It was Brogan, arms outstretched in a loud Hawaiian shirt and Ray Bans. His hair was combed back like some Italian mobster in a cheap Channel 5 movie and a cigarette hung from his lips.

He was wearing his trademark flip-flops. "ARE WE GETTING DRUNK UP IN THIS MOTHER FUCKER OR WHAT?"

The barman realised it wasn't a psycho wanting to smash his bar up and ducked back down under the bar muttering to himself. "Fucking arsehead, loud as shit, wanker, get his fucking head kicked in."

Brogan hopped over to the table and grabbed hold of me; he was like a dog that hadn't seen its owner all day. "How the fuck have you been, eh? It's been too long Billy boy."

I did my best to push him away. "Yeah, I'm okay, good yeah; I take it your well."

"Feast your eyes." His arms were outstretched again. "Feeling great, me old pal, on top of the world and ready to take a huge piss over it. What are you drinking?"

I pointed to my beer. "Something called Wolf Trap, its okay, but stay away from the Tar-Pitt whiskey; it's a bit of a shocker."

Brogan winked and threw me a 'six-shooter'; it was the second time that had happened today.

"Well, set them up and I'll get a round in." He sped over to the bar and shouted down to the biker sorting the stock out. "All right, chief!"

I went back to dropping the pool balls into the black plastic triangle. I was starting to regret the two shots beforehand and decided to finish the third. I knocked it back. I had the feeling I would need numbing up for the night ahead.

The balls broke with a whip crack, the white came spinning up the table, and two reds fell into the dark mouths of the pockets with heavy thunks. The balls glided down into the belly of the table and rolled to a stop in the windowed shelf on the side.

Such a nice table.

Brogan came back with a tray of drinks, two more beers, a couple of packets of salt and vinegar and four more shots of the killer whiskey. He was grinning from ear to ear. I shook my head.

"Not more of *that* shit?"

"What? I need to catch up." He was still smiling as he hit the first shot like it was nothing. His face soon changed as the fire hit his gag reflex. He spluttered into his hand and let out a line of drool as he dipped his head forward to stop it from hitting his bright shirt.

"The fuck is in this shit, piss and petrol?"

"It has got a kick to it, I did warn you."

"Fuck it." He put the tray on the table and necked the second shot with a grimace. "Smooth."

I continued to pot balls, laughing at my friend's discomfort. "You're a fucking idiot."

Brogan wiped the saliva away from his mouth. "Come on, your turn." He was holding up the last of the shots and nodding at it knowingly, still looking pained from the vile beverage.

Reluctantly, I took the little glass. "Here's to swimming with bow-legged women." I was tempted to hold my nose, but I didn't want to look like a pussy. It hit the back of my throat and I did all I could to sink it.

Brogan shot me a look. "Better?"

"Not really." I took my cue back to the table and tried to take my mind off the burning with more pool. It didn't really work. I could feel it gurgling away in my empty stomach and was sure that it was giving me an ulcer.

Another ball in the pocket. "So what's this restaurant like?"

"Pretty damn good." Brogan sipped his beer to get the taste of whiskey from his mouth. "Took that waitress from that Italian place there last week, brilliant food."

"Oh, yeah?" Another ball disappeared.

"Oh, yeah, proper dirty cow too, fucked her at the train station on the way home." He raised his beer to his lips. "And she took it in the arse… filthy."

My next shot wasn't as fruitful as all I could think of was the waitress's well-fucked arse. "Dirty fucker." I handed the cue to Brogan. "But the restaurant's good then, yeah?"

Brogan smashed the white ball into a pack on the bulk cushion, nearly sending it off the table. "I'm fucking shit at this." He guzzled more beer. "Yeah, great place, cheap, and the menu is outstanding; it's just around the corner too." He took another shot on the table, just as bad as the first.

I laughed to myself at the pathetic attempt to play pool and swigged more of my pint. "I'll get another round in, then we can hit the restaurant."

"What's the rush?" Brogan's arms were outstretched again. "Might as well get tanked before we go."

"Okay, but no more of that shit whiskey."

"Yes, more of that shit whiskey; might help my game." As the white ball was sent spinning off the table and onto the sticky floor. The barman didn't look best pleased.

So we stayed on and drank more beer and, reluctantly, a few more shots of Tar-Pitt until we felt we were going to throw up.

Then we drank some more.

After several rounds and many games of pool we decided to leave. We hadn't even noticed that the bar had got a lot busier. The area by the bar was almost packed, but we were far too drunk to care.

We staggered out into the street, which was still crawling with people. We laughed and shouted at a hipster on a bike with no brakes as he nearly ploughed into the side of a taxi. We both simultaneously shouted "WANKER!" Paused for a second, looked at each other, then fell about laughing. The hipster was less than impressed.

We were still laughing when we rounded a corner into a grotty little side road that was covered with litter. Huge wheelie bins sat outside the restaurant and bar service entrances and the whole place stank of piss and the late night laundry on the corner.

It might have been the whiskey churning away with the beer inside me, but the street looked straight out of a crap film. Brogan was in his element. Close enough to the classier side of town, but in a sleazy back road where drunks threw up, prostitutes gave out blow jobs, and tramps got stabbed over crack.

Brogan pointed to a shady doorway with a red light in the window. "That's the place."

"How the fuck did you find this dump?" I shouted over my shoulder as I pissed up the side of a wheelie bin.

"On one of those underground London websites, pretty mental, isn't it?"

"It looks like a brothel." I zipped myself up.

"Maybe it is?" He shouted back as he disappeared through the door.

I followed and was greeted with the tinkle of a bell above my head as I stepped into a room straight out of James Bond. It was a throwback to every Chinese restaurant of the 70's. It had either been here for years or was designed by some crazy genius to be deliberately retro.

It was a low-ceilinged room with red paper lanterns hanging over each of the low tables. Patrons sat nibbling away at piled plates with chopsticks and forks. Smartly dressed waiters buzzed around tables, taking orders and dumping down massive bowls of rice and noodles and dishes of all kinds of delights.

At one end, a vast buffet service table was laid out. A couple of people picked over it, shovelling great ladles of food onto their huge white plates. A man in a white vest, apron, and paper hat came out through some double doors by the buffet with a tray of rice accompanied by the sizzle of cooking food. He poured the rice into one of the steam trays and scuttled back through the doors to fetch more.

Then the smell hit me.

It was the greatest smell I had ever smelt. Garlic, ginger, chilli, lemon grass, grilled meat, seafood, steamed rice, noodles, soy sauce; all coming together, sending my brain into a foodgasm.

A stunning Chinese girl stood behind a well-stocked bar in a neat white shirt and black waistcoat. She smiled at the both of us and bowed a little. "Table for two?"

Brogan approached the bar, leaning in as if to tell some kind of secret. "We are looking to sample the 'special' menu... if you know what I mean?"

The waitress bowed again and held up a hand. "Of course, gentlemen, follow me." She led the way through the restaurant, to the double doors of the kitchen, and held them open for us to pass through. We entered, followed by the waitress.

"If you could make your way through, to the back of the kitchen." She pointed to a set of stairs at the back of the stiflingly hot galley.

"Then up the stairs?" I spoke, slurring my words a little.

"Yes, up the stairs, they will take care of you in the exclusive dining room."

Brogan turned to me, gave a thumbs up, and we proceeded through the kitchen. The waitress disappeared through the doors behind us.

Woks sizzled, huge tubs of rice boiled, slabs of meat were being sliced and chopped as the kitchen staff hurried around us as we made our way to the bottom of the stairs. Through all the commotion and smells of the kitchen I caught a waft of incense coming from the floor above as we climbed the narrow staircase.

At the top, we found ourselves in a small room covered from floor to ceiling with red carpeting. Smoke billowed from bronze bowls hanging by chains from white marble figurines of men with tiger heads in each corner.

There was a single black table with two chairs on either side in the centre of the room and the wall adjacent was obscured by closed red velvet curtains. At the opposite end of the room was another door with a round porthole, similar to the kitchen doors down in the restaurant.

We sat down and Brogan pulled a couple of chopsticks from the bamboo cup which held a bunch in the middle of the little table. "Wonder what's on the menu?" He tapped the edge of the table with the sticks, like he was playing the drums, as the door at the back of the room swung open and a little waiter scuttled out, holding two black leather-bound folders.

He was dressed like a little penguin, with balding greasy hair combed over his wee egg-like head. A fat mole on his chin sprouted three long hairs and all I wanted to do was pluck them. I looked at Brogan with a smirk, knowing he was thinking the same thing.

He shoved one into my hand and then into Brogan's. "You pick, you pick, make selection."

We opened the folders and saw the crudest menu of our lives. Instead of words, there were pictures, photographs of animals, bowls of rice, noodles, vegetables and sauces.

"You pick, make selection." The little waiter squeaked as he tapped the top of my menu with his finger; impatient little fucker.

"Tenacious little prick isn't he?" Brogan scanned the menu. "I'll have these." He held up the menu so the waiter could see, pointing first at the rice, then a photo of a pig, then a blood red sauce and a bowl of chillies.

"Spicy pork with rice, you like it hot, hot, hot, yes?" The waiter nodded and turned to me.

My head was still swimming with booze and I slurred as I spoke my choice. "The cow, that black stuff," I pointed to a bowl of thick, dark sauce, "and the noodles."

"Oh, beef and black bean noodle, good choice, good choice." The waiter said, bowing to both of us. He snapped up the menus and hurried back through the door at the back of the room.

"What a weird little prick." Brogan shook his head as the door swung open again. This time it was a huge Chinese guy with two massive bottles of beer. He slammed them down on the table and sneered at each of us, grunted something in Chinese under his breath, and strode back through the doors.

I looked at Brogan. "What the fuck?"

"Bruv, that geezer was fucking massive." Brogan reached for one of the beers. "Fuck getting in a rumble with that wanker."

I reached for my beer and nodded in quiet contemplation of getting into a fight with the fucker. In my head it didn't end well.

The doors to the kitchen flew open again and the giant guy rolled a trolley out into the room. He was followed by another gargantuan, equal in size, but with a bowl haircut and glasses.

The little waiter rushed around the two men as they placed vast bowls of rice, noodles, vegetables, and cooked meat onto the small table in front of us. These were mammoth sized portions and the sauces came in huge silver jugs, there must have been a litre of each.

Brogan looked at me in disbelief and I must have looked the same right back at him.

"Eat, eat." The waiter squeaked at us and waved his hands at the banquet-sized meal. "Eat, gentlemen, eat you fill."

The two huge kitchen hands took up spots behind each of us and loomed with their arms folded. They looked down at us as me dived into our feast.

My bowl of noodles was the size of a sink. There must have been enough to feed a village. I scooped out a huge ladle full into another bowl the size of a cut in half basketball. Then a massive ladle of meat, then the steamed vegetables, then I helped myself to the sauce. I didn't hold back and poured on at least half a litre.

With another slug of beer, I started to pile into the bowl. Brogan was way ahead of me, shovelling great wads of sauce drenched rice into his face with the bowl under his chin.

"Ah, mate, there's enough for a fucking army." Brogan commented between shovels. All I could do was nod without choking on a gullet full of the best noodles I had ever tasted.

The sauce was amazing, spicy and thick, and the vegetables were cut so that you didn't have to chew on them and the meat, oh the meat! It fell apart in the mouth, tender and juicy. It was the greatest meal I think I had ever had the privilege to eat.

We were stuffing the stuff away and the waiter danced and jigged in front of us. "Yes, eat, fill your guts." He laughed and clapped, the hairs on his chine almost erect with excitement, like his mole was getting a hard on.

But there was something wrong, or at least something not quite right; no matter how much I ate, I couldn't stop myself from shovelling more of the gorgeous food into my maw. I looked at Brogan, slightly panicked, and he had a look of shock on his face too.

He was packing his mouth with spoon after spoon of rice and saucy meat. His cheeks puffed out like a giant hamster.

It was like we were possessed. There was a compulsion to get more of the food into our bodies unlike anything I had felt in my life. It was a horrific sense of euphoria; a panicked action, like it would be the last we would ever see of food.

At this point, tears were pouring down my cheeks and I could feel my belly distend. I felt like I was going to pop, but I wasn't even halfway through the vat of noodles. I could see through my tears that Brogan was struggling too, but still stuffing his face. He was shaking his head, making a bubbling noise, and trying to avoid the spoon, but to no avail.

Then the dancing waiter clapped his hands. "Mr. Ko, Mr. Lee, help the gentlemen finish." And, with that, we were both grabbed from behind by the giant kitchen hands. With no effort at all, my hands were behind my back and quickly cuffed to the chair. My head was forced back, facing the red velvet curtains. The waiter then pulled two orange plastic funnels from under the trolley and waved one in my face before passing it to the huge kitchen hand.

The other I guessed was for Brogan, who was in the same pickle as me.

"Insert the funnels." The waiter clicked his finders. "It's time for the floor show."

He scuttled over the one side of the curtains as the goliath behind me grabbed me by the jaw and forced the funnel between my teeth. I was weak from the struggle and the food intake, so I didn't put up much of a fight.

Then the curtains started to draw back.

Sitting in the middle of a small stage behind the curtain was the fattest woman I had ever seen. It was hard to tell if she was just sitting on the ground due to the size of her thighs; the flaps of thick blubber spread across the ground around her.

The only real way to tell she was a woman was by the length of her greasy blonde hair and the tiny pink bikini top stretched around her vast breasts. The straps cut into her fat like sausage ready to burst.

The vision was enough to make me feel quite sick- if it wasn't for the fact I had a funnel shoved in my mouth.

The gigantic kitchen hands then started to shovel wads of our meal into the funnels with their massive club hands, pressing it down, force feeding us as the woman on the stage got up and turned around.

She was sitting on a stool, it was wedged up in the folds of her arse and she struggled to pull it free.

With the stool out of the way, it became apparent that there was no bikini bottom.

She knelt down on all fours and presented her vacuous arsehole as, all the while, the kitchen hands stuffed more food into our funnels. I was gagging from the pressure of the food being forced into my gullet, but couldn't bring anything up with the constant flow of food. It felt like it was coming out of my ears and I could hear Brogan chocking on his force feeding too.

"Yes, yes, stuff them till they burst." The dwarf waiter clapped, span on the spot, and grabbed at his crotch like a fat, midget, Chinese Michael Jackson with a greasy comb-over.

It was then that the obese woman let go her bowels. A massive rope of turd started to emanate from her dirty brown arsehole, accompanied with the sound of escaping gasses and traditional Chinese music.

The shit was peppered with yellow nuggets of corn, slices of red pepper, and other undigested pieces of detritus. It curled like ice cream direct from the machine onto the floor between her hefty legs.

More of the feast was getting rammed into our throats when the smell of shit hit my nostrils; a rank sickly stench of rotting vegetables and cow shit. It was then that her hand came around. She scooped up a handful of the faecal matter still snaking its way out of her extensive colon, and started to eat. A whopping great mouthful of her own shit, chewing at it in quite the theatrical manner, slopping it all over her maw like it was a ripe mango.

It was then that I heard a gargling sound from Brogan.

"He's going to pop, he's going to pop." The little waiter danced and pulled a metal steam tray from under the trolley and placed it at Brogans feet.

The funnel was whipped out from his mouth and the kitchen hand behind him forced him over. The biggest jet of vomit I had ever seen burst from his lips, almost filling the tray in one hit; the second stream didn't have the same impact, but was, nonetheless, heavy by volume.

Then my own stomach flipped, with another nose-full of the stink coming from the stage. My eyes rolled towards the stage to see the obese woman licking at the shit that had spread down her arm and the vomit came.

My whole body shook as the gush of puke left, it was like some invisible giant was squeezing every last morsel of undigested food from me, into the waiting tray. I was empty on the first throw up and all I could manage was a few dry heaves and some convulsive gut lurches.

"Mr. Ko, take these trays down to the buffet, Mr. Lee take care of these two." The little waiter danced through the double doors to the private kitchen as Mr. Ko picked up the trays to take down to the waiting diners.

Then there was a crack and from the corner of my eye I saw Brogan slump forward from a punch to the back of his head from Mr. Lee. He was out cold.

The last thing I saw before the formidable Mr Lee turned out my lights was the fat woman on stage pointing and laughing with a mouthful of her own shit.

***

When I awoke, Brogan was pulling himself out of the dumpster the kitchen hands had thrown us in. He looked like I felt, completely rough as arseholes. We vowed on the spot never to talk about Feng's.

We went back to the bar where the Tar-pit whiskey was shocking and the beer tasted like piss and we sat in silence, not looking up from the bar. How could we tell anyone, who would believe us?

I nearly suggested that we should go to the police or the health authorities, but from the look of deep contemplation I knew Brogan was thinking the same thing and keeping quiet about it. 'What was the deal with that fat chick?' I could read it on his face.

For a second I thought I got a whiff of her shit.

But...

Looking back, I can honestly say, without the beating we got, all the vomiting, the shit-eating obese woman, the midget waiter with the hairy mole, waking up in an alleyway miles from the restaurant, and knowing that the other patrons of that dump were eating our puke and loving every mouthful... that really was the best Chinese food I have ever eaten.

AIRBORNE CHEMICAL MESSENGER
Donald Armfield

This bathroom is in dire need of that bald-muscular guy. Turtleheads are moving out of my anus with such haste, it feels like the seam on the back of pants will burst. Almost slipping on a used condom, I make it into a stall. The door has some kind of lock that I couldn't figure out for the life of me. So I drop chow and cop a squat.

My anus erupts with a loud bowel movement. Liquid shit is pouring out and tainting the once clear water. Not that it mattered, the toilet seat I'm grasping onto with one hand on each side has shit smeared all over it and it isn't mine. I caught a whiff of my own shit and start to wonder: What had I eaten today?

Suddenly my arm gives out and I collapse to the floor in an awkward position, stuck between the toilet bowl and the wall. Diarrhea continues to spill out from my ass. The sound of a sink turning on makes me jump up quickly. I pull my pants up and tumble out of the stall. To my surprise there is no one standing at the sink with rushing water pouring down the drain. I fall to the floor with agony, holding my stomach. The pain is excruciating. My bellowed cry for help is nothing but a hoarse whisper that falls on deaf ears.

* * *

I open my eyes after a dreamless rest and find myself lying on a cot in a hospital room. I have tubes coming out of my facial orifices and a warm/wet sensation tingles my back. A nurse dressed in white comes into the room with a clipboard under her left arm. Her hat is affixed to the tight wrapped bun on top of her head. She has golden blonde hair and is chewing gum like a grazing cow.

The nurse walks over to my bedside and holds her nose. "What the fuck is wrong with you?" she says.

I can't seem to speak, so I just lie there and stare at her.

The nurse pulls a pair of gloves over her thin pointy fingers, her well manicured nails almost penetrating the tips. She makes a snapping noise around her wrist with the second glove. The nurse puts her hands on my hips and pushes me on to my side.

"Gross, fucking gross, for reals." The nurse says, dropping me back onto my back.

I continue to stare at her, having no idea what's going on.

She opens a cabinet on the other side of the room and pulls out some fresh linen. She walks back over to my bedside and moves me onto my side again, folding the soiled bed pad and pushing it under my body.

Her rough attempt is shaking me a little too much and my stomach begins to gurgle.

"Don't you....." before she even had a chance to finish her threat, my ass shoots out more shit juices, dousing her white get-up. "What the fuck?" her favorite words yell out, this time with anger. She is screaming, holding her arms out to her side, diarrhea dripping down from her chest.

A sudden change in the nurse's stare, gives me an arousal feeling. Her breathing pattern has a purr for desire and she is looking at me with her eyes. Those *oh my god, I want to fuck you* eyes. With my feces dripping from her chin and rolling down her melon-shaped chest. She rips open her white button-up blouse. Her skirt comes down along with her lace panties and like a prowling cat she jumps on top of me. She throws aside the sheets used to cover me and slams her head between my legs.

The nurse is rubbing her face against my balls, nuzzling with hot breaths—like a domesticated cat. I'm trying to hold the urge to let loose and feculence the moment, but it doesn't happen. My feces burst out like a ruptured pipe. The nurse lets out a loud moan of ecstasy and falls back on her arms. She arches her back and raises her hips into the air. A second rupture rushes out of my anus and paints the nurse. Between her legs and up to her waist line is covered with my shit. She growls and jumps onto my throbbing member. She moves like a bull rider. I lie back with my hands behind my head and relish in the moment.

* * *

I'm walking down the isle of the nearest grocery store wearing a clean pair of scrubs from the hospital and a I'm-every-woman's-dream strut. I kick the shelf with my foot and reach out with my arms, catching two packages of adult diapers. I spin on my heel and walk back up the isle, right out the doors. Not a single person came running out behind me as I continued my strut behind the building.

I pull down the pair of scrubs and affix a diaper around my waist, Slide the scrubs back on, and let it go. My pipes drain and the mess settles in the bottom of the diaper, like a muddy puddle. I have an epiphany that just needs a little research. A striking smile, a fresh load in my pants, and a swagger in my step. Yeah, I'm the shit!

* * *

I'm walking down the street with the huge shit grin. Thinking the next lady I see that wouldn't give me the time in a day or hit me with her large purse if, all of a sudden, the crotch of my pants were engulfed in flames—never mind have sex with me-I stick two fingers into the crack of my ass, a shit smear of my muddy aroma, dripping from my fingertips. Then I see her, sitting on a bench at the bus stop. A quick slide along the bench puts our hips only mere inches away from touching. I rub my finger on the bridge of her upper lip. The elegant looking lady looks at me with disgust and holds back a gag.

"What the fuck, why would you wipe shit on someone?" The lady begins cussing out even more swears, to a point it makes no sense. Spitting and looking at me with a rage of animosity.

She bounds up from the bench and uses the back of her hand, brushing off my pheromone spread. A few fleeing steps to the street corner and she freezes before the crosswalk.

Did it work?

The lady turns and looks in my direction with desire drooling from her facial expression. She runs her fingertips between her legs, her skirt bunching up along her waist line, and then bolts in my direction. Knocking me on to the ground with a shoulder tackle, she pulls at the collar of my shirt and tears it right off. She slammed her hand into the bottom of my diaper and deliberately covered her hand in shit. She brushed her wrist over the tip of my cock, then stopped, grabbing hold of my throbbing member, smearing my own feces along the shaft. Her hands meet at the top of her shirt. With one tug all six buttons of her blouse snap and scatter in different directions. The remaining shit on her hands she uses to smudge under her neck. Grasping her breast and grinding her pelvic bone into my fully aroused cock, she lets out a moan of pleasure.

She gets my pants off with another single tug and smothers her face between my legs. My shit covered bottom does not seem to bother

her. Her sucking power is glorious, like she is trying to suck my soul out the tip of my cock.

The lady climbs back on top of me and begins bouncing up and down with vigorous movements, moaning loudly. My feces mixed with her vagina juices makes slurping noises that breaks my control of pleasure. My climax releases with a rush of spunk, filling her vagina like a custard snack. She arches her back and screams like a banshee. People passing along the street have stopped to watch, talking amongst themselves and recording the moment with their phones. I push the woman off of me and pull my pants up and walk away with my-shit-doesn't-stink smile.

* * *

The chemical factor in my feces gave me the power to seduce any woman I wanted. The weeks of tests I ran were beyond anyone's imagination, even a porno star with a contract movie deal. Some of my shit-nanigans happened out of planned situations, and some from spurs of the moment.

One of the planned moments was when I went to the laundry mat to wash my pants, which had shit drizzle running down the legs. This woman had these tight little pajama pants on that hugged her thighs and had her camel toe peeking through the cloth. She looked at me like I was a peasant and rolled her eyes when I gave her a cool guy nod.

I let some of my special juices settle in my big boy diaper and was ready for the smearing. I ran my finger right across her lips and she stared at me with anger.

"Fucking Gross," she said.

Not a minute went by, but gave me enough time to climb upon a folding table and spread eagle. She rushed over to me like I was a fix for hunger. This woman was a feisty thing and used her teeth to tear my clothes from my body. I put my hands behind my head, laid back, and let her fold me in different angles, quenching her sexual desires with my shit flavored love.

Then, one time in the grocery store, standing in line with a basket full of adult diapers, I dropped the basket by my feet with intent to startle the lady in front of me.

"Do you have a fucking problem?" she said.

I took my finger out of my ass and held it to her lips and said, "Shhhh!"

The teenager standing at the cash register got his first look at a real life porn in action. He mumbled under his breath, staring off into a later thought of tugging and dirty socks---right after the lady let out a howling orgasm, "Would that be paper or plastic, ma'am?"

My whole world had changed. I was entering more caves than bears during hibernation. Giving women pure ecstasy with my excretion love juice, I am a Chemical Airborne Messenger and could make these women attack with the drop of a dime. I have this one last thought, another one of my planned fecal matter moments. Then maybe I will go to the doctors and get myself checked out.

* * *

I am covered from head to toe in my ass discharge of love. I let one go that splattered my manly diaper and ran up my back. It took two loads to get the desired look I was looking for. I caught a glimpse of myself in a reflection of a window and actually gagged. This is going to be great.

I open a door to a back entrance of an all-girls college dorm. Running down the lengthy corridor, I find my way into the shower room. I dive and slide across the wet floor and land in the center of the room. The steam built up takes affect with my chemical message: "Fuck me."

Five girls step out of separate stalls, dripping wet with soap suds clinging to their bodies. Like savage animals that haven't ate in days, they attack. Licking my shit covered body and kissing each other, swapping shit-saliva and moaning loudly. They take turns riding my shaft and rubbing shit all over themselves.

While waiting, two of the women add their own flavor to the mix and shit on each other's chests. My penis could not take another orgasm. My stomach muscles are locked up. I push one of the college girls off me and run back down the corridor, out the door I entered.

Safe at home, clean, and freshly lined with an adult diaper, I sit and wonder: Get this checked out or continue to spread my shit on woman's bodies? I'm a shit magnet. Hugh Hefner with an adult diaper and a robe. A Chemical Airborne Messenger. What would you do?

MILTON VON PUDNICK MAKES
A MONSTER
AN EXISTENTIAL TALE
Charie D. LaMarr

Milton von Pudnick was a scientist. In fact, he was a great scientist who held so many degrees he couldn't remember them all. He held the record for the most personal appearances on both Bill Nye the Science Guy and Mr. Wizard. He was mentioned several times by name on Mythbusters and CSI: Miami, New York, and Portland—the mellow version of the series. He thought he might be the guy who invented Viagra, but he'd made so many discoveries and developed so many medications he wasn't sure anymore. He took great pride in the fact that Google listed him as "The World's Greatest Nerd". When it came to science, give him a couple beakers, a Bunsen burner and some chemicals, and before you knew it, something either blew up or something important was discovered. Sometimes both. So important was he, Stamford University gave him his own laboratory, rent-free, and a hot, Swedish, blonde nurse as his assistant. In short, when it came to science, Milton was da shizz.

One day, Milton was sitting in his laboratory, one hand on the eyepiece of his microscope and the other scratching his balls. He was really going at it—raking them with his fingernails while he squirmed on the stool and cursed.

The door opened and a man in white scrubs walked in. "Yo, Doc. I got a couple more cadavers the medical school was gonna throw out. I thought I'd see if there was anything you could use first." He watched Milton mutilating his testicles. "Hey, you know, Doc, they got stuff for that now. Jock itch spray. Works miracles."

"If only that was the problem," Milton said. "You see, a while ago, I was working on developing the nanoflea. My idea was we breed about six billion nanofleas and drop them on Syria. Pretty soon, they'd start mating

139

with the local variety of flea in that shit hole at rapidly accelerated rates. According to my calculations, within two weeks, everybody there would be so infested they'd be too busy scratching to hold a gun and the war would be over. I could have won the Nobel Peace Prize."

"What happened?" the orderly asked.

"Well, as anyone who's studied fleas on Wikipedia knows, those little bastards can jump eighteen centimeters vertically and thirty-three centimeters horizontally. And that doesn't even take into consideration how far they can fall. One day, I'd completed the first set of male and female nanofleas. I was about to put them into a hermetically sealed environment with a couple rats as hosts and let the breeding fun begin. I picked them up with my tweezers and the little fuckers got away. They fell down my pants, where they've been breeding very nicely ever since." He scratched again.

"Wow, Doc, that sucks. Can't you do something? Soak in a hot tub of water and drown them or something?"

"Are you crazy, man? And destroy one of the greatest inventions ever created by man? No, I figure I'll just use myself as host. Every few days, I pick a bunch off and put them in a jar. It may take a little longer to get a few billion, but the sacrifice is well worth it. I've already written my Nobel speech. This is huge!"

"Yeah, well, if you want to take a glance at these two stiffs, they aren't getting any fresher, if you know what I mean. They came from first-year anatomy. I'm afraid some kids get a little messy when they get that scalpel in their hands the first time. Check this out."

He wheeled in a cadaver and took off the white sheet.

"My God!" the doctor said. "What happened to his head?"

"These two clowns amputated it, stuck it in a bowling bag and took it to Friday night black-light bowling. After the eighth frame, it didn't come back down the ball return. Fucking shame, too, because one of them was working on a perfect game."

"And what's this goo in the stomach cavity?"

"Vomit," the orderly said. "One of them got a little sick the first day of school. It looks like the cafeteria's bean burrito special, but I could be wrong. So, can you use him? The school has no further use for him."

The doctor sighed. "Sure, I'm sure I can use some of the parts. What else do you have?"

"Umm, this one's a bit unusual. It seems they did some after-hours work on this lady. You know how guys love it when a girl can get her legs beside her ears? Well, these asshats decided to make it easier for her."

He took the drape off the second body. Someone had amputated her arms and legs and reversed them. Her legs were pointing up from her neck and her arms went straight down from her hips.

"There's a lot of spunk inside this one. Looks like half the freshman class boinked her. Maybe some sophomores, too. Really sick."

The doctor took a closer look. "What are the nails in the sides of her neck? And how did her hair get burned off?"

"Well, it seems these enterprising young men of science tried to reanimate her using jumper cables. They were planning on booking her at frat parties."

"My God, man!" Doctor von Pudnick said. "I hope both of these sets of students received F's!"

"Well the headless ones did. They changed their major to video game technology. But the spunk-filled ones got a D minus. The professor was impressed with their suturing technique. Besides, both of their fathers are big contributors. They were given another chance, but we're keeping a closer watch on the stiffs these days."

"Thank God!" the doctor said, giving his balls another good working over—this time with both hands. "Okay, leave her. There are still some useful parts. Just wheel them into my cold room with the others."

The doctor had quite a collection of mutilated corpses, compliments of the medical school. Some students were just plain sick, and what they did to their cadavers was disgusting. The world was in big trouble if those were the doctors of tomorrow. And people thought Obamacare was bad. But he had to admit the spare parts did come in handy.

"Inga!" he called out. "I need you in here."

His lovely assistant entered the room. Her white nurse's uniform barely zipped over her huge breasts. It also barely covered her hoo-ha. The doctor was very particular about the way his assistant dressed—including the white stockings and fuck-me heels. He had no patience for today's nurses in scrubs and rubber clogs. A nurse should dress like a nurse.

"Ya, doctor. You called for Inga?" She took a deep breath and her zipper slipped down another inch. The doctor felt the pants under his lab coat getting tighter in the crotch, and it wasn't because the nanofleas were getting bigger.

"Yes, my dear. The med school dropped off two more damaged cadavers. They're in cold storage already. I'd like you make a list of usable parts and add it to our inventory. Bring it to me when you're done."

"Ya, Doctor," she said, turning and walking away from him. The view from the back was almost as good as the view from the front. Inga had several usable parts the good doctor would like to make use of. And he intended to, as soon as his new drug, Amnesiadesiac, was ready.

Amnesiadesiac was a project very close to the doctor's heart. It was an aphrodisiac combined with an agent that caused amnesia. Once perfected, he'd be able to screw Inga's brains out and she'd have no memory of it. There'd be nothing for her to take to the College President's office regarding sexual abuse or harassment. The World's Greatest Nerd didn't want to risk his standing in the scientific community. Or lose his free office space. Amnesiadesiac would taste just like cherry soda—Inga's favorite. She'd never know what hit her, or who did her. Bill Cosby personally financed the project.

She returned a few minutes later with a clipboard in her hand. "Ve got lucky, Doctor. Zere are many useful parts. Ze man is in very good condition except for ze missing head. But ve have several in stock. And he needs a good cleaning out. I believe he's filled with vomit."

She shrugged. "Not ze first time a first-year tossed his cookies into his cadaver. Ze woman—her condition is not as good. Her limbs are amputated and rearranged, and her hoo-ha is filled with za jizzom. Not ze first freshman to have sex vith a cadaver either. Although zis one seems to have been present at a first-year gang bang."

"Hoo-ha? Did you just say hoo-ha, nurse? How many times do I have to remind you I'm an internationally known scientist and I insist on proper medical terminology at all times! Her va-jay-jay is filled with spunk! Is that so hard to remember?" When he had the Amnesiadesiac perfected, he was going to give this girl a spanking she'd never forget. Well, actually, she would.

He took the list from her with one hand, his other hand busily scratching his junk. Inga blushed and turned her head away. "Please, doctor. Do not scratch ze crotch-crabs in front of Inga. She's a nice girl from a nice family. In her family, ze men go outside behind the barn to smoke and scratch."

"Damn it, girl! I've told you they're not crotch-crabs! I dropped a pair of nanofleas down my pants and they multiplied! Do you think I'm doing this because I like it? I'm doing this for science and world peace! Soon I'll have enough nanofleas to begin my breeding program. And just in time, too. The situation in Syria is serious and severe! Try saying that five times fast."

She giggled. Inga was a giggler. Doctor von Pudnick loved that about her because it caused her pendulous breasts to jiggle. He loved jiggling breasts. Sometimes, late at night when nobody was in the building, he hooked his female cadavers up to vibrators so he could feel them jiggle. The doctor was not a well man.

He turned his attention back to the list. "Good, good, excellent, very good—we needed one of those, perfect, good, wonderful. Inga, I believe we have all the parts we need now. Yes, it's all here. I'm ready to create the first human Cthulhu! Prepare the operating room! We'll begin at once! Bring me four of our best cadavers—two male and two female. Let's make us a monster!"

Inga jumped up and down. "Oh yes, Doctor! Inga is so excited! A monster! Inga never makes a monster before!"

"You go set the operating room up. Make sure the chainsaw is filled with gas. We'll be doing a good deal of amputation and the chainsaw is faster. I'll be there in a few moments. Right now, I feel the urge to write a poem. Just a little something to commemorate this glorious day. Victor Frankenstein had his creature. Today, we create Circle Fuck—the first human Cthulhu! It's a glorious day for evil scientists everywhere!"

He threw his head back and let loose with his patented evil scientist laugh. Inga jumped up and down, clapping her hands and giggling madly. Her breasts bounced wildly. This was going to be Dr. von Pudnick's finest moment. Unless, of course, it turned out he had invented Viagra. Then this would be a close second.

He quickly jotted off his poem—a masterwork, naturally. So good that after the surgery, he would record himself as he recited it for his You Tube channel. Then, he got ready for surgery. This would be long, arduous work, so he flipped on a Bunsen burner and made a couple grilled cheese sandwiches. One can never go wrong performing surgery with a stomach full of processed cheese products and gooey white bread as sustenance. Then he stepped into the operating room.

Inga had brought in the four cadavers and placed them in a row. The doctor looked at her and quickly turned away. Her black rubber apron and gloves gave him an instant raging hard-on. Rubber was one of his biggest fetishes. He decided he'd have to start performing surgeries more often—just to see Inga dressed that way.

"Ah good, Inga," he said with his back to her, scratching and trying to knock his dick back down. "I see you have everything ready. The chainsaw's gassed up?"

"Ya, Doctor," she said.

"Well, let's see which corpses you chose for this operation."

He lifted up the first two white sheets. Both corpses were male and in fairly good condition. Other than the one having a chest cavity full of vomit and missing a head, it was a good choice. It had a very large penis. The second one was also hung like a stallion, although someone had carved, "Kilroy was here" in the middle of its forehead with a scalpel. Workable. His main interest was the size of the schlongs.

The third and fourth cadavers were female. Naturally, the students had seen to it they were cleanly shaven. And he could see both were loaded with freshman spunk. They'd need to be power washed first.

However, neither one had particularly large breasts. The doctor frowned. That would mean extra work. Both would require boob jobs before the real surgery could begin. Fortunately, he stocked a large supply of oversized silicone implants for just such occasions. It wouldn't take more than half an hour each to slice their breasts open and stuff in the bags. Then he'd be able to move on to his master plan. He was already salivating just thinking about it. Or maybe he was thinking about Inga in black rubber. Either way, he was seriously salivating. And itching. Those damn nanofleas were especially active, as though they sensed the excitement of the upcoming surgery. He paused long enough for one more good, deep scratch before putting on his black apron and gloves.

"Mask up, Nurse Inga, it's time to begin."

It wasn't really necessary to mask up. There was no chance of giving germs to the cadavers, but the mask added so much to her outfit. The idea occurred to him that one day he should start producing Naughty Nurse porn videos in his surgery starring the lovely Inga. As a jack-of-all-trades, he'd probably be very good at it.

"First, we have to clean them out. They're pretty gross," he said. He turned on the power washer and spread one of the women's legs. He hit her with the water and buckets of splooge came out. He muttered to himself as he cleaned it off her breasts and face. Then he opened her mouth. More splooge.

"Turn her over, I bet they got her ass, too," he said to Inga.

He hosed her ass down. It seemed like she was filled all the way up to her colon.

"Damn first-years," he said.

The second female corpse was even worse. It appeared she'd been the subject of several first-year gangbangs. The doctor was not happy.

He moved on to the men. First he hosed out the gaping hole in the middle of the headless man. Bean burritos and beer flew everywhere. The smell was grotesque.

"What's wrong with these kids?" he growled. "A man donates his body to science and they treat it this way? By using it as a vomitorium?

144

Disgusting! Turn him over, Nurse Inga, they probably got his ass, too."

Like the women, the man's anal cavity was filled with spunk and other substances. They washed out onto the floor of the operating room in a milky white ribbon. The second man was the same, only his face was covered and his mouth was full as well.

"They really should lock these cadavers up at night. What happened to putting a thermometer up your ass, covering your boner with Jergens and jerking off into a wad of tissues while staring at a Farrah Fawcett poster in your dorm room?" he asked.

Inga giggled. "Is zat how you used to do it, Doctor? You never played fucky-fucky with one of ze dead people?"

"Hell no!" he roared. "I was too busy triple majoring. I was lucky I had time for Farrah! Kids today have no respect for education. This is Stamford! One of the best colleges in America! Chelsea Clinton went here! Show some dignity and respect for the dead! Now, Inga, would you please get me two sets of double G silicone implants? These two have very small tits for what I need."

He made an incision in the bottom of their breasts, scooped out all the goo, tucked in the extra large bags of silicone and sewed them shut with neat little stitches.

"Ah! Much better. Now that's what I call tits!"

Inga giggled.

Next, he sutured the headless man's chest cavity shut. He could just imagine the condition of his head after bowling eight frames of strikes. These first-years obviously weren't getting enough assignments. If he was teaching, he'd make sure they had enough assignments to keep them busy. They wouldn't even find time to head off to Florida for a week of sex, drugs and rock and roll during Spring Break. They were going to be doctors! Doctors never get time off! These kids needed to work harder, toughen up. The professors were treating them like little girls. He'd talk to the Dean about some revisions in the curriculum that would have those kids crying like babies. First year med school should be like boot camp. The weak shouldn't be able to make it. The drunks, druggies, and masturbators should find another major—like art or English. Med school wasn't for everybody.

"Okay, Nurse Inga. I'm ready for the chainsaw."

Holding it over his head, he gunned it like he was in a Tobe Hooper movie. Then he neatly lopped off one of the men's left arm and shoulder. Blood ran onto the floor in buckets. He grinned and tossed the limb into the corner. Then he did the same to the other three corpses. By the time he got to the fourth one, he was wielding the chainsaw like a ninja while he sang and danced—positively giddy.

"I stretch the left arm out, I cut the left arm off, I pick the left arm up and I shake it all about. I do the hokey pokey and I throw the arm away. That's what it's all about."

Inga laughed and clapped along. Blood, muscles, and chips of bone covered the floor.

"Go put the arms in the cold storage, Nurse Inga. Maybe I can use them for something else. While you do that, I'll suture up the wounds. And I need a head for the guy. The best looking one we have. I want our monster to be good looking."

"Ya, Doctor," she said, gathering up the bloody arms and heading off in search of a nice looking head. There were many to choose from. The good doctor had a very nice display of heads, all lined up in a row, swimming in jars of formaldehyde. She picked her favorite. He looked like her first boyfriend, Hans, in the old country. Hans the Roman Hands, she called him because his hands were always roamin' all over her tender young body.

Back in the operating room, the doctor had arranged the four bodies in an X pattern, sitting up on a large table with their legs stretched out on their gurneys. They were sitting boy, girl, boy, girl. It looked like they were playing musical chairs.

"Okay, Nurse Inga. Now we begin suturing them together into a monster. We sew them together all the way up to the arm and over the shoulder. Grab a needle and start stitching."

The two of them worked until the four corpses were sewn into a circle. The monster had eight legs and four arms. It resembled a hermaphrodite octopus with two penises, two vaginas and two very nice sets of boobs.

When they were done, he handed Nurse Inga a razor. "Now I need their heads shaved—including the one in the jar."

When they were bald, he used his skull saw to cut off the back of each head and connect them together via nerves, arteries and veins. He sewed the extra head onto the headless man and hooked it up. Then he stitched them together behind the ears, into one large head with a hole in the top.

"Oh, zat is a very ugly monster, Doctor! But what good is it? Ze bodies, they're all dead. You cannot do anything with it."

"Watch and learn, dear girl. They don't call me a mad scientist for nothing!"

The doctor put a funnel into the hole. Then he took an empty jelly jar, opened it and turned it upside down in the funnel. The nurse looked at him like he was crazy. She wasn't that far off.

"I know what you're thinking, Nurse. That I'm crazy. But I assure you this jar isn't empty. It contains millions of nanocells. They'll start at the brain and work their way through the body, replacing dead cells with living nanocells. Gradually, the creature will come to life." He let out another mad scientist laugh as he removed the funnel, stuck a wire into the hole and covered it with a piece of skin, which he sewed into place.

"We'll be able to watch on this computer screen. Soon, you'll see brain activity. I'll speed it up so the hair grows back quickly. Gradually, you'll see the entire body come to life, right down to the toes. It will be alive! Circlefuck! My human Cthulhu! They'll be talking about this for years to come! I'll be written about in science magazines! They'll want me on Nova and The View! I'll do podcasts! I'll become famous!"

"But vhy do you want a human Cthulhu. Doctor? Vhat vill you do with it?" asked the nurse, now covered in blood, spunk, and other types of goo.

"World domination, of course! This is only the first of many human Cthulhu! I'll be able to train them to do four functions at once! One will be a scientist, one a mathematician, one a computer specialist."

"And vat about da fourth one?" Inga asked.

"I don't know. The fourth one can always write books and try to get them published. Or become a telemarketer. Plus, it's one badass-fucking machine. You can go all around Circlefuck and take your pick."

"Zat's a good idea," she said. "Telemarketing is good. Zay can sell something good—like termite inspections or penis enlargement devices."

"Good idea," he said. "Now, it takes about an hour for the transition to live cells to start. So we can start cleaning this place up. It looks like a shit hole in here. Get a mop and a squeegee."

Inga started to mop the floor, but slipped in the blood and goo and fell on the floor. The doctor made believe he slipped, too, and landed right on top of her.

"Oh, Doctor!" she said.

"Call me Milton! Soon you will be screaming it!" he said, unzipping his pants.

"Vat are you going to do to me?" Inga asked.

"Oh, Nurse Inga, I cannot resist you. That white uniform! Those natural breasts! That black rubber apron! You're making me so damn hot! I must have you!" he said, scratching his balls.

"No!" Inga said. "You vill give me ze crotch-crabs! Zen I'll be scratching ze pussy all ze time like you're scratching ze balls!"

"I told you, they're not crotch-crabs! They're nanofleas! Okay, so I can't fuck you. But I can at least get on top and dry hump you, right? And among my many other talents, I have a very talented tongue." He stuck it out and wiggled it.

The doctor snapped his fingers and ABBA music filled the room. "I can't resist you, Inga, you Swedish meatball. I must have you." He jumped on her and stuck his tongue down her throat. They rolled over and over in the blood, spunk and goo until both of them were covered—their bodies slick and hot. For the first time, the doctor regretted letting the nanofleas jump into his pants. It was preventing him from fucking his sexy nurse. He didn't want her to have nanofleas. The thought of seeing her digging at herself with a hairbrush was simply too much for him to handle.

Finally, he looked up at the computer screen. It was very small, but he could see some live cells moving. "Look, Nurse Inga! It's alive!" He threw his head back and did his evil laugh. "It's alive!"

As they continued to roll on the floor, kissing, licking and touching each other, the live cells moved down in the body. Hair began to grow on their heads. Eyes began to flutter. Lips began to move. Soon, arms and fingers twitched. Chests began to rise and fall as air filled dead lungs once again. It wouldn't be long before everyone knew the name of Milton von Pudnick—famous doctor and former sixth grade science teacher. No one would ever tell him his work was shit again. And he'd get paid for what he did.

When the nanocells reached the sutures in the shoulders and arms, the wounds quickly healed. Nipples perked up. When the nanocells reached the groin area, the two males sprung huge erections.

"Oh my!" Nurse Inga said. "Look at zat! Zey have great big woodys!"

"Go ahead, pick one," the doctor said. "Give it a ride. See if it works. You're my assistant, assist me! Surely you don't think I'm going to go that way, do you? Go on, do it!"

Inga walked around the monster and looked at both of the men. She selected one and stretched out on the gurney in front of him, sliding off her panties and spreading her legs. The monster grunted and fell forward, impaling itself on her as it began to thrust in and out.

"Herregud! Knulla mig älskling! Fuck me, baby! Slip me zat great big dick! Oh yes, yes!" she said, and then switched to full Swedish, although Dr. von Pudnick got the idea. The monster was a regular sex machine. And the great part was when one side was done, it could flip over and do it all over again. Inga could even stop in the middle for a little girl on girl action if she went that way. The monster could handle four people at once. It was a regular human Cthulhu orgy. And it could handle every possible combination and every kink.

The doctor couldn't stand it anymore. Just as the toes of the monster started moving he joined in the action, licking one of the women while scratching his nanofleas. She was hot, and her side of the head began to moan. As the nanocells developed, speech would return. Then he'd be ready to unleash Circlefuck on an unsuspecting world.

It took about three days to teach the monster to move in synch. When one walked forward, two were always walking sideways and one was walking backwards. At first, the arrangement seemed to work pretty well. The monster seemed to be a success. But then speech developed and the doctor's problems began.

From the very beginning, the four of them hated each other. One of the women was a bad-ass butch lesbian. She despised one of the men who was a handsome, macho stud, and it pissed her off that the woman opposite her was in love with him. The other man was a cross-dressing homosexual, which meant the only one the lesbian was interested in was out of her reach, and the gay man wasn't interested in either one them next to him. And the two of them were seriously annoyed that the stud constantly had his hand on the other woman.

"Umm, hello? We're in the room, you two sluts," the lesbian said. "Don't you even care we're watching?"

"What would you like us to do, bitch?" the man asked. "Get a room? As if that would be possible. I'm fucking attached to you."

"Yeah, shut up," the other woman said. "Why don't you and the Cher impersonator hang out? I'm sure he'd enjoy giving you some makeup tips. I can't see you, of course, but from what my friend here says, you fell out of the ugly tree and hit every branch on the way down."

"Who are you calling Cher?" the cross-dresser asked. "Cher is old. Do I look like Cher to you? No fucking way. I'm a Gaga, girlfriend, one of her little monsters. Got it? Call me Cher again, and I'll bitchslap you back to the 1960s where you belong. Fuck Cher."

"You can't bitchslap me, whore, you can't reach me!"

"No, but your dickwad boyfriend can bitchslap you, and he should. Who are you calling a whore, you skank?"

"Shut up, Gaga, you're giving me a splitting headache," the lesbian said.

"Who are you calling a dickwad? You pansy jerk-off!" the stud asked. "Don't you be talking shit to this lady, got it? I may not be able to punch you out, but she can grab your balls and twist them in ways they're not meant to go."

"And you shut up, too, Chazz Bono. Who cares if you have a splitting headache? How did you happen to get hooked up to the rest of us anyway? You belong hooked to Lindsay Lohan and Bruce Jenner—face forward," the woman said.

Finally, Dr. von Pudnick could take it no more. The monster was a huge mistake. And one day, like Dr. Frankenstein, he slipped away and left Stamford, leaving it behind, tripping over its own arms and legs and spewing shit from all four of its mouths. But unlike Victor Frankenstein, he hoped he'd never see the thing again. It was the world's problem, not his. Fuck monsters.

CHICKENBONE MARY
Zoltan Komor

Chickenbone Mary couldn't find a husband for herself, even if she wanted to. But as she never thought about marriage, she made it easy for the men in the town, who chose another pathway so they wouldn't have to eschew the woman's bumblebee body on the street. Everybody knew— the only thing that excited Mary was chicken meat. Fried and roast chicken, chicken soup, bird legs and greasy wings, damn, even raw meat, if that was the case: her mother never stopped telling tales about the little Mary, who trained her growing teeth on the legs of waddling chickens on the porch, when she was just a baby. Drops of blood everywhere. A few gnawed legged, crippled birds couldn't even walk after the encounter, they were just sitting there, and shit themselves with silent agony in their empty eyes. *Mary, Mary*—her mother bored the crap out of her listeners—*sneaked out to the shed when she was six, and gobbled up a whole chicken alive. The little rascal.* "First, you have to cook 'em!" her mother nagged at the kid, and as the years passed, and the child got fatter and fatter, she taught her daughter how to kill and pluck the poultry. At nights the little girl murmured the best recipes in the dark room like they were prayers.

So Mary couldn't find a husband, that's sure as hell. As she ambled along in the dusty streets on her massive legs, the chicken bones on a string that she wore on her neck clashed against each other. The children mocked her whenever they saw the woman: "Ladies! Hide your damned poultry, 'cause here comes Chickenbone Mary, the chicken sucker, the one and only!"

Oh, Mary hated these kids. But she didn't take it to her heart, because she had everything she wanted in life: living in an inherited farm just outside this dirty little town by herself, but also a remarkable army of chickens. At nights, when she was lying in her bed, belly full and burping in the dark room, and the urge came, she just slid a tiny chicken bone between her fat thighs. When she screamed in pleasure, the feathers of the angels fell out of the clouds, and her tightening vaginal muscles broke the bone into pieces inside her.

This worked fine for a while, but as she was getting on in years, the thought of a man around the house struck a root in her mind. It was harder and harder every day for her to handle the work around the farm alone, and those damned kids got a bit too saucy lately: now and then they sneaked into the farm, stole one or two chickens, or just beheaded an old bird, writing filthy words on Mary's wooden door with its blood, other times pegging her windows with chicken shit. They wouldn't dare such things if there were a strong man, a proper scarecrow around her home that was for sure.

She knew, of course that it was impossible for her to find someone. She never even got a kiss from a boy, even when she was younger. But Mary simply hadn't cared at that time. Who cares about boys, when the chicken soup is boiling at home? Oh, the boys. To tell the truth, she couldn't even stand roosters as they strutted up and down, sticking their crops out. Those stupid little cocks, full of vanity and arrogance, like wicks that never stop glowing. The only thing she liked about them was their testicles, delicious in soup, which was why she always kept one rooster.

***

Cut-off bird legs crawl in the attic...nightmares ride into the moonlight court...coyotes scream behind the black curtains of the night. Chickenbone Mary screams, and a little bone cracks inside of her. Scorpions' candle-tails lighting with poisonous flames. *Hide your damned poultry, ladies, here comes Chickenbone Mary, the angel plucker.* As she moans and groans wistfully in a dark room—into the never disappearing sad ghost of the soup stream—men pop out in their distant beds, like they were just soap bubbles. Outside, pubescent boys smudge the sky with birdshit, writing their nasty words onto the clouds. The angels begin to retch from the ugly smell of the boy-words. *Darn kids, look at them, they behead another chicken, and drink its blood eagerly, happily burping.*

"A man... I wish there was man here, he would cook their goose!" Mary cries under the eiderdown filled with bird feathers, spinning the broken bone between her sausage fingers. Then her eyes round and she jumps out of the bed. Mary works in the faint light of the moon, crawling on all fours, the dry-rotten boards crackle under her heavy knee-caps as she collects the bones lying in the room and the ones she wears on her neck into a proper mound, then begins to nest one piece with another, hissing in the dark: "All my life, I did everything myself, I never needed anyone's help! I can make a man for myself, if I want to, god damn it!"

And her husband begins to take form: a real wondrous scarecrow made of bones. In the light of the moon he seems like a real man. Well, almost. Only one thing is missing. So Mary runs, holding a knife, chasing her only rooster. The animal runs like crazy, its large red comb waves in the air, but no bird ever escaped from Mary's wide hands: the glinting blade slices the scared rooster's throat and, within minutes, she runs back to the house with the chopped off head of the bird.

"Now you're a real dude, Joe!" Mary claps her messy hands, gazing at her new husband in the light of the rising sun, the skeleton with the rooster's cut off head between his legs. Blood drips from the bird's beak onto the floor, then it begins to heave, and starts to crow.

Angels with vulture wings. Everything burns here with dark fly-smoke, it's the buzzing mist of hell. The sun only rises happily over Mary's farm, where they can't stop celebrating with festive soups. Bubbles of fat explode, shreds of meat fly out from the saucepan and stick onto the wall. "What a real valiant you are, Joe. We really need to clink on to your health with some fleshjuice!"

It's night again. The pores of the desert open. Pubescent boys crawl out of their caverns, gather in front of the farm. What a flock of fuzzy-haired, dirty-faced kids. Their eyes glint, small knifes roll between their fingers.

"Chickenbone Mary, Chickenbone Mary, the skyplucker, the cockplucker!" they chant and laugh. The boys climb over the old board fence, and begin to chase the chickens. The lifting feathers tickle the round belly of the moon. They grab a few birds, and chop their heads off - clucking skulls fly over the night sky. "Chickeeenboone Maaaryyy!" Sliced off beaks begin to trumpet.

Suddenly, a strange noise comes from the dark: "Frighten them away, Joe!" Word-pebbles drop into the night's black pit, the blood runs out of the boys' faces, they drop their sharp knives, the birdshit and the dirty words from their mouths. The scarecrow draggles towards them in the moonlight. What a monster! A walking skeleton with a dead rooster's head between its legs.

"Meet my husband, you freaks!" Laughs Mary somewhere in the blackness. "His name is Joe!"

The youngsters begin to scream, running as fast as they can, jumping over the fence, squeezing themselves back to their holes in the desert.

"We never gonna see those damn fuckers again!" Mary cheers, as she claps her hands, rocks fell out from a distant mountain. She runs at Joe, cuddles him and gives him a big kiss on his bonecheeks. The man's cock begins to prance; the sharp beak of the bird head tries to peck Mary's pasty skin.

"You little eager!" chuckles the woman. "Oh well, you're a man, after all, and you really earned your prize tonight!"

The old bed crackles as Mary's hands fondle her husband's body, she finds tiny pieces of leftover meat on the bones. She plucks them off, and puts them in her mouth. The amulet of joy blinks. Oh, what days come in Chickenbone Mary's life! As the sun crawls up to the sky, the rooster head between Joe's legs begin to crow. Then the man wriggles out of the bed, and brings hard food to the birds. He chases one down, cutting its throat with a rusty knife. Mary teaches her husband every recipe she knows, one by one, and Joe's a hard learner. After some time, Mary doesn't even have to leave the bed, she just lays there, sucking leftover bones from the dinner, listening to the clucking that comes from outside, yelling: "Bring more meat, Joe! I feel hungry again!"

And Joe brings them. Soon he cuts every bird's throat, while his wife fattens more and more. The old bed creaks painfully beneath her. She eats so much poultry that a few feathers grow out in her armpit.

Desert storms come and go...numerous sundowns point their gun barrels at the sky...the dropped feathers of the night dry in the corner. "Oh, Joe! You are stuck music in the mouth organ. Please, bring more meat, my belly rumbles!" But no chicken is left in the henhouse. Mary doesn't even know where the birds come from; they just come, roasted, cooked, and tickling the air with their smelly steam. Finally, the folks in the town begin to talk about the missing chickens. More and more disappear from their courts, but they couldn't guess, who can the taker be? Not until the old grocer's wife catches Mary's husband stealing the sitting hens.

"It was real awful, I tell ya!" she squawks, while the villagers give her a glass of whiskey. "It wasn't human, that's for sure! It must have come from the grave! It took those poor hens, and headed towards Mary's place!"

Chickenbone Mary, Chickenbone Mary. The name circles in the room, so the good old citizens grab their pitchforks and head their way to the old farm. There, they find the ugly skeleton straightaway, it was just killing the stolen birds with a knife. So they captured and carried him to the sheriff, who cast a glance at the miserable thing and sent him behind bars.

By this time, Mary was sighing in her room, saying: "Poor, poor old

Joe!" Big drops of tears rolled down her round face, making the eiderdown all wet, and of course she was crying for herself too; she was just too fat, the woman could hardly go out to the craphouse alone. Mary decided to lose weight and rescue her husband somehow. As there were no more meals served in the bed, it wasn't a difficult task after all.

∗∗∗

The weeks went by, and she starved more and more, eating only smacked flies, the cushions of fat begin to reduce. She didn't became thin, nor pretty of course, but she could walk again, and when she felt that her legs were strong enough to carry her to the jail, Mary took action.

So one night the sheriff caught Mary standing before his desk, murmuring: "I'm here for a conjugal visit."

The man yawned and led her to the cell. Usually, they don't deny such visits, no matter how wild a miscreant the prisoner is—a good little screwing always calms the jailbirds down. Not that Mary's husband would needed any appeasement, just sitting on the pallet, looking at his useless, hanging cock, while rats kept chewing his bony toes. But when his wife stepped in, he got on his feet fast.

"Fear not, Joe, I'm gonna help you get out of here!" The woman smiled, then they lay down, and the sounds of moaning, crowing, and the cracking of bones filled the cell. When they finish, his wife puts a finger to her mouth, "Shh!" She hisses, while pulling a little bone out of her man, hiding it under her wide clothes. "Not a word, Joe, I'm gonna take you home, but I can only do it in several rounds!"

So it went. Mary showed up night after night to the jail, and every time she carried home a little piece from her lover. There, she joined the portions together and clapped her hands when her husband began to take form. No one noticed that the prisoner was waning. They simply didn't see him because they couldn't stand the sight, but he was less and less as the days went by. In the end he was just a dead roster's head, left on the pallet. This was the last piece Mary carried home. And when Joe was ready, she made a promise to him: "From now on, everything's gonna be different, my love! There will be no more days spent in the bed! We're gonna buy new chickens, and raise them together!"

This is how they plucked the days together. The feathers of the daylight floated over the sky, the night rooted out the most beautiful dreams from their skulls. The chickens laid their eggs, and shady wedding photos hatched from them. Their house was a palace spinning on a chicken leg. In the evening, Mary tore apart the pillows and weltered in the feathers, clucking: "Gimme some cock, gimme some cock!" Then the bed began to whimper.

But, of course, soon the sheriff noticed the disappearance of the prisoner and showed up in the old farm. Mary hid her lover in the henhouse, but the old sheriff didn't want to leave her kitchen, saying: "I've had enough of this game, woman! That ugly son of a bitch belongs behind bars!"

"Please, don't take him away!" pleaded Mary. Tears festered in her eye corners like shiny fat in the surface of a good chicken soup. "I love him!" But Mary knew she couldn't convince this old fool. What a cocky rotter he was! A real vain rooster, with a glittering badge, in tinkling spurred boots.

"So be it!" decided Mary, and yelled: "Come here, Joe! We're gonna cook a rooster today!"

And Joe came with a giant rusty knife in his hand. The sheriff shot a few bullets into the smiling skeleton, but it didn't stop him. And when the edge was cutting his throat, Mary told him: "See, mister? This is love, which conquers all."

Then the whole world turned to black, the cupola made of dark vulture feathers falling on the man.

So there boils the good, good sheriff soup. The stream drenches the dirty curtains. Bubbles of fat explode in the saucepan, bringing up to the soup's surface a golden badge or a fat testicle—a flavor Mary adores so much. And the years pass so fast here in Wasteland, like rabid tumbleweeds chasing each other. Joe and Mary draw a heart onto the sky with their names in it using chickenshit, and it will never go off. When God finally scratches down these two lovers from the welt of his ancient boots, they will be buried in the same coffin. That day tiny bones gonna rain from the sky. You'll see.

CHOSEN

Brenna Morgen

Our apartment door was wide open and so were Kaylee's legs; her stance suggested she was ready for all-comers. Janie stood behind my brother, as she twisted his arms behind his back, he yelled in pain. Hannah and Emily and three other women I had never seen before stood watching, panting, bodies writhing, mouths agape—their arms full of our belongings. Judging by their scanty clothing, festering lesions, thinning hair, and lack of teeth—I figured them for drug addled Savoys.

"What the hell is going on!" I screamed, slicing Hannah's wriggling butt with Momma's butcher knife. I kept Momma's knife sharp. The cut was deep. Hannah's fat parted and the blood poured out. She was going to have a nasty scar. Still clutching our stuff, the women scattered like flies from a turd.

"Drop that stuff, you bitches! That's ours." I chased them, brandishing the bloody knife.

Our iron skillet, some blankets, and a can of precious green beans fell to the concrete. When Momma's favorite vase shattered on the walkway in front of me, I stopped. I was exhausted from a day of scavenging with the men. I think we'd trekked at least 50 miles, by foot. My right boot had an oval hole clear through the sole.

When I got to Kaylee's apartment as she slammed the door, I kicked it open.

"Kaylee!"

"What? What's your problem, Rachel?" She came from the back room jutting her chin and chest out at me, along with her attitude.

"Just give me a pair of boots." I pushed her aside and went for her closet. We used to be best friends. I knew we wore the same size, and I knew where she kept all her stuff. "I need boots. That's all. I'll deal with you later."

"You just leave Thomas alone. No meeting up with Thomas in the park." She had to lay down some kind of demand to save face. Then, just a bit softer, "Okay, Rachel?"

"Yeah, sure. I'll take these."

So what if I satisfied the men in the park behind the apartments. I had to take care of my brother and me. Nobody had enough to eat. There was no gasoline, no electricity, and barely enough water. Ever since The End, the idea was supposed to be that people banded together in groups with their neighbors for help and support—not to rob each other.

Dan and I lived in The Commons Apartment Homes. The name sounded warm and comforting—but now it was anything but. Built in the 70's, The Commons looked like two motels facing each other, the old cars were parked in front of the apartments.

None of the Commons women liked me very much. All of the men did. When the other women got hungry, they got mad and laid on their beds, waiting for food, like it was the men's fault we were in this predicament. Like, if you had a man, he was supposed to take care of you. If he didn't, you didn't take care of him.

I had to be independent, though. If I was hungry I had to do whatever it took to survive. In the beginning, I'd gone out scavenging with the men, but the day I came back and found our apartment ransacked by the other women, our own neighbors, and my brother no longer innocent I knew that times were different. The rules were different. That's when I changed.

The robbery had been engineered by Kaylee. She was in cahoots with some of the nearby neighbors—the people who lived in The Savoy Apartments. I don't even know why she hooked up with them unless she was into some weird sex or they had her on some kind of drugs.

The Savoys were known, even before The End, for being dirty, nasty and disease ridden. They manufactured and used every drug available. Now there weren't any drugs—once they used up their stashes, unless they could scavenge more, they were going to go through some hellacious withdrawals.

I fortified our apartment like a castle. I vowed never to leave my brother alone again and to use our neighbors for whatever I could get from them. After all, they had taken everything we had.

Being continually hungry not only brought out my cheekbones and sunk in my waist but I think it gave a lusty, predacious glint to my now giant eyes. To complete my new bad-ass image, I shaved my head.

Nobody's windows faced the park behind The Commons. The park was surrounded by trees, like a secret meadow. I used that area to let the half starving men feel as if they were eating, but that was all, there weren't any children left and I wasn't about to bring a child into this bereft world.

It actually started with Matt Moore. He'd always been a big guy with a hefty appetite. He was really suffering from the lack of food. As his head disappeared between my thighs I thoughtlessly remarked, "Oh, what I would give for a big juicy hamburger right now." Just as I said hamburger, I felt the long caress of his tongue and he moaned.

"Oh, god, Rachel, say it again."

"What, Matt? Say what?"

"Hamburger. Hamburger, Rachel, and maybe steak. Ribs, sirloin, pork chops...mix it up. Don't stop." He buried his face. "Just don't stop," he mumbled. "Just keep repeating those words."

And I did, when I wasn't screaming.

So, as the men ate at my pale pink plate, I would whisper and moan those special words, magical words, words that drove the men mad. So mad that I made sure to have Momma's butcher knife in hand, just in case they got carried away.

I only had to kill one man. I lopped off his head and threw his body over a low limb in one of the trees to bleed out, just to show how cold I could be. Then the rest stayed in line. They always wondered what happened to his head.

Good thing my Momma was dead. Well, gone. The elders and the children were gone. Everyone assumed they were dead. But they were gone for sure, just like the food, the animals, the gasoline, the electricity, and most of the water.

The End had happened the day after my 21st birthday, May 19th, 2021. It was like an earthquake combined with one great blinding flash of lightning. No one knew exactly what had happened, they just called it The End.

As Zac White's face disappeared between my thighs, I whispered, "Pork chops... ribs... sirloin."

Then I tossed and bucked as I moaned, "Steak, steak, steak!"

Finally, my body stiffened as I squealed, "Biscuits and graveeeeey!"

I let him collapse on me for a moment, for, naturally, he had been pleased. Then, knowing the rules and aware of Momma's butcher knife, he left. Of course, I had received a generous gift in advance.

All of the men brought me offerings, portions of whatever they had. Gifts of whatever they had scavenged to eat, drink, or keep warm. Luke Harris always brought coffee from his secret stash. He was allowed a few extra pleasures at my breasts. So my brother, Dan, and I were able to survive.

But I was ashamed. I didn't want Dan to know how we came by the meager offerings that kept us alive. I didn't have enough water to wash away the foul scent of saliva, so I stayed in the moonlight with my feet in the air and my legs in a V most of the night, letting the moon cleanse me of my secret shame.

I kept the knife in my hand and slept lightly, if at all. During some nights dark shapes, perhaps Kaylee or Janie, or the Savoys, had tried to sneak up on me, huge rocks in their hands, evil intent sparking light into their eyes, but I'd always got the drop on them and chased them off.

One night as I was snoring faintly, my body glowing like porcelain in the moonlight, the ground shook. I grabbed the handle of the butcher knife as I leaped up.

A block, a bit larger than a gallon of milk, sat glistening in the middle of the park a few feet from where I had been airing myself. It shone like a rainbow in the moonlight. Cautiously, I crawled over to examine it. Was this a present for me? It was as if I had been chosen to receive this gift in exchange for the view I shared with the sky. I smelled it, hmm. It smelled rather like gasoline.

I ran to get Dan. He touched it.

"Is it gasoline, Dan?"

"I don't think you can freeze gasoline." Dan had read a lot before The End. He had spent a lot of time on the Internet—he knew things. "Possibly bio-fuel, but I don't know about freezing that either."

"I think it's gasoline." I have woman's intuition, I am smart, too. "Let's take it home and pour antifreeze on it and see if it unfreezes, then we can put it in the car!"

"No, I'm pretty sure that won't work." Dan made a face. "I think the car has to be set up for bio-fuel."

"You can't be sure unless you try it, Dan. Come on. You're always so pessimistic."

Dan carried the block home, and we put it in a large plastic bowl. I poured anti-freeze on it.

"Nothing's happening." Dan turned to go back to the living room, back to his well-worn books.

"Dan. Dan. Come back. It's bubbling. See. There. There on the edge."

Dan came back to the table and bent down to see the miniscule reaction that was taking place at the edge of the block when it suddenly collapsed—the whole thing melted at once.

"Wow." I jumped back. "Maybe we didn't need that much antifreeze."

"Wow." Dan jumped back. "That shouldn't have worked."

"Well, it did." I hugged Dan. "Get a pitcher."

We snuck outside and poured the fluid into the gas tank of our parents' old car.

"If this works, the neighbors are going to hear the engine start up. They'll just take the car from us. Then they'll beat us up to find out where we got the gas," Dan whispered.

"You're such a pessimist, Dan. We'll push the car down the road to the top of the hill so no one will hear what we're doing – then we'll let it roll down the hill. When we're far enough away, I'll start it."

"Yeah, then when it doesn't start we can walk back and they'll all want to know where our car is." Dan shook his head.

We pushed the car down the road to the top of the hill anyway– then let it roll down the hill. When we were far enough away, I put my hand on the keys. I winked at Dan.

"It's now or never, Brother!"

Dan gave me a sad smile.

I turned the key – and it started! We drove for exactly five miles, Dan clocked it. Then we drove back, and hid the car in the brush at the bottom of the hill.

Only then did we realize we had both been holding our breath the whole time.

"Seriously, Rachel, that shouldn't have worked. There's something funny about that gasoline. Where did it come from?"

"It just fell out of the sky. I think it was sent special for me, Dan. I don't want to tell you why, but don't worry about it." I smiled.

We were hiding from the neighbors the next day to avoid questions about our missing car when someone knocked.

"What?" I leaned against the wall beside the door. I had covered the peep hole with lead.

"It's Kaylee. She needs to see you—bad." It was Kaylee's partner, Thomas.

"Yeah, right. Kaylee needs me?"

"No, really, Rachel, please."

I rolled my eyes. Once Kaylee and I had been best friends. Before. I still liked Thomas. Still trusted him, so I went.

Kaylee's apartment was dark. I was on guard. I half expected to be jumped by a bunch of Savoys, but the hairs weren't standing up on my back, nothing was making me tense.

"Where are you, K?"

"Back here, Rach. In my bedroom."

Touching the wall, I found my way to the bedroom as my eyes adjusted to the dim lights.

Kaylee was sitting on the bed, the covers pulled up over her chest. Her shoulders were bare.

"What's the matter, K?"

"It's my breasts. There's something bad wrong with them."

"Do they hurt?"

"No. I mean, yes, but that's not it. Not the half of it. Will you look at them?"

"Ah, well, sure. But—"

Kaylee dropped the covers. Her breasts immediately began to glow. A soft ruby glow at first, then they became brighter and larger until it was as if they could stand it no more and the nipples protruded. The nipples became ruby then yellow as they elongated and swelled until finally they burst open into petals and stamens shot out of the centers.

"Oh my god! How beautiful," I cried.

The stamens dripped fluid and the flower on each breast enveloped me in such a tantalizing aroma I was leaning in with my mouth open when Kaylee pushed me roughly away.

"No, Rachel, wait, there's more."

The flowers continued to grow, drip, emit their aroma and then began to pulsate in tune with my heartbeat. I started to pant. The room was getting smaller. It was growing hotter.

"Please, Kaylee, just a little bit. Just let me taste it. Just let me suck for a minute. I'm almost there already."

I straddled Kaylee and tore off my own top. I envisioned pressing our breasts together.

"No! No! Rachel, it might be contagious! Thomas, get in here, get her away from me."

Thomas ran into the room and grabbed me, one arm across my chest, his hand squeezing my breast, his other arm between my legs—to ensure a secure hold. I struggled frantically against him—to get free.

Once I had struggled enough, for the moment, I looked at Kaylee again.

The lights were dimming on Kaylee's breasts. The odor had turned to something foul and rancid. Worm heads with tiny black eyes had begun to poke out of the flowers. The flowers were shriveling and receding into her breasts. Her nipples were folding inward. The worms were slithering out and spreading across the bed. Kaylee was writhing in agony, grabbing the bed sheets, biting the pillow. Then she passed out.

Thomas pulled the covers over her naked body.

"She's out for the rest of the night." Slowly, Thomas stripped me, shook my clothes, smelled my underwear, and rubbed his hands all over my skin to ensure that there were no stray worms on me. He checked everywhere. Deeply.

"Have you had any symptoms?" I looked him in the eye for any sign of dishonesty.

"No, I swear. She got it from the Savoy's. I haven't touched her since she began visiting them."

"Good, because I have no idea how to help her and I'm really hot." I led him into the other room.

* * *

The next night Dan and I went to the park to wait.

"It's not necessarily going to happen every night, you know," Dan, ever the pessimist, said.

"You're right, it might not happen tonight." I was thinking that was a good possibility as I wasn't spreading my legs to the moon tonight.

"And, uhm, I was thinking, it might be wise if we waited under the trees, just in case it does happen." So Dan wasn't entirely a pessimist.

We moved under the trees just as twenty blocks of frozen gas fell from the sky.

"Oh, my god, Dan! There's tons of it. More than we could ever use, or ever hide. Let's get everybody." We woke all the neighbors and told them to bring containers.

Some of the neighbors didn't have antifreeze. Fights broke out over antifreeze. Some used too much and used up all of their antifreeze. Some fought over the gasoline. A few people died in the great antifreeze/gasoline fights. A few people were careful as Dan had been, to only drive out half as far as their gas would take them but some drove until they ran out of gas and walked back cursing Dan and me, eager to get more gasoline the next night to bring their cars home.

* * *

The next night everyone from the Commons apartment complex,

and the Savoy, was waiting in the park again with their containers.

"Nothing is happening tonight," Kaylee said touching her breasts.

"It was a fluke," Janie scoffed.

A cloud passed in front of the moon, the park became very dark.

"There's no moonlight anymore. It's too dark out here. Let's go home." Kaylee walked under the tree canopy.

Everyone had begun to leave the clearing to return to their apartments when the ground shook. It felt as if The End was happening again. Two dozen more frozen blocks had landed in the park. These blocks were the size of washing machines! Cautiously, the people came out of the trees. If they hadn't given up and started back for their apartments, they would have been crushed.

This time the blocks were definitely not frozen gasoline.

In the dark, the people sniffed the blocks. They smelled like soup. They touched the blocks with their fingers and licked their fingers gingerly. Then they licked the blocks directly. Yes—food! For a bit they attempted to chew and lick right on the icy blocks, but they were frozen solid. Teeth broke or fell out and tongues got stuck or burned. So they chopped out pieces from the softer top of the blocks and went home and all ate heartily.

They were so hungry they ate the soup slushy frozen while it was being warmed and once warmed, they drank bowl after bowl then laid down to sleep with stomachs so full they had to lie on their backs or prop them up if they laid on their sides. Partners patted each other's stomachs and smiled at the sloshing sound, happy that their stomachs were filled with food for a change. They poured the soup in and on each other's bodies and licked each other clean.

The next morning, they jumped out of bed eager to consume the broth that remained, they licked the bowls and implements until they shone. Again, they patted and rubbed each other's stomachs in their joy.

Absolutely everyone went back in the daylight to see if there was any left, any that hadn't melted. The sun shone down into the park. The day was warm. Yet, from a distance, through the trees, they were overjoyed to see the blocks of broth had hardly melted at all. They could feast again and again.

But as they drew closer, the stench hit them. Then they saw, bits of green and grey dangling from the ice and through the clear, frozen broth – pieces of meat. In the dark of the night before, they had taken from the top of the blocks, but the larger pieces were on the bottom.

Scanning the closest block from top to bottom—they saw first the clear broth they had so eagerly consumed. Then, further down, an eyeball, as big as a human head, half shrouded by a scaly violet lid with strands of nerve ending that had once floated behind but were now frozen in place in the broth. Greenish-yellow lumps, some small, some huge—dung shaped lumps, were interspersed throughout, along with the intestines that they had spewed from. Then, what could only be an arm, though not a human arm, much larger than a human arm, severed from its host. And toes, bits and pieces of toes the size of human torsos, were frozen in place below the arm. Oh, and there was a face, if it could be called that—with no head—staring right through them. The blocks were filled with bits and pieces of the innards of grotesque giants, ogres or monsters and their feces, bile, and the bowels themselves. The broth the Commons and Savoys had consumed that morning began to feel uncomfortable in their stomachs.

Indeed, the broth began to separate from the stomach lining of Janie Johnson as if it did not want to remain in place or proceed on its pre-ordained journey to her bowels.

The broth being warmed within the confines of Matt Moore began a strange undulating of its own accord.

One of the greenish-yellow dung-shaped lumps that had somehow been consumed whole into the belly of Kaylee Taylor began to twirl like a log being rolled at a lumber festival.

Luke Harris had followed his broth with a spot of his secret coffee stash and never noticed the huge fingernail that floated in his bowl but which he could now feel scraping every inch of his throat as it rose like the steam coming up, up, up out of a tea kettle. Luke's broth and coffee mixture spewed into the air—a fine mist that spattered everything in the park.

The smell of Luke's mist freed the twirling log in Kaylee Taylor's belly. It shot up into the air only to plop down at Matt Moore's feet. Obviously Matt Moore had much more meat in his broth than he realized, for chunks flew from his mouth covering everyone in the park. Slushy chunks of giant extra-terrestrial feces and cadavers. Janie Johnson's stomach lining and her bowels both gave way at once. The stench was unearthly and deadly. Indeed.

It was later determined that apparently—right behind their tiny apartment complex—their little park had been chosen to be an extraterrestrial dump—most of the debris the refused of a morgue. A morgue with a very lonely and bored—male—attendant.

So it happened that then, even as they thought their stomachs were clear, masses of white goo splattered down around them from the sky. They ran into the trees at the edge of the clearing to escape the globs. Then, instead of separate globs, one great putrid milky sheet fell that covered the meadow to the depth of one foot (as it was later measured by the few who survived).

"What the hell was that?" Dan stood under a tree and wiped the splatter from his face.

Rachel, at the edge of the clearing, spied darling white creatures that looked like baby seals cavorting in the waves of goo and laughed in delight.

Then she saw the top of one of the cubes sticking out of the whitish goo. A grey-green piece of intestine covered with the chunks from Matt Moore's stomach and the throw-up coffee spray from Luke Harris plopped out of the cube as it melted. And to think both of those men's mouths had been on her!

The raw muscles on the inside of her belly rippled as the stomach acid tickled the inside of her throat again. She bent repeatedly and dry heaved like a wind-up toy as the white baby seals that were not baby seals at all descended on her in a great white wave. But only one was destined to succeed.

***

JIZZAPALOOZA

Sebastian Crow

It was barely noon, the festival had just started and things were already getting crazy at the bukkake pavilion. Two rather Rubenesque young ladies were on their knees, mouths gaped wide while a circle of men surrounded them, pulling frenetically on their cocks, spraying copious amounts of semen on the girls' upturned faces and exposed tits. The girls were already cum-soaked, jizz dripping from their lips and nipples, but the more man-juice splashed on their faces, the louder they moaned and begged for more.

Randy and The Cumquats were blasting out their catchy fusion of metal, swing, and pop and those that weren't partaking in the orgy were bobbing their heads and tapping their feet in time to the music. The atmosphere was wired and the festival promised to be the biggest Jizzapalooza since the festival's beginnings ten years ago, when a couple of ex-porn promoters got the idea to combine a music festival with sex. Featuring the best current bands, separate pavilions were set up to spotlight an array of sexual practices and fetishes; bukkake, anal, acrotomphilia, and menophilia were just a few of the exotic tastes on display. This year they had even added a vorarephilia stage, where cannibal enthusiasts, The Flesh Eaters were set to perform. Even the Christian protestors picketing outside the festival were not causing too many problems. Everything pointed to a terrific, fun, sexy event.

Marky D. Sade, draped in black leather, curly black hair hanging to his waist and arms covered in tattoos, looked every bit the rock star he was. He stood watching the bukkake party, amused, but totally unaroused by the jizz fest. It looked like everyone was having a ball, but bukkake was a bit tame as far as Marky was concerned, he had tastes that were a bit more eclectic.

He pulled on Justine's hand and led her away. "Come on dear, we have our own show to do and richer delights to explore."

Justine, dressed in an ankle length, black velvet dress, smiled and

167

nodded. "Indeed we do dearest."

They drifted towards the back of the stage as a new group of men replaced the ones who had already spilled their spunk. They were due at the BDSM pavilion where their band, de Sade was set to perform later that evening. It was shaping up to be a memorable festival.

* * *

"Things are going to get bad quick, just you wait and see." Lew Giles was pacing the band's tour bus, rubbing his bald spot, and chain smoking Marlboro Reds.

"Relax," Marky replied. He was stretched out across the bunk he used on the bus, tuning his violet Ibanez RG.

"Relax? Those protestors won't be content simply picketing for long."

Lew was a short, pudgy fellow who favored flashy Elton John glasses and Hawaiian shirts. Marky secretly thought he looked like a fat, demented Paul Schaffer, but he was a terrific manager which made up for his horrible fashion sense and an over-motherly attitude towards his charges.

"And I even heard that Reverend Ped Phillips is bringing up his lunatics from the Southbro Christer's Church." Lew nodded his head as if to emphasize how serious he was.

"Oh, how nice!" Justine replied. "Maybe he'd like to play with us. I hear he likes it rough."

Beside him on the bunk, Justine had shed her long dress for a leather, under-bust corset and 10" strap-on dildo that she currently had buried to the hilt in a young fan's ass. The boy, who couldn't have been more than 19, lay trussed up neater than a Thanksgiving turkey, hands laced behind his back, wearing a blindfold and rubber-ball mouth gag. His huge cock was swollen and purple, in desperate need of some release, but Justine was an expert at this game, she would be able to bring him to the most mind-numbing, soul shaking orgasm of his young life with her skillful manipulation of his anus and prostate.

Marky put down his guitar, rose to his knees to share a deep, tongue wet kiss with Justine, and then, just for fun, he reached under the boy and delivered a vicious slap to the boy's engorged penis. The boy groaned through his gag as a huge orgasm racked his body, drenching the bed with cum.

"Now, see what you've done?" Justine laughed. "I wasn't done with the boy yet."

"Sorry, my love. I guess he needs to learn better control."

Lew shook his head and lit up another cigarette. "You need to take this seriously. The security at this festival is a joke. There's going to be trouble."

Marky stood up, stretched, and slapped Lew good-naturedly on the back. "Nonsense, Lew. Why Justine and I were out just a little while ago and security was everywhere."

"Yeah, and most of them have their pants down around their ankles, pulling on their puds. Shit, they're having so much fun they should be paying for being allowed to work here."

The door to the bus opened and Casanova D. Sade and Jay, the band's rhythm section, stumbled in, laughing and sharing a doobie. Casanova was the bass player and Marky's brother. Jay played drums and had only been with the band a short time, a replacement for longtime drummer Spanky Hardon who had died in a freak, onstage spontaneous combustion incident several months prior.

The duo threw themselves on a couple of bench seats, still giggling.

"Sex with amputees is only half as much fun as with a whole person," Casanova said.

"Been sampling the acrotomphilia pavilion?" Marky asked.

"Aye, we had a go at a sweet legless thing who works in the porn industry. She was nice enough, but you know how I like 'em to wrap their legs around my neck when I'm working down south."

"Well, sweetie, I'll wrap my legs around you if you want," Justine said. She helped her young admirer out of his bonds. The worn out youth collapsed on the bunk, now sans blindfold, and stared at her with such awe and love Marky had no doubt that Justine had another devoted slave.

Jay took another toke of the joint and passed it to Lew, who looked at it as if he'd been handed a turd. "Cassie's just upset because she wouldn't let him fuck her between her stumps."

Marky threw back his head, and laughed. "You didn't really try to fuck her stumps, did you?"

Casanova looked down at the floor and muttered, "Didn't see nothing wrong with it. Sounded like fun."

Justine stood up, relieved Lew of the joint in his hand, unstrapped the harness around her hips and let it drop to the floor, "I'm taking a shower. One of you boys mind taking care of little Johnny there? From the look of his cock I think he might just be ready for another round."

Casanova and Marky glanced at each other and smiled. They still had a few hours to play before show time, plenty of time to school Johnny in the art of pain.

Lew shook his head and lit another cigarette. There *was* going to be trouble, they were just too naïve to see it.

* * *

The Reverend Ped Phillips, kneeled naked on his knees, arms lifted towards Heaven, praying fervently to the Lord. Every few seconds he took the cattail strap in his hand and whipped it viciously across his back. As each leather and metal studded lick bit into his flesh, opening old scars and a few fresh wounds, Ped would moan in pleasure as shivers of excitement raced through his tiny erection. His back, crisscrossed with scars from decades of self-flagellation, would need tending and dressing. The penance was brutal but necessary – he was about to go to battle for The Lord, he had to be purified.

He continued with the prayers and the lashes until he collapsed to the floor, unable to raise his whip one more time. Tears welled in his eyes, from both the exquisite pain and his love for The Lord. As usual, he felt guilt for getting pleasure from his sacred act, but since he never allowed himself to experience orgasm during the ritual; he knew it was only Satan trying to pervert a holy rite of contrition.

When he had recovered enough to get to his feet, he opened the door that separated the bedroom from the rest of the RV and called for his wife.

Judy was a short, frumpy woman in her early sixties who eschewed both make-up and cologne. The bun in her hair was so tight that her eyes appeared slanted under her thick rimmed glasses and on the rare occasion when she freed her hair from its torturous pins and clips, her face would sag in relief, wrinkles pulled taut resumed their proper channel.

She pursed her lips when she saw the damage Ped had inflicted in his zeal; his scrawny back looked like he had been partially flayed by an amateur butcher. Still, it wasn't her place to criticize her husband; she knew he was only doing what God wanted. She went into the tiny bathroom, retrieved several towels, bandages, and peroxide.

"So how long before we get there?" Ped asked, stretching out on the bed on his stomach.

"Earl says about an hour." Judy sat down on the side of the bed and began to blot at the wounds with a warm, wet cloth.

Ped winced. "Good. Tonight we War against Satan himself. The sodomites and unrighteous shall feel the full weight of the Lord's wrath."

"Amen."

Judy did her best to draw out the dressing of his wounds, but an hour was still too much time. As per his usual after such a brutal act of self-flagellation, Ped was aroused and demanded she lift her skirts. Also as usual, he entered her dry. Judy lay on the bed unmoving; her skirt lifted up around her hips, white cotton panties around one ankle while Ped lay on top of her, thrusting his scrawny hips up and down. As usual for Judy, there was no pleasure for her, just some mild discomfort, but it was her wifely duty, she was just glad he had such a small penis.

It was over in less than two minutes, then Judy went into the bathroom to wash off his semen while Ped dressed himself in a dark grey suit and white shirt. They both armed themselves with The Holy Bible and prepared to do battle.

* * *

Outside the festival entrance, the protestors, almost fifteen hundred strong, marched in circles, carrying signs inscribed with slogans of divine origin like, "AIDS From Heaven," "God Hates Fags," and "Repent or Die." Some tried to pass out pro-Christian pamphlets and tracts lovingly describing the torments that await the unrepentant. Others sang hymns praising Jesus, and in between they would break out into the chant, "Hey, hey, my, my, all faggots must die."

Ped Phillips stood outside his RV and looked at the protestors with admiration. These were proper warriors for The Lord; strong, moral young men and women, courageous enough to brave the den of iniquity. They were just raw and untested, but that would change tonight. He had brought along 300 of his own, battle seasoned troops. Experts in the art of guerilla protest, they were veterans of countless such demonstrations all across the country and Ped intended them to lead the other sheep into the wolves' lair and come out victorious.

He was as disgusted by the festival attendees as he was proud of his Christian warriors. Everywhere were freaks and degenerates parading their near naked flesh, the holy vessels of their bodies defiled with piercings and marked with tattoos. It was too late to save these souls, they were acolytes of Satan and the only answer for them was death. Let them have their fun, let them play their devil music, fornicate, practice their perversities, use their drugs. They didn't know it yet, but they were almost out of time.

Southbro volunteers were setting up a podium and speakers near the gates, but far enough away so as not to evoke the ire of the festival's security. Huge wooden crates were unloaded from cargo vans and carried into a hastily raised tent. It might be too late to save these souls, but by God, Ped was not going to allow this abomination to continue. Over a hundred years ago, Carrie Nation had taken up her axe and struck a blow for the Lord when she began her campaign to abolish the evils of alcohol. Ped had better weapons on hand. These servants of Hell would soon fall beneath the firepower of Southbro's automatic weaponry.

Judy laced her arm in her husband's and, surrounded by an entourage of believers, they made their way toward the podium where Ped planned to deliver the greatest sermon of his life.

He could feel the electricity running through the demonstrators as they realized who was joining their protest. The Holy Spirit filled his heart as he took his place behind the podium and raised his arms to draw the crowd nearer.

The protestors congregated even quicker than he had hoped, but there was no way they were going to miss the chance to hear the man who had once acted as the personal pastor to a former President of the United States.

"Brothers and sisters, gather near now," Reverend Phillips said in his rich, rolling baritone. "Children of God, gather round, for The Lord wishes me to speak to you."

Even nearing 70, Reverend Phillips remained powerful and compelling. Despite being mad as a hatter, he continued to be a spellbinding orator. His voice, a powerful instrument he played like a virtuoso, using only words he painted a picture of a great battle between Good and Evil, with him and his followers on the side of God and all the festival goers as Philistines and heathens in Satan's service. It did not take him long to have the group of eager worshippers whipped into an evangelical frenzy.

Soon the crates were cracked open and the Army of The Lord was ready to be deployed.

* * *

It was 9pm when de Sade took the stage.

As the stage lights slowly brightened, two huge explosions rocked the BDSM pavilion, fountains of multicolored flames shot twenty feet into the air as smoke rolled across the stage. Behind the smoke, Marky and the band strapped on their instruments and waited for Lew to finish introducing the band. Even over the pyrotechnics, they could hear the crowd's expectant roar. This was what Marky really got off on - not the fame, the drugs, not even the sex – no, it was this nightly ritual of pulse-pounding, mind-bending rock n' roll. There was nothing to compare to having 20,000 adoring fans worshipping your every word and movement, it was better than the most intense orgasm he had ever experienced. On the stage, Marky and the rest of the band were living gods.

As the smoke began to clear, Marky raised both his arms and, on his count, Justine hit the opening power chord that began the song "Tie You Up."

The crowd went crazy, jumping up and down, casting horns and thrashing their heads in rhythm to the rapid, staccato beat. Pumped and aroused by the music, the audience was soon engaged in a full-on rock n' roll orgy. Whips and chains cut into tender flesh as their recipients moaned in unconstrained rapture. Couples fornicated where they stood, thrusting their bodies in time to the music and explosions on stage. So mesmerized by the thundering sounds of sex and music, at first no one paid any attention to the sudden eruption of gunfire and percussion grenades. It wasn't until Jay's head exploded in a crimson shower of blood and bone that the crowd realized they were under attack.

* * *

Marky stood stunned, the neck of his guitar pointed downward like a flaccid penis, watching as Jay's headless corpse fell forward into his drum set. The sound of the cymbals crashing against the floor reverberated across the stage, but it wasn't until a bullet whizzed by, mere inches from his head, that Marky's hypnosis broke and he kicked into action.

His first instinct was to protect Justine, who was also staring at the horrific sight of Jay's dead body. Shocked into motionlessness, she made a perfect target. Rushing across the stage, Marky grabbed her by the arm and began pulling her to the side, away from the fusillade of bullets that seemed to be raining from the sky.

Casanova was already at the stairs, engaged in a hand-to-hand struggle with a member of Reverend Phillips's Army. The Christer was getting the upper hand. He had Casanova in a headlock and was in the process of applying a series of devastating noogies to the bass player's scalp.

"Hey, ass-wipe." Marky yelled.

The Christer looked up, just in time to take the headstock of

Marky's guitar full in the mouth, delivering the blow with enough force that the headstock shattered the attacker's teeth, went straight through his mouth, and exited out the back of his skull. The Christer stood stunned, his gaping mouth impaled by the Ibanez RG, before collapsing in a heap at Marky's feet.

Marky stepped over the dead man and helped Casanova to his feet.

"Help me with Justine, she's in shock," Marky said, motioning to the still rigid, unresponsive girl.

Casanova nodded his head and draped an arm around Justine while Marky supported her from the other side and together they stepped out into the middle of a bloody, one-sided war.

Bullet riddled bodies lay strewn across the festival grounds. Most of the corpses were those of concert attendees who were in a state of hysterical pandemonium, their good time destroyed by the mass slaughter. Some attempted to fight back, but leather dildos, whips, and chains were no match for automatic weapons and grenades.

Not that the audience was completely helpless, many attempted to fight back with what meager weapons they could find; grabbing up whips, chains, and discarded sexual paraphernalia. As the surviving de Sade members scrambled for the safety of their tour bus, Marky saw where a trio of leather clad fans had managed to take down one of the attackers. One wiry, spike-haired youth was viciously stabbing the captured Christer in the face with a wicked 13" dildo while the other two kept their victim pinned to the ground. Marky couldn't help but grin and mentally urge his young fans on.

His grin evaporated quickly, however, as he saw their tour bus explode in flames. A crowd of Rev. Phillips's army surrounded the burning bus, singing hosannas and praising the Lord while they erected a make-shift crucifix on the spot.

Marky desired nothing more than to machine gun every last one of the motherfuckers. He thirsted to rip out their throats with his bare teeth, feast on their rancid flesh, and send their ignorant, mutilated souls back to their hateful, blind god. The thought of tearing into these religious thugs, going totally medieval on their asses, brought Marky a cold, calming comfort.

"Oh, Jesus, *Lew!*" Casanova cried.

Marky had forgotten all about their mild, bespectacled manager in all the ruckus- until Casanova shouted his name.

"Shit, Lew. I forgot about...him..." Marky's voice trailed off as he finally saw what had caused Casanova's consternation.

Rev. Phillips's Christ Brigade had finished raising their crucifix and Marky saw they ritually nailed their manager to their cross in a grotesque parody of Christ's passion. Lew was still alive and screaming, his face black and bloody from numerous cuts and contusions, his beloved spectacles, one lens cracked and frames twisted, still perched on his nose. His cries and pleas only seemed to further incite the crowd's bloodlust. They began picking up stones and slinging them at the cross. Lew's chunky body, broken and shredded by the bombardment, looked like someone had taken a meat hammer to him. A particularly well-aimed stone smashed into his head, knocking him mercifully unconscious, abruptly silencing his cries.

"Oh, poor Lew!" Justine had regained her voice, though it was cracked and strained with tears.

The band's appalled vigil was broken when a cry from the crowd alerted the mob that they were witnesses to their black sacrifice. As a single entity, the mob turned towards the bedraggled trio of rockers and Marky knew there was nowhere to run, nowhere to hide – they would have to stand and fight or lie down and die.

Marky looked at the frightened faces of his bandmates and growled, his lips twisted in the famous snarl that had melted the panties of countless groupies in the past. "Death may find us this day, *but, by God, we will take as many of these cocksucker's with us as we can.*"

Casanova and Justine steeled themselves, their fear tempered by wrath and the craving to inflict some pain on these self-righteous mass murderers. Marky reached down and picked up a microphone stand that was lying discarded on the ground. Justine reached into her boot and drew a thin, nasty stiletto she always kept hidden in case one of her many admirers ever lost control. Casanova simply took off his spiked wrist bands, wrapped them around his fists and took a boxer's stance.

As the crowd moved towards the band, Marky was delighted to see the Reverend Ped Phillips himself leading the charge, his frumpy toad of a wife beside him. No matter what happened, Marky aimed to kill the bastard.

"They mean to rip us apart with their bare hands," Casanova said. "They could just fire their damn guns and be done with it, but that ain't good enough for the fuckers. They want to feel us die."

"And I want to feel *them* die, especially that fucking reverend." Marky raised the microphone stand like a baseball bat, ready to stave in the nearest Christian head, but before Marky could exact his vengeance, a blood curdling shriek brought the advancing mob to an abrupt halt. Then all Hell broke loose.

In seconds, the advancing army of zealots were scattering in disarray as a swarm of angry, rabid rock fans descended on them like a plague of hungry wolves. Marky, Casanova, and Justine could only stare in stunned silence as Reverend Ped Phillips's well-ordered, Christian Brigade was shredded like tinfoil beneath the fans' furious attack. Marky saw members of The Flesh Eaters directing the assault and realized the vorarephiliacs had arrived. He almost felt sorry for Phillips's people...almost.

Flashing teeth and knives, the new comers tore into the mob with all the lust and abandonment of a nymphomaniac nun suddenly released from her vows. Vorarephiliacs, by the very nature of their fetish, were usually constrained by society's taboos and laws from acting on their urges. Vorarephiliacs got off on eating flesh and with so few people willing to have pieces of themselves removed for consumption; they usually had to entertain themselves with internal fantasies. Now, however, they had carte blanche to fully realize those secret desires.

The band watched the slaughter with a mixture of revulsion and triumph. While many fell beneath the Christer's weapons, the sheer number of vorarephiliacs and the savagery of their attack was enough to sway the fight in the cannibals' favor. Reverend Ped Phillips' Army of Christ was just so much meat for the vorarephiliac's machine.

Soon the festival grounds was ankle deep in gore, and it had become a challenge just to retain one's footing turning the battle into a *comédie grotesque*, an absurd slapstick with combatants slipping and falling on the slick blood and viscera. It wasn't long before everyone was so saturated in body fluids that it was hard to tell the living from the dead.

The vorarephiliacs showed no mercy, took no prisoners, continuing their fierce rampage until only Rev. Phillips remained standing, his dead wife at his feet. The cannibals hadn't killed her. She had slipped on a pile of disemboweled intestines and impaled herself on her own bayonet. The cannibals surrounded Phillips and began to converge, circling in like a pack of hungry hyenas.

Phillips, his suit and tie splattered in blood, hair wild and tangled, eyes bulging insanely as he fired a pair of empty Glocks stood facing off the approaching horde like John Wayne, screaming, "Bang, bang...you're dead."

Fil Fungus, The Flesh Eaters' lead singer, raised a small, handheld scythe over his head as he prepared to remove the abomination known as Ped Phillips from the earth. Phillips dropped to his knees, raised his arms in supplication, and began praising The Lord in a high, hysterical voice.

"LORD, LORD, HEAR MY PRAYERS. OH LORD, I PLEAD TO YOU TO

SEIZE VICTORY FROM DEFEAT. STRIKE THESE SINNERS FROM THE EARTH AND PURIFY THIS BLIGHTED LAND WITH FIRE."

A slow, ominous rumbling rolled across the sky and everyone lifted their heads towards the heavens. For a moment that might have been an eternity, the crowd held their collective breath as they waited to see if The Lord was going to answer the Reverend's prayers.

A few drops of rain fell from the gathering clouds, splashing into the upturned faces.

Grinning like a depraved clown, black mascara running down his face from the exertion of the battle, Fil ordered several burly youths to restrain the Reverend.

As they pinned Phillips's arms behind him, Fil announced, *"Vorarephiliacs, feed!"*

The crowd descended on Judy Phillips's corpse, blades drawn. The Reverend's anger turned to horror and revulsion as he was forced to watch his wife being devoured, one slice of flesh at a time. The scene was so horrific; Marky had to look away while Justine buried her face in his shoulder.

The feast continued until one vorarephiliac grabbed his gut and doubled over, his gorge rising from the amount of raw meat he had consumed.

Fil shouted, "Now!"

They dragged the Reverend, thrashing and shrieking in a hoarse, terrified voice, over to the sick cannibal. The vorarephiliac clamped his lips over Phillips's and blew a thick, steaming stew of chunky, liquid flesh into the preacher's mouth.

Reverend Phillips went ballistic, whipping his limbs madly as he tried to escape. Another three or four beefy men waded in to bring Ped under control.

More of the cannibals' appetites caught up to them and soon it was a veritable vomit orgy. Chunks of regurgitated flesh sprayed from dozens of suddenly nauseous diners, splattering the living and dead alike in a bukkake of puke. Others fed their human goulash to Phillips, his eyes bulging in revulsion as he slowly choked to death on his wife's corpse.

The surviving members of de Sade gathered around the corpse of Ped Phillips as the sky erupted in a torrential downpour that, in time, would wash away the stains of death from the festival grounds. In a final act of contempt, Marky and Casanova fished their cocks from their leather trousers, spraying hot piss on the dead preacher's face while Justine squatted and emptied a load of warm shit on his chest.

PLUG
CS Nelson

Module 1: The Perfect Soufflé & Egg Theory

There's no such thing as a hungry toilet, you little turd burglar.
Crap, I should've gone before I left the house.

Culinary Institute of America's (CIA) *Culinary Fundamentals, 9th Edition*: "7 egg whites, clean and whisked to a sheen in a copper bowl."

"Again. Whip, not beat, Mr. Krump. Whip it. Whip it to perfection." Master Chef Bui's voice sounds stifled and nasal, his scrutinizing eyeballs floating right there at my mixing bowl. Every student around me attacks his or her whites with differing pitches of masturbatory fervor. Stainless steel synergy lost in the sploosh of egg splatter. Sounds of my fellow hopefuls whisking with wild abandon.

Shwick-shwick-shwick-shwick-shwick-shwick!

A void of silence weighs between me and our instructor. Abdominal pressure builds.

There's no such thing as a starving commode, you little cum dumpster.

CIA's *Culinary Fundamentals, 9th Edition*: "Beat the whites until they are stiff, preferably standing at 45-degree angles."

"*Mis*-ter Krump." Master Chef Bui strides toward my workstation, hands behind his back. His Asian eyes squint through wire specs.

A Rubbermaid scraper spatula *plunks* into my crappy egg whites. It swings up for inspection. Molested goo, substandard, runny and full of bubbles, drip-drip-drips down the handle with the consistency of chlamydia.

Culinary Fundamentals, 9th Edition: "One part *béchamel* cream, two parts egg whites. Prepared, of course. Whipped not beaten."

Gas cramps fire through my gut.

There's no such thing as a porcelain mouth just waiting to slurp you down, you little shit for brains.

Master Chef Bui flings my imperfect whites in a mucous arc across the kitchen tile. I whisk faster.

"Stop, Mr. Krump." *Monsieur* Bui lets all disappointment deflate from his lungs. "Just. Stop." He shakes his head in wobbly circles. "Mr. Krump." He holds me with a watery gaze. "Do you even *desire* to become an accomplished master like your grandfather?" The hurt in his voice seeps through, trailing ire. Every culinary artist desires to be like Grand Master Grampa Krump.

I let my eyes convey the sentiment of hot shame over my pathetic egg whites and wince. My gut burbles.

I risk a glance past Master Chef Bui at the kitchen latrine. Occupied.

There's no such thing as a honey bucket slobbering to gobble your poo, you little pussy queef.

Bui throws his hands in a tiny eruption of Vietnamese anger. Dismissing me with a harrumph, nose to the sky, he stomps over to Ricin's beautiful egg whites.

White egg whites.

Frothy egg whites.

Sheening egg whites.

Perfect, velvety egg whites, thick with the right mixture of air and albumen. Ricin holds up a dollop of her perfection and they stand at a textbook, 45-degree angle.

Little white shark fins.

Tiny biting saw teeth.

The Culinary Institute of America's favored child.

Bui samples Ricin's whites with his bloated tongue, then gloats like a fat Vietnamese dwarf speaking bad French. Which he is.

My girlfriend bats eyelids heavy in emo-liner. A crimson lock escapes her hairnet and she brushes it out of her face.

Witness: the complete unveiling of sexy. The white culinary uniform frames Ricin's red highlights, somehow enhancing her curves despite its simple white-on-white, double-breasted jacket and black pants. Her green eyes shine with a soft porn glow. She gives me her I'ma-eat-you-all-up Suicide Girl grin.

Two parts sadist, one part conflicted love.

"Thank you, Master Chef," she says. Sultry. Heavy. In her bedroom voice. Her only voice.

She, too, curls the tip of her tongue into the egg whites, nipping off a dorsal 45 and purposefully letting it dribble down the side of her mouth. She swipes it with a finger and pokes the white perfection back into her lips.

Ricin giggles.

Bui grins.

I grunt. And clench my pelvic floor in the world's tightest pucker. A stream of new bubbles makes its way down the core of me.

I have to get out of here.

The porcelain monster within the classroom lavatory gargles through a long flush. My descending-to-sigmoid colon *squilch*es in response.

Master Chef Bui swings toward the bathroom door. His stern reprimand carries across the *shwick! shwick! shwick!* of 28 abused, copper mixing bowls, "Tell me. Did you wash appropriately, Ms. Massey?"

9th Edition: "While the Center for Disease Control (CDC) recommends 20-seconds of hand washing to ensure sterility, the CIA insists on a 32-second wash for sterility and a happy, contaminant-free kitchen."

A mousy girl with a Hummel's face freezes at the doorway. She blushes with huge, tearing eyes, and bows before scuttling to her workstation. Then it's back to my snotty eggs.

"Mr. Krump. How do you expect to advance to the next *module*," Bui asks, "if you cannot handle even a *simple* soufflé?"

Ding! The class egg timer. A chiming mixture of sweet release and intense control fight for Natty Krump inner-space. My body tries to dump my guts right there in the kitchen study.

"We," *Monsieur* Bui says, sagging, as if to shrug off an ancient mariner's albatross, "are *fini* for this afternoon. Students, restore your areas and resume from scratch tomorrow." He perks up with the twinkle of a remembered anecdote. Probably from Grampa Krump or Julia Child. I seriously hope it's Miss Child. "Remember how the word soufflé originates from the Français verb *soufflér*, which means 'to blow.' They are very delicate creatures. When dealing with a soufflé, time the process so that neither of you... *collapse*." Bui snorts once, twice, then huffs and hics through a suffocated fit of laughter.

I'm out the door before I explode, praying I make it to my own kitchen in time. I can't ruin another uniform.

And I do make it. Only to tear at my shins with bloody fingernails, screaming through each blast of bad stomach gas. After fifteen minutes of strain in the kitchen, hovering over my Cuisinart, deep glass, 8-quart wedding caker bowl, I'm rewarded with a single *plublp.*

I bend to stare into the depths of my Krump-friendly commode.

A lone floater.

A solitary sausage.

A two-inch squiggle of feculent dark-matter.

The most insignificant of tiny turds bobs in a blue felt chemical bath of glutaraldehyde and my own recipe. Four parts hydrogen peroxide, one part baking soda, a dollop of soap. Lemon and lime wedges to ring the rim. To address both odor and aesthetics.

Two weeks of a reduced calorie diet and rigorous exercise, and now I'm shitting concentrate. At least I made it two weeks this time. But I'm still shitting. And out of lemons.

I cry out and grip the floor in a downward-dog yoga pose, ass poised over the bowl. Another blast of gas roars without solid waste production.

***

"Tell me about Ricin." Dr. Libitz works at his legal pad, perched on tightly crossed legs. He adjusts his glasses and runs a hand down his trimmed mustache, but never makes eye contact.

"Well," I say, "she's pretty hot."

"You mean hot as in beautiful, or hot as in like her candle wax and handcuff soiree, perhaps?"

"Yeah. Like that."

"Go on."

I don't know what I am paying for at this point: Help in dealing with my disorder, or supplying Libitz's sick libido.

Witness: professional psychological gigolo. Dr. Libitz's ex-pat, safari-style shirt hangs open to the fourth button down, spilling gray chest hair and Brut by Fabergé. Nautica dress khaki's crossed with confidence. Soft wisps of red hair plush for petting around his bare dome. That passive amenable perma-smile.

"Where do I begin," I say, but I'm not really asking. I kinda want this to be over. I glance at the clock on the desk behind him and Libitz pulls it face down with a satisfied grunt.

"We have time, Natty. Start from your last sexual encounter."

Fantastic. "Puppets," I say. *And embarrassing.*

"Oh, my." Dr. Libitz leans back in his chair and cocks his head at his notes. He feathers his pencil, then brushes through his pornstache again. "Do tell."

"Uh, she wanted to try puppets this time."

"And what puppet did you get to play, Natty?"

I swallow and look to the ceiling. "Rimmy."

"Rimmy?"

"The pony. She likes it when I'm the pony."

"Fascinating. And Ricin?"

"Um... Cowboy."

"So, role reversal, perhaps?"

"Not so much."

Libitz stops writing, but doesn't look up. He waits.

"Cowboy likes to check the pony."

"Check Rimmy?"

"Yeah. You know. For babies." Now I find my feet. "I guess."

"And when Cowboy checks Rimmy for babies, does Ricin also check Natty—"

"Oh for chrissake! Can we please just talk about this fear-of-shitting thing?"

Libitz places his pencil flat on the pad. The reflection in his glasses looks more like art instead of a kooky psychiatrist's scribble.

I see hair.

I see cleavage.

I see a horse's behind.

I see an arm buried to the elbow. Checking for babies. Fuck.

Libitz leans forward and speaks to my knees, even though our chairs face one another. "Natty, its called defecaloesiophobia. You are afraid of bowel movements." His voice softens. "Very normal and probably a result of an incident in your youth. Perhaps," he says, voice lowering even more, "just maybe perhaps, a parent or trusted guardian touched you once." He clears his throat. "Inappropriately, perhaps."

I shake my head. My grandfather, the most successful Master Chef in greater Seattle, hated me. He would never touch me, certainly not to molest me. And make no mistake about it. That is exactly what Dr. Libitz just put on the table.

Mom? No chance. She worried over me, but I've been a burden ever since her rich father wrote us both out of his will. She worked herself to death trying to regain status after delivering such detestable afterbirth as me. Nope. Not Mom.

Mother and Grampa Krump.

One part sour cream, two parts curdled milk.

"No, I don't think I ever experience any 'bad touches' from grownups."

"Perhaps we should try exploratory subconsciousness."

183

I scowl into his off-looking glasses even though I'm just getting double doodles of my girlfriend fisting a horse.

"Hypnotherapy, perhaps."

I slump in my chair.

"Natty, it might be an opportune time to not only uncover the source of this trauma in your life, but also deal with it so you may use a nominal toilet and stop trying to defeat biology."

"Sure," I say, all vapid and lifeless. "Why not."

"Good." He dims the already dull lighting. "I want you to lie back and listen to my voice..."

Module 2: Icings & Fillings

There's no such thing as a ravenous shitter, you little shithead.

Waves of tiny razors spiral through my colon.

Culinary Institute of America's *Culinary Fundamentals, 9th Edition:* "While store brand chocolate might present a temptation due to cost and availability, perfection will only be attained by the sacrifice for quality. Premium baker's chocolate, such as Valrhona or Lindt, then, becomes a costly necessity for survival in the modern kitchen."

"Fold not whip, Mr. Krump. *Fold.* This is not the same as egg whites. Air will ruin a good *ganache.*" Master Chef Bui strolls past to Ricin. Around us, our class of now 22 culinary dreamers orchestrate creamy chocolate fillings with gentle swipes of spatulas. Ricin uses a special technique of a sensual caress, ending on a proctol upstroke. I squint and look back to the congealing lumps of chocolate in my own bowl.

Bui takes a step back. He bends to the side and leans into my work, hands clasped behind him. He tsks. I follow his cue and peer down, our foreheads nearly touching.

"Now do you understand why you fail, Mr. Krump?"

Burst air bubbles pock my folds of dark chocolate.

A brown pile of disease.

A mushy lump of failure.

A glass bowl of shit.

Dark chocolate and heavy cream, half emulsified, smudge the sides.

"And you still owe me a perfect soufflé," Bui says.

There's no such thing as a lunatic loo to suck your guts out, you little goochtard.

Sounds of my stomach's squishy solid waste fizz and grumble over the sounds of squishy bad pastry filling. My *ganache* farts, spewing chocolate. Teensy dots speckle my face.

Culinary Fundamentals, 9th Edition: "It is best to start the stirring process from the center working outward in order to prevent excess air, which can, in general, interfere with the already difficult emulsion process."

Behind Master Chef Bui, Ricin cocks an eyebrow and holds her spatula in a lax, crossed-arm salute. She drags a finger through her handiwork and smears it across her lips. Her tongue explores for each dab of deep brown. Bui turns back to her and strides quickly to Ricin's bowl of creamy dark wonderment.

They make verbal love over it.

They coo and sigh about it.

She moans into it.

He whimpers for it.

I gasp and clutch my stomach, tightening up against the next round of boiling gut grease.

Monsieur Bui and Ricin.

One part soured Pad Thai sauce, two parts spiced hard candy.

I won't make it. I have to use the classroom lavatory. Three weeks of a liquid diet has finally caught up, all of those micro-fiber particles thickening in a gruel deep within my bowels. Steeping. Fermenting. Effervescing.

I break into a cold sweat and move toward the monstrosity behind the wood panel door.

There's no such thing as a john that wants to chomp your dook, you little dick twist.

Ms. Massey is two strides ahead of me. She sees me from across the stainless steel work tables and we both stop. I squint. We lock gazes. Massey squeaks and runs for the lavatory, slamming herself in before I can make it.

"Fuck!"

"*Mis*-ter Krump!"

Ding!

I run for the exit.

Ten minutes later, I step out from behind the parking lot shrubs, head down, hoodie up, and a pile of dark soft-serve steaming from the grass. Three weeks without a bowel movement. I made it three. I can beat this thing.

***

"So how are we today, Natty?" Dr. Libitz scratches away at his legal pad. I haven't said anything yet.

"Fine."

"Oh? Any new developments with Ricin, perhaps?" Scratch, scratch, scratch.

"No."

"Still using puppets, hmm?" Scratch, scratch.

"No."

He puts the pencil down and gazes at my knees, perma-smile fixed.

"Perhaps something new, then. Tell me about it, Natty."

I stare directly at his bush of chest hair and say, "We did some cosplay."

"Very nice." His breath comes rapid and shallow. He licks his lips and half grunts, "And who did you play?"

"Cowboy." I hate this.

"And Ricin..."

"Nurse."

Scratch, scratch, scratch, scratch. "And perhaps this went better than puppet night?"

He hums as he takes notes, cocks his head, turns the pad, then nods with a thoughtful frown.

"Not really."

I want to sink into the seat. But I'm afraid to. We had more than psych issues the other night, me and Ricin. What if it gets stuck up there even deeper?

"Tell me."

"We lost Rimmy."

"Oh dear." But Dr. Libitz is consumed in his note taking, so much so, he now has to keep turning his pad different angles to capture all of his thoughts. A tiny BDSM nurse flashes in both of his lenses. "Did you do something to hide Rimmy, perhaps? Perhaps to avoid the discomfort of giving in to Ricin's domination—"

"Fuck! No, okay?" Then calmer, "No. We lost it together... kinda. Someplace else. Can we talk about my problem now?"

He raises a finger without speaking, pencil dancing across the paper. He stops. He tilts his head and nods before clearing his throat to address my knees.

"Very well. I suspect you have issues with your mother, Natty."

I kickstand my cheek against my fist and roll my eyes. "I'm sure."

"Last session we discovered she was responsible for your struggles through potty training, did we not?"

"Really?" I blink and sit upright.

"Well, it *was* her burden to bear as a single parent. It only follows the natural course of things."

"Yeah, but I don't remember any of that—"

"Don't you? The bad boy too stingy to feed the poor starving Tidy Bowl Man?"

"What?"

"Mr. Hungry who never gets a healthy meal because Little Natty Potty Pants won't make poopoo?"

"That's ridiculous!"

"The sad, sad, sad little peepoo monster Mother's little Doody Doll refuses to play with—"

"Holy shit."

"There must be a significant emotional event to cause this over attention to toilet training, Natty. And from the sound of it, she could be quite the creative verbal abuser."

I nod along, staring at the twin reflections of Ricin's sexy nurse, up to her elbow in my ass-less chaps. I'm wearing a cowboy hat.

"Perhaps we need to go back even deeper. To your grandfather, perhaps."

I swallow hard.

"Follow the sound of my voice…"

Module 3: Doughs & Pastries

There's no such thing as a starving potty, you little piss licker.
I'm too full.

Culinary Institute of America's *Culinary Fundamentals, 9th Edition:* "The dough must be allowed to rest beneath a wet towel for approximately five minutes after final cuts, which is an opportune time to flatten your butter."

Whap! Whap! Whap! Whap!

"Mr. Krump? Aren't you going to beat your butter with the rest of the class?" Master Chef Bui stands on tiptoes with hands behind his back. "Or would you rather owe me a decadent puff pastry to go with your yet to be seen, perfect soufflé?"

I lean my head against the table and raise my rolling pin.

Whumb. Whumb.

I'm not feeling this, but I am feeling the reverberation pushing against my bulge. Every one of our 16 remaining wide-eyed sponges puts whole heart into wailing the cream out of their butter sticks. Bui snorts and strides to Ricin, nostrils first.

Ricin lays into her puff pastry with the fury of a heavy metal drummer.

Witness: sex and leather goddess in her element. Her hair falls in shimmering scarlet locks from her net. Butter stains her white double-breasted uniform in an amber Rorsach insanely close to the shape of two outward looking horses. Her white cheeks and khol eyeliner blaze with each strike of her rolling pin. She issues a passionate battle cry as she assaults her puff.

I glare at the toilet from beneath my sweat-plastered bangs. Occupied. Not that it would matter.

Hot lava rises to the bottom of my esophagus.

THERE'S NO SUCH THING AS A HUNGRY TOILET—why didn't you go here, at home, instead of Grampa's restaurant, you little cum stain?

Silence. I look up. All around, everyone is still beating the brakes off their butter sticks, but I can only hear my inner asshole. And now his voice sounds weirdly female. And familiar.

Bui leans on the counter and Ricin feeds him wads of her well-fondled dough.

He chews.

She smirks.

I slip out of my chair into a hunchbacked shuffle for the exit.

"*Mis*-ter Krump!"

Pain ratchets against the blockage in my sigmoid colon, vibrating through five weeks of a bolus effigy, one wad of calcified waste after another stacked well into my descending colon. The toxins agitate my system, stirring bile and mucous production until the churning maelstrom of stomach fluids splashes higher and higher into my gut.

I need to get it out.

In the bushes, I puke on the weeks-old coil of my *ganache*-shit being daily reconstituted by the Culinary Institute's sprinkler system. I wipe my mouth and take a deep breath before returning to my puff pastry, Ricin, and Bui.

I feel so much better. A month without a dump. Chunks may be the way ahead for me. And it's all organic ingredients.

Primo.

Top shelf.

The best.

One part backed-up plumbing, two parts stick-to-itiveness.

Why is my mother in my head giving me shit, now?

***

"Natty."

Dr. Libitz looks at me. For the first time, he really sees me. And I see his legal pad. It's empty and that's a good thing.

I really don't want to have to look at tiny doodles of me in fishnets and garters. Me Roman Showering Ricin on her command, strings of empty bile and mucous pouring across her face, her mouth, her *open* mouth. God, I'm gonna puke again. I think I'm becoming anti-sexual.

"Natty Krump. Grandson of Master Chef Ethan Krump of Seattle's world famous Café de Krump."

I nod.

It hurts.

He smiles and I wince.

Libitz leans in. "Natty? You don't look so good. Perhaps you should tell me the last time you experienced a solid waste bowel movement."

I want to swallow; but I'm afraid to do so. Too much bile and acid have shredded my vocal cords. And it's working! Excruciating pain aside, I haven't shat in over a month. I can live with—oh, fuck that hurts.

One part backwash, three parts acid swill.

I go through a raspy false start, then find a sliver of voice. "Five weeks."

Dr. Libitz explodes out of his chair. I grip my armrests and steel against the pressure. "Perhaps we need to get you to a fucking hospital, Natty!"

He moves to grab his coat and I do the same. Except when he sticks his head out the door to let his receptionist know, I'm already gone. Out the back. You know. Back door. I have some experience.

I also have a perfect soufflé to make and no time to dick around with this shit.

Module 4: Fondues & Founts

You cost me everything...*so SHIT YOUR LITTLE FUCKING GUTS OUT*

ALREADY! Oh…oh no. Did Mommy upset you? GOOD!

I'm bigger today. And I have a horse's tail swinging from my anus. Ricin's gorgeous green eyes burn through me because I wouldn't let her play with it last night. I'm moving like an arthritic blimp.

A blimp with a tail.

A brick balloon with a pony peeking.

A led zeppelin with Rimmy's stallion braids jutting from swollen hemorrhoids. And my girlfriend wants to work it-work it because she gets off to stuff like that.

I hate her.

She's sick.

One part freak.

I'm breaking up with her as soon as finals are over.

Bui whispers something to her and she giggles, though her eyes don't. They continue to tear me apart for not letting her yank Rimmy out of my ass. Like I had a choice anyway. I'm pretty sure his horse head got hung up between my sigmoid colon and rectum, the weird P-trap we all have in the pipes connecting our mouths to our buttholes.

Our class graduation project flows dark and glorious in the center. A chocolate fountain.

This hurts. I'll probably die. I need to shit. I don't want to shit.

Besides, now that I think about it, who would shit in a restaurant—

Do you lagg the smell, Nathaniel?

That's not Mom. A gruff male with a fake French accent.

Do this smell of sheet and sole meunière *with ma perfect* chocolat soufflé *not pleases you? Mm?*

Grampa? I shake my head and focus on cleaning my utensils. The oven timer reads 2-minutes remaining at 375-degrees Fahrenheit. I slow-pivot and open the oven. Still full and beautiful.

9th Edition: "When baking the soufflé, it is important to check consistently but often. Ensure the foil collar is still in place, in addition to checking for colour, crust, and rise."

Here. Eat this, maître de la sheet!

"No!" I scream.

"*Mis*-ter Krump—"

"Fuck off!"

Bui jerks with his hand to his heart. Ricin's eyes glow. Rimmy's tale slips out a little more and I freeze. This could get messy. Vomit rises with my perfect soufflé.

I eyeball the toilet. Occupied. *Fuck, Massey!*

The chocolate fountain burbles like a joyful brook.

It cascades with happiness—

—Ricin rubs herself up the side of her workstation table, her tongue extended and eyes closed to slits—

Overflows in euphoria.

Spills over in ecstasy.

I cry out from the two-way pressure. I'm gonna blow from both ends. A reverse Chinese handcuff.

Ding!

Silence. The kitchen holds the heaviness of a decompression chamber.

No whisks whisking.

No scrapers scraping.

Only chocolate bubba-bubba-bubbling.

My gut joins the *fontaine de chocolat*. Tiny bubbles swirling down to beat against the impaction of horse head and petrified shit, bigger ones roiling back up.

Everyone gathers in rubbernecker onesies at first, then my 9 remaining classmates huddle around my table with their bowls of graduation chocolate, keeping their distance from my writhing, swollen, brick-hard and pregnant, double-breasted white uniform. Ricin edges over to the oven.

Here! Bon Appétit, leetle sheet!

Pressure inside my stomach. Pressure inside my head. Pressure from the pressing crowd of victorious wishfuls.

"Here ya go," Ricin whispers in my ear, "stallion." She bends over with her perfect S-curve ass aimed like a love cannon at my face, and places my creation on the stainless steel table. Her full lips form a succulent O and she gives Master Chef Bui eyes about it.

He gives her a nervous smile over it.

Ms. Massey slams the lavatory door and everyone goes, "ooooh," then they go, "ahhhh," at the terror on my face. But my soufflé wobbles only the slightest against the rush of air, the vibrating table, the 9 other climate-altering breaths so detrimental to a delicate construction.

Rimmy squeezes out another thumb's serving size between my rhoids. I grunt and slip to the floor, stiff and volatile.

Ricin dips her finger in Bui's bowl of victory chocolate, and holds it to my face, groupie eyes pulsing with an internal mischief. Or maybe perhaps orgasm. Perhaps.

"No," I say. But it's more of a defeated no. My stupid, shithead, cock-gobbler, Libitz-diddled brain is going to make us go there. Fuck.

Witness: *Grampa Krump splashes through a puddle flowing from the restaurant* toilette. *A small lake of potty water and toxic deposits. He holds a fork in his crossed arms. His face scrunches into a sadistic smile, eyes focused on a little boy sitting in the mess with pants around his ankles. The smell of a lactose intolerant dairy farm wafts from behind the boy. It steams from the puddle rich in other people's poo. Patrons usher out the door. Others cover mouths to the wet sounds of* blugh, *and,* yerlbh.

That little boy is me.

"Mr. Krump," Bui says in a reverent voice, spoon raised. "This," he digs in to the wibbling top of my soufflé and rolls euphoric eyes over his first bite, "may be the finest soufflé I have experienced." He takes another bite and invites the class to join him. Ricin is in her zone, though, poised with one dripping finger ready to paint my cheeks. Bui announces, "You have surpassed even the Grand Master, Chef Krump himself..."

Witness: *Grampa squats and forks a tiny turd. He holds it up between us and harrumphs. "Eat, Monsieur Sheet. Enjoy." He shoves the little ball of rotten fudge at my closed lips. I'm crying. Mother is wailing, "Why, Natty? Oh why oh why oh why?"*

"*Monsieur* Krump," Bui says. "I can now call you an accomplished chef. I am proud to have mentored you—"

Ricin swipes chocolate over my lips and cheek. My gut swells with one building bubble.

Witness: *Grampa Krump titters hysterically as he dots my cheeks, my forehead, my nose, even my lips, with his forked turd. This is what happens in the Krump family when you stop-up the toilet at the restaurant.*

Applause. Thunderous in the acoustics of Master Chef Bui's kitchen. I made it and everyone is happy for me. I'm gonna puke.

"I'm proud of you," Ricin whispers in my ear.

I'm gonna shit.

She snakes her hand down my pants. The back, not the front.

Clap-clap-clap.

She purrs. And grabs Rimmy's tale.

My gut churns.

Bui laughs and throws his hands to the ceiling.

"Ohhh... Rimmy," Ricin growls.

She yanks.

Two months of backed up poo. A day's worth of agitated barf. I'm a *fontaine de effluvium.* Rotten eggs and bad liverwurst. Vinegar and butyric acid and spoiled yogurt.

The clapping dies. The synchronized puking begins.

Ms. Massey squeaks and runs for the lavatory. *Monsieur* Bui beats her to it, both squeezing into the water closet. The illustrious *fontaine de chocolat* thickens with chunks.

KitchenAid stainless steel bowls fill.

Cuisinart glass dessert mixers overflow.

Weilburger ceramic Dutch ovens slosh to the brim.

Everyone dives for a basin except Ricin. She softens and helps me to my feet, dark and putrid *bouillon* trailing from my pants, vomit dribbling down my chin. She kisses me. On the mouth. Open mouth.

Before we leave, Ricin sashays to the table and grabs what's left of my perfect soufflé.

One part mischief, four parts passion.

Tonight she wants to try food play. Tonight I'm going to use a real toilet. My *porcelain* throne in *my* lavatory.

No puppets, *s'il vous plaît.*

BON APPÉTIT

***

About C.S. Nelson

CS Nelson holds a BA of English and has appeared in US and Canadian ezines and anthologies. When not writing, he spends time with family, performs acupuncture therapy on puffer fish, and serves as a US Army Cav Scout out of Fort Irwin in the Mojave Desert. By the time you read this, he will already have been exiled to the Arctic paradise of Fort Wainright, Alaska. And for this, the puffer fish are happy. www.nelsoncs.com.

BLUBBER
Dixie Pinoit

Fuckity, fuck, fuck, fuck. Why were doctors and their bitch nurses always so *blithe* about assuming that their patients had nothing else to do but sit around the waiting room all day?

Using the word *blithe* almost made Larry forget how pissed he was at having to cram his fat ass on the stupid little bench in Dr. Limos' lobby. *Blithe* had been a featured word in the *Reader's Digest,* "It Pays to Increase Your Word Power" column recently, and he'd been looking for a chance to use it. Blithe. That's right. Old Lemon-Balls was fucking *blithe* about his patients' time.

His patients all paid him enough money so he could buy a watch, didn't they?

To show his contempt, Larry farted loudly.

The old lady sitting closest to him gave Larry an alarmed look and moved away.

Larry snorted and breathed deeply of his own gas, then pulled a Twinkie out of his messenger bag and ripped it open, shoving it whole into his mouth.

Mouth still open, he fished out a packet of salt from his breast pocket, tore off the corner, and poured the contents in after the Twinkie.

He moaned with pleasure as he chewed, forgetting to close his mouth completely, spraying Twinkie crumbs and salt down his already stained shirt and across his grubby pants. Gobs of cream filling mixed with his spit and started to ooze out of his lips and trickle down his chin. Someone made a sound of disgust and Bobbie, Dr. Limos' receptionist, came around the desk to stand in front of him.

"Larry, you've been talked to about eating in the lobby. Dr. Limos told you if you did it again, you'd have to wait in your car until he's ready to see you."

He frowned at her.

She was beautiful. Usually he wanted to slobber all over her. This time, her stern look made him glance at his lap. His fingers plucked at the Twinkie crumbs on his pants, and he began shoving them back in his mouth.

He tried ignoring her, but he could see her slender feet tucked into mile-high stilettos, and they weren't budging. Finally, he raised his eyes to hers, and flinched at the contempt he saw there. Normally she hid it better. He felt a spurt of hatred.

"He shouldn't make me wait so long. I got hungry," Larry said, lower lip jutting.

"You've been here five minutes," Bobbie said.

"The bench hurts me." It was twenty four inches wide, thickly cushioned and the legs were made of steel. It groaned under his weight.

She sighed. "I'll get a cushion. No more food. Give me your bag; I'll put it behind the desk. Otherwise, you'll need to go sit in your car."

Larry weighed his options. It was summer in LA, and while he had AC in the car, the building AC was infinitely better. "I'll give you my bag when you give me the cushion," he negotiated, eyes narrowing.

She studied him for a long minute, then nodded. As she walked away to get the cushion, Larry farted again. Extra juicy.

***

Dr. Limos looked at Larry Scroggin's chart one more time, mostly to keep from looking at Larry. Larry Scroggins was the most vile, disgusting pig of a man Dr. Limos had ever had met, bar none. But he had the millions. So when Larry Scroggins had shown up at Dr. Limos' clinic looking for an extraordinary amount of liposuction – medically unsafe on someone as grotesquely obese as Larry— it only took one quick credit check for Dr. Limos to welcome Larry with open arms.

Wide open arms. Anything less and the nasty asshole never would have fit.

***

Larry sprawled on the cold metal table, happily splayed and nearly naked, greasy mounds of pasty flesh on display everywhere that Dr. Limos' nurse, Holly, looked. Larry had a cotton gown to wear, but he made sure it kept falling open every time she glanced his way. It was like trying not to look at a bad car accident. And Larry's penis was following her with its creepy little unblinking eye. She could see the tip, visible under the huge

196

folds of fat that made up his belly.

Christ, how could a man let himself go like that? Thank God Dr. Limos was nothing like that. Nothing at all. Danny Limos was lean and fit and obsessed with cleanliness. He had his entire body waxed once a month like clockwork. Except for his head, of course. And his cute, fuzzy balls.

***

For his part, Larry couldn't wait for his lipo to begin. Anything that involved touching his body, feeding it, stroking it, indulging it, paying attention to it in any way, gave him a quivery, almost sexual pleasure. Having the delectable Holly – Pamela Anderson tits, Angelina Jolie lips, Kim Kardashian doe eyes. – And the impeccably groomed Dr. Limos worship at the altar of his abundance was almost more delight than Larry could stand.

When they inserted the cannula and began to actually suck out the greasy yellow fat, Larry's eyes bulged with awe and an unexpected feeling of loss. Suddenly, his world tilted. What was joy became grief in the time it took to flip a switch.

That was him – him! Being sucked away into clear receptacles, bloody greasy bits that had been part of him for years, until forcefully ripped from his stomach under the watchful eye of Dr. Limos and his sleazy, big-titty nurse. Larry felt like weeping. He'd been afraid of this. His therapist had warned him. His body! His precious body, his lovely fat, his wall against all comers. No one understood. Why had he decided to do this? At the moment, he couldn't remember.

When they were done with the first session, fifty pounds of Larry vacuumed away forever, the incisions closed and bound, he pinned the doctor with a commanding look. "I want to keep it."

"Excuse me?" said Dr. Limos.

"My fat. I want to keep it."

Holly froze.

"That's ... No one's ever requested that before. I don't ..."

Larry smiled slyly. "I'll pay for it, if that's the problem."

The mention of money got Dr. Limos' brain functioning again. "I'm sure we can work out something. Holly, be a dear and see if we have enough of those stainless steel containers to hold Larry's ... excess matter?"

"No need," said Larry. "I brought some cryogenic containers with me. I'll call my chauffeur and he can bring them in."

Holly, looking like she was going to barf, said, "I'll let Bobbie know to send him back," and fled the room.

"We'll have a technician come help with that." Dr. Limos gave Larry an uncertain smile, handed him the bag containing his clothes, and left right behind his assistant. He didn't even stay long enough to remind Larry to book his next session.

The receptionist delivered Larry's canisters while Larry dressed. When he was done, Larry opened the door to look for Holly and Dr. Limos. The technician hadn't shown up yet, and there was no way he was leaving without his precious fat.

They jumped apart when they saw him, Holly's face flushed and guilty, eyes looking everywhere but at him, Dr. Limos with a pasted-on smile even Larry could tell was phony. He wondered what they'd been talking about.

Dr. Limos stepped forward and steered Larry back into the procedure room. "Larry! Let's get your …" he paused and swallowed, "… your souvenirs packed up so you can go home." He fished a bottle of pills out of his lab coat pocket and handed it to Larry. "Here are some supplements for you to take to help support you until your next appointment. Vitamins, immune boosters, muscle builders, all good stuff. I recommend it for all my patients who've embarked on a positive lifestyle change! Now where is that tech?"

***

By his fourth liposuction session, Larry had lost nearly two hundred pounds. "I don't get it," whispered Holly to Dr. Limos out in the hallway. "Forty pounds extracted each session equals 160 pounds. Where did the extra forty-pound loss come in?"

Dr. Limos smiled at her knowingly and pulled out the refill of Larry's 'special supplement.' "Right here, gorgeous. Little appetite suppressant, little antidepressant, little bit of steroids, little bit of MDMA. All guaranteed to keep him coming back for more."

Holly's eyes widened, then she burst into a fit of giggles. Dr. Limos quickly shushed her, but with an indulgent smile. Larry was still in the procedure room, after all, waiting for his grotesque 'souvenirs' to be packaged up.

***

Larry looked in the mirror as he changed back into his street clothes. He was making great progress – but he didn't look nearly as good as he thought he should. His eyes were still piggy under folds of drooping flesh. Skin under his chin hung and jiggled, as did the skin under his arms, along his thighs and – he slowly turned – yep – his ass.

Furious, he crammed his legs into his pants. Dr. Limos had practically promised that liposuction would be the answer to all his weight loss problems. He was just buttoning up his shirt when Dr. Limos walked back in. Larry whirled angrily on the doctor, then choked it down when Limos took a startled step backward. "Ah, sorry, doc. Didn't mean to scare you. Look, there are a couple of other procedures I'd like to talk to you about."

* * *

By his tenth lipo, Larry was walking through the door with a bounce in his step. His eyes had been lifted, his tummy had been tucked, his throat had been tightened, and the skin on his arms, legs and buttocks had been pulled, trimmed and gathered like an expensive suit. Thanks to contacts, his baby blues were mesmerizing. At least, they would have been to anyone who didn't remember his creepy Twinkie-fart moves. Or the follow-you-with-his-penis charmer.

"Is it my imagination, or is Blubber getting kind of hot now that he's lost all that weight?" asked Bobbie. "Your boyfriend is a miracle worker."

"It's more than just the weight, though," said Holly, as they watched him walk toward Dr. Limos' office. "Even his voice is different. How he speaks, the way he says things."

"I noticed that, too," said Bobbie. "You think he's got a speech therapist? And maybe … a lifestyle coach?"

"He's got muscles, for sure," said Holly, eyes narrowed on his tight butt. "I bet he's got a personal trainer. Pretty soon he's not going to need us anymore."

A thought struck Holly and she looked at Bobbie, a smile creeping across her face. "Hey, Bobbie, does your sister still do that Medical Marijuana gig?"

* * *

It took a little convincing, but her darling Dr. Limos eventually saw the wisdom of removing the steroids and appetite suppressant from the supplements he gave Larry and replacing them with a hefty dose of powdered marijuana concentrate, enough to boost his appetite back into the stratosphere.

But this wasn't the old Larry.

He *felt* things now. Like withdrawals from the steroids and the speed, even though he wasn't sure why he was feeling what he was feeling. He *thought* about stuff. Like why he was suddenly so *hungry*. Had the doc changed something in his pills? Left something out, maybe? Doctors never admitted when they made a mistake. Too afraid of malpractice suits. He knew that.

Larry'd never bothered to question what was in Limos' special supplement before. Just like that stupid Limos has never bothered to question where all of Larry's money came from. He was about to learn the mistake he made in not looking any further than a bank balance.

Larry called Max, his driver/bodyguard. Celebs were so stupid. They thought their employees were going to be loyal to them because they were so *cool*. Larry paid Max enough money to *buy* his loyalty. And to insure he stayed bought.

"Hey, Max, I got some work to do. Make sure I'm not interrupted."

"New Monsanto contract?"

"You really care?"

"You gonna keep payin' me?"

"Yep."

"Then no, not really. Just makin' conversation."

"You want conversation, call a phone sex line."

"You gonna pay for that?"

"Yep."

"Cool."

Larry went into his home lab and started testing the contents of a couple of capsules – one from before Limos changed his supplement and one from after.

When he got the results, he did something he had never done before. He punched a wall hard enough to make a hole in it.

For a minute, his own power and ferocity distracted him, then he got back on task. Limos. And Holly. He couldn't say why he was so sure, but somehow he knew that stuck-up bitch had something to do with it.

Larry was going to make them pay.

***

"Listen, Doc, I know I'm all done here, but I wanted to do something nice to say thank you for all your fantastic work," Larry said, giving Dr. Limos an earnest smile.

Dr. Limos frowned at him. Despite two months of the marijuana infused supplements, Larry showed no signs of gaining weight, and, in fact, looked healthier than ever.

"Doc, did I say something wrong? All I wanted to do was invite you over for dinner. And please, bring Holly. I feel like I owe her so much."

Dr. Limos quickly wiped away the frown. Maybe dinner at Larry's was just the opportunity he needed to learn what was killing his golden goose. Or, actually, keeping him so slim and healthy.

"I'm sorry, Larry, I've given you the wrong impression. Holly and I will be delighted to accept your kind invitation. You are my greatest success story." He stood and held out a hand for Larry to shake, nearly causing Larry to bobble the small microphone he was planting under the lip of Dr. Limos' desk.

Larry stood too, and clasped Dr. Limos' hand. "Friday night, then. Seven o'clock. I can't tell you how happy you've made me." He kept a straight face all the way out to his brand new Jag, which, unlike his previous rides, didn't require a driver, then laughed like a madman all the way home.

***

"I'm not going to his fucking *house*," said Holly. "I've seen him eat. It's disgusting. I'm not sitting through a whole meal of him slobbering and drooling and farting."

"Darling, it may be the best chance we have to figure out why the supplements aren't working," said Dr. Limos. "Besides, I think his manners are greatly improved. Everything about him has improved. He plays soccer now, can you believe it?"

"Something's not right," insisted Holly. "Why isn't the pot derivative working? When I got it from Bobbie's sister, she swore it was the highest dose they make, guaranteed to work for cancer patients getting extreme chemo."

"And that's why we need to go to dinner," said Dr. Limos, his sharp tone coming clearly over the hidden mic to Larry. "We've made well over a million dollars off of Larry, and our cash cow is about to slip right out of our grasp if we don't figure something out. So put on your big girl panties, stop arguing with me about it and go buy something distracting to wear."

There was a moment of silence, and then the slamming of a door, but Larry wasn't worried. Holly was on the hook, he knew it. And he knew something else: Holly was absolutely, positively complicit in the whole scheme to drug him up – first to lose the weight, and then to gain it all back. But *this* cash cow had turned into a bull.

And they were about to get gored.

***

Friday night, Larry sent Max and a limousine so lavish that even Holly was temporarily mollified. More so when she saw his house. She nudged Dr. Limos and whispered, "How on earth did Blubber-boy get all this money?"

"I have no idea," Limos said. "I always asked for payment up front, never had any problems. I Googled him way back in the beginning. Nothing showed up. He's a nobody. Family money would be my guess."

They looked at each other and smiled. Clever, secure, superior.

From his office, good old nobody Larry smiled, too.

***

Dinner was winding down. Larry had shown an almost embarrassing degree of enthusiasm in presenting each dish, but Holly had to admit they were unforgettable. She had somehow been charmed into a warm and nearly snark-free glow, no doubt helped along by the endless supply of excellent wine. They'd failed to learn anything meaningful about Larry's failure to gain weight on the new supplement, despite the distractibility factor of Holly's dress.

"The night, alas, is drawing to a close, and I'd like to propose a toast," said Larry, rising to his feet and pouring a measure of wine from the bottle that waited at hand. He handed out the glasses and raised his own. Holly and Dr. Limos followed suit, happy and relaxed in the wake of their wonderful meal.

"To friends," said Larry. "To those who are honest and kind. To those who go out of their way to help their fellows, to do what is right, no matter what."

"I'll drink to that," said Dr. Limos, beaming. He tossed back his glass with flush-faced abandon.

Holly quickly did the same. "So," she said, setting her glass on the table and licking her lips, "what's for dessert?"

Dr. Limos tittered. "I hate to say it, but after all I ate, I'm still strangely hungry," he said. "Is there something amazing still in the kitchen?"

"Max will be bringing it out in just a second," said Larry, gauging their reactions to the wine. "It's a recipe I got from the dessert chef at Lincoln Ristorante in New York, and as a chemist, I couldn't resist trying my hand at it —"

"They let you eat there?" asked Holly.

"You're a chemist?" said Limos at nearly the same time.

"Actually, they gave me the recipe in exchange for my promising to *never* eat there again," said Larry, giving her a good-natured smile.

"Now, where was I? Oh, yes, chemistry. It's a lot like cooking, in a lot of ways. Both a science and an art. The science part, for instance, led me to the chemical composition of the supplements you've been giving me, Dr. Limos. First, appetite suppressants, antidepressants, steroids. Ecstasy, even. Felt great, stopped eating so much, and I loved everyone I came in contact with, Doc. Really did. Best I've felt in years. Have to thank you for that. Although I have a few recommendations I might make to the next guy I run into trying to pull this con. The stuff you were using is awfully hard on the heart."

"Larry. I had no idea," said Dr. Limos, breaking into an earnest sweat. "The man I get the supplements from ... he ... wrong batch. Mistake somewhere. I would never ..."

Larry made an easygoing *shush* motion with his hand as he walked around the table to stand between them.

"But *you*, Holly. You were the one who came up with the plan to change out the steroids and the appetite suppressants for synthetic THC once I got slimmed down, so I'd start packing on the pounds again. Weren't you?" Suddenly, Larry didn't look so easy going. "You just couldn't wait to see me torn back down again, could you, bitch?"

He was bent over, screaming in her face, drops of spit flying, and she could see the old Larry, the nasty, smelly, farting, penis-chasing, fat, greasy, scheming Larry looking her right in the eye. She tried to jump out of her chair and run away.

But she couldn't move.

Gleeful, Larry straightened up and sneered at her. She could see Danny, her lover, her hero, struggling and failing to rise as well.

Larry made a 'tsking' sound. "Paralytic in the wine, so sad," he said, not looking sad at all. "Targeted. Didn't want to keep you from talking. Or swallowing. Hope you're still hungry."

Max chose that moment to come in, bearing two exquisite dessert plates crowned with rich chocolate cake and creamy gelato.

"Help us," said Holly.

"Please!" said Dr. Limos, always the more polite of the two.

Max rolled his eyes. "Like the 'please' would make a difference," he said. "I'd be all impervious, but the 'please' would warm my cold, cold heart."

Larry chortled as he wedged Holly and Dr. Limos apart and fit another chair between them. Sitting down, he gestured for Max to put down their plates. "Come on, we all know what a softy you are inside. It shows in your warm, mushy brown eyes,"

"Still payin' me ten for this?" Max asked his employer.

Larry nodded.

"Good, then, and I'll steel myself," said Max. "Now that that's out of the way, where do you want me to dump the limo and the bodies?"

"Oh, God, no," said Holly. "All this for ten thousand dollars? Dr. Limos will pay you more than that. You can't just kill us and dump the bodies. People know we came here. Lots of people. Right Danny? Tell him!"

"Not ten thousand, you stupid bimbo," said Max. "Ten million. For me to make it look like all three of us died in a horrible accident. You, me and Limos. I get a face job and a new ID though." He turned politely to Dr. Limos. "Can you beat ten mill? Now, tonight? Got it in your pocket? 'Cause I ain't waiting around for you to call your bank and your mommy and shit."

Limos hung his head. "No," he whispered.

Max grinned at Larry. "Your offer's the best one on the table. I'm outta here." Whistling, he walked out the door.

Holly looked up at Larry. "What did he mean, he's making look like all three of us died? If you aren't going to kill us, what are you going to do with us?"

Larry smiled and opened a door from the massive sideboard at one side of the room. He pulled out four sets of leather straps and cuffs and began carefully securing Holly and Dr. Limos to their chairs.

"Here's the thing, Holly, Doc." Larry was grinning again. "You don't mind if I call you Doc, do you? I feel that we've reached a new level of intimacy in our relationship – in a few minutes, you'll know why."

Dr. Limos nodded, his eyes rolling with fear.

Larry sat down between them and scooped up a small spoonful of gelato and cake. Holly's stomach growled. He gave Holly a bite first, then Dr. Limos. Hunger overrode their fear.

"See? I'm still treating you nice. Very nice. Now, isn't that good? Tasty, huh?"

Larry scooped up a spoonful of dessert and paused just short of her open mouth. "How's your appetite?"

Fat, mascaraed tears leaked down Holly's face. "I'm ..." she sniveled. "I'm hungry. Really hungry. You put something else in the wine, too, didn't you?"

"I borrowed some super-weed from a friend of mine from my old alma mater, and created a tincture out of that, which blows your friend's product out of the water. I think I may have to patent it. It's quite amazing, really."

Holly stuck out her tongue, attempting to lick the spoon.

"You really want this?" said Larry, waving it temptingly in front of her.

"I do," she said, crying harder, attempting to catch it with her mouth. "It's delicious. Like everything you made tonight."

"And just wait till I tell you the secret ingredient," said Larry, offering her another spoonful of cake.

They were just finishing dessert when Max got back.

"Deed's done," he announced cheerfully.

Holly regarded him with hostile eyes.

"Now," he said. "Don't look at me like that. I've been working for this guy since he graduated from Yale. It's a habit I've gotten into, doing what he tells me."

Dr. Limos frowned. "You two were at Yale?" he asked, glancing from Larry to Max.

"Well, I was there as a fix-it man for those Skull and Bones guys, kinda watched over them for their dads," Max said. "Met Larry when he joined the Society. When he graduated, he made me an offer I couldn't refuse and stole right away from the whole lot of 'em. Been together ever since, huh, boss?"

Larry nodded complacently.

"But Dr. Limos Googled you," said Holly. "You're nobody. He checked."

Larry grinned. "Not nobody. Just nobody that wants to be found on the Internet."

He scraped one last spoonful of cake frosting together and popped into Holly's mouth, admiring her slender neck as she swallowed it.

When she was finished, and had licked the last bit of chocolate buttercream from her lips, Larry tapped his temple thoughtfully with one finger. "Now, let's see. There was something I wanted to tell you, and I just can't remember what it was ..."

"The recipes for all these delicious dishes?" said Dr. Limos.

Larry smacked himself on the forehead. "The recipes! That's what it was. Thanks, Doc, guess I'm gonna have to keep you around for a while. Now, let's see, where do I start? Oh, yes. I wanted to make this dinner extra, extra special after I found out how far you two were willing to go to keep me hooked, to extract every last dime you possibly could, to risk my health and well-being, even my life – just to keep me coming back for your treatments, while you mocked me behind my back, made fun of me, called me Blubber-boy, for Christ's sake, fed me dangerous drugs –"

"Larry," interrupted Dr. Limos. "We never did those things. I swear to you. Whoever told you that was lying. Trying to disrupt the doctor/patient relationship. That's all. Look. Let us go. Let's talk this through."

Larry looked at Dr. Limos in complete disbelief. So did Holly. The level of the doctor's denial was unbelievable. "I *bugged* your office, Doc. And I'm a *chemist*. One of the best on the planet. I analyzed your drugs myself, once I got suspicious."

"Danny, give it up," said Holly. "He knows everything."

"It was her, I swear to you. She drugged me, too," said Dr. Limos but it was more of a question. No one bothered to reply.

"See, here was my problem," said Larry. "I've been living this super healthy lifestyle. No fats, no oils, no butter. Good for me, but not what most people go for when they think of a fancy dinner. So I go to start cooking, and there's no butter. Likewise, no lard, no olive oil, no cream ... well, you get the idea. How was I supposed to create the luscious menu I had planned for the two of you?" Larry's eyes widened in mock horror.

"Me, I opted for the Big Mac meal, myself," said Max, nonchalantly. "I don't for go for the fancy stuff, so much."

"Go to the store?" asked Dr. Limos, with a stoner glint in his eye.

"Turns out, Max had already taken the car out to pick you up for me," said Larry. "I was stranded here at the house."

Holly began to shake her head from side to side. "No," she said. "No, no, no, no, no."

"Oh, yes," said Larry. "I thought of all that fat that the two of you had lipoed off of me, that was just sitting around her in cold storage, and I thought, what could bring us closer than using my own fat in each and every dish I prepared for you tonight? So I got out one of my cryogenic storage containers and ... well, here, see for yourself."

Larry stood and walked back to the huge sideboard, where a TV was also nestled and picked up the remote that waited there. Bringing the TV to life, he started a recording of himself, waving at the camera and mugging as he used his own body fat in each and every dish he made.

"There you go," he said. "See how well it heats, what a lovely sear it put on that swordfish? And oh – look! It blended in so beautifully to the buttercream you just gobbled up, Holly! It must have been really good, because buttercream isn't even cooked, now, really, you know." He turned back to her.

Her face flushed and her throat strained. Tears rose to her reddening eyes. Her mouth opened, but no words came out. Instead, she began to vomit, a copious outpouring of all the dinner she had stuffed into her gullet throughout dinner—great gobs of chocolate cake and frosting she had eaten last, mixed with melted gelato, followed shortly by flakes of garlicky swordfish and whole capers she'd wolfed down without chewing. She was retching so hard now that bits of polenta and rock shrimp were coming out of her nose as well as her mouth, bringing long strands of mucus with them, mixed with salty tears.

Mixed with everything was the bitter wine she'd drank much, much too much of, burning now as it came back up, chunks of squash that caught in her throat and made her gag again and again as her stomach forced it out.

Larry watched her with distaste as Holly gagged and retched until her stomach was empty and everything she'd eaten and drunk that night lay on the table before her.

Holly's puking set Dr. Limos off and he began to puke as well, his vomit mixing with Holly's on the table, course after course splattering his nice understated tie and cobalt blue shirt, her beaded jet dress and copious cleavage. Max made a face and stepped away from the table, then looked apologetically at Larry. "Sorry, boss, but these shoes are brand new. I'm not offending you or anything am I?"

Larry shook his head, "Not at all, Max. They are pretty fucking revolting, aren't they?"

"Fucking pigs, boss. We gonna whack 'em now?"

Larry looked into Holly's blurry eyes, the snot and vomit covering her mouth and chin, then down at the table. "Sorry, babe. That's not how this works. Max, Wheel in that laughing gas, okay? And grab a syringe of that THC tincture. We need to get them ready for what happens next."

"What happens next?" choked out Holly.

Larry smiled down at her and made a circular motion with his pointer finger to encompass the vomit she and Limos spewed on the table. "Around here, Missy, we expect you to finish your dinner. One way or another."

He looked toward the door Max had disappeared behind and raised his voice. "Max? Fetch me that funnel and a pair of latex gloves while you're in the lab, okay? And I'm going to need a medium – ah, make that a large bucket and a scraper, to get all of this off the table, too."

It took three attempts to get Holly to hold down all of the food she'd vomited back up. Just when they thought they'd succeeded, she'd turn around and heave it up all over again, but eventually, her body stopped fighting the inevitable, and Holly's dinner stayed where Larry wanted it to.

Limos only took two tries.

Then, and only then, did Larry allow Max to cart Holly and Limos off to the specially prepared rooms he'd prepared for them, where they were carefully cleaned up and transferred to their new beds, hooked up to IV's that supplied them with a steady infusion of drugs that Larry had concocted to keep them docile, hungry, but decidedly unhappy.

It took months to build Holly and Dr. Limos' weight up to what Larry's used to be, even on a steady diet of high fat foods supplemented with Larry beautiful blubber.

Larry enjoyed spending time every day with Holly and Dr. Limos – separately, of course; he never let them see each other – stroking their fattening limbs and talking to them about how beautiful they were. Their rooms were mirror free. Even with the drugs, they seemed torn between resenting each other and clinging to happy memories in the cesspool of misery into which they'd sunk. Neither appeared to have considered the impact their imprisonment had had on the other. They were each totally mired in their own degradation.

With Larry's diabolically clever drug supplements it seemed like it took no time at all for Holly and Dr. Limos to reach their target weights. One morning, Dr. Limos waddled onto the scale, and lo and behold, the scale chimed softly, indicating his goal weight had been met. Holly had met her goal several days before, and surpassed it.

Slowing, he began changing the supplements so they'd experience their full quotient of wretchedness when they met again. Once he was sure they'd shaken off the fog, he explained he wanted to have a talk with them – together – about their futures.

Holly looked in one of the many mirrors in her room and burst into tears. "He'll never be able to love me now," she sobbed, tears running down her fat cheeks.

Limos, on the other hand, regarded his image more speculatively, but kept his mouth shut. He'd had a hefty chunk of change tucked away in a couple of offshore accounts, Larry knew. No one knew better than a man, and a rich one to boot, that chicks cared more about the wallet than the looks.

When they were all together, the two former lovebirds separated only by a curtain, Holly looked at Larry fearfully. "Are you going to kill us now?" Tears began to roll down her cheeks. Larry, sitting in front of the curtain where it ended, so that he could see both of them, offered her a Twinkie from the bowl on the table. She quickly forgot about the waterworks as she reached for it and crammed it in her mouth. On the other side of the curtain, he offered the bowl to Dr. Limos, who immediately shoved one in his mouth, too. Larry beamed with pride. He'd taught them well.

"Are you kidding? This is where it gets fun, kids. Okay, here's the deal. I'll let you go. I'll even give you five mill apiece to start over again. But there's a couple of conditions. You ready to hear them? You interested? And Limos? You may be interested to know that we produced a phony will leaving your entire estate to an imaginary nephew and collected all your assets when you 'died'. I've been holding it all for you. So that five mill is in addition to all your holdings prior to your death. You won't have lost a cent on any of this."

"Not bad," said Limos, looking thoughtful.

"And yes, that includes the offshore holdings," Larry continued.

Limos flicked a look at the curtain.

"You had offshore holdings?" she asked.

"I didn't want you to be involved in anything shady," he said. "That's all."

"Very noble," Larry assured him.

"What are the conditions?" Holly asked him.

"First, you take a new identity. I'll take care of that for you. You never tell anyone what happened here, or I take the money back. I'll be monitoring you against that possibility. Closely. Condition two: you get married and you stay together, married, for the rest of your lives. Condition three: I get to meet with you in a public place whenever I want. And condition four: you will not lose the weight, ever. Five pounds variation max, or you come back here for a tune-up."

They both stared at Larry for a beat.

"Why in public?" asked Dr. Limos.

Because you've *never been fat in public before, you stupid schmuck,* thought Larry, but he kept his thoughts to himself. "I've really developed a fondness for fresh air lately, that's all," he said, innocence incarnate.

"Sounds good to me," said Limos, shrugging as he reached for another Twinkie.

"Now, you ready to see each other again for the first time in oh-so-many months?" said Larry.

"Okay," said Limos, spraying a few Twinkie crumbs.

Holly muttered something under her breath, then shrugged.

Larry flung back the curtain.

That's when the screaming *really* started.

THE EVIL THAT MEN GOO
David W. Gammon

Somewhere on the other side of Depravity, Canada 1996

From between pursed, chapped lips a sigh of resignation drifted into the stagnant air. The scent of cheap aerosol air freshener, copper, and despair lingered. All time and significance ceased to exist within the four walls of The Trigger Finger Adult Emporium.

Dane stared in disbelief across the threadbare carpet at the spectacle before him. The mark (as his boss Mitch Savoy so affectionately referred to browsers or customers) scanned the aisles of eight by twelve video boxes as though this were the most crucial decision of his existence.

Seemingly infinite photos depicting women from all walks of life, in every conceivable dirty little position, and scenario proudly graced the covers. Gang bangs, midgets, pregnant women, geriatrics, teen-aged fantasies, inter-racial, leather and latex, bondage, and just about every other sick and twisted perversion one could desire beckoned the consumer, to *come on in big boy, and give me a try*.

Dane strummed his fingertips along the glass surface of the display case. Shaking his head and rolling his eyes, he couldn't remember the last time he'd had a smoke break or the luxury of taking a piss without interruption.

Restlessness consumed him. He paced back and forth behind the counter wishing the freak mark would hurry up and make his choice. The video cassettes were one and the same anyway. Fucking, fucking, and more fucking. One didn't need to be consumed in desperation to realize that.

Squeezing his eyes shut while clenching and unclenching his fists, he couldn't believe the girth on his prospective customer. He had to have been as round as he was tall. An undeniable wheezing and panting succession enveloped the stale cloud around the triple-x thrill seeker. Perhaps most fittingly was the fact he lingered dangerously close to the anal section. A formidable chorus of crackling pops and creaks ensued as the mark bent to retrieve a laminate box title.

Dane smirked in cynical recognition. He knew he had this one hook, line, and stinker. It seemed every asshole lurked in the Anal section sooner or later. He grimaced in revulsion at the predator's immodest track pants, descending down his over indulgent backside, revealing a cluster of matted dark hair and clusters of acne.

Although he hadn't been a clerk at The Trigger Finger for long, Dane wondered how he'd found vocation at the thirteenth acre of hell. It seemed like only yesterday he had life by the balls and not by the same manner that the same-sexed models of 'that other section' frolicked so shamelessly in a celebration of flamboyance.

Dane had everything going for him. A young, beautiful, insatiable girl named Tara, a well-paid civil servant job, a nice car, flashy threads, and a nice crib. It seemed as though he'd had everything a twenty-two year old man could ever dream of. So where did everything so suddenly go to shit?

Dane knew the answer without cause to search for very long.

They say that behind every successful man stands a woman, or something like that. Dane didn't know how true or not that was, but it seemed ever since he was unceremoniously dumped everything had gone to hell. Just like a bad country song on a vinyl forty-five, skipping perpetually, he'd lost everything one by one.

The one and only place that would take him seriously for job prospects was The Trigger Finger. He supposed he'd always be indebted to Mitch Savoy for eluding certain financial disaster. Still, he wasn't sure how much longer he could take this indignity.

Counting to ten in his head, he cleared his throat tentatively. Such a brash and excitable manuever often had dire consequences. You couldn't startle the timid, the sexually oppressed. Such an overt expression would cause the marks to engage in fight or flight according to the words of wisdom from proprietor Mitch Savoy. You had to treat customers with delicate precision. Make them comfortable, put them at ease, was his motto. Everyone that walked through the door wanted, desired, needed something. It was our mission at The Trigger Finger to help them execute their shot and go home with a bull's eye every time.

Dane was not in the mood for any philosophy, perverted or otherwise. He wanted a smoke, damn it. Even more so, he wanted this creep out.

His telepathic rays of banishment must have worked on some level. With a grunt and greasy fart the mark stood at last and pivoted towards the cashier. On tree trunk-like legs the mastodon waddled. A flimsy jersey rode up his torso, unveiling cellulite tattooed, paisley flesh. His navel had to have been so descending it was as dark and desolate a mystery as his very presence within these four walls.

Dane psyched himself up for the inevitable interaction. The list of things he hated about the job far surpassed any fringe benefits. Having to actually touch and speak with the marks made his stomach lurch.

The parade of jiggling flesh, left then right and repeat, almost shook the room. Behind the cheap dot matrix computer, Dane took his post. Silently, he blessed the three feet of aluminum, glass, and press board barrier between them.

Thick, sausage like fingers gripped the film case before gingerly placing it on the counter. *Carwash Debutantes*, how original. Dane struggled to refrain from sighing once again. Onto the laminate side he flipped the case, searching for its call number. As he strode past hundreds of numerically filed video cassettes he reached to retrieve its match.

"May I have your phone number, sir?" He refused to meet any kind of eye contact and was willing to bet Baby Huey here felt exactly the same with relief.

"Ah, ah, ah," he stammered at once and Dane recoiled from the sour stench of coffee, sour milk, and rotting flesh. The mark seemed to be searching his cerebral cortex for just the right, most profound proclamation.

For a brief moment Dane thought his mark was considering buying the tape. Rare, yet not entirely unheard of, some smut connoisseurs actually paid top dollar- forty to sixty bucks- to own these things. These would-be wankers would actually shell out enough cash for Dane to easily live off for a week. There was no accounting for taste, or sanity, for that matter. Besides, if his sales figures didn't start getting closer to the quota of four hundred dollars a shift, he'd be out of a job in no time.

"No, no. I'd like to um..."

For a second or two, Dane actually felt pity for the mark, as filthy and repulsive as he was. Clearly, he was struggling. "I'd like to watch it here."

A flurry of sucker punches just about keeled Dane over. He hadn't seen that coming. The mark's face was crimson with embarrassment.

It was one thing to buy or rent these tapes, often times returned with unidentified mysterious sludge on the plastic; it was a complete crime against nature to watch them *here*.

A couple of weeks ago the fearless leader of The Trigger Finger contracted to have a total of eight Beater booths installed. These state of the art, erotic viewing destinations boasted the ability to watch a full length colour feature within the luxury of your own private seating area. You could fast forward, rewind, pause, and play until your heart—or willy—was content, as Mitch Savoy would so eloquently put it. One could also purchase tokens to watch three minute clips of any of six featured channels.

Dane had heard of this sort of thing in New York City and thought they were called Peep Shows or something like that. He'd thought they were an urban legend or exaggerated.

Never in his worst nightmares would he have believed what goes on in there. The primal shrieks, moans, and cries were enough to drive any man around the bend. And the stench that came waffling out of there? Forget about it.

Dane grew instantly nauseous at the thought of having to clean, disinfect, and deodorize after this trailer park behemoth had his way with himself. *Carwash Debutantes* or not, he just knew this mark's disregard for personal hygiene was a surefire indicator of how he'd leave a jerk off junction.

Their eyes met in a taboo, impervious stare. Mere seconds passed that could have equated eternity. Dane could justify just about everything within the confines of the reputable Trigger Finger. The rubber dildos, the thirty five varieties of vibrators, butt-plugs, strap-ons, anal beads, prosthetic vaginas; even the ludicrous inflatable dolls staring infinitely with their patented O mouths had their place for the sexually adventurous and deviant. He far from condoned everything, but at least understood their ultimate purpose. Those infernal beater booths, on the other hand, that was where he drew the line. The filthy mongrels had to have some other sort of escape.

Submissiveness prevailed at last as he set the cassette down and muttered.

"That'll be eight dollars, sir."

"Eight dollars? You've got to be kidding me."

All of a sudden, the timid browser became the irate consumer. Was he kidding? He was *actually* going to argue economics within a seedy porn shop?

"I'll have you know Candyland downtown charges six. This is..." He stammered, growing increasingly red by the minute. "Highway robbery, no other term for it." From seemingly out of nowhere he produced a stick of beef jerky, chomping and grinding through yellow stained incisors.

Dane was tempted to retort that his fat ass wasn't in Candyland

and maybe if he didn't indulge in quite so many bon-bons and ginger-bread houses he could go on an actual date instead of getting better acquainted with the *Carwash Debutantes*.

Instead he resigned to inevitable reason, apologized for the prices, and said he'd speak to the manager about it. The mark seemed to calm a little at this. Thank God for small favours. A coronary was the last thing Dane needed on his hands at the moment.

"Well, see that you do." He slapped a crinkled twenty down on the counter. "Queue me up, will you, buddy?" He gnawed into another chomp of gristly, greasy beef. "But give me five minutes. Got some pork rinds in the car, nothing like titties and snacks, am I right?"

He actually winked.

Dane grappled with the urge to purge and run.

The clock's digital face read 10:35, which meant he'd only been open for an hour and a half. To obscure the view for minors and protesting religious activists, the store's windows were tinted. It could be pitch black outside and Dane would never know the difference. The Trigger Finger seemed to have its own principals of relativity and reality.

It wasn't long before the mark had returned from his pork rinds expedition. He waddled back in through the exit door and crept around the pressboard configuration of the viewing rooms.

Dane felt a silent expression of gratitude after being spared another awkward confrontation with the morbid mark. Into the VCR he set the tape, making sure it was rewound. After all, it was only kind to rewind. He chuckled a little at the thought. Even the realm of smut had its moral codes, and failure to rewind was clearly an infraction of such.

The paper-thin separation wall between the counter and the beater booth left damned little to the imagination. Pork rinds and jerky had made his way around the corner and was shutting the booth's door with a loud creak and moan. At first Dane feared the mark would get stuck. Visions of heaving a sweaty, distressed customer with tattered grease-stained track pants around his ankles through the door made him shudder violently.

It wasn't until he heard the tell-tale sound of the latch clicking that he eased a little and proceeded to push play.

A plastic rustling sound echoed through the remaining seven empty chambers. It seemed even the pork rinds were protesting the lewd conduct about to unfold before them.

Crossing his arms, Dane closed his eyes and leaned against the wall behind him. Something was unsettling, something out of the ordinary. He had the sinking feeling that he was forgetting something.

He opened his eyes in a burst of panic and frantically checked the calendar.

"Oh shit. Shit, shit, shit!" Today was the fifteenth, which meant his car insurance was supposed to come out of his bank account. He had completely forgotten. What with the break-up, move, and change of jobs he'd neglected to make sure he'd socked enough away for this month's insurance. It wouldn't be such a big deal ordinarily. If this had been the first infraction, a simple phone call and assurance to make up the overdraft charges would make all well. This was, in fact, the third infraction, and he'd surely have his coverage revoked.

The only saving grace made his heart sink and acid lurch into his throat. He'd have to call his mother.

She could make the deposit and he'd pay her back. Simple enough right? Maybe in anyone else's family. His mother would not out and out refuse, but she'd be sure to make Dane sweat it out after thoroughly expressing disappointment. A guilt trip would surely follow, with pleas of how she'd done him so wrong in his upbringing.

Dane considered letting the payment bounce anyway, but if she heard about it, she'd never let him live it down. Talk about a rock and a hard place.

He clenched his eyes shut and gripped the bridge of his nose with his thumb and finger. A headache of epic proportions was forming.

With the receiver cocked between his shoulder and cheek, he dialled the number from memory. Then the inconceivable was unleashed.

From the perimeter walls, the speakers ignited into a celebration of funky, disco-type beats, threatening to level the entire Trigger Finger from the foundation up.

Startled into reprieve, Dane yanked the phone away from his ear. It rang once. Twice.

The techno symphony segued into a barrage of banshee-like cries of ecstasy and agony. Dominant male verbal pillaging seethed and frothed.

"Take it, you sudsy winch. Scrub my crankshaft."

"Yes! Yes! Yessss!"

"Hello...hello?"

Dane heard a distraught voice faintly over the cacophony. He slammed the receiver back into the phone cradle.

Oh, dear God. Don't tell me she heard all of that.

He thumped his forehead into the wall over and over. Just when he thought it couldn't possibly get worse!

The skin flick's overbearing audio ceased just as quickly as it had begun.

A moan foreign to The Trigger Finger's typical utterances ricocheted off the plaster walls. Mumblings of "Not feeling so good." bombarded Dane's disbelief. Further moans, now increased in volume and intensity.

The phone chirped into life next to Dane's quivering arm. He laughed at the notion of almost having a heart attack. Still giggling a little with embarrassment, he retrieved the receiver. "Hello Trigger Fin—" He began to spout, smiling.

The speakers burst into life, impossibly louder than before.

"My, my, we *do* seem to have a very dirty undercarriage!" purred a sultry, faceless vixen, undoubtedly stacked with peaks of silicone.

"Dane? Dane...whatever is that awful racket?"

He slammed the phone into its cradle again, cursing.

A further vengeful onslaught of moaning eclipsed the soundtrack. Dry heaving followed. Slurring and sputtering ensued behind a thin vale of gagging.

"Going to be sick," came the anguished voice from the beater booth.

Dane dashed down the electrical tape and cigarette burned carpet. Musings of no, no, no, no cascaded down his gape.

Make no mistake about it, The Trigger Finger did its best to discourage any unsavoury behaviour behind closed doors in the viewing area. Suffice to say, at least they did come prepared in the event someone were to employ such disregard for personal hygiene. Wastebaskets were placed strategically inside each booth, along with tissues and disinfectant. Why nine out of ten people decided to deploy their misgivings wherever fate would find it was beyond Dane.

A wet, gurgling yack exploded into the stale air. Splashes of half digested grime ... jerky and pork rinds, painted the walls and cheap linoleum floor below.

Dane smashed his fist against the wall again and again. Nothing was worth this. You couldn't pay enough to mop up sludge and filth and peddle perversity. And for a slave's wage? He was *so* done with this place. And now, mopping up puke from some asshole? Against the cheap pressboard, he bounced his forehead, rolling it back and forth. Little did he know a tiny, miniscule crack in the linoleum floor, unseen to the naked eye, opened up ever so subtly. The bile, chunks of half-chewed jerky, and wisps of rinds spiraled into the abyss like a drain before the crack closed back up, tighter than it was before.

"Well, I guess it could have been worse," Dane gargled from behind his mask. Doing his best to sound amicable, he scrubbed with gloved hands and ammonia. Scents so overbearing they made him cringe each time he inhaled assaulted him. The mark did precious little to help, hovering over him, refusing to leave.

"Look, why not call it a day and I'll credit you a free rental for your trouble," Dane offered while hacking and gagging. Silently, he cursed his coworkers, Curtis and Frank, for being so insolent and useless. Would they do something so undignified as to scrub these walls? He thought not. Somehow, he couldn't shake the uneasy feeling that there should have been more of a mess. From the sounds of things, he was certain to find a tsunami of spew all over the place. Thank God for small favours once again.

The remainder of the morning was at least uneventful. *As uneventful as life in a porn shop could possibly be*, Dane thought sourly. A couple of marks came in to buy magazines and rent a few flicks, it being two for one Tuesdays and all. It was nothing out of the ordinary, really.

Just when he was about to step out for that much needed smoke break, the overhead door chimed, signalling another potential customer. Dane did his best to summon a warm salutation without coming across as pretentious or creepy. His mark was quick to the draw, wasting very little time in making a selection. In no time flat he honed in on the European locale and chose a leather and latex type soiree. *Hey, whatever floats your boat.* Digging out his change, the jittery mark laid out several dollar coins. For some reason, he refused to meet eye contact which was more than fine with Dane.

"These god damned Limeys always get the hottest tail. Ever notice that?"

Grabbing the corresponding cassette, Dane barely registered what the mark had said.

"I'd do just about anything to be one of those dudes. I mean look at these bitches."

While Dane opened his mouth to retort he was cut off. "Eight bucks to watch it here, right?"

It was next to impossible not to show his frustrated disapproval. "Sure. Take booth two … best sound in there."

Once the mark made his frenzied retreat around the corner, Dane laughed to himself and hoped the kink enthusiast enjoyed the smell of vomit.

Along with a menial job, there were, of course, menial tasks to do daily. If there's time to lean, there's time to clean, Savoy always said. Through the ridiculously outdated dot matrix computer, Dane sent a series of commands to generate a late list. Calling customer's homes was always a big deal and had to be treated with the upmost confidentiality. Yet when some deadbeat took the liberty of withholding some of the hottest releases for days on end, they had to be notified.

Depressing *69 to block the store's phone number on the recipient's call display, he called the first tardy perpetrator. It was no surprise to receive voice mail. In Dane's humble estimation, someone who rented and horded *Transsexual Bus Stop Tales* didn't deserve such a courtesy, but protocol was protocol. Regardless of his politics towards depravity he left a brief, vague message resisting disclosure and checked the item off the list.

By now he was sure the second peepshow mark of the day was working himself into a sweaty tizzy. Dane stifled a laugh while moving onto the next caller. Maybe the freak considered regurgitated jerky and pork rinds an aphrodisiac. At least he was good enough to turn the volume down to virtually mute.

The remainder of the short late list was pretty much no answers, busy signals, and one out of service number. There were previsions one could take to deal with AWOL renters. The sympathetic side of Dane hoped it wouldn't come to such embarrassing measures.

Inside the beater booth, the PVC fan must have made quick work of his European splendor. From the black and white security monitor, Dane saw him saunter around the corner, towards the rear exit, in that tell-tale stride that looked like one was trying just a little too hard to walk without conviction. The walk of shame was one in the same, regardless of who possessed it. In the end, they were filthy animals and no amount of overcompensation could hide their dirty little secrets.

Despite the mark's swift retreat, Dane was oblivious to the copious globs of spunk trickling down the stained linoleum floor. He was spared any impromptu cleaning as the jizz flowed like a ravine into the canyon-like crevice, which devoured its prize before closing back to the surface.

Early afternoon hours in the Trigger Finger saw a little more traffic. There weren't any paying customers, but at least there were a few deliveries, like the magazine guy and a couple of video distribution reps who dropped off a shipment. Dane really didn't mind the arbitrary tasks of the job. He'd much rather consume his efforts in the mundane than serve whack job customers – pardon the pun – that discouraged his faith in humanity. It was closing in on two o'clock and he hadn't even thought of that smoke break he was fixated on earlier. His shift quota was pathetically low, but what could a guy do? It wasn't as though he could stand on the street corner and solicit customers in. That's all he needed … to be arrested and charged with lewd conduct. No thanks.

From out of his inner leather jacket pocket he went to retrieve his smokes and figured it was well deserved. As though a psychic radar was mounted on the outside front door, the infernal chime burst into life, signalling another mark.

Dane groaned in defeat and stuffed his smokes back into his pocket. Oh great, just great. *This* guy he recognized as a regular. Dane wanted nothing to do with the likes of Julian.

It was never officially divulged what exactly Julian's sexual orientation was. Not that it mattered, of course, in a place like the Trigger Finger. Julian was a metrosexual at very least. Bronzed in a perpetual spray-on tan, he always sported an expensive haircut, wore expensive, trendy clothing and was drenched in high-end cologne. His gestures were flamboyant and flighty and he was a drunk. Three sheets to the wind on cheap wine. Dane couldn't recall ever seeing a time when Julian was even remotely sober. He always rented all guy compilations, the kind where nothing but GQ-type models bludgeon one another's backsides in excess of four hours. Yet, on occasion, he'd rent all lesbian flicks. To say Julian was a sexual enigma was a mild understatement.

"Wassup, Cherry Cheese Danish?" Julian slurred while colliding with a turnstile of DVDs. If it were anything else, Dane would've been furious. *These DVD things will never catch on anyway.* Tried and true perverts were fixed in their ways. No way they'd subscribe to a flash in the pan technology like a DVD.

"Julian, you know I hate it when you call me that." There wasn't much use in arguing, but he really didn't have the patience for drunks right now.

"Oh lighten up, buttercup. You're always so tense." Julian stood three feet from the counter, yet somehow managed to defy physics, leaning casually. From seemingly out of nowhere he plunked down a VHS tape, slipped, and dropped it to the floor. A hysterical round of laughter ensued as he struggled to bend and pick it up.

After three or four tries he was semi-successful and slid it back across the counter. With an effeminate wave of the hand he stifled a belch and began to giggle. "I need you to do me a flavor," he said.

Oh, for the love of God.

"What, Julian? What exactly do I need to do as a favour?"

"Hey, hey. Easy now, big guy. You owe me. I'm like your bestest of best customers ever."

To fully illustrate his point, Julian waved his arms in windmill fashion.

Dane felt sour bile rising in his throat.

"I'm listening...."

"My condo's being fumigated. Can't go back in until tonight. Do a brother from another mother a serious solid and let me watch this here, huh?"

Dane reluctantly inspected the discarded cassette on the counter. *Cruising*. How appropriate.

"Julian, this isn't even our tape. I can't let you watch this here."

He swayed back and forth before the cash register, nearly colliding with a lubricant and condom display.

"I know it's not your tape." He leaned in uncomfortably close. "This is high end, *caballero*. Jeff Stryker." He actually squealed a succession of notes even a choirboy had no business reaching. "The package...." He gestured towards his crotch while gyrating his hips.

"All right, all right! Jesus, Julian." Dane snatched the cassette and queued it into the player. "Just promise me you'll never make me watch that spectacle again."

Julian's assent came beaming through an onslaught of uncontrollable applause.

"Booth number four and-"

"I know. I know handsome. Best sound."

Dane grimaced as he watched the drunken fool blow him a kiss.

It wasn't long after Julian had not so unceremoniously exited the display area and retreated to the private booths that the phone rang. A long distance tone, Dane was puzzled. He picked it up on the fourth ring. "Trigger Fin—" was all he managed.

"Dane? Dane is that you? I heard your voice hours ago, but we were cut off. What on earth is going on over there?"

"Mom? Oh my God, Mom! I'm so sorry. Listen, I'm really sorry about earlier..."

"All that wretched screaming and moaning. Were you calling from a brothel? I never raised my boy to be associating with the likes of such."

Dane's brow furrowed as he rubbed his temple with his free hand.

"Mom, no. I can explain. The walls are really thin here. Those were the Gordons next door. You know, the one's that just got married?"

"Daniel and Michelle? Oh my yes. Lovely couple, how nice for them. Why can't you meet a nice girl, Dane?"

"Come on, Mom." He groaned, agitated and embarrassed for such a bold lie.

"Then again, she didn't sound so nice while enamoured, now did she?" A burst of mischievous laughter ensued.

"Mom!" Dane gasped, nearly choking.

He'd just about forgotten about Julian. Thankfully, there seemed to be no audio attached to the Jeff Stryker aficionado's tape.

"Oh, Cherry Cheese Danish...."

"What on earth?" Dane's mother intrigued.

"What the hell?" he spewed simultaneously.

Once again, the singsong chirping that only the truly flamboyant ever achieve.

"Cherry Cheese Danish...Daddy's got to tinkle."

"Dane, for the love of all that is holy, what is going on over there?"

"Mom, hang on. Better yet, let me call you back."

"Sonny boy, I haven't all day to sit beside the telephone and—" Dane clicked the receiver before his mother could finish her thought.

"Come on, big guy. I really have to twinkle."

"Julian, I swear to God if you make me come over there..." Dane was outraged now. Veins bulged on his neck like venom-filled snakes ready to strike. Commotion ensued. Blundering bangs, crashes, and curses followed. It was evident Julian was trying to exit the infamous booth and having damned little success in the process.

Storming down the floor, he charged towards the booth. He wasn't entirely sure what he was going to do, but he'd had just about enough.

"Julian, if you don't get it together right now, I'm calling the cops. I mean it. I..."

He never had the chance to finish his threat, empty or otherwise. Standing on the threshold of the forbidden, marked by carpet and decrepit, worn linoleum, Dane stood frozen in disbelief.

A steady stream of yellowish liquid came pouring onto the floor from inside booth number four. And was that *steam* rising from the discharge?

Rage roared within his blood.

"That's it, Julian. That's fucking *it*. You've really done it this time." Dane raced toward the phone. "I'm calling the cops right now, and if I were you, I'd get the hell out of there."

He raced to the other side of the counter, nearly tripping on a tattered piece of lifted duct tape. His trembling hands fumbled over the keypad. An audible click ignited with authority. The room hung in eerie silence. Door number four creaked open with methodical unease.

"I'm sorry," came a faint mumbling. "I'll go."

"For God's sake, Julian." He returned the telephone to its cradle. "Just who exactly do you think has to clean up this mess?" On very tentative legs, he whisked back towards the beater booths. A resounding chirp bleeped above the door. Dane whirled his view towards the front door.

Nobody was there.

It must have been the back door. Slowly, with one cerebral, methodical step after another, he approached the waiting disaster. If he'd been a fraction of a second earlier, Dane might have marvelled at the formidable crack in the floor acting as a sponge, absorbing every last drop of the urine induced puddle before stitching itself back together, imperceptible to the naked eye.

With mop in hand, Dane stood on the viewing room floor, beyond absolute puzzlement. He scratched his head and glared, unblinking.

It just doesn't make any sense.

Muttering to himself, he tried to piece it together.

What if it was all just a sick joke?

It wasn't beyond Julian to pull such outrageous behaviour. But clearly he had heard and seen him pissing a steady stream onto the floor. He kicked his sneakered toe back and forth.

Nothing. The floor was dry as a bone. It wasn't entirely inconceivable that Julian somehow wiped up the mess before his hasty retreat, but would he just leave his prized video behind? Dane didn't think so. Julian was a lot of things, but forgetful was not one of them. At last, Dane sighed and swung the mop handle over his shoulder. Thank God he didn't have to clean it up.

Good enough. It was done.

It was that time in the day where Dane could finally begin to get excited about blowing this popsicle stand. At three thirty he was a half hour away from shift change and leaving the day from hell behind like a bad memory.

Some customers came and went, nothing too eventful. More movie rentals, a couple of low-end vibrator purchases, and a nutty guy who blew seventy five bucks on digest magazines. You know the kind, with campy titles like *Lusty Layover* and *Wet T-Shirt Wenches*, penned by such inspired authors as Dick Givens and Rick O'Shea? Who made up this drivel anyway? All in all, it wasn't a bad shift. Nowhere near enough to make Savoy happy, but what the hell. Dane would deal with that another day.

The cash register was ajar, while each of the coin trays were sorted through. Dane languidly counting through each. He always liked to be more than prepared when judgement time came. Just off to his side, the phone burst into life once again.

Shit! He'd totally forgotten about calling his mother back. She'd be livid by now.

At this stage, he didn't know if he had it in him to have to endure yet another lecture about effective budgeting and his failure to achieve it. On the third ring he picked up, taking a deep breath.

"Mom, listen, I'm sorry I never called back. I just got really busy and—"

A sputtering round of hacking and coughing cut him off at the pass.

"Hello?" A groggy voice groaned through the receiver. "Dane? Is that you?"

"Curtis? Holy crap you sound awful dude."

"Yeah." He wailed and moaned a little more abundantly than necessary. "Listen, man. I'm not going to be able to make it in." He emphasized each word with dramatic flair.

"Not coming in? What do you mean? It's three thirty already. You need to call Mitch about this."

"I tried. His cell phone is off. Dude, listen to me. I'm dying over here. I can't even get out of bed."

"Curtis. Brother, come on, man. Did you call Frank?"

"Out of town, remember? Some Comic Con shit or something, booked it off weeks ago."

Dane bit his lower lip enough to make him wince.

"No way. Uh-uh. Don't do this to me, Curtis. I can't do a double. I'll lose it."

"Sorry, thought I better call at least."

"Curtis, don't you hang up. *Curtis? Curtis?*"

Dane was screaming at a dial tone.

"Shit! God damn it, no!" He threw the receiver against the wall and the entire phone flew off the counter, dangling precariously above the floor.

Sighing in complete defeat, he picked up the phone, once more returning it to its mate.

If he'd had the strength, Dane would have wept like a baby as he pushed the cash register in and slumped down to the floor.

He had no idea how long he'd been sitting there. When a man gets lost in his own darkened thoughts, re-evaluating his life, succumbing to simmer within the juices of his own mediocrity, time ceases to exist. Dane was so submerged in his bout of self-pity he didn't even finch when the overhead chime went off. A muffled chorus of giggling gradually lifted him from his self-loathing séance.

"Buddy? What you doing down there? Having a party-of-one circle jerk?" A hyena-like cackle scraped his nerves.

Dane braced his hand to his side before rising to a kneeling position. He clutched the edge of the counter with a bone-white grip and pulled himself to his feet.

"What can I do for you?" He muttered under his breath and looked up at his potential paying prospect. A grimy looking biker type with a long beard, bandana, and every other accessory in what must be a standard biker's handbook glared back at him. Decked out in leather and denim, the girth of his upper arms far exceeded that of Dane's thighs. Around one python-sized arm he squeezed a nattering blonde bimbo, equally decked out in leather and denim.

"Tube's on the fritz at home. Want to watch some quality A flicks with my old lady here. What do you say?" He flopped down a copy of *Blue Movie*, the latest Jenna Jameson feature that had taken the XXX world by storm as of late.

Dane opened his mouth to retaliate.

"Is there a problem?" Biker dude began to crack one knuckle after the next.

"Yeah, is there a problem." His blonde bimbo imitated in nails to chalk board fashion. She resembled Jenna Jameson in a way. If you took away the acne, frizzy hair and crooked teeth they could pass for sisters. All right, sisters from another family. Maybe. She smacked her chewing gum, then inserted her finger into her mouth, hooked a piece of it, and twirled the stretchy gum impatiently around her index finger.

Dane shuddered. He wasn't up for another confrontation, especially one of this magnitude.

"No, no problem at all." His face began to redden from sheer frustration.

He tried to walk casually over to the wall of tapes where its match would be and nearly tripped. Couple of the year gabbed on about something, giggling to themselves.

Dane wondered how this day could possibly get any worse.

"There you go, sir. Why don't you take booth number four?"

Man mountain Harley Davidson slapped down a twenty.

"Here, buddy. Keep the change."

They walked hand in hand in the direction of the beater booth. "Oh, by the way, how's the sound?"

"Oh it's the best sir! The absolute best!" This time it was Dane's turn to duck and conceal a round of vengeful snickering.

A tattered old office chair is where Dane decided to perch after firing up *Blue Movie* for the match made in Hell. It may have only been five o'clock, but at least he could sit and read the latest Stephen King novel. He'd be damned if he invested one more iota into this hole for the rest of the day. The extra hours might have been nice if it wasn't pigeon feed to begin with.

The read was turning out to be a most welcome escape from his personal hell. It didn't take long to get completely engrossed in the adventure. Leaning back in his chair, he allowed the literary odyssey to take control. The overheard chimes hadn't ignited in what seemed forever and Dane drifted further away.

The last thing he wanted to think about was what could have been going on in that scuzzy little cubicle. *Blue Movie*, by God's grace, had a great deal of dialogue between baloney pony scenes. He wasn't sure if he could take any more debauchery at this moment.

Just when he was getting completely fixated on what was going on in Castle Rock, squealing erupted from the booth's corridors.

Dane wished for a set of headphones, a lobotomy, cardiac arrest. Anything.

"Um, yeah, Daddy you know that's how I like it. Give it to me, big boy."

This was beyond surrealism.

A guttural roar burst into the stagnant air. Dane shuddered and dropped his paperback. The primal sound of flesh pounding upon flesh consumed him. No longer could he discern whether the porn tape was accountable for such atrocities or the biker was reaming the holy hell out of his chosen squeeze.

Testosterone-fuelled grunts and submissive wails shook the plaster within the Trigger Finger.

"Oh, oh, oh God, yes!"

Dane rolled his eyes and was tempted to stand up and just walk out the back door, never to look back. At very least he hoped the portly biker was a minute man and would do his business and dispatch the premises as soon as humanly possible.

No such luck.

The clapping, smacking sounds grew in volume and intensity. If Dane had not known better, he'd swear he was killing the trollop.

"Oh, *yeah*, Daddy! Yes! Yes! I'll bet that slut Clarice never gave it to you like this!"

The sound of wet denim being ripped, amplified

"Ouch! Fuck. You son of a bitch!" Further banshee like squealing resumed, not unlike a sow being led to slaughter.

"If I told you once, I told you a god damned thousand times, Vinny, the exit door is off limits. You shithead, look what you made me do!"

A burst of maniacal laughter.

"Oh, so it's funny, huh? You want to be the one to tell that sorry sap that he's got to clean up shit off the god damned walls? Stop laughing, you prick. I'm not going to be able to sit for a week."

Dane shut off the VCR. As riveting as the dialogue between Jeanna Fine and Jenna

Jameson was, these would-be Hillbilly sweethearts far surpassed anything they'd conjured

up. On shaky, quivering legs he stood.

"Look, I don't want any trouble. Why don't you two clean yourselves up and get on out of here? I have to close soon and I don't want the two of you to be inconvenienced in any way."

The closing part was a lie.

"I'm going to step out the front door for a smoke. Why don't you two head on out the back?" Dane swept into the adjacent makeshift bathroom and grabbed his leather jacket. He hoped to God that their ability to see reason was as crystal clear as his own. Taking a leap of faith, Dane exited the front door in search of sweet nicotine release.

Little did he know the vagrants of choice had fled through the rear entrance in silent compliance. Along the linoleum floor, the hairline fracture descended into abyss. Sinewy, crimson appendages slithered out onto a parallel plane. Blindly grasping for substance and life, all remnants of fecal matter were being swept towards the cavernous gap. An unearthly shrill pierced the night before descending back to the depths below.

By the time Dane had returned, his head was more than a little swimmy with a head rush.

Something sinister had taken place in the infamous booth number four and he cared not to charter that territory. At some point before the end of the evening he'd surely have to give a thorough once over to the viewing rooms.

Anytime but now.

For now he was content in doing his best to distract his notion that something very bizarre was going on with the viewing rooms.

Dane did his best to keep busy for the remainder of the late afternoon to evening. He figured if he was trapped here until eleven o'clock, he might as well make the best of things. Time only went by faster that way. No point in brooding over his misfortune.

It wasn't as if Curtis or Frank maximized their efforts in order to provide sufficient upkeep to the shop. Dane decided to fill a bucket with soapy water and give the box covers a once over.

Lugging over his bucket, a rag and some paper towels, he decided to start by the front door. An extravagant selection of amateur movies donned the dusty walls. Dane chuckled a little over the absurdity of it all. Imagine someone who fornicated before a video camera having the audacity to call herself an amateur. Something about doing the nasty with a complete stranger with a crew of onlookers in attendance positively screamed professional slut.

Wringing out the soaked rag he hummed a little tune to lighten the mood. The disturbing behaviour of the vagabond couple unnerved him still. Just what kind of degenerates bumped uglies in public, anyhow? He supposed there might be some kind of psychological thrill at the risk of being caught; he knew full well some people got their ya-ya's from knowing others were watching. But to actually try to forcefully add anal probing to any repertoire, especially when one participant wasn't exactly in full consent—that was just flat out disturbing.

Dane dreaded the notion of inspecting the booths for projectile stool. He'd get to it eventually, just not now. The booths always gave him the heebie-jeebies, and if there was a mess it wasn't going anywhere anytime soon.

The amateur section was as close to pristine as anyone could hope for. A white glove test would surely reveal not the faintest indicator of dust.

Dane proceeded into the Couples Appeal section. Here were a bevy of beautiful women dressed in every conceivable outfit, from pirates to schoolgirls, even sanatorium garb. He supposed this is where overzealous boyfriends and husbands tried to convince their significant others that porno video watching was right for them.

Bending down to retrieve his bucket, Dane was startled when the front door whooshed open, nearly colliding with his backside.

"All right, where is he?"

Dane stood staring, mouth agape, paralyzed in amorous awe. An Amazon, buxom and voluptuous, stood before him.

"You may want to close that before you drool all over yourself." She smirked through quivering lips. Shimmering emerald eyes pierced directly into Dane's core. Her bronzed complexion was flawless, accenting golden corn rollers that dangled precariously down her back.

Dane shook his head, felt his face flush. "Where's uh, who?"

"Don't give me that. Did he pay you to shut up? God damn, Vinny," she muttered to herself. "Need me to spell it out for you?" She glared at him with hands on hips, leaning in close. An aroma of vanilla and strawberries plumed from the nape of her silky smooth neck.

"Fat, greasy biker guy? Long grey beard, leather and jeans?" Each syllable sounded like poison on her tongue. "Did he come in here with some cheap looking crackhead whore?"

"Uh—look miss. There was someone here earlier, but I don't know what that has to do with—"

"Oh, so he *was* here!" The goddess pinwheeled her arms. "Good boy." She placed a tender hand upon his shoulder that made Dane shiver with ecstasy.

Suddenly an epiphany hit him with such monumental understanding his eyes just about burst from their sockets.

The Amazonian was already making her way into the display floor. She scanned the display shelves, seething.

"Um, say, aren't you, um-"

She whirled around so swiftly her corn rolls just about whipped Dane's face.

"Yeah, yeah. Janessa Del Rio. Get over it, buddy."

A smile of gratification flashed upon Dane's profile, so intense it was a wonder his lips didn't split. Del Rio was a renowned feature exotic dancer who travelled all over Canada and the United States. Her shows were legendary with a burlesque type feel and, of course, an erotic subtext so undeniable she rendered men into gibbering, drooling school boys. Dane had never had the pleasure of seeing her show, but had seen her on covers of countless softcore magazines in the store.

"Wow. I've never had, like, a celebrity in here or anything-"

"Look, kid. Celebrity or not, I'm just a woman who puts on her pants one leg at a time, just like everyone else." She sighed and closed her eyes. "I'm sorry. I don't mean to be a complete bitch."

Janessa placed one tender hand upon his shoulder again. Dane was certain if this kept up much longer, he'd cream his jeans.

"It's just, that disgusting slob that was in here? Vinny? He's my manager and fiancée. Or at least he *was*. Just wait until I get through with him. He's been chasing these skanks around lately. I followed his hog earlier tonight and was sure he came in here. Please tell me he didn't fuck her in here."

Her eyes were so angelic at that moment, so blissfully scorned it made Dane feel light-headed and spaghetti-legged all at the same time.

"I don't know what to tell you, Ms. Del Rio. I-" Before he could finish, Janessa had taken his hand and led him towards the viewing rooms.

"I'll bet the creep did her in there, didn't he? Such a scumbag." Tears welled up in her eyes.

"Look, miss I-"

"Don't you dare lie to me, kid. I don't care what he gave you or what he said. He did, didn't he?"

She now had both hands on his shoulders, pleading, gazing directly into the windows of his soul. Dane could do nothing but nod solemnly and look down at the floor.

"Well, well. And the truth shall set you free." Janessa paced back and forth, whipping her corn rolls into a frenzy. She whipped back around, nearly crashing her exquisite peaks into him. "What's your name, kid?"

"Oh-ah, sorry. Where are my manners? It's Dane." With a shaky reflex, he held out his hand.

"You know what they say, Dane. Two can play at that game." She swirled her index finger on his chest and gripped the back of his neck. Into his ear she purred. "Now how about you go ahead and lock up for a few minutes. I assure you, this won't take long."

Dane gulped and just about bowled over the display counter, frantically searching for his keys.

After Janessa twisted his rubber arm, she asked him to put on some sexy music, something a girl could grove to. Dane had only the radio, but was ecstatic to find Toronto's local alternative station was playing Nine Inch Nails' "Closer."

He'd wheeled out the decrepit swivel chair from behind the counter. Janessa insisted she commence a little show of her own, close to where Vinny had defiled that skank.

"I wanna fuck you like an animal..."

Grinding and gyrating to the techno beats, Janessa's thighs caressed Dane's torso. She leaned in close, licking his ear, purring sensual hot breath. With the grace of an angel, she swirled the chair around with her knee. Dane's heart thumped in his chest. He stared at the cheap pine wall. Janessa peeled out of her white tank top and shimmied her tights down to her ankles in one fluid motion.

Kicking the chair back around, Dane couldn't possibly suppress his exhilaration at the sight of her mammoth mocha mammories. The vixen leaned dangerously close, swaying what God and likely a couple of gifted surgeons had given her. Her areolas alone, puckered and glistening, had to have been the size of Dane's entire face. Clad only in a glittery, skimpy g-string, she turned around and ground on his eager lap.

Contorting her hips, she bobbed and swished this way and that. With trembling arms, Dane raised his hands. Janessa sensed his enthusiasm, interlocking his fingers with her own and navigating each digit onto the swell of her chest. She moaned with unbridled approval, leaning her back into him. Just when things couldn't possibly get hotter and heavier, a heavy pounding started at the back door.

"Damn it!" they both shrieked in unison. In one fell swoop, Janessa stood and retrieved her top. She was dressed once again before Dane could even catch his breath.

"Hey, come on, open up. I know you're still open."

Dane could have screamed in frustration.

"Look. I don't want to get you into any trouble. Thank you for your honesty. You're a sweet kid, Dane. Janessa leaned into him. Her dazzling aroma sent shivers up his spine. When her lips met his in an elegant, appreciative kiss, he just about blew his arousal gasket.

She produced a business card from seemingly nowhere.

"Why don't you call me. Or better yet, come to my show tomorrow night at Caddy's. I promise you this, kid, you won't regret it. And as for Vinny..." She growled, an utterance so primal and inhuman it made Dane flinch. Onto the linoleum she spat a thick wad of indignity. "As for Vinnie, he can go crawl under and rock, fuck off, and die."

With a naughty wink and smile, Janessa walked to the front door. Stiff and blue-balled; Dane could barely register what the hell had just happened.

"Janessa, wait!" He flew after her towards the front of the store. It was already too late. She'd turned the key hanging out of the door and made her escape into the elusive night.

More than a little disappointed, Dane gazed at the front door. Still, he couldn't wipe the shit-eating grin from his face.

Janessa Del Rio. Hot damn.

The day wasn't an entire write off. The brief interlude with Janessa revitalized his spirits in ways he never thought possible. It wouldn't be long before this night was over. He was so captivated with their interaction he was completely impervious to the writhing entity buckling the floor inwards to devour the vengeful secretion. The cavernous gape closed in once again without a trace of ever appearing.

The pounding continued at the back door and was making Dane livid by the minute

"All right! All right, keep your pants on." It wasn't as if the smut was going anywhere anytime soon. In the last few strides towards the steel door, Dane pondered. Something wasn't quite right. He hesitated before turning the dead bolt. Just a goose walking over his grave, he supposed, and laughed to himself.

At the precise moment he turned the latch, the florescent lights sizzled and flickered overhead. Great, what next? The lights went out as the entire store was enveloped in darkness. The door burst outward with a fury. Dane couldn't react fast enough to retrieve it.

"Look, mister, the power just went out. I can't let you in. It should be only a few min-"

"Shut up, mother fucker." To convey the severity of his command, the stranger shoved the barrel of a forty five in his face. "Get inside and give me all your money," he screamed, shoving Dane to the floor. There was only a split second for Dane to see his face, and he could make out very little in the darkness. Plus the robber had a bandana to conceal his identity. "Move, move, move!" He bellowed, kicked and shoved, sending Dane scurrying in panic.

"All right, okay. Just take it easy, mister." He waved trembling hands in defeat. "I'll help you. Just be cool and let me get up."

The stranger's retort was wordless. He clutched a fistful of hair with his free hand and yanked his victim to his feet. Thrusting his pistol into Dane's spine, he screamed again.

"Now move it, and no funny shit! Keep those hands up where I can see them. Push any buttons or call for help and I blow your brains out."

"Okay, okay. I'm trying," Dane whimpered. "It's pitch dark in here, I can barely see two inches in front of my face."

"Yeah well, if you don't give me all your cash in two minutes in this bag, you'll never see again, shithead."

Dane was already behind the counter, thankful he was so accustomed to the layout he never really had to second guess his steps.

"Hurry the fuck up, fucker."

He popped open the cash drawer and was about to hand him the fist-full of paper. The stack of fives, tens, and twenties were already ripped from his grasp and shoved somewhere unseen. The robber reached across the counter and grabbed the plastic cash tray. A rain of coins came spiralling onto the floor in a shower of jingling and jangling. Dane pondered for a brief second if the security cams were catching any of this in the dark.

"Stupid fuck. The safe! Open the god damn safe!"

Dane was about to burst into tears. "There isn't one. I mean there is, but I can't open it." His voice reverberated in octaves like a teenager in puberty. "Honestly I-"

"If you're lying, you're dead." To punctuate his growls the robber got another fistful of hair in his grasp and yanked Dane until he pulled him clear over the counter. With his other hand he pressed with incredible pressure into the back of his head. Dane squirmed and wriggled to no avail as the thief dragged him towards the back door and beater booths.

"Now be a good dog and play dead." He shoved Dane face first into the viewing room entrance. "Lie down and count to a hundred before you think of doing anything stupid."

Dane turned his head slightly just to assure his assailant he wouldn't dream of such things. In the reflection of the viewing room's display case, he caught a glimpse of the robber's profile. Oozing, open sores riddled his cheeks and nose, dripping puss everywhere.

"Night, night, jack ass." With a whirlwind swipe he pistol-whipped the back of Dane's head. A kaleidoscope of speckled colors was the last memory Dane had before his entire world went black.

Of course being unconscious one never has a clear conception of how long they've been out for. Dane moaned on the linoleum tile. A wave of vertigo washed over him as he grappled with the discarded chair, the prop in his impromptu lap dance from Ms. Del Rio. It resisted his efforts, rolling backwards as he stumbled in his climb. With one hand he felt the back of his head and winced. Clusters of matted hair and blood stained his palm. He bent over, gagging.

The overhead light fixtures hissed and sizzled, flashing blinding shots of light. On uncertain sea legs, Dane bumbled towards the counter. He found himself surprised that he had dismissed the telephone and walked directly into the washroom. In the dim light he stood at the sink, staring into the mirror.

Where had it all gone so incredibly awry? How had he fallen so vastly from grace and ended up in this forsaken place? His reflection held precious little insight. Seemingly aged ten years overnight, he could barely stand to look at himself. Some serious life changes were in order and fast. He had to get out of this cell he had constructed for himself.

He took a deep breath, looking down, and ran the faucet. Tomorrow he'd start fresh. He'd quit this piece of shit job or at least give his notice. Despair washed over him, sank him further into the abyss.

Through Dane's self-loathing and resign he failed to see the stalking entity behind him. An alien creature, its grisly glory illuminated with sinewy strands of clotted blood as it moved closer to him. Dane would never see that the entity was a carbon copy of his own demise. The gape opened wide as, with rotted teeth, the creature made its inevitable feast.

***

About David W. Gammon

David W. Gammon is a columnist, film and novel critic for horrornews.net. His most memorable experiences have been interviewing the late, great Marilyn Burns (Sally, *Texas Chainsaw Massacre*) and sharing laughs with two actors who have played Jason Vorhees, Derek Mears, and Ken Kirzinger. As a contributing writer for hellnotes.com under the pen name Rick Amortis, Dave began his modest journey in that less than modest of genres, erotica. His debut novel, *Lusty Layover*, was written under yet another pen name Rick O'Shea and is available from Blueline Publishing. He resides in Niagara Falls, Canada where he gets inspiration from the perpetual oddities.